THE WATCHERS OF ASTARIA, VOLUME ONE

THE WATCHERS OF ASTARIA, VOLUME ONE

PATRICK DUGAN

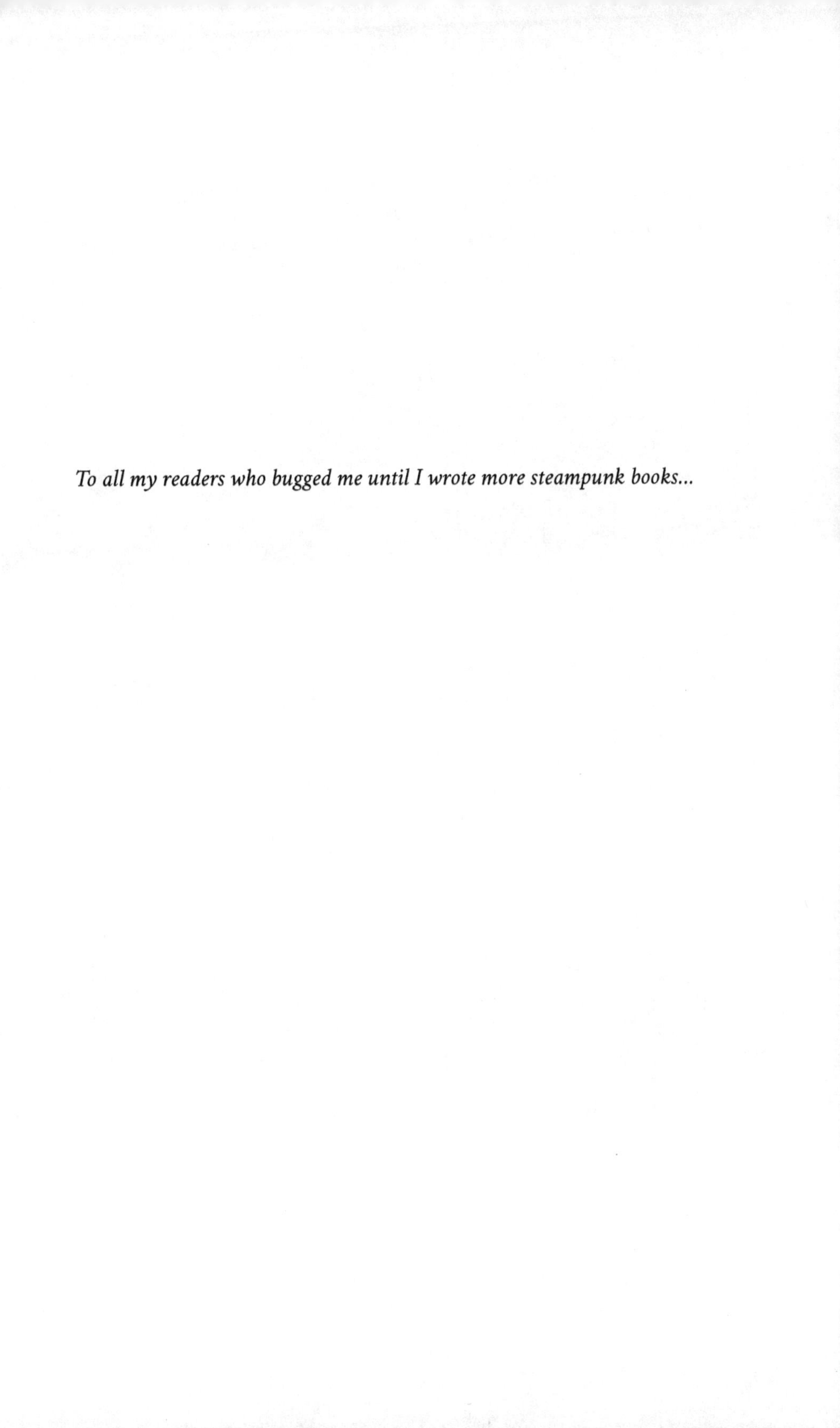

To all my readers who bugged me until I wrote more steampunk books...

Praise for Storm Forged

"Storm Forged is a superhero coming of age story with a truly innovate structure for both power and politics."

-Hugo & Nebula Award-Winning Author Seanan McGuire

Praise for Fate & Flux

"I was totally swept away by this story! Once I picked it up, I couldn't stop until I finished it."

Praise for Unbreakable Storm

"This second book in the series is even better than the first. I couldn't put it down. "

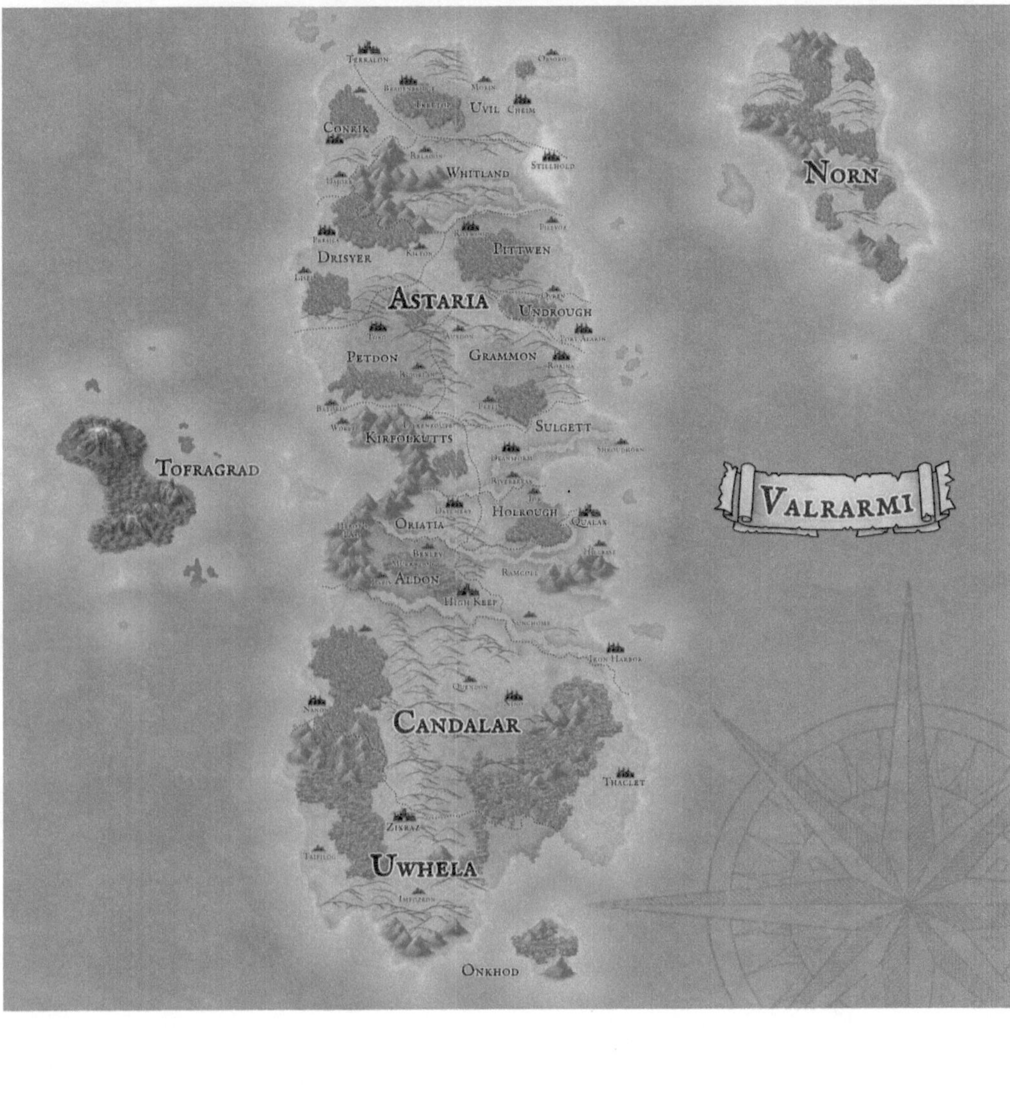

NORN
VALRARMI
TOFRAGRAD
ASTARIA
TERRALON
ORSORO
MOKIN
UVIL CHEIM
CONRIK
TREETOP
WHITLAND
STILLHOLD
DRISYER
PITTWEN
ASTARIA
UNDROUGH
PETDON
GRAMMON
KIRFOLKUTTS
SULGETT
SHROUDROKN
HOLROUGH
ORIATIA
QUALAX
ALDON
RAMCULL
HIGH KEEP
IRON HARBOR
CANDALAR
NANO
THACLET
ZINRAZ
TAIPILON
UWHELA
ONKHOD

OF COGS & CONJURING

BOOK ONE

*To my wonderful family, Hope, Emily, Nicholas, and Blaze. Thank you for all
your love and support.*

With a loud shriek of metal on metal, the last of my former living area collapsed from the side of the workshop forty feet to the ground. I eased myself over to the edge of the workshop and peered over the edge. Next to the massive tree trunk that supported my workshop, the metal frame shattered like an overheated knife. It had once been a small bedroom and storage closet. While not part of my duties as a Watcher, this was when my personal kind of fun began.

I adjusted my metal arm, making sure the straps were tight before starting on the next portion. An impervious arm worked great in a fight or blacksmithing, but normal people didn't have to worry about having an arm drop off if the straps failed. The receptor ends in the cup that held the stump of my right arm allowed me to throw lighting and fire blasts when I used my combat arm, not that either would help with this operation.

The new structure would become the kitchen and my living quarters. I'd assembled the addition's frame on the ground. Roland, my mentor, and the previous owner hadn't been much for comfort, but I needed a place to cook and sleep. He'd left me a series of books on the art of architecture. He insisted that these were the true masters and hacks like Bakker's treatise on building was garbage. Did I really need an addition?

No, but if I was being honest with myself, the project kept my mind off Roland's death six months ago and all my failures.

"Master Quinn," Jabber called from down the hall. His metallic voice sounded raspy, meaning I'd need to tune his voice box gears again soon. Before I'd joined the Watchers, I'd always thought of automatons as golems, creatures created from magic that did the bidding of their masters. Most were machines, but Jabber was far more intelligent, knowledgeable, and…naggy. He could be a real mother hen at times, a quality not found in other golems I'd encountered. He was definitely more than a box of gears, and I had no idea how Roland had produced him. "I heard a crash. Is everything all right?"

"Yes, Jabber." Roland had named him such since he tended to never stop talking. "As I said earlier, I'm adding the new wing today."

"Wouldn't it be easier to use your magic?"

I turned to face him. He'd been constructed from bronze, which gave him a copper tint much like my own skin. He measured five and a half feet tall and was built like a lanky teenage boy instead of stout like most automatons. Roland had even added a bowler hat and a monocle for some reason I didn't understand.

"Sure. If my magic actually worked," I said, rolling up the plans, careful not to tear them with my metal hand. A wizard named Usorin had sliced my arm off in a fit of anger. In a way, I owed him for my current position. Roland had found me close to death, nursed me back to health, and built me a new arm. He'd also recruited me into the Watchers. Every silver lining had its cloud. "I've got the rigging all set up to raise the new addition."

"Very well, sir." Jabber returned to doing whatever he'd been doing before the commotion had distracted him.

I took the lift down to the small cabin below that hid the access point to Treetop from casual viewers. The cunning inner workings appeared to be part of the tree itself. Granted, being a day's travel from the closest town meant few passers-by—merchants bringing their wares to Bradenbridge or bandits—but an ounce of prevention and all that.

The camouflaged cabin held a small table, some game traps, and other features of a hunter's lodge. It had been ransacked a couple of times, but they'd never found the lift to upstairs or seen the workshop or stable thanks to spells Everard had done to conceal it. With the new coded lock I'd installed, they'd never get into the lift even if someone found it.

I pushed those thoughts from my brain, focusing on the task at hand.

I'd hooked up guiding rigs and Roland's small airship to the add-on and hoped that would give me enough power. By myself, it would be tricky, but it wasn't like I had neighbors to come help me.

It was a calm day with a slight breeze. I'd only get one chance to attach the addition to the frame I'd built to hold it since I doubted it would look much different than the previous section if I failed. After double-checking the two winches I'd attached to the tree and the main lifting ropes under the airship, I fired up the furnace, watching the envelope enlarge as the steam-filled it with hot air. At a similar size to a lifeboat, it took a lot of steam to lift it.

Twenty minutes later, the airship I piloted bobbed over the structure below. I engaged the winches, lifting the structure upon a series of pulleys affixed to supports above the destination. I shuddered at the groaning sound from the ropes as my new living quarters rose into the air. I'd computed the strain and found it within the safe range, but with any engineering project, you could never account for all the variables.

The minutes crept by as the new construction inched toward the rest of the structure forty feet above it. The airship rocked as I adjusted the fins to keep it steady. Adding to the challenge, the wind picked up, nudging the structure into a ponderous swing. A quick look at the sky made me sweat. Dark clouds scudded toward me.

The wind rocked the airship, bobbing it around like a twig on the sea. Of all the days for a storm to roll in. I needed another twenty minutes to get the piece in place and settled on the foundation and another half hour to secure the structure. From the looks of it, I didn't have that much time.

The airship was attached by ropes to the tree. I ran across the deck to check the tension on the ropes. The safety line would hold me, but I wasn't looking forward to the ride. I hooked my metal arm over the rope and slid down to the tree, dropping the last couple of feet to the workshop. I ratcheted up the winches. The smell of burnt rope and grease filled the area as the strain intensified on the steam engine that powered the rig. The add-on bucked and swayed. The pace and wind increased. While I understood Roland's decision to hide his workshop in the treetops instead of on the ground like a normal person, it made projects like this a lot more difficult.

The add-on hung over the support structure now, ten feet from success. I'd planned in using the airship to nudge it into place, but hard drops of rain pelted me as I climbed along a support beam. At the end of the structure, I used the strength of my mechanical arm to pull, dragging the add-on toward me. With my legs wrapped around the strut, I shimmied back, guiding the piece.

"I've got this," I said as I continued to move the addition.

Yet another gust of wind struck the Treehouse and addition alike, knocking me from my perch. My stomach lurched from the sudden acceleration. The ground sped toward me before I caught myself. I clutched the edge, dangling over a forty-foot drop. It seemed a lot closer now than it had before. The straps around my chest slipped as the weight came full on my metal arm.

Well, hells. I was either about to lose my arm—or myself. The connection with my stump separated, locking my fingers into place. My body swayed dangerously, held to my arm by the leather harness. I kicked desperately, swinging like an idiot until I grabbed hold of the metal frame with my left hand.

The rough metal tore at the skin, and blood made my grip slippery. Without the leverage of my right arm, I couldn't pull myself to safety. My brain raced as I tried to think of a way to not fall to my death.

"Jabber!" I screamed trying to force the panic out of my voice. I failed. No answer. The only time the automaton wasn't around.

"I'm sure the mighty engineer has everything well in hand if you'll pardon the pun, but might I be of service?" a voice called from the ground below me.

I glanced down, wishing I hadn't. Everard, the Arch Magus of all of Astaria and the head of the Watchers, stood with a wicked smirk on his face. He wore a red cloak over his leather jerkin.

"I can come back if this isn't an opportune moment." He laughed while I swung from my less than useful arm.

"Help!" I yelled. I hated to admit it, but I was in a bad spot.

"As you wish," Everard said.

I wondered if it would be less embarrassing to die.

2

Everard helped me into the workshop, and I connected the new partition to the original structure. I needed to hook up the water to run the kitchen and bathroom, but that would have to wait. Jabber might have cleaned the blood from Roland's bedroom, but... I still couldn't force myself to go into his space.

"You certainly are ambitious," Everard said as he walked through the addition. "How are you coming with your magic?"

Fire crept up my face. Over the past few months, I'd been driven to complete the living space and hadn't spent much time practicing magic.

"I see," Everard said before I could make up a good excuse. "Lady Maelyrra gave you magic so you could protect Astaria, not so you could squander it building your fortress and hiding from the world."

"It's not a fortress," I said with a bit more sulk in my voice than I liked. Roland's murder had shaken me to the core, and I'd neglected my duties as a Watcher as I convinced myself the new workshop had to have better quarters if I was going to be able to perform at an adequate level.

In reality, the magic eluded me. I couldn't even do the basic spells Everard, a mage who'd burned an entire army to ash, had taught me. Spells that were merely warm-up exercises, not the more useful enchantments. Who cares if I could rattle a glass or burn a piece of paper? Practicing the magic I supposedly possessed was a frustrating, humiliating experience.

9

Everard sighed, taking a seat on the floor. The Arch Magus gestured for me to join him. I dropped down and across from him. He didn't say anything for a few moments. "I know this is hard on you, Quinn. You've lost more than most people do in a lifetime, but I need you, and more importantly, Lady Maelyrra requires your protection."

"Why would she need me for anything?" I asked. The whining tone in my voice sparked a throb of guilt knowing in the six months since Roland died and I received my magic I'd done nothing. "She's more powerful than any of us. She could destroy anyone who threatened Astaria in a heartbeat. For that matter, we could hand out enough alarium-powered devices to the magus to fight anyone who attacks."

"No," the Arch Magus said, shaking his head. "Maelyrra is bound to her realm and only ventures here at great cost. She grants a mage magical powers to protect Astaria and the alarium that holds the magic. Only you and I have real magic"

"Don't you mean magus?" I asked, assuming he'd misspoken.

"No. Mage is a person who has true magic. Magus is a title and gives the bearer the right to the alarium-powered devices that conceal when we don't have more magic at our disposal."

My jaw dropped as what the older man said registered. "How are alarium and magic related?"

"The magic we tap into is contained in the alarium beneath Astaria. Once it's gone, the magic will cease. It's why we mine so little of it."

"What?" Like most of Astaria, I had been raised to believe that the magus were magic users and they ruled because of that power. After Roland brought me in, I learned that alarium devices were the true power.

"I guess I should have explained things more thoroughly. If the Candalarians or the Norns realized there were vast veins of the precious metal that we hadn't tapped, they would seek to destroy them to eliminate our magic."

"Why? They have magic of their own."

"Norn magic is derived from death. They sacrifice people to fuel their resurrection magic."

"And the Candalarians?"

"They tap into the energy of the spirit realm to power their spells. It's unreliable but powerful in the hands of a trained Walker."

"Walker?"

He smiled at me. "I forget how new you are to all of this. The Wind

Walkers are the mages of the Candalarians. They convert spiritual energy into magic."

"Oh." Every time I thought I had a basic understanding of the world, I found out more I'd not been told. Why had Roland picked me to be a Watcher? I knew nothing beyond the forge. Maelyrra had wasted her magic on a one-armed blacksmith. After six months, I couldn't move a mote of dust with magic. Sure, I could build alarium powered weapons and items for the other Watchers, but I'd never fulfill the responsibility she'd laid at my feet.

"Enough on the topic for today, though we will obviously need to discuss your formal training soon," Everard said with a pointed look. "We have a situation I need you to deal with."

"Are the Norns back?" I asked. I'd fought their leader and killed him. I'd left him roasting like a gutted pig on a forge fire.

"No, nothing that large, but there have been incursions into the Aldon region. Something has attacked two villages. The Watcher there, Aurelia Salwey, was killed in the first attack on Herot's Pass," he said, pulling out a map to consult. It showed the thirteen regions of Astaria, each with a Lord Magus to lead and a Watcher to take care of issues Everard wanted handled. From Terralon far to the north all the way down to Aldon in the south. Everard's finger stabbed the map. "Herot's Pass and Murkwood reported their inns destroyed the day after magus Quiliel of Aldon made his quarterly visit. He hasn't had any luck locating the perpetrators. Honestly, the man is an imbecile and couldn't find his butt with both hands and a map."

"Sounds like a great leader," I said dryly. "What do you need me to do?"

Everard shot me a mirthful glance. He did his best to tolerate magus' royal tendencies. "You'll be meeting up with Cian, the Watcher from Ramcoll, in Murkwood. He's an experienced ranger so he'll be of use in tracking down whatever is killing people."

"Whatever?" I wasn't sure whether giving me help was a vote of no-confidence or the situation was worse than I thought.

"There weren't a lot of witnesses to the deaths. In both cases, the inn was attacked, and all the inhabitants were killed. The timing troubles me. It seems beyond circumstance that the towns are assaulted the day after the magus left. According to Quiliel, a boy saw a monster."

"A monster? What kind of monster?"

"I don't know, but we need to find out what is happening. Aldon borders the Candalarian territories which always makes it more important." He shook his head. "Astaria is in greater danger than I've ever seen. The Norns are building more ships, and the Candalarians have been gathering the horse clans at Thaclet. The magus leaders are demanding more alarium weapons to protect them from the threats."

"Why me? If Cian is a ranger, won't he be able to track the people responsible?"

"He probably could," Everard said, rubbing his forehead with the palm of his hand. "You need field experience. You've handled your artificer responsibilities well, but you need to be a complete Watcher."

"You mean murdering people that piss you off?"

Everard glared. "That is a small part of the job, but yes it sometimes is required. More often your missions will be to protect the people of Astaria by any means necessary."

"And Roland sacrificing his life was just another necessity?"

"It was unfortunate and I was far closer to him than anyone else. I know he explained the risks to you. Are you walking away from the Watchers? Does Roland's death mean that little to you?"

I shook my head. "No, I swore an oath to Roland and I'll not let him down. I still don't like your methods."

"We do what is needed to ensure the people of Astaria are protected, even the ones we don't like."

"I guess we better get started. Something is killing our people and I mean to stop them." I didn't add if I could to the end.

I wondered if I was strong enough to stop the killing or if I'd be joining Roland in the afterlife.

3

The smell of blood, fire, and death clung to the dank night air like scale forge to a piece of molten iron. Behind us smoldered the burning remains of a small farmhouse, and behind that, the remains of the family who had lived there. The fire didn't look intentional, but the people had all been torn to shreds. My guess was the fire got out of control as they tried to scare off the bear.

It turned out the kid from Murkwood had been right. The perpetrator of the attacks was a monster. Now all I needed to do was figure out who was creating them.

The moon peeked out between the roiling clouds as the wind picked up from the west. My leather mask with specially created optics enhanced the dim light, making it easier to see. It also protected our identities since Watchers tended to make powerful enemies. I adjusted my cloak and moved out into the night. Cian scouted ahead, searching for a trail to follow.

Lapis, a small town on the southeastern coast of Astaria, was our destination. According to Cian, it was a sleepy village nestled in the hills overlooking the sea. Thatch huts and broad-beamed buildings housed the town of two hundred or so, and nothing had ever happened here to put the town into the history books besides its incorporation.

I cleared my mind, picturing the monster as it had been described to me by the Murkwood boy who'd survived its last attack. Once Cian and I stopped the killing, there would be time to find who was behind these atrocities.

I pulled the tuft of fur I'd retrieved from the Murkwood attack and concentrated. I crossed my hands in front of me and said the words Everard had taught me to cast a finding spell.

"Dilna op nata." I spread my hands wide, tossing the fur into the wind.

Nothing happened. I retrieved the fur, tried again.

Frustration and irritation flared hot when the spell failed a second time. After two more attempts, I gave up, stuffed the remaining fur in my pouch, and waited for Cian to return from scouting for the trail.

Magic was effortless for Everard, but I'd been more successful at the forge than casting any spells. Maelyrra might have given me magic after I'd stopped Orvo from stealing it through the machine he'd created, but the power wouldn't respond to me. I followed Everard's instructions to a T, and nothing.

When I was given the magic, I'd been able to feel it inside me like the heat from the sun. When I cast spells, I might as well have been taking a nap I felt so empty.

I found a stump and took a seat. Might as well be somewhat comfortable while the ranger sought traces of our prey. I pushed up my Watcher mask and looked at the stars. Was Roland up there, guiding me? I could almost hear him telling me, "Get a move on, lad." Without him, I'd have been a one-armed man with no prospects beyond begging or robbery.

He'd saved my life and I'd let him down when he needed me. I'd failed my family, my mentor, Everard, and Lady Mylerra. The least I could do was save the Astarian people from this unnatural predator. I refused to fail my oath as a Watcher, even if it killed me.

My mask had smudges on the eyepieces, so I pulled a cloth out and carefully cleaned them. A marvel of ingenuity, their lenses compensated for both darkness and bright light. They protected our identities from the public so we could move about without being harassed in our real lives. The mouth slit filtered out dust and toxins.

Once the lenses gleamed, I checked the status of the enhancements I'd made on the mask since Roland had died. I might not be able to cast spells, but I could improve on the designs Roland had created, at least.

"I found the trail," Cian called, striding across the field. I adjusted the secondary chest strap that helped to hold my arm in place, which I had designed after the embarrassing incident with Everard a few days ago.

"Let's go," I replied. Cian led the way to some trampled grass and other markings of the bear's passage. One thing was sure, Cian was an amazing tracker. "Follow my directions when we confront the monster."

Cian frowned at me before scouting the area for more signs. "How in the hell did we get a monster out here?"

I increased my stride to keep up with the taller man. "I don't know, but from the little I've heard it is at least partially mechanical."

"An abomination is what that is," he said, his gaze flickering over the ground in front of us. We made steady progress over the uneven terrain, on the trail of our quarry. "Thing has to be twice the size of a horse, given the prints."

I swallowed hard. I'd faced off against men and machines, but never a creature the size Cian described. "How far behind are we?"

Cian stopped, knelt, and studied one of the immense paw prints that were mostly hidden by the clumps of grass around it. I knelt beside him, examining the deep impression in the ground. I hadn't noticed the print before he pointed it out.

Cian traced the outline with his finger. "I wouldn't think too far. See how the print is pressed into the soft dirt, but there is only a bit of water? After a few hours, the groundwater will seep in to fill the depression."

I cleared my throat. "We should pick up the pace. I don't want any more people killed by this thing." Bile rose in my throat at the thought of finding more bodies tonight.

Cian snorted a laugh. "It already killed one Watcher. You're assuming we won't be part of the dead after going up against this monster. I've dropped a couple of big animals in my time, but nothing to rival this one. He must be over a thousand pounds."

However dangerous the threat—mechanized monsters, psychotic Norns, or rogue Magus—it was the job of the Watchers to protect the people of Astaria. Fear thrummed through my body in time with my hammering heart. Regardless, people were dying, and it was up to me to save them. So much for starting off with an easy mission. I wished I could have stayed hidden like I had since Roland was murdered six months ago.

Over the next hour, we followed the trail of the giant bear across the rolling hills. Luckily, we didn't happen across any more farms or other folks the bear had visited. The moon shone brightly overhead, making it easier to move quickly. As we crested the top of the largest hill yet, the quiet town of Lapis appeared in front of us.

It was not so quiet this evening. The villagers had built a long bonfire across the road leading into the hamlet. I pushed my mask into place and the scene illuminated as the goggles enhanced my sight. Dead bodies and farm implements dotted the ground around a massive bear who lurked a short way away from the barricade. So much for a monster. The bear had mechanical eyes and armor platting. Obviously, the villagers had charged the monster and hadn't fared well. I'd heard the descriptions, but I wasn't prepared for just how massive this beast was.

Shadows flickered around the flames, making the illuminated faces of the villagers look contorted in its light. The tension in the air could be cut with a knife.

A bestial roar shattered the still night air. The bear lumbered toward the town, trampling the corpses as it went.

"We've got to get there." I set off at a run, only to be halted by Cian's barked order, louder due to his Watcher's mask.

"Stop!"

I skidded to a halt and gestured impatiently. The people of Lapis weren't armed to take on such a huge foe. For that matter, nothing in my blacksmith training had prepared me for this. Roland had taught me the basics of fighting, though my education was far from complete. "People are going to die if we don't stop that monstrosity."

Cian jogged to my side, down the slope of the hill. "Quinn, use your head. Run the whole way and you'll be too tired to fight. The fire will hold the bear back until we get there and draw the animal off."

I hated to admit it, but he was right. "Fine, but we need to get there quickly."

Cian grinned before settling his mask in place and setting off at an easy pace. I tried not to fall flat on my face as the uneven footing threatened to trip me. If the townspeople occupied the bear for ten minutes or so, I could use my armaments to drive it to a safe distance before we killed it.

A bolt of lightning streaked from behind the fire into the approaching bear. Lightning, and not the natural sort. Another of the blue-white streaks followed.

Was that Magus Quielel, the ruler of Aldon? I increased my pace, which Cian easily matched. With a Magus on hand, we'd have more firepower, but alone he was vulnerable.

The bear stood on two legs, bellowing its challenge. Arcs of blue-white lightning crackled around the beast. The strikes did little damage to the armor but seriously irritated the bear. With an earsplitting roar, its front legs came down and it charged the magus, absorbing the lightning strikes with no sign of slowing.

The barrier of flame burst as the monstrosity drove through it, sending villagers screaming away from their attacker. Magus Quielel stood his ground.

Cian and I got there in time to see the bear's massive jaw clamp down on the magus' head. Blood spurted in all directions as the animal shook the corpse until the body tore free, landing in a pile at its feet. The head bounced across the ground.

We slowed to a halt, panting. The bear grasped the headless corpse and began to drag it away from the fire. I readied my arm and gauntlet for the fight. The glow from the alarium shimmered around my arms. I turned to Cian. "Do bears eat humans?"

He shook his head, as bewildered by the spectacle as I was. "No, not usually."

The bear lifted a massive paw and struck repeatedly at the corpse. "What is it doing?"

"I've no idea." Cian pulled his hood up over his head. He gestured back toward the fire. "We've got other problems, though."

I followed his gaze. The town's people were dissolving into a panicked mob. Some ran for cover, others thought to challenge the monstrosity that had killed their neighbors. Some carried farm implements, others flaming torches, but they were determined to fight. The bear ignored them dragging the corpse along the ground.

So much for this being an easy mission.

4

creams of anger and fear erupted from the villagers. Women and children rebuilt the barricade fire, sending sparks off into the darkness. The men, determined to save their families from the beast, braced for a fight and shook pitchforks and hoes, a few shoving long torches into the fire.

From our vantage point just outside the firelight, we watched the bear tear an arm free from the Magus and set it aside. "What is he doing?" Cian asked while we watched the morbid display.

I shook my head, having no idea myself. "Do we just leave him be and wait for him to move off?"

Arrows tipped with flame rained down on the bear, bouncing harmlessly off the armor. One lucky shot found a weak point and sunk its barbed head into meaty shoulder flesh. The animal roared in pain before charging toward the town. Shrieks of terror sounded as the giant plowed into the fire again, sending burning logs skittering like dice at the local tavern.

We headed toward the carnage. The angry animal swatted anyone within reach, throwing them like rag dolls. The fire had wisely been built far away from the majority of Lapis's buildings. Otherwise, the whole place might have burnt down.

Cian outpaced me, his long legs covering more ground than I could

18

ever hope to. He became a blur in the shadows. Pistols appeared in each hand as he fired at the beast's head.

A few moments later I reached the fight. Cian danced around the monster like one of those fancy acrobat performers. He flowed in circles around the attacker, firing into the massive body over and over again. The tang of the projectiles striking armor filled the air.

"Stop!" I yelled at the townspeople, backing them off from the bear.

"I'll keep him busy, you figure out how to stop him," Cian yelled as he continued harassing the bear. A series of shots pinged off the armored bear. As with any great plan, it fails once the fighting starts.

The bear ignored Cian and spun toward me. His mechanical eyes twisted to focus on me. How I was supposed to stop a rampaging gigantic bear?

First I'd need to be close enough to strike it. I dashed into the melee, throwing a ball of flame from my mechanical arm. With a yell, I hiked up my shield and blocked one huge swipe. The bear continued the onslaught. Its claws sparked as they raked the alarium generated field. The force of the blow shoved me across the clearing. After an awkward landing, I collapsed to the ground in an undignified heap.

Cian's guns fired at the animal, ricocheting off into the night.

The bear reared on his hind legs, lurched forward, and heaved itself atop me, attempting to crush me beneath its massive frame. Or it almost did. I rolled away from the blow. Could my shield could absorb the force of that much weight? The bear continued its pursuit, now focused on me and nothing else. Clambering to my feet, I backpedaled away from another slashing blow. I didn't see Cian, but then again, the bear took up most of my field of vision. I tried to outmaneuver my foe, but a piece of log tripped me. I went down hard as the bear pounced.

My shield held as the animal's incredible bulk pinned me to the ground. White cracks appeared in the blue energy as claws fought for purchase. When the shield failed, the bear would smash my head like an overripe pumpkin.

A flash of flame appeared above us, and the bear staggered to the side. Cian shoved the burning branch closer to the animal, giving me a chance to stand. I scrambled away, flicking off the shield before the damage overloaded the alarium core.

"Did you shoot his mother?" Cian yelled as I increased the charge to my lightning attack. The bear stopped in its tracks with its head at an odd angle as if it was listening to us speak. "He seems to be on a mission to eat you, my friend."

"No idea." This close, the optics that had replaced the bear's eyes glowed with a strange red light. "The real question is what are they trying to accomplish?"

"I see you don't share Roland's sense of humor."

The remark stung like I'd been shot. "Roland is dead. We've got to handle this our way or we'll be joining him." I tried to keep the hurt and anger out of my voice but failed miserably. Any further comments were cut short by an ear-splitting roar the bear launched toward us.

Cian leapt to the left, firing his pistols at its flanks while I opened up with a burst of flame, scorching the fur around the bear's muzzle. It reared up and slammed back down, clipping me with dagger-like claws.

I took the blow on my metal arm and immediately wished I hadn't. The new restraining strap popped, leaving my appendage hanging limp and numb at my side.

"Quinn!" Cian yelled over the roar of the angry grizzly.

I dodged left, holding my mechanical arm in place so the connections could reestablish. Without those, the arm was virtually useless. Feeling returned, much to my relief. I opened up with a barrage of fireballs, forcing the enraged beast back.

Cian appeared next to me. "What happened?" He fired a series of quick shots at the massive head, cracking one of the mechanical eye lenses.

"Strap broke. See if you can reattach it." The bear circled us cautiously now, and I tracked it as Cian knotted the broken strap.

"It won't take another blow, but it should hold until you can repair it."

I reached into my belt pack and grabbed my latest invention, the sonic bomb. "When I tell you to, push the button, throw it at the bear, and cover your ears."

Cian held the ball by a wire poking out of its bronze casing. "Is it going to sing off-key?"

Instead of answering, I charged the bear, firing two arcs of electricity from my reattached arm. The lightning wouldn't do anything to the animal, but if it momentarily blinded him, Cian's chances of a hit increased. "Now!"

The device bounced off the bear's snout before landing directly under it. A loud whistle erupted as the sonic blast reached its full potential. The bear shied away from it, giving me my opening. I leapt onto his back, my hands latching onto the strap holding his armor in place.

The response was immediate and terrifying. The beast roared and shook. My body swung wildly as I fought to hold onto the straps. He bucked uncontrollably, but I stuck to him like a hot weld.

The bear dropped to all fours, nearly jolting me off. The bear lumbered toward Cian, hardly slowed by the additional weight. The tracker danced just out of reach and kept the bear engaged so he wouldn't focus on ridding himself of his unwanted rider.

I worked furiously at the buckles. Success! Pieces of armor rained down as the plates were freed. The bear didn't appreciate my work. It jerked sideways, again unsuccessful in dislodging me.

We'd moved closer to the remains of the fiery barricade. The increased light revealed a piece of metal about the size of my hand embedded in the bear's fur between its shoulder blades. Tubes ran from the plate into the bear's body.

I wedged my fingers under the plate and pulled. Blood and a blue liquid spurted. I yanked what turned out to be a metal box out of the animal's flesh.

As soon as the wires broke, the bear dropped onto its belly dead. After a few moments, I leapt free, the box still in my hands. Cian joined me as I ran farther away.

A group of villagers charged to join us. The leader inclined his head. "Master Watchers, is the beast dead?"

Cian turned to them. "He's dead. The Watchers have done their duty."

A cheer went up, but no one else approached. The Watchers might save your village or they might arrive to dispense the Arch Magus' justice. The safe bet was to stay away, far away.

"Everard said you were in charge. What do we do now?" Cian asked once he made sure all the others had gone. He had a smile on his face and looked ready to fight again.

With a pop and the clanking of metal, my arm fell to the ground.

"I'm going to invent some better straps."

5

The sun was about to set as I pulled the cart with the supplies I'd purchased in Bradenbridge into the small barn that stood at the base of the massive tree that held home and workshop. The sigils Everard had used to hide the barn flared in my sight as I crossed through the hiding spell. At least I could see his magic now, that was an improvement.

When I'd first arrived at Treetop, the lift had been hidden, but after Roland's murder, I'd added a mechanical lock to guard against intruders. I moved the interlocking pieces until they clicked into place and the door slid open. Working methodically, I stacked each crate of supplies on the lift's floor until the cart was empty.

After I pressed the button for the upper floor, it shuddered and jerked to life, another thing I'd have to fix one day, but it worked for now.

"Good day, Master Quinn. I assume your mission was a success?" Jabber asked as I entered.

I handed a wooden crate full of vegetables to Jabber. "It was. Any word from Everard?"

"Indeed, there is a word." He followed behind me as I carried more supplies to the new kitchen. I hadn't had time to finish the build, but the shelves were mounted on the wall. For now, I'd rigged up a small burner for cooking.

I realized Jabber, who took questions literally, wasn't going to tell me what word we'd received from the Arch Magus. "Jabber, what did Everard say?"

"He said Watcher Atwater had reported in. He congratulated you on stopping the bear and directed you to find who is behind it. He also inquired on your magic and insists you come to Vario to continue your education."

I sighed, not wanting to think about magic, killer mechanically enhanced bears, or anything else. All I wanted to do was cook myself a large dinner and go to bed. I'd been on the road for over three weeks hunting the bear and now had more questions than answers. "Respond to Everard. Tell him I will be investigating the source of the box and will track down the perpetrator. Afterward, I'll be in Vario for training." Maybe.

It took a while to stash my provisions and cook butter-poached chicken and mashed potatoes for dinner. My cooking skills had increased during my solitude.

Jabber sat across from me at the table as I ate. had that been the automaton's habit when Roland lived here? "Jabber, how long did Roland live here alone?"

The automaton cocked his head as he processed the question. "Master Roland only came here to work or train apprentices. He did not live here as you have been."

I chewed the slightly overcooked chicken. "Where did he live?"

"Master Roland had a residence in River Cross. I do not have further details," Jabber answered. I'm sure he had details, but Roland would have locked them away in Jabber's memory.

"I didn't realize he had other apprentices." I'd been with Roland for a few months before the attack that killed him, but he'd never mentioned taking on other assistants. It still shocked me how much I didn't know about my mentor. He'd saved me after I'd lost my arm and I'd barely gotten to know him before he was murdered.

"Roland had three apprentices before you. Two have retired from the Watch. One was killed in an explosion."

"Explosion?"

"I do not have details of the mission, only the entry notifying the Arch Magus of the outcome of the mission."

"Interesting." I finished eating, cleaned up, and headed for bed. The next few days would be busy as I tried to decipher the metal box I'd torn out of the bear.

Three days later after disarming numerous traps, I finally opened the box without damaging the interior. Whoever built the device had wanted its secrets to die with the bear. They'd installed several small explosives and a vial of highly corrosive acid which I had removed before the attached explosives could trigger.

A wire casing fed into a small box covered in runes like the Norns or the Candalarian Hordes used to control their magic. Too bad shaman magic was as much a mystery to me as my own.

I set the box aside, checking out the series of gears attached to a syringe that pushed the blue liquid through the tubes. With a set of crimpers, I closed off the tube before I removed it. Luckily some of the fluid remained in the syringe. The gears were set to rotate at a small increment and deliver more of the fluid. How often and how much fluid was delivered would determine how long it had been since the animal had been with its creator.

The blue liquid-filled half the syringe. The big question still hadn't been answered. What did this do? How could I run tests to determine what it was? I needed an expert which was definitely not me

I rummaged through the tomes on the rebuilt shelves until I found a book of maps. I spread it out on the workbench and cranked up the alarium lamp. On the page showing the Alolon fiefdom, I traced the bear's progress from Lapis to Murkwood to Herot's Pass where the first known attack had occurred.

According to the map, Herot's Pass provided the best passage to the grasslands of Oriatia, though the forest and Kirfolk mountains certainly didn't lend itself to an easy trek. Most likely the bear had originated there, but you could hide a lot in the treacherous mountains.

Jabber entered carrying a steaming teapot and a cup. "I thought you could use a bit of refreshment, Master Quinn."

"Thank you, Jabber."

The automaton poured the tea and placed it near enough for me to reach, but away from my work. "Might I be of some assistance?"

"Only if you can identify what the liquid in the syringe is or what these runes mean," I said peevishly, waving my hand over the disassembled device. Three days of work and I barely knew more than I had before.

"I'm afraid not. Master Roland's notebooks contain the list of Watchers and their specialties."

"I hadn't thought to check there." The notebooks had been housed in the workshop, but Jabber relocated the books to Roland's old room while I repaired the workshop.

I hadn't been in his room since the day I'd found his body. The horrid images flashed before my eyes as I considered having Jabber fetch them. While the automaton could do a lot of things, reading Roland's atrocious handwriting left a lot of room for error.

Dread struck at my heart, but I had to do this. I opened the door to the musty smell of the unused room. Jabber had cleaned all the blood and viscera from the floor and burned the carpet, but my gaze was drawn immediately to the spot where Roland had been hung from his arms. I stood frozen in the doorway, unable or unwilling to enter the place where my mentor had been murdered. A rivulet of sweat dripped down my back as my anxiety climbed.

His oversized bed, nightstand, and the alarium core that powered Treetop occupied the back wall. A small desk and set of drawers stood off to the right. Bookshelves covered the left wall from floor to ceiling. Jabber had piled the workshop's library in front of the shelves. I swallowed the bile that threatened to climb up my throat and forced myself into the room.

Giving the center of the room a wide berth, I crouched in front of the first stack, searching for the notebook Jabber mentioned. Books full of alchemical and metallurgy theory, sketches of new inventions, and every message Roland had received from Everard were in the first pile. The other stacks on the floor were the same. Nothing.

Next, I examined the books on the shelves. More tomes on every possible subject filled these shelves. I didn't recognize most of the names, but I was surprised to find a copy of Bakker's treatise on architecture. What was this doing here? Roland had said Bakker was an idiot who didn't know the first thing about architecting a pigpen, let alone a building.

Curious, I pulled the book and heard a loud click. A section of bookshelf swung away from the wall, revealing a tiny hidden room.

Lights flickered to life as I stepped through the opening. Roland's cloak and Watcher mask hung from a hook on the wall. A larger desk than the one in his bedroom was covered with papers and an enormous black book. The back wall held a metal plate the size of a shield. I pulled the steel handle to expose a hole that was deeper than the light in this room could penetrate. Hm.

I pulled a coin from my pocket and tossed it into the dark. The sound echoed as the coin bounced down what I guessed was a slide. Roland always had a plan, including a secret escape route from Treetop. I wished he'd used it that day instead of fighting.

I shut the hatch and took a seat in from of the desk. The book was open, face down. I flipped it over and saw Roland's familiar scrawl detailing the process he was using to double harden copper to increase its strength.

The other pages contained more drawings for completed projects. I paused at the familiar diagrams for a heating system, the one he'd built for Usorin. At the bottom in Roland's scrawl was written, "Keep an eye on Quinn." I'd never met Roland until the day he saved my life, so had he jotted down this note before or after I'd lost my arm? At this point, I'd probably never know.

With a huff, I turned the page, searching for the Watcher's list. No luck. I set it on the floor and rifled through the papers until I uncovered a small notebook. The Watcher's eye insignia graced the front cover, and inside was the list of Watchers.

Roland was listed as the Artificer for the Terralon territory under Usorin. I skimmed the other twelve entries. Atwater was noted as Ranger, as was someone named Brull, though his name was crossed off. An explosives expert, Doctor, and others were here, but alchemist was the one I needed. The name beside it was Wyndham and the region of Whitland. Thirteen districts and only eleven Watchers. How long since had the list had been updated? At least since Roland had started training me, I presumed, since my name was scribbled at the bottom with Artificer beside it.

Mission accomplished, I headed for the door when I noticed Roland's watch on the shelf. It stopped me in my tracks. As hard as it was, I tried to envision Roland in here instead of the corpse I'd found in the other room. I'd sworn to avenge his and all the other murders of the people I loved. After fruitless months of searching, I was no closer to finding Roland's killer, but the bill would come due one day no matter how long it took. One day the coward would rear his head again, and I'd be ready.

6

I spent the next week poring over reference books about the Candalarian Horde. The horse clans of the Verdant Plains were masters of hit and run raids on outlying settlements and traders. The southern Astarians called them the white ghosts since they were of pale complexion. I found volumes on fighting styles and culture, but only trace amounts of information regarding their magic.

Jabber interrupted an excruciatingly boring section of Cuttle's "Warlords of the Candalarian Hordes," much to my pleasure. The author stated facts but didn't connect them back to the actual people and how their ways impacted their society.

"Master Quinn, I contacted Watcher Wyndham as you requested via the telex. You are to meet in four days at the Broken Spoke in Stillhold. You will know the Watcher by an onyx stickpin in the lapel. You are expected at noon."

I nodded. My knowledge of geography outside of Terralon was sketchy at best since I hadn't left Bradenbride in the twenty-five years before becoming a Watcher. "Stillhold should only take a couple of days to get to."

"If you take the airship from Bradenbridge to Stillhold, you will reach it in three days, two to ride to Bradenbridge, one on the airship. Riding a horse from here would take four to five days, depending on how hard your push your mount. I'd suggest the airship."

I didn't respond to the obvious fact I'd just said as much. "Is there anything else I need to know about the meeting?"

"When you approach Watcher Wyndham, the passphrase will be 'What should you do with a dead chemist?' and the appropriate answer is 'barium'."

What an awful joke. This Wyndham fellow was an odd cog for sure. "Thank you, Jabber. I'll leave in the morning."

Jabber didn't answer but stood there shaking. No, not shaking. Laughing. Since when did automatons have a sense of humor? Roland must have spent a great deal of time teaching Jabber.

"Barium…bury 'em," the automaton repeated to himself as he left.

⸺⸺◈⸺⸺

I waited impatiently for noon to arrive before leaving my room at the Broken Spoke. The night before, I'd caught a ride from the airship to the inn with a steady wind whipping dust at my back. I'd had to use a makeshift mask to help me breathe. Stillhold was a farming community, but the bartender told me that in stopping the Norns, the magical battle had diverted the river that fed the town, leaving a dustbowl in its place.

After affixing my everyday arm, I clopped down the stained and scuffed oak stairs into the common room. This arm didn't have built-in weapons, preferring to not call attention to my absent arm or the weapons I carried to fight with. The onyx stickpin pierced the lapel of the coat I wore over my white shirt.

Once I reached the common room, I glanced around for any sign of Watcher Wyndham. A large fireplace dominated the wall to my right and the bar took up the left. A bored serving girl swabbed out wooden mugs with a cloth I wouldn't have cleaned my anvil with. I wouldn't be eating here if it could be helped. Twelve long tables filled the center of the room.

A couple of trappers in roughhewn clothes sat near the fire, laughing and swapping stories. The table held their drinks and two pairs of goggles with attached respirators. I wished I'd have known to bring the same with me. My Watcher's mask would handle the dust, but it would also mark me.

After examining the trappers, I concluded Watcher Wyndham wasn't a member of that party. Two men wearing bowlers and dark coats, and a woman wearing a coat, but no hat, sat near the door. While they appeared to be discussing business, the woman watched the door like a hawk while the other two sized me up in a not-so-friendly manner. None of them wore an onyx stickpin.

I took a seat on the other side of the room from the unfriendly group, closer to the trappers. The far door opened. As the air billowed across the room, making me realize I should have chosen a different table when the smell of the trappers reached me. All three of the tough's heads pivoted toward the open door.

A tall woman strode in, slamming the door behind her. Her long dust streaked coat nearly concealed her black shirt and pants. While it wasn't unheard of, a woman in pants still elicited scowls and comments. A respirator and goggles hung around her neck like an elaborate necklace. She scanned the room before walking straight toward me. "What do you do with a dead chemist?"

I groaned, still hearing Jabber's laughter ringing in my head. "Barium."

Yep. Onyx pin in her lapel. Before me stood Watcher Wyndham, alchemist, adventurer, and a woman. I'd have to inform Jabber. "I'm Quinn. Nice to meet you, Watc--"

She cut me off. "None of that. Didn't Roland teach you anything? Call me Victoria. Follow me." She pivoted on her heel and headed toward the front door. The trio had risen to block her path. I stepped up behind her.

"Master Spencer would like to have a few words with you, Lady Yorke." The lead man's smile never faltered as his hand went to the knife at his belt. The movement revealed hardened leather armor under his duster. The other two, the man with a long, greying beard and the woman had long dirty brown hair braided down her back. Both held short clubs in their hands. The woman's eyes darted toward me and back to Victoria, clearly nervous.

"Aren't you going to introduce your companions?" Victoria asked, her tone was more appropriate for a garden party.

Granville smirked. "Why of course. Allow me to introduce Miss Laurel Anne Hill," he gestured to the woman who nodded at us. "And Mr. Silas Tanner."

The older man grunted in response.

"A pleasure, I'm sure. Now if you allow me and my associate to pass, I'll bid you all a good day."

"All you'll be doing is coming with us to speak with Master Spencer," Granville said.

Victoria snorted a laugh. "Please, Granville. Jed Spencer has never been and never will be a master of anything. Run back to your boss and tell him his money is coming and not to bother me again."

Granville's smile turned feral. The knife slipped out of the sheath. "Laurel Anne, watch the door. Silas, take care of her friend." The ruffians flanked us. Silas, whose long grey beard hung halfway to his belt, came closer to me.

"Granville, you are making a serious mistake," she said softly.

"The only mistake was mouthin' off to the boss," Silas said. A sneer consuming his ugly face.

"Madame, I won't ask again. Will you come with us?"

"Stay out of this," she said to me in a low voice over her shoulder. Without waiting for a response, her foot lashed out and struck Granville squarely in the crotch. The knife clattered to the floor as he grasped himself, groaning. She executed a right turn, driving her fist into Silas's gut, dropping him like an ox at the slaughterhouse.

Laurel Anne swung her club at Victoria's back, but she danced aside. Swift as forge hammer, she snatched a mug off the trappers' table and slammed it into the woman's head. She joined his friends on the floor.

"Hey, that was my ale!" the trapper complained.

Victoria flipped a silver coin onto the table. "Next round's on me."

She swept out of the pub and I followed. As my first "official" mission since Roland's death, I'd wanted something easy. How hard could killing a rogue bear be?

Obviously, a lot harder than I expected.

7

Outside the wind had picked up, sending sheets of dirt and debris down the street in waves. Victoria snapped her goggles and respirator into place. "Lots of wind and not a lot of rain in Stillhold. Pays to be prepared."

I tied a cloth across my face before following my fellow Watcher down the street. The dust, undeterred by my makeshift mask, found its way into my lungs, making me cough. The impending storm whipped the town like a mule driver in a hurry to get home. My eyes fought to clear themselves of the grit. Victoria's stride increased as she turned down a small alley I'd have missed.

For the next half hour, we stalked between buildings, dodging the worst of the dust storm, hiding in the dark recesses until Victoria was confident we weren't being followed. "Can't be too careful, " she said. "Spencer's goons are getting more determined by the day. I'll have to do something about him sooner or later, though I might need a bit of help."

We continued on. Wyndham slid between rancid piles of trash, which made the stinging wind a pleasure. I held my breath as I navigated the lumps of unidentifiable debris. The light dimmed as we pushed deeper between two warehouses. Victoria stopped and worked a concealed lever to open a hidden door.

Inside, alarium lights dotted the white walls of the laboratory. Victoria's workspace was controlled chaos, with glassware and other instru-

31

ments I didn't recognize stacked all over wooden benches and tables. She hung her long coat, goggles, and respirator on the wall before tying on a leather apron similar to mine for the forge.

She turned to face me, an annoyed look on her long, thin face. She must be a few years older than I, maybe thirty, but her experience placed her far above me. "Do you know how stupid it is to mention the Watchers in a place like the Broken Spoke? If you want to return to Treetop, you need to think first and talk after."

My cheeks heated as I was scolded like a child, but if the shoe fit, you nailed it in place. "I guess I was surprised."

She looked down at her body and leapt back as if startled. "Oh my, I'm a woman," she exclaimed in a mocking tone. Her eyes locked on mine. "Listen, junior--"

"Quinn."

"I don't care if you're Everard. Have you never seen a woman before or did you think the Watchers was a boy's club?" Her eyes blazed like a stoked fire and I was the iron she was about to liquify.

My head dropped, breaking her glare. "I've only met Cian, Everard, and Roland."

"Well, Roland should have…" Her voice trailed off and she tapped her chin as she considered me. "Roland died before he'd fully trained you, didn't he?"

"Yes, ma'am."

"Call me Victoria. or Mistress Wyndham, if you're feeling formal." After another excruciating minute, she said, "You mentioned you needed me to examine a substance you found?"

"Yes, ma'am, err, Victoria." I fumbled in my sack for the blue liquid, which I unpacked carefully out of its box. It had survived the trip intact, which I couldn't say about my nerves. I held up the stoppered syringe.

"Where in the world did you get that?"

"From an armored bear that killed a lot of people."

"I need to hear this story." Victoria took the syringe from me, holding it up to the light. She motioned me to sit on the stool across from her and we both sat. "Let me hear your story, Quinn."

I told her about Cian and I fighting the bear before we were forced to kill it. She murmured her approval. I described the process I'd used to examine the device and how I thought the mechanism worked.

"What do you think is behind the attacks?" she asked. "What do the three towns have in common?"

"Nothing as far as I can see," I said, absently scratching the spot where my mechanical arm met skin.

She noticed, quirking an eyebrow.

I stopped scratching and settled my hands. "Usorin tried to kill my mentor and took my arm instead. Roland found me and, once I was healed, brought me into the Watch. We built a replacement arm. I modified the design to mimic the magus devices for combat."

Victoria nodded, her lips pursed. "Roland was a good man and a great Watcher."

"Yeah," I said glumly. "I've got big shoes to fill."

"So did Roland," she said with a chuckle. "We all have our strengths and weaknesses. You'll learn."

"And if I don't?"

She cocked her head, a strange expression on her face. "Then you'll die, I assume. Now, let's take a look at the present you brought me."

I stood up, startled at the abrupt change of subject. Victoria was a unique person to be sure.

She unstoppered the syringe, emptying the contents into a glass tube on her workbench. "I'll need a day or so to ascertain the nature of this elixir. I'll call on you at the Broken Spoke when I know more."

"What do you think it is?"

She shook her head, "If I knew that already, I wouldn't need a day to research, would I?"

"True."

She smirked at me, a twinkle in her eye. "Do you know what happened when the red ship crashed into the blue ship?"

"No."

"They were marooned." She burst into laughter. I left, shaking my head the whole way.

<hr>

I backtracked to the main street of Stillhold. The winds hadn't stopped, but they weren't trying to knock me over as I walked, either. The sun was beginning to set in the west. I shielded my eyes from the worst of the dirt and wandered around until I found the general store I'd seen earlier. If I was staying in Stillhold, I needed goggles and a respirator. I pushed my way against the wind until I reached the heavy wooden door and, with an effort, wedged it open enough to slip inside.

"Don't let the door--"

Boom! The door slammed behind me, the force of the wind driving it into the frame hard enough to shake the floor. Luckily the frame held under the assault.

"Slam," finished the woman behind the counter. She wore a plaid shawl draped around her shoulders over a dark dress with a long white apron. "Did your ma not teach you about slammin' doors?"

"No, ma'am," I stuttered. "She died when I was young. I didn't mean to let the door slam."

The woman scowled a bit before relaxing. Strands of dark hair snuck out from under her bonnet. Her goggles and a respirator hung around her neck. "Well, can't be blamin' you if' in you weren't taught. What can I do ya fer?"

Supplies of all types populated the store's shelves. The store displayed blankets, bags of oats and flour, cans of oil, along with an assortment of farming supplies and tools. Metal mining lanterns, block and tackle, and other gear hung from the rafters. A curtain covered an exit that led to the rear of the building. Behind the counter were various canned goods along with an assortment of goggles and respirators.

"I'd like to buy a pair of goggles and a respirator," I said, approaching the counter. An ancient mechanical cash register was positioned behind a set of glass jars filled with candy.

She gave me an appraising look before retrieving a dull grey set of goggles and a respirator from the shelf behind the register. I picked the goggles up. Tin. If I put any pressure on them, they'd dent. The respirator was even more flimsy, without mesh or weave to keep the dirt out.

"Seriously?" I asked, trying to keep the irritation out of my voice. My Watcher mask would be far more effective, but a Watcher couldn't exactly walk around town without causing a ruckus. When there was an emergency everyone was glad to see the Watchers, the rest of the time we were viewed with suspicion if not outright hostility.

She shrugged. "You don't look like you've got a silver to your name, let alone the three those cost."

"Three silvers? These are tin. The lens will crack in a stiff wind, and without a filter, I'd choke on the dirt."

She grunted, putting the tin pieces back. The next set appeared no better and I had no patience to spend all day doing this.

"Give me the brass fitted ones on the top shelf."

"Those are two gold. I'll need to see your coin." Her eyes narrowed like a street fighter watching their opponent.

I held up my hands. "You're wasting my time, I'll do without." I turned on my heel and headed toward the door.

I heard her sigh. "One gold for the set?" The note of uncertainty rang out in her words.

"Let me see them." I returned to the counter as she stepped on a short stool and pulled them down. She wiped them on her apron before handing them over.

The goggles had real glass lenses and mechanical fittings so they could be replaced if damaged. The sides contained a small set of grates to allow moisture to escape without allowing in dirt, smoke, or anything else. The respirator held a bag of charcoal that smelled slightly sulfuric. It would neutralize odors and gas. Overkill for what I needed, but I'd quenched my iron so now I was stuck paying for it. "These are better quality, but still not worth a gold."

She cast an appraising glance at me. "How do you know?"

I explained the craftsmanship of the piece and pointed out the benefits of such a setup. She nodded along as I spoke, interrupting to ask a couple of questions. I was in my element, discussing metallurgy, design, and fabrication.

"Are you a tinker?" she asked suddenly, cutting off my lecture on the benefits of using brass instead of bronze.

I shook my head. "No, I was a blacksmith, until my mentor died."

She chewed her lip for a second. "I'll give 'em to you fer half a gold if you'll fix my register. Hasn't worked for a spell and I can't get it open."

"Deal. I'm Randolph." I said, supplying the alias I'd taken for this mission. I reached out my hand and she took it with a firm shake.

"Millicent Habsburg. I appreciate you fixin' this old hunk of junk."

She stepped aside to let me see the register, if you could call it that. It looked like a cross between a metal box and a steam engine. Pistons, gears, and rivets were on every available surface. A glass window showed a "No Sale" chit displayed within. Millicent peered over my shoulder as I pulled out my traveling kit.

She whistled softly as I unrolled the oilskin, displaying my tools. "You must be a tinker, carryin' stuff like that."

Having a quality set of tools had come in handy more times than I cared to remember. When you depended on a mechanical arm, being able to effect repairs was a necessity. "I trained as an artificer when I was younger. You never know when you'll need to fix a mudstone lamp or a register."

"Lucky for me, then. Dang thing's been locked up for months." She pulled a stool over and perched on it, straightening her white apron over her knees.

I checked the drawer mechanism. The locking pin was engaged, but not jammed. The easy fix would be to depress the lock and open the drawer, but that wouldn't prevent the issue from recurring. Plus the return key was frozen in place, which was strange because it wasn't in disrepair. I finished my inspection of the device and nothing else appeared out of order.

"Can ya fix'er?" Millicent asked, doubt heavy in her tone.

"Probably." I rounded the counter, looking for the machine's internal access panel. The candy jars blocked my view of the register's rear plate.

"You break even one of those and I'll tan your hide."

I nodded, carefully setting the jars off to the side. From the back of the register, two small pipes ran down through the counter. "Where do these pipes lead?"

She shrugged. "Don't know. Mr. Habsburg always took care of the store."

"I'm sorry for your loss."

She barked a laugh. "Loss? He's a drunk and ran off on some damn trading adventure. Left me with nothin' but this shop and a lot of debt. Best thing ever happened was him leavin'."

Well, at least I hadn't put the wrong shoe on the horse. "Mind if I look around?"

She clenched her hands together, but said, "Suit yourself."

I searched the room, trying not to trip over the piles of supplies. Millicent had quite the selection for being so far away from a large city. After a few minutes, I found a half door in the wall behind a decent quality mechanical harvester the size of a small donkey. The door revealed an old generator.

This was an old version of a generator, but instead of alarium, it ran off mudstone that didn't last very long. It wasn't running. I primed the pump, but nothing happened. After a couple of minutes, I found the compartment that held the power source. I unscrewed the couplings and removed the top. The chamber held nothing but faint brown dust. It had simply run out of fuel.

I straightened and returned. "Mrs. Habsburg, do you have any mudstone on hand?"

Her eyes narrowed, but she nodded. She took down a tin labeled mudstone from the shelving behind the register and produced a sizable chunk of the semi-precious stone. I placed it in the chamber, reassembled the housings, primed the pump, and started it up. Lights flicked on overhead and the register banged open with a clang. Coins scattered across the floor, all of them gold.

That was when I noticed Millicent pointing a small crossbow at me.

I'd fallen from the tongs into the fire.

8

The curtain at the back of the store swished open, and Granville from the Broken Spoke, flanked by Silas and Laurel Anne, sauntered out. Granville pulled an older woman behind him. Her hands were tied before her and a gag was shoved in her mouth. Tears rolled down her plump cheeks.

"Mrs. Habsburg, are you all right?" I asked gently as I sized up the situation. The crossbow was the biggest threat, but only until the woman fired it. I doubted she could reload it, given the pull of the bow. I was more concerned about the bruised, battered, and probably resentful men holding the real Millicent Habsburg.

Case in point, Granville pulled her in front of him and placed a long hunting knife near her throat. Since I hadn't brought my weapons, I'd have to rely on other skills. Roland had trained me in hand-to-hand combat, and it was four on one.

"Of course, she's all right, lad," Granville said, though I noticed he stood a bit gingerly. "Imagine you just strollin' on in here when we spent the day lookin' fer ya. Unless you want the old woman to get sliced up, you'll be taking us to see Lady Yorke once we're done here. Do that, and we'll let you go. Decide to be a hero and you'll bleed. Either way, you'll take us to her. Understand?"

I nodded, keeping my eyes on the floor, acting like a good mouse. I

38

needed to get within arm's reach of the knife. Then the real fight would begin. "I can take you to her, but only if you release Mrs. Habsburg."

The leader waved the knife in my direction. "See, the lad is reasonable and we've no gripe with him." He pushed the old woman to the side, where Silas caught her. He had a small club, not a knife, making my job easier. "Edwina, gather up the coin our young friend was nice enough to free up for us."

Millicent, trying to talk through her gag, protested the robbery I'd facilitated. Granville raised his baton to strike her.

Guilt at being fooled so easily galled me. "Leave the coin. She's done nothing to hurt you."

Granville brandished the knife, gesturing at me to emphasize his point. "You're a stranger here, lad. This woman has stolen from the poor people of Stillhold as if she'd put a knife to their throats herself. Ask her how many farms died after the river broke?"

"What do you mean the river broke?"

He smiled at me like I was an ignorant child. "Boy, them wizards got into a fight upstream. When all was said and done, the river stopped flowing past Stillhold and flooded out the down country."

This must be what the bartender was talking about. Was Everard involved? He had to be. The magus' all used the alarium powered sleeves to effect their "magic" and there wasn't enough power in them to divert a river. "How does that make it Mrs. Habsberg's fault?"

"Did she offer equipment to drill wells to irrigate? No, she just let them starve or bought up their lands and offered to rent the land back to the farmers with a well—at a ridiculous price. Does that sound like a saint?"

"Sounds like a business. How many debts did your boss excuse during the hard times? I would guess zero." His cheeks flushed. Behind me Edwina tossed the previously trapped coins into a burlap bag, giggling the whole time.

"And why should he? Master Spencer lends to those in need, but he expects his money returned to him. The Lady Yorke owes him a right sum, and I'm going to make sure he gets it. Now let's finish this. Master Spencer is a man of little patience."

I nodded. The crossbow rested on the counter next to Edwina. She'd lost her focus while loading up the coins. "Why are these all covered in grease?" Edwina complained. She cleaned one-off with the hem of her dress. "I told you Lemuel said there was a fortune stuck in here and I was the only one smart enough to figure it out."

Granville rounded on her. "That coin is for Master Spencer, not a trollop like you, Edwina. Don't you go forgettin' it."

I doubted I'd get a better chance. I dove at Granville. He twisted at the last second, my punch landing on his shoulder instead of his jaw. He bellowed in pain as my metal fist struck.

Edwina's burlap bag crashed to the floor with the jingle of spilling coins. She grabbed the crossbow and fired without aiming. The shot ricocheted off my arm and pierced the woman's chest, dropping her.

"Laurel Anne!" she cried, running to the fallen woman.

Silas charged at me faster than I'd predicted given the number of things in the way. His baton struck me across the face, hard enough to knock me back from him and his weapon. He advanced, launching another blow at my head. The fight would have been over except my foot caught on a bag of flour and I crashed to the floor, avoiding the finishing blow.

"Don't kill him," Granville yelled over Edwina's anguished screams. "We need him to find the woman."

I don't think the man listened. He swung overhanded at me. Using my metal arm as a shield, I blocked the attack. With a swift kick, I struck his knee, buckling the leg. Baton and man alike fell to the ground.

In hopes of a quick knockout, I threw a punch at his head. He rolled aside, pulling a knife from his boot before he climbed to his feet.

"Now we'll see how well you bleed," Silas said between gritted teeth.

The knife flashed, and a rent appeared in my sleeve, revealing the bronze metal underneath. "What kind of demon be you?"

"Not a demon, just an injured man."

Silas lunged, the knife held like a spear. I caught the blade in my metal hand and snapped it clean off. While he stared at his broken weapon, I punched him in the jaw, dropping him like a bad habit.

Before I could reach her, Granville grabbed Millicent and held his knife in his left hand while his right hung uselessly at his side from the earlier punch. "I'll kill her if you come any closer, stranger."

I had been taken advantage of and underestimated and my patience had run out. It was time to put an end to this. "Let her go and you can walk out of here."

He shook his head, anguish and fear reflected in his eyes. "I don't bring in Lady Yorke, I won't live to see tomorrow, lad. Master Spencer doesn't brook well with failure."

Which meant he had nothing left to lose. Before I could do anything, Millicent Habsburg nodded forward as if she would faint.

With a flick of my wrist, I sent the broken blade sailing over Granville's head.

He laughed when it missed, but it wasn't long-lasting. The knife sliced through the thin cord holding a mining lantern in place. He looked up in time for the lantern to crash into his face. When he fell to the floor with a hiss of pain, Mrs. Habsburg stumbled free.

I pulled my belt knife and cut Millicent's bonds. She pulled the gag from her mouth and proceeded to kick the man who'd threatened her life. I led her behind the counter, pushing the crossbow out of the way, and settled her onto a stool. "Did they hurt you?"

"No, son. Thank ye for saving me. My husband's been gone for a few years. I'm glad you got the register opened. That money was for me to run the place, but the register stopped working right after he left. Let me reward you for saving me."

I smiled at her. "I'm going to finish this." Edwina sobbed on the floor next to Laurel Anne's body. The quill had pierced her heart from the looks of it. I knelt next to her. "How much does Lady Yorke owe Master Spencer?"

She flinched away from my touch. "Granville would know." She gestured toward where the leader lay on the floor clutching his bloodied face. I left her in her misery and pulled Granville to his feet. "How much does Lady Yorke owe?"

Blood spattered me as he slurred out the answer. "Twelve gold, but Spencer wants her more than the coin."

"Gold will have to do." I dragged him behind me. "Mrs. Habsburg, I hate to impose..."

She held out a handful of gold coins. "There are fifteen there. Spencer is a hard man, so be careful."

"I will. Thank you." The coins were slick with oil, not grease. I looked to her for an explanation.

"I tried to oil the lock, thinking it was stuck. I guess I used too much."

I chuckled. "Well, these won't stick to anything now. I'll pay you back as soon as I can."

She shook her head and handed me the brass goggles and respirator.

"You'll need these. The least I can do is help you get your friend out of debt."

I nodded, knowing I was done with the easy part of my day. As a Watcher, I should have taken Edwina into custody for murder. Unfortunately, they'd seen my face and I couldn't risk revealing I was a Watcher. It would be up to "Randolph", not Watcher Quinn to set this straight.

It was time to walk into the lion's den and face down the king.

9

I half dragged, half carried Granville through the maelstrom of the oncoming storm, thankful for the goggles and respirator Mrs. Habsburg had given me. Granville stumbled and cursed as I propelled him into the teeth of the wind. I may have 'forgotten' his gear back at the shop. No skin off my nose, but his nose was in rough shape at this point.

After a few minutes, we reached a wooden building sporting a faded sign proclaiming it the Gilded Lily. I pushed our way through the heavy wooden door into the main room of the brothel. A few girls stared at us, glassy-eyed, as I shoved Granville down on the floor in front of me. He squawked, landing with a thud. I'd have dragged his accomplices with us, but they were taking Laurel Anne to the morgue.

The room was well appointed with brass fixtures and mirrors covering the walls. Stairs led up to a walkway that wrapped around the main room. Glass chandeliers hung low, casting a soft light that made the room feel richer than the furnishings alone ever could. Small tables dotted the area before the mammoth bar which was made of polished brass, glass, and a series of gears across the front. What happened when the gears turned? My professional curiosity would have to wait.

A large woman in a silk robe and elaborate hairdo strolled across the room toward us. Her gaze fixed on Granville. "You ain't lookin' so hot, honey."

Granville lifted his head. "Mama Rosalie, I ain't feelin' so good." His words were muffled by his broken nose.

Rosalie's gaze meandered over me. I didn't take off the goggles but slipped the respirator down so I could speak.

"You here on business or pleasure, sweetheart?" she asked pointedly. "Maybe a bit of both?"

I tamped down on the flush that tried to color my cheeks. "Business, ma'am. I need to speak to Master Spencer."

"Such a shame. Well, follow me." When I stopped to grab Granville, she added, "My boys will take care of the trash."

Granville whimpered but didn't say anything. I followed Rosalie past the opulent bar and through a doorway into a large office. The walls were paneled in a dark wood, broken only by a large stone fireplace that contained a roaring fire. A thick rug covered the floor in front of the mahogany desk with two alarium lamps. Master Spencer must be worth a small fortune.

A man leaned back in his chair, puffing on a cigar. A glass of amber liquid rested in front of him. He was a larger man, not fat, but sturdily built, like one of the haulers I'd known as a boy. His hairline receded from an oversized nose that ended in a vicious hook.

When he spoke, it was in a deep, booming voice. "Allow me to introduce myself. I'm Master Spencer, owner of the Guilded Lilly. And you are?"

I ignored the question. "I've come to settle up Lady Yorke's debt to you."

"So, you must be the companion of Lady Yorke I've heard about. Why have you abused my men and come here? Mayhap you wish to die?"

I pulled twelve gold coins from the pouch on my belt and tossed them on the desk. "There's your coin. You and Lady Yorke are square, as I see it."

Spencer laughed as he raked his hands through the scattered coins. He examined his oily fingers before cleaning them on his handkerchief. "Boy, you come into my place of business and declare a debt been paid? That's not how these things work. Lady Yorke owes me twelve gold and a favor. You can't repay that."

Rosalie simpered like a schoolgirl at the implications. I glared at her, though I doubt she could tell with my goggles on.

I was about to speak when the door opened and Watcher Wyndham herself strode in. Her apron had been replaced by a sturdy leather coat, leather gauntlets, and a large revolver. "Spencer, our game has been fun, but as usual, you've gone too far."

Another bout of laughter erupted from the big man. "Ah, my Lady Yorke. To what do I owe the honor of your visit?"

I wasn't sure what her game was, but I was fascinated by how she spoke to Master Spencer.

Victoria's eyes burned like a hot and uncontrollable coal ash fire. "How dare you sic your mutts on the Widow Habsburg? I knew you had few morals, but this is beyond reproach."

Spencer's fist struck the top of his desk, jangling the coins and threatening to topple his drink. "It is you that goes too far, Lady Yorke. I lent you coin in good faith and this is how you repay me?"

The fire in her eyes went out like a bucket of water had doused it. "You're right. Instead, I will offer you a gift." She pulled a small glass vial from the inner pocket of her coat. It held a green liquid that sparkled in the light cast from the alarium lamps. "I bestow upon thee the elixir of life."

"What foolery is this?" Spencer demanded, but his eyes clung to the vial in her fingertips. "Even with your alchemical skills, there is no such thing."

Victoria cocked her head, considering his words. "True for most, but this truly is life for you, Spencer." She spun the vial neatly in her fingers. "Master Randolph paid my debt. Did you touch the coins?"

Spencer's face grew concerned as he held up his hands, noticing the residue from the oily gold. "Why?"

Victoria must have spoken with Mrs. Habsburg before following me here.

Wyndham smiled brightly. "Contact poison, I'm afraid, and this is the antidote. Well, at least the first one."

"First one?" Rosalie's eyes widened like she'd touched a hot iron.

"Rosalie's got the picture. The poison will stay in your system. Every week, I'll leave a vial of the antidote with Widow Habsburg. I'll leave it up to her if she'd like to deliver it. Vex the poor woman, and your life will be over. Do we understand each other?"

Spencer's gaze went from the vial to Wyndham to me. His eyes lit up as he said, "What about your man there? He touched the coins. You're bluffing."

I held up my hand, covered in a leather glove. "I took precautions."

Spencer's shoulders slumped in defeat. "Name your terms."

"You may keep the coin, though you may want to wash them. As you correctly stated, I did borrow it from you and I have returned it with the interest as agreed."

Spencer didn't say anything so Victoria continued. "Second, if your men come after me or the Widow, your supply of antidote will cease and you will die a horrible, excruciatingly painful death."

"Anything else?" Spencer mumbled as he placed his elbows heavily on his desk.

"No." Victoria slid the vial across the desk to Spencer, who uncorked it and drank it greedily.

Spencer leaned back into his chair. "We're done here. Get out of my office."

Rosalie approached, shooing us. I stepped toward the door, but Victoria held her ground.

Wyndham's voice was light and airy as she asked, "Spencer, what kind of tea is hard to swallow?"

His face darkened. "I have no time for your foolishness. Get out."

Victoria smiled sweetly. "Reali-ty." With that, she pivoted on her heel and strode from the room.

The woman could definitely make an exit.

10

Victoria escorted me back to the Broken Spoke and asked me to stay out of trouble. I thought about arguing with her, but given the day I'd had, I just agreed and ate an early dinner in my room. I spent the evening maintaining my arm, though one-handed was always a challenge.

The next morning, I was eating breakfast in the common room of the Broken Spoke when Victoria sauntered through the front door. She wore a long, dark coat over a peacock green shirt and grey pants. She slid her goggles and respirator down as she approached my table and took a seat across from me.

"Good morn, Randolph." Her bloodshot eyes hinted at a lack of sleep.

"Good morning, Lady Yorke." I set my bowl aside and wiped my hands on the cloth napkin. "Did you find out about the package I left with you?"

She smirked. "Why, yes, I have. If you're done with your breakfast, there are things we need to discuss."

No jokes or wordplay. Worry seeped up my back into my brain. I dropped a couple of coppers on the table and adjusted my goggles and respirator as she opened the door. While the storm wasn't as intense as the previous days, it was still enough for me to be thankful for them.

Wyndham took a different route to the laboratory, stopping three times to ensure we weren't followed. I didn't say anything, and given the whistling of the wind, conversations were best held indoors. After she was assured we were alone, we entered her hideout.

Her coat and goggles were hung on a hook. I pulled mine off as well, setting them on a small table near the door. A gunpowder revolver sat on the workbench near the door. "Expecting trouble?"

Victoria perched on a stool. "Quinn, tell me how you got this again?"

I repeated the story about the bear Cian and I had defeated outside of Lapis. This time she fired off questions, picking at details as if looking for the hidden seed of truth.

"I am forced to say I believe you, but what you've brought me is highly troubling, to say the least." She grabbed a piece of parchment and handed it to me "I've run a series of tests and have reverified the results to elimi-nate any false positives or testing errors."

I waited as she collected her thoughts. Concern etched her face like the design on an artificer's plate. After a moment I prompted her. "And?"

"Sorry, lack of sleep is making me a bit foggy." She adjusted her leather apron. "The fluid in the vial is benzodiazepine mixed with a cyclopy-rrolone."

As an artificer, I knew my fair share of large words, but Victoria may as well have been speaking Nornish. "I don't know what any of that means."

"I didn't think you would," Victoria said as she set the paper back down on the workbench. "Both are strong drugs, used to treat patients in asylums. They make the patients more pliable, open to suggestion. Mixed, they form a drug that borders on hypnotic. If the device on the animal's back was pumping this into its system, someone could easily control the poor thing's mind to force it to follow simple commands."

I pulled the pouch off my belt and removed the mechanical piece I'd taken from the bear. I handed it to Victoria, who studied it carefully before returning it to me.

"What is it?" she asked.

I shook my head. "It is probably how the bear was controlled. If no one was nearby to direct it, then this instrument must be how they forced the bear to attack the villagers."

"Makes sense," She pushed her long black ponytail over her shoulder. "The real question is why attack the villages in the first place?"

I'd been wondering the same thing. None of the towns were overly wealthy, nor traded in products that were scarce. No large merchant routes ran through them. The magi rulers weren't known for atrocities or mismanaging their holdings. In fact, Nigel of House Hawk had a reputation as a bit of a philanthropist, giving to the people of Aldon far more than Usorin had ever given Terralon.

"I've been over the attacks in my head, but there are no common denominators. If it was revenge, why attack three towns? None of the towns hold strategic or political value. I need to find out who is behind this."

Victoria nodded her agreement. "It is a sticky situation. With Aurelia Salwey's death in the first bear attack, there isn't a Watcher in Aldon. I guess that's where you come in."

"Then why didn't Cian handle the latest attack? Aldon is on the other end of the country from me." Why I'd been sent to deal with this situation perplexed me since I was only responsible for Terralon. And if I recalled correctly, Roland had traveled all over the country. "I thought the Watchers served Astaria as a whole?"

Victoria sighed. The dark rings under her eyes told the story of how exhausted she was. "Those would be questions for Everard, but my guess is you have a skill he needed. Each of us has abilities that we use in the defense of Astaria. The trick is to use your specific skills to carry out the mission of protecting the Astarian people. You couldn't use alchemey to solve a problem any more than I could forge a solution. You have to approach things from your point of view, not someone else's."

What had Everard expected I could do more than an experienced Watch member? I definitely would be discussing this further with him at his earliest convenience. "I appreciate the information, both on the fluid and on the Watchers. I doubt I'll ever understand all of this."

She laughed. "You will, Quinn. It's only been six months. Most of us apprentice for years before we move to our own region. Time is the coin of our trade."

My mentor had been killed before I'd had much training. Sometimes iron breaks and ends up in the scrap pile. That doesn't stop you from forging a new piece. "Speaking of coins, how long until Spencer realizes you didn't poison him?"

She cocked her head. "Who says I didn't poison him?"

"Well, the coins were coated in oil, not poison, and you gave him the antidote."

She smiled, mischief dancing in her brown eyes. "Did I now? How do you know it was the antidote?"

"You told him it was."

"I did," she said, shrugging her shoulders, her hands spread out in front of her. "And of course, a lady would never lie."

After a moment, I realized what she'd done. "The vial was the poison."

She clapped her approval. "Spencer is a rabid animal, but if I remove him, someone worse might take over. By poisoning him, I can control him and keep him from killing more innocent people. This is what I mean by using your skills to solve problems. Dead, he's no good to me, but poisoned he'll do as I say or he will be gone."

Ruthless but practical. "Thank you, Victoria. Today has been very educational."

"A child comes home from school and is asked, 'What did you learn today?'" Victoria said as I snapped my goggles back into place.

"And the child says?"

"Not enough, I have to go back tomorrow."

I groaned and headed out the door into the wind.

The words rang true, though. I'd have to keep learning tomorrow if I wanted to find the person responsible for the bear attack.

11

I caught the airship back to Bradenbridge, staying overnight at the Brass Gear before riding the two days to Treetop. On my way out of Bradenbridge, I stopped to buy some supplies I'd need. No sense going home empty-handed.

The puzzle of the bear, the drug, and the mysterious magic device ran circles in my brain as I steered the cart along the path I'd come to know quite well. The answer was in front of me; I just couldn't see it. Victoria had said to use my talents to solve issues, but blacksmithing or artificing didn't get me any closer to catching the person responsible for the attacks. At least as far as I could see.

I stepped off the lift contemplating my dilemma. No Jabber. He always waited at the door for my return. "Jabber?" I said, setting down the provisions and entering into the living area. The door to the workshop stood open with no signs of Jabber or anyone else. The last time I'd returned to find Treetop empty, I discovered the corpse of my mentor. A mix of fear and energy throbbed through my body as I turned the corner that led to the sleeping areas and the kitchen.

"Quinn," Everard yelped as he jumped back. The stew in a wooden bowl slopped over his hands as he adjusted his grip. Jabber followed behind the Arch Magus with a small cask of ale. "Good to see you, Master Quinn, but I hadn't expected you until tomorrow."

"What are you doing here?" I asked, my voice trembling from the shock of seeing another person in my home. Jabber was part of Treetop, but Everard was an unexpected guest.

"Let me put this down before I spill it all." He stepped past me, heading for the long table in the living area.

Jabber approached me. "The Arch Magus is authorized to enter Treetop," the automaton said, his voice neutral as ever. "Is that not correct?"

I shook my head in disbelief. Why would Everard be here? "He's allowed to enter, just wasn't expecting anyone else. Can you put the provisions away while I talk with Everard? I'll take the ale."

"Of course," Jabber said with a slight bow. He handed me the cask and the cup. I needed to figure out how to adjust him to be a bit less formal, but that would have to wait. I walked down the hall and retrieved a second mug.

Everard sat at the table eating the stew. I took the stool across from him, poured us each a mug of ale, and waited for him to explain why he was at Treetop.

He sipped at the ale and nodded approvingly. "Good beer. You asked why I've come to visit, as it were," he said in a joking tone. "Two reasons, really. Cian told me about the incident in Aldon, and you need to practice your magic, so I am here to teach you."

I groaned inside. Everard had been Arch Magus since before I was born. Unlike Roland's patient lessons, Evarard's idea of teaching was constant repetition until it worked or you fell over from exhaustion. Not exactly the best learning environment. It might be better to bang my head against the table until I got the hang of magic.

Everard held up a hand. "I realize we've been less than successful in our other training sessions, but I've got a few ideas. First off, tell me what you've found so far about the bear."

I took a swing from my mug, collecting my thoughts. I had to agree, it was a good beer. "Where do you want me to begin?"

"From where you encountered the bear."

I launched into the story, going over the fight and how pulling the box free had stopped the rampage and killed the bear in the process. I shared the information Victoria had given me and the conclusions I'd had that the device was being used to control the bear from a distance. He sipped at his beer while I spoke, stopping me to ask questions.

He refilled both our beers when I came to the end. "Can I see the device?"

I fished it out of my pouch and handed it over. He studied the runes and inscriptions carefully, before placing it on the table. He muttered a few words as he made a series of gestures over the device.

Nothing happened for a few moments until a raspy male voice emanated from the air above the small box. "Kill the magus and bring me..."

The voice dwindled to nothing.

"Interesting," Everard said. A single bead of sweat rolled down his cheek. "Not much to go on, but we know it's a male who was directing the bear. The real question is why concentrate on you when Cian was the greater threat?"

I started to agree, but then remembered. "Maybe, but one of the Aldon magus was onsite. He threw lightning at the beast before it killed him and tried to drag his body away. The townsfolk threatened and the bear attacked them."

"Why would a bear drag off one corpse after killing so many?" Everard asked.

I couldn't answer that question. Each piece of information held nothing in common with the rest. I had a bench full of parts and no plan to show me what to build. I took another drink and waited for Everard to say something.

"I'll sleep on it and maybe in the morning I'll have a better idea of what to do next," Everard said.

"Next?"

Everard scoffed. "Come now, Quinn. You can't believe someone who went to all that trouble to kill a bunch of villagers would stop that easily, did you?"

The Arch Magus was right. It was only a matter of time before another bear, or something worse, showed up. But when and where...and why? "What do they have to gain from killing villagers?"

"Well that certainly is a question we'd like to answer, but we'll need to keep searching until we find it." He clapped his hands as he rose. "Now, let's try a couple of simple spells to warm up."

I forced myself to stand. Everard straightened and breathed deeply which I mimicked. He paced me through the exercises his master had used to teach him about magic. In my observations, magic was altering energy to accomplish your goal. What deep breathing and arm-waving had to do with it, I didn't know, but I was game to try anything at this point. At least he was trying something different than the last set of lessons.

"Now," Everard said when I was sufficiently warmed up. "Start with Lenthal um Tral. It will levitate an object. I tried magic too complex last time, so this is as simple as it gets."

"Lenthal um Tral," I said, envisioning my mug rising off the table. Nothing happened.

"Quinn, you need to use gestures to unlock the magic. Watch." He crossed his wrists, hooking his thumbs together so they looked like a bird. He spoke the words as he curled his fingers, and his mug rose smoothly into the air. As he uncurled his fingers the mug settled back to the wooden table. "Now you try."

I repeated his steps as exactly as I could and still, nothing happened. "Maybe my metal arm interferes with the magic."

Everard shook his head. "Try it again, but make sure your thumbs are interlocked." I did and still no results. For over an hour I tried to float the mug, but voice inflection, finger position, and everything else yielded nothing but frustration.

"You have to believe it will work, Quinn. You must be doubting the magic or yourself. I can't think of anything else that would be stopping you."

"Maybe it's his teacher," a soft voice said from behind me. I pivoted to see a woman in a blue robe, silver runes surrounding the cowl and wrists. She pushed back her hood, exposing deep golden skin, lavender eyes, and features so delicate they could have been made of glass. Long black hair draped behind her.

Everard knelt on one knee and I followed suit. "My lady Maelyrra. To what do we owe the honor of your visit?"

"You are ruining my mage, Everard, and I want you to stop."

12

I remained on my knees, head bowed, wondering what to do. The Lady Maelyrra had bestowed my magic upon me to defend Astaria from our common foes. I still had no idea which dimension she came from or why she had chosen me to aid Everard with true magic. The nobles used devices such as my shield generator to mimic magical abilities, but if I could ever get my powers to work I would be far more effective.

"Stand up, Quinn. I would converse with you."

Thunderstruck, I stood. What was so important to risk the danger of crossing over to our dimension? She could have summoned me instead.

"Everard, leave us." She dismissed the Arch Magus with a wave. "I have need to speak with Quinn, alone." The emphasis on the word "alone" would have pierced even the dimmest of listeners. Everard, being far more intelligent, huffed once, bowed to Maelyrra, and proceeded to leave the room.

"Lady Maelyrra, how can I be of service?"

She floated just off the floor, the hem of her blue robe billowing slightly as if a gentle breeze stirred it. "Your mastery of the magical arts has not progressed beyond rudimentary. I came to find out why, but I would like to know your thoughts on the matter."

A headache crept up my neck as my heart pounded. Would she take away the magic if I didn't master it? I felt like a child who'd been gifted a

55

wonderful machine with nothing to tell them what it did or how to operate it. All of the parts were on the table before me, but there was no way for me to make them work. Honestly, I'd stopped trying out of frustration. I sighed. "I have done everything the Arch Magus has demonstrated and nothing works. He's left me notes and practicums, and I can barely light a candle with my magic. I feel like I have failed you."

Maelyrra nodded, her eyes full of warmth and interest. "Let me ask you a question. Would you put a horseshoe on a cow?"

My spinning thoughts halted at the unexpected question. The shock must have shown on my face for a gentle smile graced her lips. "No, of course not."

"Why?"

"Horses and cows have very different hooves. Even if the shoe fit, hammering the nails in would hurt the cow. It would be cruel to the animal."

"Exactly. So why would you learn magic the same way Everard did?"

"I..." Words fled as my brain failed to produce a reason. I floundered and finally spit out, "Because he learned it that way and that is how magic works."

Her eyes glittered in the afternoon sun that streamed in the windows. "Are all blacksmiths trained the same?"

I shook my head. "No, my lady. Some take to it quicker or have an eye for how the metal moves under the hammer. You adjust the training to suit the student."

"Agreed. So again, why learn magic the way Everard did? It is possible an off-handed solution would be more effective." Her serene expression informed me she wasn't upset or angry at all.

Why was I learning Everard's way? Everard's magic was strong and had saved lives, thwarted Norn and Candalarian attacks, and kept the Astarian magi in check. Not to mention there weren't any other true magi in Astaria. In the absence of another source, you returned to the fire you had.

Except...I never had been willing to sacrifice the quality of my work because of limitations. I would build a bigger forge bed or add mudstone to increase the temperature if that was what it took. I wouldn't settle for the fire I was given. Why should I do it with magic, when I didn't do it with the rest of my life? My master blacksmith had always told me a true artisan had to go his own way, not recreate what others had already done.

"Well?" she asked, though I was guessing she knew what I'd been thinking. Whether that was through her own magic or common sense I doubted I'd ever know.

"I shouldn't be learning Everard's way," I answered.

"Correct. Everard is a showman, brash and charming, able to convince others of his vision. You are an artificer. Magic for you won't be a system of words and gestures or runes inscribed on an object. Your magic is directly tied to your essence. It will work when it joins with your other skills."

"It sounds like you are telling me to use blacksmithing to do magic," I said.

"All the mages who've wielded power through the ages have had their own specialty that made them unique. Quinn, you design and build devices. Let the magic flow through you and into your work, and you will know success."

"Thank you, Maelyrra."

She acknowledged me with a slight dip of her chin. "If you would allow me, I'd like to show you one thing before I leave you."

"Of course."

She held out her hand to me and I grasped it gently, afraid my metal hand would damage the delicate woman. A cool sense of peace and harmony flowed into me and lifted my spirits. I hadn't realized how much grief and anger I'd been carrying until it was taken off my shoulders. Without a word or a gesture, we shifted into a dark room somewhere other than Treetop. The room's only feature was a spinning blue globe the size of a cart that cast enough light to push the shadows back, but not dispel them.

"Where are we?" I asked as I stared at the globe, noticing the scudding clouds, the rippling waves of the ocean. Astaria opened out before me, from the northern reaches of Terralon to the high plains of the Candalarian Horde spread out to the south. The Norn Empire stood off to the northeast of Terralon. I circled the globe, but the rest was hazy and nondescript.

"We are on my plane of existence. The source of Astarian's magic bound by the alarium in the ground under your country." Her voice sounded miles away and yet so close that I expected her to be next to me.

"This is our world, but I can't see what else is here."

"There is much you do not know, and I cannot reveal things about the world you have not learned on your own." The globe spun and grew until I stood outside Lapis the night of the bear attack. Everything was frozen in place, but I could walk around the scene. Maelyrra stood next to me as I studied the details I hadn't had time to notice in the middle of the fight.

"Magic takes all forms, Quinn." Her gentle voice was the only sound. "You are on a path to either save us or doom us to the darkness. Fate has chosen you to be her tool in righting what once went wrong."

Me? I didn't want to believe her, but it was Lady Maelyrra. Magic emanated off her like heat from a forge. I felt an urge to protect her at any cost, making it impossible to deny her. I'd come to realize there must be a reason she chose me. I'd have to trust her judgment until it became clear that I could do the job. "What do I need to do?"

"You will know when the time comes, but you cannot do this alone. Pick your allies carefully, for there are forces at work seeking to end the light for good."

"Is the bear attack part of it?" I asked, my voice hesitant. The enormity of it all set my head spinning. "If I find the responsible party, will the threat be over?"

"I think not. This may have ties to the enemy, but may only be coincidental." She stared off into the darkness for a moment before continuing. "The future is unclear, but you are resourceful and strong."

As we stood in the dark outside of Lapis, watching the bear dragging the magus's corpse across the ground, I felt neither strong nor resourceful. Then an idea struck me. I fumbled in my pouch, producing the rune-covered device I'd taken from the bear. I held it out to her. "My Lady, do you know what this is?"

Her eyes widened as her fingers touched the piece. "This is strong magic. Where did you get it?"

"It was in the box controlling the bear. Watcher Wyndham analyzed the liquid I found in the box along with this. It turns out it is a drug that puts the victim into a hypnotic state. Someone was forcing the bear to kill people."

Maelyrra flipped the device, studying the engravings. "It is not of our type of magic," she said after a while. "My guess is a Candalarian Wind Walker enchanted it. The Norns use runes but these are not theirs. It is complex magic meant to be cast from a distance, but I can glean nothing else."

It was more than I'd had before. If the bear controller was in league with the Candalarian Horde, it made sense the attacks happened on the border between Candalar and Astaria. If this was the start of a larger invasion, more attacks would be coming and I'd need to be prepared to face them. I was about to ask Lady Maelyrra to return me to Treetop when something caught my eye.

I strode across the ground to examine the bear more closely. The images felt real enough that I half expected the bear to attack me. It had torn the arm from the magus who had tried to stop it. The arm, wrapped in the metal armature the magi used to emulate magic, dripped blood onto the grass under the bear. Why that body—why that part of the body? What if it was after the technology? Had the same happened at the other two towns or if the attack was meant to lure the magus out to fight the bear?

If they were after the artifacts and not just killing villagers, this changed everything.

13

My mind flooded with all new questions. Who would benefit from stealing the magus' gear? What were they using it for? Why employ an animal instead of ambushing a magus and taking what they wanted? Too many unknowns and no answers.

Maelyrra returned us to Treetop without a word or a gesture. "I know the path may be difficult for you, but you will grow into a tremendous mage."

In the blink of an eye, Maelyrra was gone and I was alone with my thoughts. How does being an artificer lend itself to magic? I built devices, not magic spells.

Everard emerged from the hallway carrying two mugs, Jabber following closely behind him with a tray of food. "Good to see you are back. Jabber and I prepared dinner since you can't work on an empty stomach."

To illustrate the point, my stomach growled at the smell of roasted chicken and potatoes. I pushed the papers to the side, making room for the meal. Everard placed a mug of ale in front of me. I took a quick drink while Jabber set out the food. I noticed the clock on the wall and flinched. "I didn't realize I'd been gone all day."

Everard nodded, setting down his food. "What did you and Maelyrra discuss, if you don't mind me asking?"

I reviewed our conversation, told him of the room with the globe, and

60

how we'd watched the scene of the bear attack. He interjected a couple of questions for clarification as I went. In the end, we came to the same conclusion—the attacks were intended to steal the alarium powered magus armaments.

Jabber interrupted me. "Master Quinn, your food is getting cold and you've not eaten today."

My mother had died when I was a child, but now I had a mechanical mother to watch over me. Obediently I bit into the chicken, juice running down my chin.

Everard groaned. "We should teach you table manners." I started to protest, but he cut me off. "You eat. I'll talk." He took a swig of his ale as Jabber cleared his plate. "I need you to make me an automaton."

"It's not all it's cracked up to be," I said with a snort.

"I heard that." Jabber's voice came from down the hall. "You would be lost without me to take care of Treetop."

Everard chuckled. "He's got you there. Over the years, Maelyrra has shown up to speak to me a handful of times, and only twice have I been invited to the viewing chamber. Both were when Astaria was in the most danger."

"Viewing chamber?"

"The place with the globe in it. It is a powerful artifact that brings you to what you need to see most. This situation must be important for her to take you this early in your training."

"I still don't know how to use my magic any better than I did, and now you are telling me the situation is worse than we'd guessed. None of this is making me feel any better."

"Tell me again what Maelyrra said about learning magic," Everard said.

"She said I need to approach it as if it was an artificer's problem."

"How would you solve any other problems?"

I scratched my chin as I thought. "I'd examine the problem, decide what tool I needed to fix the issue."

"Exactly," Everard said, reaching across to fill my mug. "Let's start with something easier than the bear and all that. Design something to lift a box."

"But I need to—"

"No, just a device to lift something. Build a machine and let me know when it's ready. No arguments, just do it."

I started to disagree that I didn't have time to waste, but until the hidden enemy made his next move, I had nothing but time. As my old

Master Blacksmith used to say, you had to build the fire before you could bend metal, and he was right. "I'll get on it."

"Good." Everard left the room.

I retrieved my sketch pad and began to draw new plans for a lifting device. Jabber collected my dishes, placed an alarium lamp on the table, and retired to the other side of the room in case I needed anything.

Hours passed as I designed a piece to attach to my left arm gauntlet. It was a flattened cylinder with a dial so I could adjust how high I wanted to raise the object. I went into the workshop and lit the forge fire. I started with rough shaping the pieces of the lifter. Energy flowed through and around me as I worked, setting the hairs on my arm on edge. I'd never experienced anything like that before. My focus was razor-sharp, noticing small imperfections in the metal.

Jabber silently operated the bellows as I cast the base from bronze. Once the clay mold was filled, I used silver stock to craft the dial. I wasn't sure how the magic I could now feel would be incorporated, but I was too focused for such concerns to affect me. Everard said to build a device and I was making it, even though I wondered if it would work.

Swirls of energy spun around me while I hammered out the forms even as an icy sensation covered my body. Invisible strands bound me to each piece I created. Somehow it was as if they were alive in my mind. Was this how Everard felt when he did his magic? As I worked, the completed form hung in my mind like a kite on the wind. I knew it would work.

I set the silver disc aside and broke open the clay mold to examine the casted piece. It needed to be smoothed out for easy turning, but it was not cracked or warped. I drafted a small hole through the bottom for the pin that would bring the two pieces together. Once the screw was done, I heated the silver and set the thread pattern so when it cooled the two pieces would connect.

"Master Quinn, you should go to bed," Jabber said as I dozed in the armchair outside the workshop waiting for the pieces to be ready.

I stretched and stifled a yawn. "I'm going to put the pieces together and then I'll go to bed." Sleep would have to wait. I wanted to see if the device I made did anything at all.

My energy waned with each passing moment. I felt drained to the point of collapse, but I forced myself to keep going. The burden of failure and worry hung over me like a storm cloud. The metal looked cold, but metal was unforgiving and a piece hot enough to burn you looked the same as a cold piece. Once I ensured they were room temperature, I picked them up.

I staggered to the finishing bench with a strong alarium lamp and a magnifying glass for delicate crafting. The creation of weapons, lamps, and other devices required finesse to ensure everything interfaced smoothly. I spent longer than I should have cleaning up the screw threads, but my eyes could barely focus through the bleariness. It did make threading the screw into the housing a lot more difficult.

"Master Quinn," Jabber said. "Might you be better off waiting to finish until you've slept?"

"I would, Jabber, but it's done." At last, the thread caught in the hole dial. I tightened the screw and turned the dial. Nothing happened. I concentrated and pointed the device at the screwdriver on the table. "Lift," I said as I rotated the dial. Still nothing.

Lack of sleep, frustration, and failure were like a strong drink when you've already had too much. I threw the piece onto the floor.

"I'm going to bed." I stumbled out of the workshop, ignoring Jabber, who continued to call my name as I skulked down the hall. *Once a failure, always a failure.*

I reached my room, opened the door, and slammed it behind me. Maelyrra and Everard had told me to use my artificing to access my magic, and I'd come up short. You didn't find the defects in your metal until you heated it. Well, the heat of the forge had brought my flaws to the surface and I'd cracked.

Now, I dreaded the hammer strike that would shatter me.

14

BOOM! BOOM! BOOM!

I pulled the heavy blanket over my head to blot out the noise of Everard knocking, not that it was doing much good. Thoughts of my failed device pushed at me, but I shoved them away and tried to go back to sleep.

BOOM! BOOM! BOOM!

I tossed the blankets off and stormed to the door, throwing it open so that it crashed into the wall. "What?" I yelled at the startled Arch Magus, failure and lack of sleep replacing my healthy fear of the man.

"Good morning, Quinn," he said, a quirked eyebrow the only sign he found my behavior less than acceptable. "I'd like for you to explain something to me. If you don't mind, follow me."

I held my head in both hands, trying to squeeze the headache out. What could be so important that he couldn't leave me to sleep? "Let me put on some clothes first."

He glanced down and I followed his gaze. I still wore the forge-scented, wrinkled, sweaty clothes from yesterday. I groaned as I added washing my bedding to my list of chores. "Fine. Let's go."

What was this about? Had he found the useless device in pieces on the floor? The last thing I needed this morning was a lecture on how to relax my center so I could do better magic. "Everard, I'm not a mage, I'm a blacksmith. Lady Maelyrra was wrong about me."

The abandoned project lay on the workshop table. A mug of tea sat in front of one of the stools. He gestured for me to take the seat with the tea.

"This one didn't work?" Everard said.

I shrugged wearily, unwilling to look him in the face. Maelyrra had even visited our realm to help me and I'd still failed. I wanted to scream or hit something or maybe just leave. A war raged in my head of all the feelings I couldn't express.

"It was your first attempt," Everard said as he spun the dial. "My first spell took me months of practice before I could do anything of consequence. Light a candle, lift a napkin, were easy."

I really wasn't in the mood for the 'better luck next time' speech. Everard's failures were far behind him. I sipped the tea and stayed silent.

"Do you know why Maelyrra gave you magic?"

"Because I saved you." I hated the sulky tone in my voice, but I couldn't push past the sense of failure.

"No," he said, a sad smile playing across his face. "I'm dying. The magic requires a price and soon it will end me. I've held it off until a replacement could be found, but my time is almost done here. You don't need to be Arch Magus, but you will need to protect Astaria."

My mouth dropped open like a starving man staring at a haunch of lamb. First Roland and now Everard. Was everyone who came into contact with me jinxed? "Can't Lady Maelyrra fix it?"

He snorted a laugh. "There is nothing to fix. My body is worn out and rotting on the inside. In a couple of months, I'll be dead."

Dark circles ringed Everard's normally youthful eyes. I hadn't noticed the ashen skin and the stoop of his shoulders like he carried a great burden on his back. The realization hit me with the force of a forge hammer in the head. I was a blacksmith, not a magus. How in the world could I learn to protect the whole country, when I'd barely learned the basics of being a Watcher? "There has to be a mistake…"

"You know in your heart there isn't," Everard said, affixing me with a penetrating gaze. "Lady Maelyrra could have chosen anyone, but it was you she chose to follow me as the protector of Astaria. I have spent hundreds of years protecting the land I love, and now you will succeed me. You have the potential to be very powerful."

Powerful? Me? I wasn't suited for this kind of power, but would I want it granted to one of the petty magi that squabbled over supposed slights and pouted when they didn't get their way? No. My whole life, I'd been taught that hard work and keeping your word was more important than my pride. "If I don't take the Arch Magus title, who will?"

"Usorin will ascend—"

"What?" I shouted, rising as rapidly as my anger. "The maniac who cut my arm off is going to be Arch Magus? He doesn't even have any magic."

Everard held up his hands and I returned to my seat, glaring at the older man. He cleared his throat. "Arch Magus is a governing term, not a rank granted though ability. Most of Astaria's greatest mages were unknown to the people. Usorin is much changed since he attacked you. He's mellowed and takes his place far more seriously now. You have the option of stepping up to be the next Arch Magus if you so choose. Once you display your power, no one will question you. Think about it, though. Do you want to give up this life to be tied to governing Astaria?"

I'd thought of what it had to be like to spend all day managing the thirteen regions and foreign disputes. Political intrigue, boot lickers, and all the rest that Everard put up with. Not for me. "I'm not cut out to lead. Usorin will have to be the one who takes over."

Everard shrugged. "He's one of the few that know the true secret of alarium. He won't trouble you regardless of your decision."

"Without magic, there is no decision," I insisted, trying not to let the hurt and anger into my voice. I failed.

"Do this for me. Try again. Pick something to work on. Think about what you want to happen and how it should feel when it succeeds. Traces of magic fluxed through the pieces of the device. You just need to find what inside you will fuse them together to achieve your goal."

He was right. I could sit here feeling sorry for myself or I could get back to it. "What happens if I can't get it to work?"

"Nothing," Everard said after a moment. "My guess is Lady Maelyrra makes few mistakes, but she will pick a new champion if you are unable to take over."

The thought of losing my magic, even though it eluded me, was appealing and terrifying at the same time. As much as the magic frustrated me, I wanted to protect the people of Astaria. Victoria said we each have skills to contribute. I'd continue building weapons to protect the people, but not to the extent that Everard had. I couldn't build a weapon big enough to take out an entire Norn fleet or shatter an invading Candelaria army. To do that I needed my magic. "I've got to get the levitator to work."

"You'll be a great mage. Trust in yourself. I certainly believe in you. Maelyrra wouldn't have chosen you if you weren't worthy."

"Will you be here later?"

"No," Everard said slowly. "I'm afraid this will probably be the last time I speak with you. Even now I can feel my body deteriorating. I used most of my magic to come here and have just enough to return home."

I nodded, feeling my heart break. The older man hugged me tightly in yet another goodbye. Yet another death. He whispered something in my ear and the world went dark. When I woke up in bed later, he was gone.

"Thank you, Everard."

15

With renewed determination, I returned to the levitator. The original model went into my slag pile so I could melt it down later. I selected a couple of stock pieces, examining each piece carefully. Everard had spoken about "feeling" the magic and seeing the transformation I wanted. Nothing.

I selected a couple more pieces and tried the same thing. Still nothing.

"Excuse me," Jabber said from the doorway.

I'd been so deep in concentration, I hadn't heard him approach. With a small jolt of shock, I dropped the pieces on the floor. I bent down to retrieve the metal. "What is it?"

"I was wondering if you'd be breaking for lunch?"

"No," I said. My left hand grasped the fallen stock and I gasped. A shock ran up my arm. I moved the piece to my right hand and the sensation ended. I'd been using my artificial arm to touch the metal I'd worked with.

I switched the metal back to my left hand and the jolt of energy almost caused me to drop it again. I straightened, examining the metal. Pulses of magic ran up and down my arm. Without warning my skin began to ripple under an unseen force. Blue energy seeped out of the skin from my hand to my elbow. A torrent of force flowed into the metal with me being pulled along like a rider with a foot stuck in the stirrup of a galloping horse. I willed my grip to loosen, but my fingers were welded to the metal. The glow from my arm intensified until I could no longer look at it. With a deafening crack, the metal burst into shards falling to the floor.

"Are you ill?" Jabber asked. If his eyes could have widened I'm sure they would have.

"I'm fine." A wave of fatigue struck me like a sledgehammer driving spikes sending me to my knees. Jabber caught me before I fell completely. He carefully escorted me to my room. I was asleep before my head hit the pillow.

A few hours later, I pulled myself out of bed and stumbled to the kitchen. I grabbed an apple and some cheese which was gone before I realized I'd eaten it. After a second apple, I felt more like myself. Time to see what I'd created earlier.

The door to the workshop stood open. I entered and saw the remains of the metal stock I'd touched earlier. It pulsed a pale blue light around it. Well, at least I hadn't dreamed it. My left arm looked normal.

"No time like the present," I said into the quiet of the shop. I selected a new piece of metal with my forging arm, sensing the design I was planning wanting to emerge from the bar. I set the piece on the anvil and touched it with one finger. A tiny trickle of energy leapt out and encompassed the stock. I pulled my hand away not wanting a repeat of my earlier experience. The glow faded after a few moments. I tried again, touching the piece longer to allow more magic to pour into the inert metal. After a couple of hours of trial and error, the metal glowed like it had been pulled from the forge.

I grabbed my tongs and the rounding hammer and set to work. The metal responded like it had been properly heated, but wasn't hot to the touch.

I set to making a new levator, sensing the difference in the metal, the forms buried inside beckoning to be released. For the next day, I labored over the device, taking a short break to eat and sleep. Finally, I held the new device in my hand. "Jabber, come here, please."

Jabber appeared in the doorway after a minute. "Yes, Master Quinn."

I pointed the levitator at Jabber and turned the dial. He rose a few inches off the floor. I snapped off the dial, whooping in joy. Finally, I knew it was working.

I'd done it. I did have the magic Lady Maelyrra had granted me. I was worthy.

"Master Quinn, that was unexpected," Jabber said, his tone tinged with disapproval.

I grabbed him by the arms. "Jabber, it worked! It worked!" I danced around the shop, using the levitator to pick up and drop things back on the bench. Everard would be so proud if he were here.

I spent the next week building on a device to neutralize the hypnosis machine. Everard trusted me to stop these people, and I refused to let them win. If it took every drop of blood in my body, I'd complete the last mission he'd given me.

After a lot of bad designs, I settled on a pistol to deliver the magic. This way I could pinpoint the animal and disrupt the hypnosis. I crafted a pistol body, envisioning the spell fired like a bullet and calibrated the trigger. I certainly didn't want an area effect for the magic, since I had no way of determining what would happen. The directional vector of the pistol design should limit the effective field. The main problem was that I couldn't test it. The control device from the bear lay in pieces since I'd removed most of the parts to study it. I wouldn't know if it worked until I faced down the next monstrosity.

***

Over the next week, I created a freeze bomb. It took a while to build the spherical casing so when I pressed the button and threw it, it would freeze everything in place after two seconds. The Norns used fire-bombs to soften up defenses, but my bomb should halt an opponent in their tracks for at least thirty seconds. Literally. It would have been handy against the bear.

After three tries I was setting the firing pin in my new bomb design when Jabber entered. He held the neutralizing pistol I'd left on the table. "Master Quinn, I'm looking at the plans for your newest project and I have a few suggestions for improvements."

The liquid bronze in the crucible bubbled and steamed. I poured it carefully into the spherical mold, each half ready to lock together around the activation button. Without taking my eyes off the casting I said, "Those are old. The final plans are on the workbench."

He laid the old plans down and retrieved the new ones, studying them carefully. "This won't work."

I groaned. Jabber took full advantage of his freedom to discuss things ad nauseum. I finished the pour and straightened. "Why is that, Jabber?"

He pointed at the pistol device I'd created earlier. "The trigger mechanism is not correct. See the second pin here? It should be further back to balance the force of the trigger pull. This could break if any torque is applied during the firing of the weapon."

I frowned. "The trigger isn't connected to any other mechanical parts, so the resistance is low enough to avoid torque. With black powder pistols, the trigger has to be secured, but this is for magic."

"The application doesn't change the fact that the trigger is not properly reinforced to allow for the user to hastily fire the weapon as one would in a combat situation. Master Roland espoused the adage 'Better to over plan than under-deliver.' And in this case, moving the pin would alleviate the stress point and ensure a smooth mechanical function."

He had a point. The fix wouldn't take long, and the last thing I needed was a mechanical failure in the field on top of trying to learn magic. "You're right."

"Besides, given the mechanical hand…" Jabber fell silent. "Did you say I'm right?"

"Yes," I said, fighting to keep the grin off my face. For all Jabber did to maintain Treetop and me, he was childlike in his perception of the world and the strange people in it. "You brought up some good ideas. I'll make the change now."

"Thank you, Master Quinn," he said, sitting on the stool by the workbench.

I retrieved the pistol from the holster I'd found in the weapons locker. Removing the pin involved some swearing and a couple of failed attempts, but I eventually tapped it out. I verified it was still structurally sound, re-drilled the hole through the trigger assembly, and completed the revision. Jabber didn't speak through the whole process, just watched my every move.

"Jabber, feel free to make any suggestions you find necessary. I might not agree with them, but I'd rather discuss it than miss something. A man can't see his own blind spots."

Jabber nodded, rose, and exited the workshop. As he went, I swear he stood a bit straighter. I went back to work.

***

The sun had set by the time I'd popped the sphere out of the mold so I could file down the rough edges and assemble it. Jabber entered, though this time he didn't carry any of my plans. "Master Quinn, Watcher Cian has requested you meet him in Bradenbridge in two days. There has been another attack on Oriatia, near the Aldon border."

How fast could I finish up here? The freezing orb, as I'd come to think of it, needed a few more hours before it would be ready. To reach Bradenbridge in two days would require leaving early in the morning, but I could forego some sleep in order to complete the orb. Depending on what we were facing, it could come in handy. "1 hour to go before I'm done here. Can you pack my rucksack and layout my combat arm and the new gauntlet?"

"Absolutely, Master Quinn," Jabber said softly. "I will attend to Treetop in your absence. I hope it won't be a long one."

"Me, too," I told him and realized I meant it. Treetop had become home and Jabber was part of that. Did he get lonely here by himself? Surely not. Automatons didn't have feelings, at least I didn't think so, but the image of Jabber walking out, head held high after I'd complimented his suggestions, made me question that.

"Very well," he said crisply, the old Jabber reasserting himself. "I'll have your things ready for your morning departure." After he left, I affixed the button to the sphere casing. I'd built the button to trigger the magic, hoping it would work like the levitation wheel I'd added to my gauntlet.

I wasn't sure if any of my gadgets would affect a rampaging, hypnotized bear or anything else the madman behind this threw at me. If worse came to worse, my mechanical arm and gauntlet and the artificer tricks I'd built into them would come in handy.

I always had my wits if things really went bad. I hoped it never got there.

Because then I was really in trouble.

16

Three days later, Cian and I rode horses from Herot's Pass into Oriatia and the small town of Bexley's Crossing. From what Cian had said, the town was a bridge over the Itugar River and not much else. The Oriatian magus, Eva Pelham, had reported an attack against her men on the road outside of the village. Pelham had been scheduled to return by carriage from her mountain home to her estates but had taken an airship when her father fell ill.

"We've got a long journey, and we've got time to kill," Cian said as the sun passed noon time and started her journey toward the mountains. "I know you worked with Roland. How did he find you?"

I told him the story of Usorin cutting off my arm and Roland finding me barely alive. I regaled him with the boring details of building my new arm, the more interesting parts of fighting the Norns, and the heart-breaking events around the murder of Master Ruari and the rest of the blacksmiths. I left out Walden Ovro's attempted assassination of Everard as we'd agreed to not discuss Ovro trying to steal Everard's magic and Lady Maelyrra bestowing magic of my own. Though the Watchers "knew" I had magic, they didn't know how or why the magic worked.

"Interesting." We rode for a few minutes in silence. The slope of a large hill slowed our progress but pushing the horses into a trot up an incline would wear them out. "When did you get magic? You didn't mention it earlier in your story."

I'd hoped he'd ignored the omission. Cian was a fellow Watcher, but I didn't want the knowledge about how I got my magic public. "Everard thinks I always had it, but the stress of stopping the fight and the deaths of the people I loved brought it out. Whatever happened, I'm not very good at it." I left out the 'I can build magic items' information.

Cian nodded. "Makes sense. The Wind Walker of the White Ghosts think all souls are magic and we are projections of our true beings. Those who connect to their true selves can bring the magic here. Maybe they are right."

"White Ghosts?"

Cian snorted. "They barely have any skin coloring."

"Do you know a lot about the Candalarians?"

"Enough," Cian said with a sigh. "Guess you don't know 'bout me." He glanced at me, and when I agreed he kept going. "Old Brull was the Watcher in Ramcoll when I was a boy. When I was young, the Candalarians bought, or stole, me from my parents and made me a slave. That's how I learned their language. I was being auctioned off near the border to Astarian farmers—"

"Wait," I interrupted. "Slaves are illegal in Astaria. The Norns and Candalarians allow it, but anyone in our country would be freed."

"Quinn, you haven't been a Watcher long, but out on the plains of Aldon and Ramcoll, there's no law other than the magus and they are more interested in taxes on grain and corn sales to look too closely at who does the farming." Cian tried to smile, but it wavered.

"The farmers in Bradenbridge don't use slaves," I countered. I'd known many of the local farmers as an apprentice blacksmith before I'd become a watcher.

"Maybe not. But a few hours' ride south of Iron Harbor you'll find Thaclet. It's the largest slave market on the continent. Some of the slaves the Norns sell end up in Terralon."

I'd spent my whole life in Bradenbridge and the subject never came up. Granted, the farm holdings were hours away from the city, but the farmers ventured to town frequently to sell their goods and buy supplies. Ruari had repaired and maintained farm implements all winter long to ready them for the spring. "I've never seen any slaves or heard rumor of them."

Cian held up his hands. "I haven't been to your neck of the woods, so I don't know for a fact. Just tellin' you what I heard."

As unpalatable as it was, I couldn't see any reason for Cian to lie about it. "Why don't the Watchers free the slaves?"

"Brull drove it into my head that we weren't here to fight every evil in the world, but to keep Astaria safe. I concentrate on the mission at hand regardless of my feelings."

"And Brull?"

"He died in a fight with a White Ghost Wind Walker. Everard promoted me to Ramcoll's Watcher. I've been here ever since."

Like me, someone else's death had been involved in his promotion. How had Victoria Wyndham been recruited into the Watchers? I'd have to ask her when I saw her next. The idea of him being a slave rattled me like a loose screw in a perambulator. I'd seen excesses and cruelty from the magus of Bradenbridge, but we were all free. If Ruari hadn't taken me in and taught me a craft, I could have ended up on a farm, worked to the bone, though at least I wouldn't have been a slave.

Cian cleared his throat. "Anyhow, Brull taught me to read and how to hunt. Being able to track across the grasslands is a skill few possess, so I can use it in service to protect people. I can track the White Ghosts when they enter into our territory. When they cross into Astaria I can hunt them down."

"Does that happen often?

"In Ramcoll it does. Mostly raids on livestock. Occasionally they try to kidnap people for ransom or to be sold off. Most of the farmers have walled compounds to keep themselves safe."

What a difference from Bradenbridge, though the port city Cheim sported walls to keep the Norn raiding ships from entering the harbor. Astaria was a country with enemies, and our mission as Watchers was to protect the citizens and keep the rulers of the regions in line. "What do you do when that happens?"

Cian's grin reminded me of a wolf. "I rescue the Astarians and kill as many of the bastards I can in the process."

"What does Everard say about all this?"

Cian's eyes swept the area around us while he slowed his horse to get him around a large hole in the path. "I don't know and don't care. The White Ghosts are animals who kill and maim without provocation, and it's our job to keep rabid animals away from Astaria."

I was about to answer when the thunder of hoofbeats rolled over the hill ahead of us.

And that was when the Candalarians showed up.

Four warriors on large black horses crested the hill, facing us. Cian and I readied ourselves for a fight, angling our horses until we were side by side. The animals shied and pranced from the sudden intrusion. The Candalarians were known to be fierce warriors who rode their horses like they were born in the saddle. An array of lances, bows, and a couple of swords stuck out in all directions? The warriors were clad in leathers, but the horses were decorated with bright colors and baubles. I stopped examining them when I realized one of them had a string of fingers around his horse's neck. I readied my arm while the riders moved to flank us.

"This isn't good," Cian muttered.

I grunted in response. Which one was the leader? If they attacked and I killed their leader, the rest might think better of harassing us, though the odds of that were about the same as steam billowing out of my nose.

And that was a device I hadn't invented yet.

The largest of the warriors with broad shoulders, long black hair, and a beard down to his waist cautiously approached us. His white skin shimmered in the sunlight. I now understood where the term 'White Ghost' came from. It was like the inside of an oyster shell.

He held up the spear and the rest of the riders spread themselves equally behind him to ensure they had room to maneuver. He studied us for a long moment before he spoke. "I Dakao. We speak of you. Looking for our Huallia."

"Huallia?" I asked Cian. The leader sat tall in the saddle, but he must have been shorter than me. Height wasn't necessary for riding horses, and the smooth way he guided his with his knees proved that fact.

"It means Wind Walker," Cian whispered before responding to their leader. "Ja latta non Huallia. Ju gryra jey truio."

"What did you say?

"I told him we didn't see their Wind Walker and to leave our lands."

Dakao laughed as did his men. "You not speak as warrior." He addressed me, dismissing Cian. "We seek Huallia. Gemaki." He indicated the warrior to his left. She nodded her head in my direction, but I kept my eyes fastened on Dakao. "The Wind Walkers take us to place and find metal arm man." It sounded like he said kin in his broken Astarian, but I knew he meant me.

As hard as I tried, I couldn't stop Cian's hard words from echoing in my mind. These were the people who sold him as a slave and still did so today. Was he wrong to want to kill them on sight? If I ever found them selling a human I know I would burn them to the ground. Under the circumstances, I needed to follow where this was leading.

Cian bristled. "I told you to leave our lands. You have no right to be here."

"We not speak to slave, we search for our Huallia," Dakao said in a casual tone.

His cheeks flamed red at the insult. "We are Ostarian guards and I demand you leave."

This wasn't going well. If I didn't step in, Cian would rise to the provocation and blood would be shed. I pulled back my sleeve to expose the metal of my arm. "I am Quinn, but I have no information on your missing Wind Walker."

Gemaki answered instead of the leader. "You will lead and we will find Huallia."

I inspected each member of the group. Dark circles, like iron rings, hung under their eyes, blotching their pale skin. Their leathers were matted with dirt and sweat, telling me they'd been searching for a while. Cian muttered to himself as I examined the situation and came to a decision. "It is getting dark. Let us camp for the night and discuss what to do."

Cian whispered. "I'm not spending the night with these savages."

Dakao ignored Cian and swung off his horse. He approached me, his arm extended. I looked at him, wondering what I should do.

"I offer peace on my ancestors, Quinn of Astaria," Dakao said simply, his arm still reaching for mine.

Cian sighed. "Grip his arm at the elbow and repeat the words."

I clambered down from my saddle, a landslide to the flowing water of Dakao's dismount. I took his arm and repeated the words as his calloused hand gripped my elbow. The leader then pulled me close and kissed me full on the mouth.

"What?" I stammered, caught completely off-guard.

Cian laughed as Dakao said, "We have shared breath. We are as family until the next moon rises."

I cast a sour look at Cian, who tried to smother his grin. "You knew about that, didn't you?"

The older man kept grinning. "I told you they were savages. I'll not break bread with these murderers."

I pushed the urge to test my freeze bomb on Cian out of my mind. I pushed down the uneasy feeling that had settled over me. "They don't appear to be hostile, just looking for their Wind Walker."

"Quinn, you're a fool. They would as soon murder you as spit on you. We need to leave now." Cian's voice was hot with anger.

"You need to go back to Herot's Pass and send a report to Everard." I couldn't have Cian causing bloodshed because of his personal grudge, even though he had every right to hate these people. Was I being a fool for not just killing them instead of working with them?

"What?" Cian said, almost at a shout, drawing the looks of the Candalarians. "You can't be serious."

"I am. They will follow us if I leave with you, but we need Everard to know so he can send more Watchers."

Cian scowled. "Quinn, this isn't smart."

"It's the only way this works. I'll help them search while you get help." I sounded crazy even to myself, but there was no way they had heard of me through non-magical means. There was something here and I needed to stop the attacks. That had to take priority even over my own safety.

After a long moment, Cian agreed. "I'll ride to Herot's Pass and come back with more men to even the odds."

"It's settled. You head out and I'll wait for you."

Cian wheeled his horse around and rode off the way we had come.

Once he was gone, I approached Candalarians. "We should find shelter for the night."

I followed the riders into a small copse of trees at the base of the hill where we found a clearing to make camp in. Dakao's people started a fire and placed reed mats around the far side of it. I set out my tarp and blankets, glad to be in the temperate southern portion of Astaria. As fall crept closer to winter, sleeping outside became less and less pleasant.

I pulled a pan to cook the bacon and beans I'd packed. Across the fire, I saw each of the warriors gnawing on pieces of meat with no cooking utensils in sight. Cian had mentioned they don't cook their food. With a huff, I stored the bacon and beans, pulled out some jerky, and joined Dakao's people with my meal.

As I approached, Gemaki waved to the patch of ground next to her. I nodded my thanks and sat near enough to her to talk, but not so close as be within reach. She smiled as she looked at the space between us. After a moment she held out a piece of the meat she was eating.

"No, thank you," I said as I shook my head so she'd understand. The thought of eating raw meat did nothing for my appetite. She pushed it toward me more emphatically. With the realization that refusal could be seen as an insult, I smiled and took the proffered meat. She waited until I tore a piece off with my teeth.

I chewed the meat, which tasted peppery and carried a bit of heat. Rather than being tough, it fell apart easily as I ate it. "This is good," I told her between mouthfuls of the spicy meat.

"Why did Golacka leave?"

My brows knit together as I tried to puzzle out the meaning of the word. Gemaki gave me the answer.

"Low-born. He speaks the tongue of the fields."

"He went to report to our master." She meant slave, but I didn't correct her. We ate in silence as the sun slowly dissolved behind the mountains. I handed her my water skin which she took a long pull from, as did I. The heat on my tongue intensified as I ate the food.

"The charga cooks the meat while we ride and does not destroy the animal's spirit as fire does. Those who are spirit-blind do not see the dishonor in putting meat on the flame. We weep for those such as you."

That might have been the nicest insult I'd ever received. I had nearly finished our shared meal when it dawned on me I had an expert sitting next to me. The device I'd found was supposedly Candalarian magic. It was a risk to be sure, but what if the risk paid off? I wiped my hands on my pants and retrieved the leather pouch from my belt.

Gemaki's eyes followed my every move as I extracted the device and held it in my palm. "Do you know what this is?"

Her eyes grew as large as quenching barrels as she scrambled away from me. Gemaki screamed something in her language and the other Candalarians pulled weapons and jumped between us. I stood, sliding the box into my pocket.

Dakao's face darkened in the flickering light of the fire as he stared at me, spear in hand. I readied for a fight, but I needed answers, not bloodshed. I held up my hands in front of me. This was getting out of control quickly.

"I'm sorry. I found this on a bear that had been turned into a killing machine. I need to know what it is before it happens again."

A series of conversations flowed between the four Candalarians. Gemaki's voice still held a tremble of fear as she answered Dakao's questions.

I eased back away from the group and out of stabbing distance of Dakao's wicked-looking spear.

After a few minutes, Dakao returned without his spear. "We talk in morning. Evil best not talked in dark." He went back to his people who sat huddled together, whispering frantically.

I sat watching the Candalarians and the dark. What in the hell was this device, that it terrified hardened warriors such as these?

I wondered which I should be more scared of, the Candarlians or the device that scared them.

18

The sun rose over our strange camp. Dakao's band ate breakfast and stored their belongings. Gemaki watched me from beyond her people as I packed my gear and gnawed on hardtack. If the Candalarians didn't open up discussions of what had happened last night soon, I would have to do it myself.

Dakao strolled across the intervening space, his gait swaying from spending so much time in the saddle. He stopped at a respectful distance.

I felt my shoulders tighten with anxiety.

"Quinn, I explain. The piece is evil. Soul Stealers control people with such things, make do horrible things. Where get it?"

I told him the story of the bear. "I am sorry to have startled Gemaki. I had no idea what it was to you."

"It is you not understanding. I speak with my people." He returned to the Candalarians. He wore a metal breastplate over his coat this morning. In fact, they all did. Seeing the evil magic had certainly shaken them to the core. Their hands lingered on their weapons now, where last night they had relaxed.

As Dakao spoke, Gemaki's eyes flicked back and forth from him to me. She scowled and fired off a string of words that, from the tone of them, should have burnt Dakao to the ground. He weathered the storm with a calm I found amazing. The other two warriors, Mojuro and Akaru, stood to the side. Mojuro had strung his bow, Akaru spun throwing knives around his fingers as he listened.

I brushed down my horse, checked his shoes, pulling out pebbles with the tip of my metal finger. After a once over, I gave him a small apple from my sack. He crunched happily as I stroked his mane.

My morning routine was cut off as Dakao and Gemaki returned. She appraised me. "Quinn, I now know you were stupid as to what the nathal was. It is very evil. If you will give to me, I can follow the evil to the source."

Finally, a break. I'd found someone who could help locate the culprit behind the bear attack. If we removed the people behind the attacks and the drug, we'd never have to face this threat again. The question was could I convince her to lead me to the evil and defeat it?.

"We both want the same thing," I said, keeping my tone as neutral as possible. "I know we are traditionally enemies, but if we work together, we can end this evil once and for all."

The Candalarians agreed.

"May I have the nathal?" Gemaki asked, her hand open before her.

I retrieved the device and gave it to her. Gemaki took a deep breath as if to steady herself before she closed her fingers around it.

"I'm on my way to examine the scene of another attack about a day's ride from here. We think it is connected to the bear attack, but don't know for sure. I'd appreciate your assistance."

"We will follow until we find our Huallia. The spirits have told us so." Dakao said, turning on his heel and returning to his horse.

Gemaki went to do the same but stopped. "Quinn, this is very danger-ous. Know this." She headed back, gracefully mounting and bringing her horse around.

I swung up into the saddle and started for Bexley's Crossing. They kept a bit of distance between us as we rode. I turned the problem over and over in my mind, trying to find a link between all the facts I had. None of it made sense.

We ate while we watered the horses. Every hour we dismounted and walked for a bit to conserve their strength. I appreciated the chance to stretch my legs. Gemaki watched me on several occasions, but she turned away if I approached, and Dakao didn't seem to welcome my company so I kept to myself.

We reached a small forest, which according to the map contained the site of the attack. I reigned in my horse to speak with Dakao. "We received a report of a group of guards being ambushed in the woods. I want to examine over the area to see if it is linked to the bear attacks."

Dakao looked up to check the position of the sun. "Can we reach before dark?"

"I think so. I don't know exactly where it happened, but it should be under an hour's ride." I waited for his agreement before starting off again. Something felt wrong, but I couldn't put my finger on just what it was. A case of the jitters, I hoped.

We had been taking the road through the trees for almost an hour when I saw the first body. I dismounted, tying off my horse on a branch. The horse's eyes rolled back as he whinnied. Something besides just the body was spooking him, and that wasn't good. Dakao and his warriors joined me, weapons out and readied. Their horses stood stock still, but their eyes flicked around nervously.

The scene reminded me of the last attack on Murkwood. A carriage with the Pelham crest emblazoned on the doors. Two horses were still attached to the stuck carriage. They snorted and stamped their fear and tried to pull free to no avail. Three men's lifeless bodies littered the ground. Stains where the blood had soaked into the ground surround each person.

The closest body I turned onto his back. The bearded man's throat had been ripped out. I stepped over the corpse and approached the empty carriage the guards had been escorting. Tracks interlaced all over the place, and I moved cautiously as I approached. No sign of the horses, but a man in an Ostarian guard uniform lay on the ground, mauled beyond recognition.

As I examined each person, it was evident that something closely resembling the bear attack had occurred. All had their throats torn out and bite marks riddled their bodies. All these people were killed for no reason.

Dakao joined me. "We need to go. Those wolves markings," he said softly. His spear was held loosely in his right hand, though I was sure he was ready and willing to use it at a moment's notice. His eyes peered into the darkening woods. Animals rustled in the underbrush.

"We'll never reach Bexley's Crossing before nightfall." I removed my coat to prepare my arm and gauntlet for a fight. "We should find a defensible position, secure the horses, and get a fire going."

"Agreed." We walked back to the horses, eyes everywhere as the sounds in the underbrush increased. Within minutes Dakao's people had a small fire burning in the center of the clearing. Mojuro stacked dry tree branches nearby while Gemaki, stick in hand, circled around the group drawing inscriptions in the dirt.

"Do not step on the wards," she warned, her voice echoing through the near silence of the clearing. A snapping noise from the woods, louder than the pops of the fire caught my attention, but I saw nothing

Gemaki waved everyone inside the circle she'd created and finished the wards. "Stay inside the circle. Your weapons may cross but not your body."

The runes were similar to the ones on the control device I'd taken from the bear. A ripple of power tingled my senses, but it was much different than the feel of my magic. Ghostly apparitions flickered at the corner of my eye but fled when I tried to look at them directly.

The first howl in the distance stopped any thoughts of magical theory. Each of us faced away from the fire, preparing our weapons. Dakao added wood to the fire, increasing the range we could see. I longed to put on my Watcher's mask so I could see better, but I didn't want to give away my identity. The Candalarians were still enemies even if our goals coincided for now.

The sun had gone behind the mountains, plunging the clearing into complete darkness. I wished we were in open land where the moon could illuminate the area, but the canopy filtered the light there was. Red sparks flicked into and out of view as the wolves howled outside the range of our light.

Dakao said, "Those mountain wolves."

Mojuro scoffed. "They are strong but die like anything else."

"The bear we fought took down two magus before we took care of it. We'll be lucky to survive the night if there are a lot of them."

"I can hear they are just wolves." Mojuro sounded less confident than before.

A louder growl came from in front of me as the red, glowing mechanical eyes pushed through the scrub and into the clearing. The wolf was the size of a pony. It loped toward us, unnatural armor reflecting the light. When he reached the circle Gemaki had etched in the ground, it yelped and backed away.

Would it be enough to keep the wolves at bay? And would this be a good time to test my magical devices?

An unbelievably large, armored wolf emerged from the trees and howled, summoning the rest of the pack. They slid like ghosts from the trees, hard to distinguish in the dim light of the fire. The animal growled in greeting. The horses whinnied and thrashed as the scent of the wolves reached them.

"Will the circle hold?" I asked Gemaki, The wolves darted toward us in waves before retreating from the spell.

"I know not," she answered. "I've never warded for beasts such as these."

As if to answer her question, a smaller wolf charged, throwing itself at the barrier. It bounced off the invisible shield. I let out the breath I was holding when the shield flared brightly before subsiding. The alpha stood across from me, its head cocked as if listening to something.

"Get ready," I said when the alpha snapped his teeth. The wolves stormed the circle, striking it with their bodies over and over. I fired lightning, and the arrows and knives from Dakos's people flew through the barrier, hitting the wolves. One wolf reeled to the side and fell, an arrow piercing its right optic.

The alpha charged at Dakao. He rammed his spear through the barrier, attempting to kill the animal. The wolf dodged to the side, latched on to the spear, and dragged the blade down. As the Candalarian leader tried to dislodge his weapon from the wolf, Gemaki screamed, "Do not disturb the wards."

It was too late. The blade scraped on the ground in Gemaki's inscriptions.

The barrier broke apart. The wolves attacked.

I fired my flame weapon at the alpha, forcing him back, but the fire did little more than singe the fur around his armor. He backed off, scared of the flames. I whirled and punched down, striking the wolf who darted in to try to hamstring me. His steel teeth clamped down on my mechanical wrist, but instead of yanking back and possibly losing my arm, I set off the lightning.

The teeth acted as the perfect conductor, frying the wolf before he could do anything. The poor animal slumped to the ground. I hated to kill them since they were being forced to attack us, but I had little choice in the matter.

Around me, the fighting intensified as the wolves darted in and away. They tore at the Candalarians. Mojuro lay on the ground, blood seeping from gashes on his leg. Akaru swung a short sword at two wolves, keeping them at bay, as Gemaki stabbed in from the side. Her sword found a gap between the armor plates and dropped the wolf. Another of the pack dove at the distracted Wind Walker. I fired flames at it, driving the animal back before it could strike.

We'd managed to kill three wolves and lose one of our own and the fight had just started. They seemed to vanish then appeared where I least expected them. The alpha charged at me again. I grabbed the magical pistol from my belt and hoped it would eliminate the control device on the wolf's back. I pulled the trigger and the damn thing snapped under my finger.

When he struck me in the chest, the wolf's momentum carried me backward. He'd have torn out my throat if I hadn't wedged my metal arm between his jaws. I stumbled over the edge of the fire, the wolf on top. Thrusting with all my strength, I propelled the solid creature off of me, leaving a mixture of blood and saliva spattered across me. The animal crashed into the brush as I pulled myself to my feet.

Gemaki swung her sword at another attacker but didn't realize her mistake until too late. As she swung at the first animal, a second sped in and grabbed her leg. She shrieked. The sword tumbled out of her hand, leaving her open for the killing blow from the first wolf. Dakao hurled himself into the fray and killed both wolves with his spear, spinning like a weathervane in a storm.

The alpha flashed into the clearing, heading directly for me. I pointed the levitator at him and cranked the dial. Which would have been a great plan, but the beam missed, struck the ground, and it threw me backward through the air across the clearing. The wolf jumped to land on me. I engaged my left gauntlet's shield just in time, and he bounced off the glowing blue barrier.

The blow dazed the wolf, and he landed on his side with a whimper. I dove forward and wrenched the control box from his back. The wolf howled as the box came free, dragging blood and wires with it. He righted himself, shook his massive head, and ran toward the forest. He collapsed dead after only a few steps.

I limped back to the fight to find Dakao fending off the last of the wolves. I pointed to the levitator and carefully turned the dial. The wolf rose off the ground slowly, feet scrambling in mid-air. I pulled my belt knife and cut the control box from his back. Once it returned to its senses, I set the wolf back down and it ran off.

The bodies around the clearing told the story. Three dead Candalarians and eight dead wolves. Dakao knelt next to his fallen warriors.

"My fault. I broke the circle," he said as I stood next to Gemaki's lifeless body. He picked up the nathal and threw it into the dark woods. "Evil has found us. You must stop this."

"What will you do?" I asked, hoping the big warrior would help me track down the Soul Stealer. It was obvious after this attack that it was not a one-man job. But from the look on his face, I knew he was returning home.

"I will take warriors back to families. It is duty."

I stood and left the grieving warrior to deal with his people.

Concern welled up inside me. Would Cian come back with reinforcements before I was attacked again? How could I hope to stop the people responsible for this by myself? I resolved to push forward and do the best I could do. It was what Roland would have done.

The only way forward was through.

19

The Candalarian warrior had the bodies of his deceased companions tied over the backs of their horses. I approached him to offer my help and express my gratitude and sorrow at the loss of his people. They'd refused to allow me to touch their fallen. Dakao helped me load the guard's corpses into the abandoned carriage so I could bring them back to civilization. He harnessed one of his pack horses to pull the rolling morgue.

"May your travels bring you to new places," Dakao said as he took my arm. "When next meet, may us not be enemies."

"Thank you," I said, not knowing how to respond to him. He pulled himself into his saddle and led the horses off to the south. I loaded the dead body of one of the wolves into the carriage with the men. I needed to be able to examine the attached control box.

The magus of Oriatia rode in comfort. Heavy steel springs supported the white and gold carriage. I thought about all the needless loss. All I could do now was make sure the guard's families could say goodbye, and I'd have intact devices to study. I searched every inch of the clearing for anything I'd missed but came up empty.

After the search, I put on my Watcher's robe and mask, since I needed to deposit the carriage and corpses with the authorities. Once I'd tied my horse and the pack animal to the carriage and checked the tethered team I

88

was ready. I climbed into the driver's seat and set off toward Bexley's Crossing.

The trip took no time at all, including a stop to hide the wolf carcass outside town. Much sooner than I was ready for, I encountered the appointed Sheriff of Bexley's Crossing, Aaron Inchcombe. His thin, grey hair draped over his bald head, though it did little to hide his scalp. His long handlebar mustache had gone completely white, and his circular glasses were chipped in a couple of places. He eyed me up and down as I stood in the center of his office.

"So, you be a Watcher?" he asked, scorn coating every word like grease on a ball bearing. "Why not take the bodies and the coach back to her Eminence the Lady Pelham in Datchery?"

"Sheriff Inchcombe, I am a member of Arch Magus Everard's Watchers, not an errand boy. It is my responsibility to return these men to the local authorities, which is you." My voice sounded very different coming through my mask, lending it a properly menacing tone. "You will assign one of your people to return the carriage to Lady Pelham and deliver a note from me explaining what I found."

The sheriff pulled his pants up, but the girth of his belly made them retreat south as soon as he let go of them. "Well, Watcher..." When I didn't supply a name, he continued. "I'm not in the position—"

I'd had enough. I raised my left arm and turned the dial on the levitator. A trickle of icy energy raced down my arm. This close there was no missing, and the sheriff squawked like a startled goose as he rose into the air. Behind my mask, I grinned like a schoolboy who'd filched a pie. "You will do as I ask or I will replace you, understood?"

Inchcombe's arms and legs flailed as he tried to free himself from the levitator to no avail. He stammered out, "I agree, now put me down."

I turned off the levitator and let him land. Hard. Patience wasn't in my toolkit today.

The sheriff stumbled as he hit the wooden floor, grabbing his desk to steady himself. "Ya didn't need to do that. I'll get a couple of the boys to return the carriage." He glared at me as he said it.

I produced the note I'd written and handed it to him. The Watcher seal was evident, but I didn't trust the sheriff. "If the seal is broken by anyone other than Pelham, they'll die."

He dropped the paper onto the desk as if it was a snake. "I'll take care of it, sir."

I pivoted on my heel and ignored the itching between my shoulder blades. I was sure he'd love to shove a knife there, but I'd scared him enough to keep him in line. At least the levitator had worked correctly and I had better aim. I strode out of the sheriff's office, mounted my horse, hooked the lead rope of the packhorse to the pommel, and rode back to where the wolf carcass was stashed.

An hour later, I reached the hiding spot and cooked a quick lunch of bacon and beans. The flame attachment on my arm made starting a fire much easier than flint and steel. While I ate, I considered my plan to craft a device to track the nathal.

In Bexley's Crossing, I could probably find a blacksmith that would allow me to rent space from him. If I could craft the device I needed here, it would save a lot of time. After cleaning up and dousing the fire, I concealed all my Watcher-specific gear and entered the town from the far side.

I smelled the forge smoke before I saw the smithy. The complex sat on the edge of town, which suited my purposes. Everything looked to be well maintained and orderly, just the way I'd been taught. I tied the horses to an iron ring embedded in the wall over a watering trough and walked into the forge.

"Silas, work the bellows, boy," I heard as the blacksmith shoved some dully glowing metal back into the fire. "Silas, boy, get over here."

I went to the unmanned bellows and pushed them together slowly so as not to throw sparks or impede the fire. The rhythm of the work came naturally to me after so many years of being an apprentice. It felt like I'd returned home and I felt my mind clear and focused on the task at hand.

"When did you learn to control the fire like that? Yesterday, you just about set the place ablaze." The blacksmith clearly hadn't spotted me yet. I smiled as I continued. The blacksmith was a smaller man than I was but built like a bear. Thick arms, covered in tattoos, turned the metal in the forge as he waited for it to reach temperature. He pulled the billet from the fire and took the three-pound hammer to it, bending it around the horn of the anvil into a rough horseshoe shape. He kept at it until the metal cooled and then he replaced it in the fire.

"Da, there be a dead wolf out here!" A boy of about twelve ran into the forge, yelling at the blacksmith. Unless my guess was wrong, that would be Silas.

The blacksmith's head came up, and he noticed me working the bellows. "Silas, get over here. The fine gent shouldn't be doing yer job fer ya." The blacksmith walked over to where I stood as Silas took over the bellows. "Thank ye fer the help. I'm Matthew Redsmith. Can I assist ya with something?"

"Name's Zeke Smith," I said. "I'd like to rent some space to build a piece."

A frown crossed his bearded face. "I'm not much fer rentin' out my place. I've not got time fer teachin' you how to smith."

I pointed to the horseshoe in the fire. "May I?"

"Guessin' you mean to either way," he said, but the smile on his face told me he thought I'd make a fool of myself. Lots of people assume blacksmithing is just banging a hammer on metal. "Silas, can you work the pump?"

The boy clamped the bellows together, the flames leaping from the flood of air. No wonder his father had been so startled by Silas' 'improvement'. Master Redsmith demonstrated how to ease the air into the forge. The flare of sparks subsided and I set to work.

The metal had heated to glowing, so I pulled it out with the tongs and asked the smith, "Do you have a jig for this or are you hand bending it?" I already knew the answer, but I wanted to show my experience.

"Hand forging is the only way to get them right," he said with a smirk. We both understood it wasn't the case. If he'd been a farrier and shoed a lot of horses, he'd have a form to bend the metal around. I took the time to properly shape the shoe and drifted the nail holes. When it was perfect, I set the piece on the anvil to let it cool.

Master Redsmith examined the shoe, picking it up with the tongs. Rule number one in the forge —never pick up a piece of metal by hand. Hot metal looks the same as stone-cold, but the mistake has cost new smiths a lot of burnt fingers over the years. He set it back. "You know yer way around the forge. I could use some help instead of the rent."

Usually, I'd have jumped at the chance to work with a master smith, but time was of the essence. "I wish I could, but I need to forge my piece and be off." I pulled a gold coin from my pouch and tossed it to him. It would take him months to earn that much. He tossed it back.

"I don't take money from a fellow smith for usin' what's here. You wanna start now or in the morn?"

My brain said now, my body tomorrow. My body won the fight. "In the morning."

He smiled. "You look tuckered out. Head three doors down and tell Olivia I sent ya'. She'll put you up. She'll have supper on before long and you look like you could use a good meal."

I thanked him and followed his directions after laying the wolf out behind the forge where a casual passerby wouldn't see. An hour later, I sat at a table, enjoying a bowl of stew and a mug of ale. I'd examined the pistol I'd built to disrupt the communication device. The magic still flowed through it, but when the trigger broke it didn't discharge. Apparently, the function of the piece was as important as the magic tied to it. I pondered on if I reinforced the —

Without warning the door to the common room opened and Victoria Wyndham strolled through.

Of all the run-down inns in the world, why was she here?

2O

"Phineas Overclock, I don't believe my eyes. You've returned from the Southern Tier and quite unexpectedly as well," Victoria said for all to hear as she crossed the dimly lit room.

I ducked my head and sank deeper into my seat. She practically danced toward my table. Luckily, I was in the back of the room, so everyone got a good look at her. She wore a purple paisley coat over a teal green blouse and dark pants with knee-high boots. Her dark hair was pulled up in an elaborate set of combs, and her goggles hung from around her neck like a statement piece. The clack of her boot heels echoed through the stunned silence of the small inn. Everard himself couldn't have made a grander entrance.

"Will you sit down?" I hissed through clenched teeth. "I'm going by Zeke Smith."

Her smile was that of pure sugar. "So I've heard. Stashing an armored wolf behind the smithy has gained more attention than you would guess. Phineas is a renowned explorer of the occult and famous for going undercover on his adventures. Would you rather be known as the eccentric adventurer or some sort of lunatic toting around dead animals?"

I rubbed my face as the day caught up with me. She wasn't done by a country mile.

"On top of that, Sheriff Inchcomb is telling everyone about the Watcher that appeared and cursed him for not assisting him fast enough."

She tsked. "You have the manners of a sow, my young friend. Everard must see something in you to keep you around, but we definitely need to polish you up a bit."

"Is it really that bad?" I took a large swallow of ale, hoping it would wash away the stinging rebuke Victoria had just delivered.

She flipped her hand at me. "No, but it could have been. I decided to mention to the sheriff the newcomer to town was none other than the world-renowned adventurer Phineas Overclock. The incident with that nasty Watcher was gone in the blink of an eye. Our good sheriff is a huge fan."

"Is Phineas a real person?" I asked, taking another pull on my ale. The serving lass skipped over and set another mug on the table. "The gents at the bar sent this over." She glanced around conspiratorially. "Is it true you captured a giant crocodile and rode it to escape the Talu?"

Before I could answer, Victoria dove into the breach. "Actually, it was a sea serpent, but the editors didn't think people would believe the tale. The Talu still call him the Serpent God."

My jaw hung open at the audacity of the lie. "Well..."

She patted my hand like I was a slow child. "Phineas is shy about his adventures, which is why I follow him and chronicle his deeds. Other-wise, the world would never know of the exploits he gets himself into."

The maid's eyes grew wide as barrel rings. "Humble and cute. If I do say so." She leaned in and kissed my cheek before scampering off behind the bar to a chorus of cheers and catcalls.

"See? No one will remember the strange man and ask questions. You've hidden in plain sight. There is a time and place for subterfuge and times for boldness."

I couldn't think of anything to say so I shoveled another bite of the spiced stew into my mouth and followed it with a swig of ale. Victoria's grin widened as the silence stretched on.

"You are so much fun to play with." She stole my fresh mug and sipped. "Not bad for the backwoods of Oriatia. Now, fill me in on what you've been doing, since I have some very interesting things to share with you."

The next half an hour I went over what had happened with Cian, the Candalarians, and the wolves. I ran down my plan to craft a device to track the nathal once I'd examined the wolf. She prodded my story, elic-iting more information or shaking a detail loose I'd overlooked in the chaos of the fight.

"Interesting. I need to see the levitator work," she said as she tapped her finger on her chin, looking more like the Victoria I'd met in Stillhold than the peacock I sat across from now. "You don't strike me as the type to make mistakes in design. Before we're in a fight, you need to know why it malfunctioned."

"We?"

She reached over the table and patted my cheek. "Dear boy, you will definitely need help with this, and if you think I'm missing such a grand adventure, you've sorely underestimated me."

"No, ma'am," I replied out of habit.

She laughed. "Lady Eloise York appreciates your understanding, Phineas."

I laughed as well. Victoria's wild sense of humor was infectious and much needed after everything that had happened.

"After you left, I returned to my lab and ran more extensive tests on the drug and broke it down into how I believe it was synthesized. I attempted to trace the components back to the source. Two elements of the drug aren't available in Astaria. One I found with a Candalarian merchant who smuggles the substance into Iron Harbor, but the other comes from the jungles of Uwhela."

"Uwhela? I've never heard of such a place."

"I'd be surprised if you had. Uwhela is south of Candalar. It's mostly jungle and the home of the Talu. They're cannibals and use human sacrifices to power their magic. Nasty place, but if we are to stop this drug from coming into Astaria, we need to find where it is coming from."

"You mean we need to travel through Candalar, find a cannibal mage, and stop them from creating the hypnotic drug?" I shook my head in disbelief. "Not much to it, huh?"

"Not we, me," she said with a grin. "I fabricated the drug without the unknown element. While it is an excellent sedative, it does not lead to the overwhelming hypnotic effect of the substance used on the animals. Now you probably need both the drug and the nathal to control an animal, but it's a start."

"How do you know that?"

"A bird flew into the lab and told me, of course," she said with a smirk. "Why, I took the drug and had my apprentice Letitia command me to do things. My version had no effect, though I did want to fall asleep."

"You tested the drug on yourself?" I asked a bit more sharply than I'd meant to.

Victoria rolled her eyes. "Science demands risk. I was fairly sure there was no danger, and I needed to know if it worked like the original."

"You didn't take the original, did you?"

"Of course. Letitia had a fine laugh as she made me cluck like a chicken and do some silly folk dance. Afterward, I had her clean every bit of our lab equipment, but she was still laughing."

"Are you crazy?" I asked, appalled that she would risk her life, sanity, and health on a drug being used to turn animals into killing machines. "What if you had turned violent and harmed your apprentice?"

"She had a syringe of sedative and a loaded pistol if it came to that. As I hypothesized, the animals only turn violent when instructed to, and Letitia was to not give any command that could be construed that way."

"The more you try, the more you do," I said, reciting a favorite quote of my mentor Roland. When I made mistakes, which was often, he would tell me that.

Victoria cocked her head. "Where did you hear that?"

"Roland. He said it a lot during my training."

"I haven't heard that since his previous apprentice died years ago."

I frowned. "I didn't know Roland had another apprentice."

"Mortimer was his apprentice before you. He died in a fire trying to rescue a family. It took Roland a long time to quit blaming himself."

Knowing Roland, he'd never gotten over it, just hidden it better. I'd have to ask Jabber about Mortimer when I got back to Treetop. For now, I needed to forge a locater to find the person behind these attacks. I fought down a yawn.

"It's late and we need to start early," I said as I pushed away from the table.

"What did the mother cow say to her baby cow?"

I rubbed my forehead, waiting for the answer.

"It's pasture bedtime."

I groaned and left the common room to find my bed.

21

In the morning, I descended the stairs and found Victoria seated near the door, book in hand, waiting on me. The sun had only been up for a few minutes. Did she ever sleep?

"Morning," I said as I crossed the room. The place smelled of sweat, stale beer, and burnt stew. She stood to greet me. Today, she wore a leather vest over a grey shirt and pants, the tops of which were stuffed into her boots. Her hair was pulled back into a ponytail.

"Let's go." She turned on her heel on headed out the front door. I followed along, too tired comment on her appropriating my mission to stop the attacks. She'd proven to be smart and flexible. I could do far worse in a partner.

We walked in silence, rounding the smithy to retrieve the wolf. I pulled the corpse away from the building and pried the top of the control box off so we could see the inside of the device. The same syringe of the blue drug rode next to a larger device similar to the first, but I could feel the magic rolling off this one like clouds churning over a lake. I'd missed the magic signature on the original. My skills must be making me more sensitive to magic in general.

"So that is a nathal?" Victoria asked as she probed the inner workings of the metal container. The copper tubes ran forward toward the brain, as did the wires. I followed the visible scar until it reached the ears. When I

97

turned the wolf's head, it revealed a device embedded in the ear canal. After a bit of fishing, I retrieved a small piece of metal, inscribed like the piece in the control box.

Victoria picked it up. "This must be how they told it what to do."

The idea of an animal being able to understand so many human commands struck me as unlikely, but two attacks later what else could it be? "At least we know how they are coordinating the attacks."

"This is barbaric. To what possible end could they be using these poor animals to harm people?

"Every ambush has been in a place where a magus should have been. The bear attacked the towns where it killed the Watcher and one where Magus Hoadley of Aldon had been the day before. Magus Pelham had been scheduled to be in the carriage the wolves ambushed. Either someone knows about the devices the magi use or they are trying to eliminate the magus of the southern regions." I still couldn't produce an argument for either hypothesis. Neither made a lot of sense since the control boxes on these animals far surpassed anything the magus carried. How could magus be a threat to people who knew how to create this sophisticated magic?

"I feel we are missing something." She traced the scars along the back of the wolf's neck with her finger. "This is a merging of flesh, magic, and technology. Whoever is behind this has an advanced understanding of things you and I are just touching on. Given enough time they could control Astaria itself."

Which made my mission to find this person or people and put an end to it even more urgent. After that, we could establish if they were after the magic artifacts or another reason.

Victoria stood and I did the same. "Can you really create a device to locate these people?"

"I think I can," I said, wishing I was more confident in my abilities. My failure of using the levitator during the fight had rattled me. "I still haven't figured how I missed with the levitator."

She stepped back from me and spread her arms wide. "Lift me."

Of course, Victoria would volunteer instead of pointing out an object that couldn't feel pain. Of course, I hadn't asked the Sherrif and he'd been fine after. I did as she requested, though. I raised my left arm, aimed, and slowly turned the dial. She rose smoothly into the air. For the next few minutes, Victoria put me through my paces. Left, right, up, down, push, and pull. The whole time she clapped and laughed at the experience.

"Set me down gently, please."

She bumped on the ground and joined me. "Lift the wolf."

I did and it floated into the air before returning just as gently.

Victoria clapped me on the shoulder. "It seems to work. Try lifting the wagon."

I pointed and turned the dial. I felt an immense pressure pushing down on me. After a few seconds of the wagon not budging the pressure turned to pain as I sunk into the ground. I twisted the dial to off and the pain subsided.

"You're a bit shorter than I remember," Victoria said with a wry tone in her voice.

My knees were even with the dirt now. "It looks like I can't lift anything heavier than I am."

Victoria helped me out of the hole I'd created. "Well, that illuminates a few things. During the fight, you said you missed the target?"

"I assume so," I said hesitantly. In the chaos of the fight, I wasn't sure what had happened. "The force threw me across the clearing."

She tapped her chin as she thought. "Try pointing at the ground and see what happens."

I did, turning the dial carefully controlling the lift. This time, I was the one who rose in the air as the force of the magic pushed against me. My spirits rose along with my body. I had created magic and it worked. All those months I thought I was a failure. and now I was levitating both other things and myself with my own power.

The things I would be able to do with this—like fly! If I added a attachment it would let me—

"Quinn, play time is over. Now be a good sport and come down from there."

Reluctantly, I turned the dial to off and landed on the ground.

She shrugged. "It makes sense. You don't have the leverage to move the earth, so the force rebounds against you.With the wagon you were exerting an upward force, thus you sank. Luckily, you weren't standing on stone or you'd have broken your legs. The faster you turn the dial, the more violent the repulsion."

"This will come in handy when we find who is behind all this," I said trying to not sound over proud of myself.

"You've definitely piqued my curiosity." She cleared her throat. "But none of this gets us closer to stopping these attacks."

"Right." I headed for the smithy. The master blacksmith was already hammering away at a shovel head. Up with the light was how smiths worked. I greeted him as did Victoria.

I waited for him to place the shovel into the fire before I interrupted further. "I need to build a piece and will require the forge. It is truly life or death, but I don't want to cost you trade by delaying your work."

"I appreciate the thought, but I'll be fine. I've heard rumors and wild stories about you. The whole town is abuzz. Don't matter though. You're a fellow blacksmith and I'd be honored for you to use my forge."

"We would be happy to pay you for your time," Victoria added, but I shot her a look as the smith's face darkened. He had already refused payment and she was insulting him, albeit unknowingly.

"I appreciate your generosity," I said over her before she made things worse. She might be an expert on the outside world, but I knew the smithy. "What can I do in return?"

"I've been thinking since our talk last night. If you'd come back and help me catch up, I'd be in your debt," Master Redsmith said.

"Consider it done. Once I finish the next portion of my journey, I'd be proud to work by your side," I said, all the while wondering if I'd live to fulfill this promise.

"I'll be your assistant for as long as you need me, master smith." He pulled the piece he'd been heating and set it aside, freeing the forge for me.

Without more words, I started to work. I took the nathal out and placed it on the anvil, feeling the magic flowing from it. The magic drifted off to the east, the path almost visible when I concentrated on it. I picked a piece of metal stock and trickled magic into it. Once it was charged I set it in the coal forge. I didn't want any awkward questions about forging "cold" metal. Master Redsmith worked the bellows, fetched tools, and assisted with the finer details as I bent my will to find where the magic came from. Victoria sat on a bench, out of the way, watching like a hawk.

While the metal heated in the forge, I found a slender piece of iron and crafted three pins to repair the pistol. I'd need it for this adventure, I was sure. Once that was done, I returned to the tracking device.

The sun had just started to set over the mountains as I put the pieces together. The pointer on the crude compass never wavered from what I believed was the source of the magic controlling the animals. If it worked, we could put an end to these senseless killings, but that was a giant if.

I thanked Master Redsmith for his assistance and we returned to the inn. I barely made it to my room before I collapsed into an exhausted sleep. Working with magic was far more draining than just using the fire and hammer. Tomorrow we'd track the person responsible for these attacks.

I only hoped we were up to the task of defeating them.

22

An hour before sunrise when I silently entered the common room, Victoria already lounged by the common room's door, bright as the morning sun. She cast me a cheeky smile as if she knew I'd been trying to arrive before her this time.

"Good morning," I said.

"The horses are saddled out front and I've seen to the provisions for the mission. I refuse to eat the jerky you live on."

I ignored the comment and thanked her before we mounted up. Victoria sat astride her horse with the packhorse tethered to her pommel. She'd packed enough for three missions from the looks of it. I checked the compass and it still pointed east.

I tapped my horse's flank and we headed out as the sun crept up from the horizon. We crossed the bridge over the Itugar River, guided by the compass. Victoria rode by my side as we left the road and entered the forest.

After a couple of hours, we came across a game trail. I wished Cian were here to identify the tracks, but to me, they looked like a mixture of horse hooves and paw prints. It was as good of a sign as any. The compass pointed in the general direction of the trail so we stayed on course.

"Do you have a plan for when we find the people responsible? If you don't I have a few ideas." Victoria asked. The birds sang as we rode, which was a good sign since during the attacks the forest had gone silent.

"I won't until we see what we're up against. Who knows what other animals they've perverted? And they may have magic we haven't seen yet. What are you carrying for weapons?"

She slid matching pistols from under her coat. I'd seen similar ones back at the workshop, but they weren't the new models Cian wielded. "I always come prepared for trouble."

I checked the compass again and it wobbled back and forth, reorienting. We must be close. After an hour, we spotted a small compound of buildings set in a valley below the ridge we had just crested.

Victoria produced a pair of binoculars and studied the scene before handing them over. Men armed with swords and clubs walked between the buildings. There was a large whitewashed house in the foreground. The shutters were missing, or hanging loose, giving the impression it had been abandoned long ago. A massive barn, its once red paint faded to grey, stood behind the house. One of the doors lay off to the side near a dilapidated shed. Two wagons sat outside the barn doors, loaded with cages containing wolves and a small bear, probably a cub from the size.

"This looks to be the place," I said as I handed back the binoculars. "Do we ride down and take them out?"

She shook her head. "We are outnumbered, and if they release the animals, even more so. There must be at least ten armed guards and who knows how many others? We need to attack at night so we have the element of surprise."

I hated to delay, but she was right. After I tethered my horse and removed the saddlebags. Behind the deadfall tree was a good place to watch while we waited for the sun to go down. Victoria rifled through her pack pulling out bottles filled with a variety of colored powders.

"What are you doing?"

She didn't look up as she continued her search. "I thought it might be a good idea to have a couple of tricks on hand."

"Surprises are good," I said as I pulled out my toolkit to adjust my gear. "As long as they are surprises for them, not us."

I put a new piece of alarium in my arm. If my arm went dead in the middle of a fight, it wouldn't be so great for me. I checked the shield, fire, and lightning weapons to make sure they were operational. The levitator and the broken disrupter pistol wouldn't need alarium—only my magic, as miraculous as that seemed.

"Rest assured, I am well versed in fighting," Victoria said with a wicked grin.

After seeing her drop the three toughs at the inn, I had no doubt, though she looked more like a librarian than a fighter. I retrieved the pins I'd made at Master Redsmith's forge and repaired the disruptor pistol. Then I set to carving a couple of wooden stakes. You could never be too prepared.

Victoria continued mixing potions, sitting across from me, behind a fallen log. "You know how good things come to those who wait?"

"They do?"

"Yep, unless you're waiting on death."

When would I learn not to ask?

23

The hours crept by as we watched the people of the compound go about their business. We ate from the provisions Victoria had purchased and I hated to admit they were much better than what I'd brought. The farmhouse bell rang announcing dinner. We needed the darkness to help us fight so many men.

As darkness fell, Victoria took her pistols and checked the sights for the fourth time. We both wore our Watchers masks, so we were able to see in the darkness of the new moon. When the lamps were extinguished in the main house, we put our plan in motion.

"I'll take care of the house, you lock down the barn so we don't have to fight any more animals," I told her as we descended the slope toward the compound.

"Affirmative," she replied as we separated to handle our tasks.

We hadn't seen any additional people join the ranks of the camp below. Security was definitely lax given how long we'd been here and not one person patrolled the treeline. Given the distance to any roads, I doubted anyone was worried about intruders. At least I hoped so. Between my armaments and Victoria's pistols, we should be able to handle anyone who tried to stop us, but my confidence fled when it came to the animals hopped up on the control drugs.

I reached the farmhouse as Victoria slid through the night toward the barn. Up close, it was plain the whitewash had flaked off long ago. Two windows flanked the front door. I stalked around the house to the back where I found another exit. As quietly as possible, I wedged the spikes I'd cut between the door and the jam to stop anyone from leaving this way. Once I was satisfied, I set fire to the rear of the house and ran to the front. The ancient structure went up like a soot-filled chimney from the ball of fire I threw at it. I stood off to the side of the front door and waited.

Screams of panic erupted inside as the fire spread through the derelict house. The front door slammed open. A worker ran out into the night and I shocked him with a lightning blast from my gauntlet, knocking him out cold. I repeated the process on the second and third men who fled, but my luck ran out as I shocked the fourth man. The man behind him leapt over the prone form and landed beyond my reach. While I tried to fire on him, three more emerged, pulling knives and swords when they saw me.

The first swung his short sword at me, but I blocked it with my metal arm. He dropped the sword from the impact, cursing loudly as his compatriot charged in with a knife. I hit him with a blast of flame followed by a swift kick to his crotch. He screamed as he fell off the porch, landing hard on the ground, clutching himself.

Another man darted in, a sword the ready when pain jabbed through my side just above the hip. A knife. The first man had awakened and charged in to join the melee. While it wasn't a deep cut, the wound burned along my side. I lost focus for a second, and the running man slammed into me, knocking me off the porch and onto the ground. The breath fled at the forces of the impact.

I had just caught my breath when a foot slammed into my injured side. I rolled away only to have another man dive on me. I wrestled with my attacker with a combination of metal arm and curses. I fired lightning at my opponent's head. He screamed as he reared back, grasping his ruined face. I rolled to the side, avoiding another kick as more people emerged from the burning building. I swept flames at them to keep them at a distance.

The sound of breaking glass and coughing came from behind me. I glanced back to see a cloud surrounding two of the men who were in the process of vomiting on the ground. A third man screamed as a slug from Victoria's pistol took him in the shoulder. The other two rushed me.

I activated my shield, stopping the bigger man's sword strike. I lashed out, catching my other opponent under the chin with a metal fist. A loud crack accompanied the blow. He fell backward and lay still. I fired a bolt of lightning into the sword-wielding man, knocking him out.

Victoria ran over. "We've got a big problem."

I looked over her shoulder and saw what she meant. Cian turned the corner, two wolves flanking him as he stalked toward us.

"Quinn, come with me, and I'll let her go," he said. He stood holding the struggling alchemist about ten feet from where I was.

"You've got to fight the hypnosis," Victoria said. "We'll find whoever did this to you."

Cian threw back his head and laughed. His mask hung around his neck, swaying as he mocked Victoria. "You think I'm being controlled? Don't be stupid."

"You're a Watcher," I said, "How could you betray your duty? We protect the people of Astaria."

"The Watchers are Everard's toys and he doesn't care if we are broken, he just gets new ones. All we do is keep the false magus in power. Once Everard is gone, we'll take over and use the alarium to destroy Candalar once and for all. Then the people of Astaria will be safe."

It suddenly made sense why they were doing this. "The attack on Lapis was to steal the alarium from the magus' arm piece?"

Cian laughed again. "You think you're so smart, but you need the truth spelled out for you. You will build us the weapons to eliminate the Candalarians and the Norns. Astaria will take its rightful place in the world."

"You're a traitor." Victoria spat at his feet. "We don't negotiate with your ilk."

Cian grinned. "You always thought too much of yourself, Victoria." He pointed at us and commanded the wolves: "Attack."

I recognized the alpha from our earlier fight, an ambush I now knew Cian had orchestrated. Lady Pelham's guards had been slaughtered so I would investigate with only Cian by my side, but the arrival of the Candalarians had messed up his plans.

I was a fool.

Victoria and I pivoted so our backs were protected by the other. The wolves ran at us. The alpha leapt at me, but I knocked it away with my fist. Victoria fell beneath the other wolf. The animal pressed down, teeth snapping as it sought to rip out her throat. I kicked it in the side, driving it off her. The alpha darted in from behind and cut my legs out from under me. I went down hard as it landed on my back.

"Just say the word and I'll call them off." Cian's voice was harsh. "Why die to protect Everard?"

"I honor my word," Victoria said as she kicked the attacking wolf in the jaw.

I struggled to my knees but the alpha pounced, knocking me to the ground again. He pulled at the leather hood of my cloak which, thankfully, blocked my neck for the time being. I pushed my arm into the ground, readying to levitate myself. The wolf's paw knocked the dial out of my hand before I could turn the dial.

I swore as the wolf tore at the material blocking him from my neck. My hand found the dial and I twisted it. Magic surged into me, taking my breath away. With a blast of blue energy, the magic shot me and the wolf straight up into the air at an accelerated rate.

After a few seconds, I turned off the dial which did two things. First, the wolf kept rising, as its momentum wasn't tied to the device but to my body. Second, I fell.

From my new vantage point, I spotted Cian racing toward Victoria who still fought with the other wolf. I engaged the levitator to slow my descent. I threw a fireball at Cian to prevent him from reaching Victoria. He danced away from the flame as I landed feet first with a thump.

Cian threw a knife at Victoria, clipping her shoulder as she dodged, but it was enough of a distraction. The wolf pounced, driving her to the ground. She shoved her arms against its neck, but she didn't have the strength to hold it off. Cian sauntered up, pulling his swords from their sheathes. I was too far away to reach her, and she'd be hurt by anything from my arm. I grabbed the disruptor pistol from my belt and fired it at the wolf.

Nothing happened. Again.

Frustration crashed on me and I threw the useless pistol at the wolf. It struck it in the side and exploded with light.

The effects were immediate. The wolf stopped snapping at its prone victim. After a great shake of its head, it fled into the night, leaving a scratched and bloodied Victoria behind.

I dropped to my knees as the same overwhelming cold as before enveloped me. My teeth chattered as my body shook uncontrollably. I forced myself to my feet. My mechanical arm spasmed as the connection failed.

Cian sprinted across the space between us. His long sword arced in, overhand, and I jerked to the side. It clanged against the metal of my arm.

Cian kicked me, throwing my balance off. My arm detached, crashing to the dirt. The lack of weight caused me to overbalance and land on my side avoiding the short sword thrust.

I heard another bottle break near my feet, releasing billowing smoke. With the Watcher's mask, I was safe, but Cian hadn't been wearing his. He retreated, coughing as the vapor found his lungs. The thick smog obscured my vision but gave me time to shake off the freezing effects of the magic. I tugged on the straps and restored my arm to full use.

A form appeared in front of me and I barely had time to block Cian's sword as it arced overhead. He'd gotten his mask on before the fumes had overcome him. We now fought in a swirling mass of smoke. Pain flared in my good arm as the short sword bit into my gauntlet. Something broke and blood flowed down my arm, but I couldn't pay it any attention.

I jumped back to avoid a strike that would have gutted me but snagged on the leather strap of my pouch. It gave me the opening I needed. I grabbed the sword with my metal hand and snapped it off the hilt. Cian released the sword, jumped up, and drove both feet into my chest, sending me backward out of the smoke. I hit with a jarring thud and felt my arm loosen. The sensation flickered as the connections yet again lost contact with my skin. I needed to use my magic to attach my arm so it would stop falling off.

Cian stalked out of the fog, short sword in his hand and blood lust in his eyes. When he noticed my hand spasming, he smiled. "I'll be taking the alarium now, Quinn."

I tried to push myself up with the semi-attached arm but collapsed. I was a fish out of water with the hawk bearing down on me.

Thud.

Cian crumpled, revealing Victoria right behind him, pistol gripped like a club.

"Well, he's certainly a knockout," Victoria said.

I groaned, but somehow we'd won.

It didn't feel like a victory.

24

Victoria helped me reattach my arm and bandaged my elbow where Cian had cut through my gauntlet. That treacherous bastard, now trussed up like a pig ready for the spit, was still unconscious from the knock on the head. The freed animals had already fled. We tied the arms and legs of the men who'd been helping Cian. After we removed Cian's weapons, Victoria confiscated his mask, checking his eyes.

He moaned as she prodded his skull harder than necessary. "Don't seem to be any fractures, so he'll recover. I have just the thing to encourage his cooperation." She rummaged through her bag, examining each until she found what she wanted. After all the fighting, I was amazed they weren't broken.

Cian stirred and I pointed his own pistol at him. "You've got a lot to answer for."

He looked up at me with bleary eyes. "You stopped me, but there are more to finish the job."

"Yes," Victoria said brightly. "And this will make you feel really friendly and want to help us."

He shook his head. "I know all about your tricks, Victoria." He opened his hand to show a syringe of the blue drug. He shoved the needle into his leg and depressed the plunger before I could stop him. His head sagged back as he passed out.

"Is he dead?" I asked as Victoria tried to rouse him.

"He's still breathing. Too much of the drug can kill you. I don't know if there was enough there to overdose on."

"Dead men tell no tales."

Victoria nodded. Cian was alive but non-responsive. she tried again to awaken him, but he stayed absent. "I'll have to make an antidote first. For that I have to find the compound in its pure form," she said once she'd finished with Cian.

"He wasn't doing this alone. We need to find the other people behind this and stop them," I argued. "Cian may recover and tell us. I'll take him back to Treetop and Jabber can nurse him back to health or maybe Everard could use magic to "persuade" him to help us find the people behind this."

She snorted. "Everard can stop an invading army, but delicate work to remove the effects of this drug are beyond him. I'll travel to Uwhela, find who created the compound, and destroy their ability to do so. If Cian stays alive long enough after the overdose, the antidote may bring him back to answer for what he's done."

"Aren't you being hasty?" I asked, not wanting her to go, at least without me. Just as my task had, in the end, required her help, perhaps hers would require help as well. "He could recover in a few days."

"You can handle him if he does. Regardless, I have to destroy the manufacturer of the compound or we'll never be free of this drug. You think there won't be more people willing to create mindless slaves to do their bidding?"

She was right and we both knew it. She packed away her things. "I'll be in touch when I return. You'll have to stop the upcoming attacks, but at least you can warn the magus about the dangers."

I nodded. "Be careful and good luck."

"I'm always careful." She turned to leave but then faced me. "You know the problem with a two-headed horse?"

"No."

"You can never tell if it's coming or going." She laughed.With a smirk and a wave, she left to start her mission. I'd miss her jokes. Well, maybe not a lot. And off Victoria went. I wondered if the people she hunted were ready for her.

I seriously doubted it. She angled for the tree line where we'd secured our horses. I'd use Cian's horse to tote him back to Treetop. As I sat on the ground next to Cian, I realized he'd broken my levitator when he struck my gauntlet. I'd have to remake it since there were a lot of other uses for it, like putting an unconscious man on the back of his horse.

The groans of the other men roused me from my thoughts. I loaded Cian and the men into one of the wagons and set off for Bexley's Crossing. As the sun rose, I rode toward the town so I could turn them over to the authorities.

The longer journey would be in stopping whoever was behind this whole plan in order to protect the people of Astaria.

Because that was what Watchers did.

THE END

PISTOLS & POTIONS

BOOK TWO

To all of the dreamers who create fantastic new worlds.

1

―

A hoy, the ship. Please tell Captain Breachcolm that Lady Yorke wishes to book passage."

I studied the Maiden's Kiss for a moment while I waited for the captain to appear. The airship impressed me with how well-crafted it was. The balloon floated above the ship, secured by a series of ropes. The ship appeared to be ocean-going, except for the massive propellers that were attached to the back, bottom, and on arms out to the sides. Each could be used to turn or accelerate the ship.

Stillhold stretched out below the single airship tower. Unlike the major cities like Terralon or Iron Harbor, with their major trading centers, Stillhold only got airships infrequently. Lucky for me, the Maiden's Kiss made frequent stops here or I'd have had to track them down.

I spotted the new additions Captain Breachcolm had added since the incident with the sky pirates. It looked far better than when the mission had ended, what with the whole pirates attacking the ship thing and all. You could barely make out the burnt timber and the new rails were an improvement over the old rickety ones. Breachcolm should thank me for paying for all the repairs to his ship.

After I'd gotten him attacked by pirates in the first place, it was the least I could do.

"The captain says we're booked."

The owner of the youthful voice should have been home with his folks, not on an airship traveling the world. So much for being thankful.

"And what exactly does that mean?" I asked, placing as much scorn into each word as possible. I hated dealing with the crew, but one does what one must in the service of Astaria.

The lad at least had the decency to flush with embarrassment. "The captain said—"

I cut him off with a wave of my hand. "I have no time to deal with trivialities. Get the captain or load my bags onto the airship."

"But..." He paused to look over his shoulder. "Lady Yorke, the captain said you aren't allowed on."

"Travis Breachcolm," I yelled up to the ship that swayed against its mooring ropes in the slight breeze. "Face me like the man you should be instead of the cowering dog you are."

The deckhand gasped in shock, but I ignored him as a salt-and-pepper-haired man threw his leg over the side of the airship and climbed down the rope ladder to the docking platform. He strode toward me, eyes alight with his ever-present anger. Really, Travis needed to deal with his issues, but not on my time. Or, rather, the time I intended to purchase from him.

"Victoria," Travis said. He dismissed the deckhand, who took to the rope ladder like a monkey traversing a tree. "You've some nerve showing up here, belittling me in front of my crew, after you almost blew my ship out of the air with your fire elixir."

I scoffed at him. "You didn't seem to mind when the same elixir destroyed the pirates who were attacking us. How is it my fault you brought your ship too close after I warned you that the mixture was highly flammable?"

His eyes almost burst from his skull. "Too close? The master cannoneer had to deliver your attack. How were we to know the backlash that the explosion would cause? It cost me a lot of gold to repair the Maiden's Kiss after that fiasco."

"Actually, it cost me a large sum, since I included the repairs in my payment. We can quibble over he said, she said all day, but in the end, you will transport me to Uwhela. I'm on official business and you are headed in the same direction. Now be a dear and load my luggage and let's be off." I resisted rolling my eyes at the man. I plucked a leather pouch out of my pocket and tossed it to Travis. "That should more than cover your fee to take me where I need to go. All other business is canceled until I complete my mission. You know how official business is, don't you?"

His eyes narrowed. "I do. And if I say no? Are you going to take over my ship?"

I patted his cheek. There were other airships, but Travis Breachcolm was two things. Honest and dependable. Other airships fled the moment trouble reared its head, but not the Maiden's Kiss. Travis would fly through the underworld if he had agreed to do it, and moreover, he'd make it out again. "You know how the Arch Magus is when he has to personally get involved, don't you? I won't have to do a thing."

His face blanched, no doubt remembering the last time he'd crossed paths with Everard. The Arch Magus could be quite persuasive when he needed to be. I doubted Travis would ever forget that encounter. "Get on board. I'll have your bags put in the hold."

"Oh, no," I said with all the sugar I could add to it. "Place them in your quarters. You can kick your first mate out of his cabin. I need the space to work."

"Why did you have to pick my ship? There are plenty of others headed to Uwhela."

I met his eyes dead-on. "Travis, you are the best pilot in Astaria and one of the few somewhat trustworthy men who fly these lanes. I have no doubt you will stay with me until the mission is over and I'll give you another pouch to match the one in your hand. How long will the trip take?"

He seemed to brighten at that, though whether it was the compliment or the offer of more gold, I couldn't say. As long as he did what I needed, I didn't care.

"Two weeks to get there, assuming good weather. Always a pleasure to do business with you, my lady."

He turned to leave but stopped when I cleared my throat.

His eyes narrowed slightly. "Yes, ma'am?"

"Tell me, why don't sailors play cards?"

He groaned. "Why?"

"Because the captain is standing on the deck."

Travis shook his head before striding to the rope ladder. I distinctly heard him say, "There isn't enough gold to listen to her awful jokes."

I smiled and followed him on board.

My bags were loaded into my room. While it was the captain's cabin, it was more of a glorified closet. I secured my small trunk to the wall to avoid accidents and to keep it out of plain sight. The crew of airships was worse than tea socials in regard to gossiping. The trip to Uwhela would be about two weeks, given good weather. I'd sent word to Everard of my plans to take the Maiden's Kiss to Uwhela via Thaclet. I needed to find Mac Tan in Thaclet to get intel on who concocted this new drug. I had to stop whoever was using drugged animals as weapons against Astaria. He'd come in handy over the years, and while he was an awful person, his information was top rung.

Most of my luggage contained my mission bag and various supplies I might need. I'd considered a small setup given the distances involved in my travels, but if the last trip with Captain Travis had taught me anything, it was to be prepared for the unexpected. I'm sure the pirates hadn't been as pleased as I'd been that I'd had the makings for the firebomb with me.

The airship lurched upward, dropping me onto a mattress so thin it could have been a sheet of parchment. The walls bore the signs of hard living aboard a merchant airship. Gouges and stains dotted the room like a broken palette. Seriously, couldn't the captain afford a nicer setup? Everything was so minimalist, but I'd dealt with far worse in my time as a Watcher. I'd gotten a bit comfortable spending the majority of my days in the lab instead of traipsing around Astaria like my fellow Watcher, Quinn did.

"No time like the present," I said to the empty room and set to making things as comfortable as possible. The wardrobe still held the captain's clothes, but there was enough room to hang my duster, a couple of outfits, and my mission bag.

I opened the leather satchel so I could arrange the contents on the bunk next to me. Roland's voice rolled through my head. *Lass, you check every piece of equipment 'fore you take a step on a mission.*

I knew all my gear was in perfect condition, but the routine beckoned. I unholstered my pistols, a gift from Roland when I'd become a Watcher. They were works of art, both in form and function. The set of custom alarium powered pistols were clean, charged, and ready for business, though I hoped to avoid any unpleasantness. I couldn't test fire the weapon while ensconced in the captain's quarters, but I'd fire off a couple of shots later to ensure they were operational.

From my bag, my Watcher's mask emerged first. The alarium had to be checked to make sure it hadn't been damaged in transit. Once I examined the mask, I placed it over my face, and the eyepieces and respirator worked perfectly

"No one wanted a broken piece of equipment when your life depended on it."
Thanks, Roland.

My belt and its assortment of pouches rattled a bit. I took it off and carefully examined the contents of each. Fire potion, samples of the hypnotic drug Quinn had discovered, a couple of poisons and antidotes, and my favorite—the forget-me drug. My assistant had accidentally smelled the forget-me potion and couldn't remember anything for days. It was a fun party trick, though. Those I secured before setting them aside.

I found the rattling noise when I reached into the pouch with extra ammo. The container had opened, and the pellets clinked when jostled. Far better than the alternative of not having ammo on hand.

The rest of the travel bag held holsters, emergency medical supplies, and food and water just in case. I hated the extra weight of carrying susten-ance, but it had saved me quite a few times. I holstered the pistols across my hips where they'd been covered by my duster. Given my last flight on the Maiden, I hoped there wouldn't be any incidents, but the men and women of Travis Breachcolm's crew were far better than the pirates, but only a fool travels unarmed.

The other items went back in the satchel, and I returned it to the cabi-net. I secured it to the wall so there weren't any accidents. After I settled the duster in place, I left my cabin and went up on deck.

The city of Pillvor, the capital of seafood as they claimed, could be seen off to the East, but the airship sped by. Whatever else Captain Breachcolm might be, he handled the Maiden's Kiss like a lover on their first night together. The ship barely swayed in the stiff breeze that carried us farther south with each passing moment. We flew over the Allernora river which separated Astaria from Candalar. While there were places you could ford the river, airships made the journey so much easier. If only the gorges that protected Iron Harbor and High Keep ran the whole length of the river, we wouldn't have the Candalarians raiding so often.

I'd never been to Uwhela before, having to rely on rumors and innu-endos from travelers. Stories of invisible cats, men who topped seven feet tall, and the wild magic of the Uwhelans must be exaggerations. I'd heard similar tales of the Arch Magus's exploits, which I knew to be everything from far-flung hype to straight-up lies.

I stood at the rail wondering if I'd be able to stop the people responsible for the atrocities against the people and animals of Astaria. I swore I would end this before any more people died or became turncoats like Cian. A Watcher's job was never easy, but it could be rewarding to save the lives of innocents from evil.

I wondered if I was up for the mission. Only time would tell.

2

The sun woke me as it crept through the porthole. I washed my face and straightened out my tangled hair before donning my clothes, pistols, and duster. A quick jaunt up the stairs and onto the deck to see the sun rising in the east. The breeze had picked up from yesterday, but the ship barely rocked. With the trailing wind, we might just make it to Uwhela in the promised two weeks.

"Lady Yorke," the captain said. He came down from the quarterdeck. "We are stopping in Thaclet as you requested. I promised the crew three days of leave while we unload and bring on goods for the trip to Uwhela. It will break up the trip and allow you a few days of comfort before we continue. You know Thaclet has a lot of different forms of…um…entertainment available. Astarian law doesn't apply there."

"If I were looking for comfort, I'd be being replacing the atrocity you call a mattress with a feather one. But I understand the need to stop in Thaclet. You can have one day, no more." Truly, we had killed everyone involved with the mysterious drug at the farm, except Cian, who was in a coma the last time I'd seen him. Quinn and I hadn't left any witnesses when we attacked the cultist at the farm. The best our unseen opponents could do was send someone to find out what happened and then return with news. I should have enough of a head start, but why deal with needless risk when a good plan and a ready supply of elixirs would take care of most situations?

"I understand, my lady…"

I quirked an eyebrow at the use of my fabricated title. My given name, Victoria Wyndham, didn't strike the fear into the hearts of men, like that of Lady Victoria Yorke, daughter to Reginald Yorke, the Magus of Holrough. The fact that the real Lady Yorke had been killed in a foolish attempt to climb a rotten apple tree wasn't common knowledge. Her father was more than willing to back my story. He'd lost his only daughter and his oldest child and allowed me to use the family name to keep the focus off his young son who'd take over the fiefdom. "And?"

"My crew is expecting three days of shore leave," the captain said, visibly relieved by my agreement. He turned to leave, but I stopped him with my hand on his arm.

An idea tickled the back of my brain. "Absolutely not. Eight hours, no more."

His face flushed. "Now, look here. I am the captain. My men have families in Thaclet, and canceling shore leave will be a major problem."

"I am not unreasonable," I said, holding up my hand to forestall the avalanche of excuses. Luckily, Everard had granted me a tidy sum of gold to complete my tasks as well as the profits to be had from selling potions to the locals of Stillwater. "I will triple the men's pay and give a gold bonus per man for the inconvenience once my mission is done."

"That is a generous offer, my lady," the captain said. The glint of greed lit his eyes like an Autumnfest demon gourd. "What do I do if they refuse?"

"That isn't my problem. Find a new crew, throw them overboard, whatever gets us to Uwhela the fastest. You do not understand the importance of my mission. I'm sure the Arch Magus will be pleased with your cooperation, which is far better than the alternative, I assure you."

All the color left his face. "I will make it happen." He spun on his heel and returned to the quarterdeck. He might be willing to ignore my requests, but Everard had a reputation for incinerating anyone who got in his way. In reality, Everard only fought when all other options were gone. Not that the good captain needed to know this.

The first mate passed me, gathering up the crew to talk with the captain. She kept a wide berth since she'd been on the last trip. The fact that I'd treated a nasty stab wound that would have cost her an arm made no difference. They were all wary of me.

I climbed the steps to the forecastle and watched the scenery fly by below us. Angry shouts floated to my ears, not unexpectedly, but Breachcolm would handle it in his own way. My hair flowed behind me in the wind. A leather tie took care of the nuisance.

The land rolled along below the ship while I stood at the rail. In some ways the captain reminded me of Cian, which irked me to no end. It still bothered me that Cian had turned on the Watchers. What could have made him join forces with people wanting to overthrow Astaria? Did he think he'd become powerful in the new land? Without Everard or another powerful Arch Magus to protect us, Astaria's army wasn't large, and we didn't have enough alarium weapons to stand against our warrior nation neighbors. If things went poorly, Astaria would end up split between the Norns, the Candalarians, and every other nation who thought Astaria to be weak.

Everard stood between peace and destruction. With him dying, who would step into the void to protect the Astaria? I wondered if Quinn would be strong enough to take the lead.

The loud stomp of boots caught my attention, bringing me back to the present. Five of the crew came up to the forecastle. The large man in front wore no shirt, but his skin was covered with tattoos to the point I couldn't make out the skin below. They spread out in a semicircle around me, forcing me to put my back to the rail. Not optimal, given the ease of throwing me overboard in this position.

"What's all this? We don't get shore leave," the leader said. His accent was thick, but I got the picture. I didn't recognize any of the small group from the previous mission with the pirates.

Captain Breachcolm and his first mate, Zora, descended from the quarterdeck. Both had knives out. I shook my head, and they stopped, though the captain looked less than pleased.

"Gentlemen, do you know what you call a boat that comes in second place?"

They exchanged confused glances. Obviously, they weren't prepared for my jokes.

"What?" asked the smaller man with a hook nose and a scar down his right cheek.

"The rudder-up. Get it?"

This was where they should have groaned but didn't. No accounting for humor.

"What's that got to do with anything?" a hefty man on the left asked. He'd been the strong arm in his early days, I guessed, but age had caught up with him. "We want our shore leave."

"I understand," I said, catching the leader's eyes. "This mission is a matter of life and death. I've offered a large sum of coin for your trouble. How many times do you get a gold coin for a trip?"

The men glanced at each other again. These men would work for years before they earned a gold. The tattoo artists in Thaclet would make a small fortune, assuming any of the crew had space for new ink.

A few of the crew had been on the last trip, but these were new as far as I could tell. It would be great to play the Watcher card, but the crew would spread the news all over and I'd need a new alias, so I withheld the information. The Watchers had a reputation, and it wasn't all good. Certain members did what was necessary, no matter the collateral damage. I wasn't sure if I was that type after my run-in with Master Spencer.

The big man's scowl deepened. "What's stopping us from just taking your coin and pitching you over the rail?"

There are times when words work best. This wasn't one of them. I stepped forward and kicked him square in the groin. He screamed in an octave reserved for angels and young children. Tears gushed down his face as he cupped himself and sank to the deck.

"Cal!" the hook-nosed man shrieked. He pulled a knife from his belt. "Bitch, you're gonna die."

Before he could advance, I had my pistols out. They retreated at the sight of the weapons since only the very rich or the Watchers had access to alarium guns like this. One barrel pressed into Hook Nose's forehead, and the other pointed at the hefty man. "You're willing to fight for my coin?"

"No, my lady," he said, panic thick in his voice. "My gal can wait. I'm sure she'll be happy with the pay."

I looked at each man in turn. They all had their heads bowed like unruly school children. "After you attack me, you expect me to still pay you?"

"It was a mistake, fer sure," the hefty man stuttered out his answer. "Please, Lady Yorke. We shouldn't have listened to Cal."

I tapped my finger on the pistol next to the trigger. The smell of urine filled the air as Hook Nose peed himself. Captain Breachcolm didn't travel with brutes or low lives, so while unexpected, they showed fire. I could use this incident to help with my mission. "While I'm in Uwhela, I may have need of a few strong arms. Agree to help me without question and I will pay you as promised, and this will be a forgotten memory."

"Yes, ma'am," they all said in unison. Even Cal, though his sounded strained for some strange reason.

"The next time you cross me, I will shoot each of you dead. Do we understand each other?"

All but Hook Nose nodded. I pulled the pistol away from his head and he joined in the nod fest. "We are sorry, my lady."

"Take Cal and let him get some rest. I will have work for you, and I expect it done."

It took two of the crew to get Cal off the deck. Jeers and catcalls followed their limping procession past the rest of the crew.

"I told you not to mess with her," Zora said from the quarterdeck as Cal passed. "We'll be having words later."

Cal nodded but said nothing.

Captain Breachcolm and Zora ascended to the forecastle. "My apologies, Lady Yorke," the captain said. "I'll dock the crew involved the extra pay for this. I'll not have this type of behavior on my ship."

"No, you will pay them," I said.

"What?" Zora said, clearly bewildered. "They attacked you and you want to pay them?"

I holstered my pistols. "They made a mistake and learned their lesson. I may need these men later."

Captain Breachcolm sputtered. "Victoria, that was not part of our arrangement."

I laughed. "Neither was your crew threatening to rob me and throw me overboard. The rules changed, and you had better get used to it."

The captain threw his hands in the air. He pivoted to leave, stepped in the puddle left by Hook Nose, and fell squarely on his ass. With a string of imaginative curses, he lifted himself up and stormed off.

Zora and I exchanged a glance. Both of us fought not to laugh at the retreating back of the soiled captain.

"Well, he didn't need to get so pissed, but at least he didn't wet himself," I said.

Zora's laughter could be heard for miles.

3

I spent the next few days in my cabin while the captain regained his sense of humor and dealt with his crew. I'd already pushed the captain and his crew pretty hard, and unless I wanted to pull out my Watcher's mask and take charge of the ship, I was better off using the time to review my research. The next day we'd reach Thaclet, and I'd see what happened with the crew.

The hum of the boilers from below was ever present but soothing in an odd way. The boilers produced the steam that powered the propellers that made the ship more than just a hot air balloon. I pushed back the memory of one of the first airships exploding mid-air over Stillwater. *No sense dwelling on the past when I had work to do.*

The sample Quinn had retrieved from the mechanized bear he'd killed had proven insightful. I had broken down the compound and isolated the main chemicals, benzodiazepine mixed with a cyclopyrrolone. A potent combination that could hypnotize an animal, but I had been missing something. After distilling the mixture down, I arrived at a floral-smelling compound that was far more potent than I'd been expecting. One drop puts the user in a state of compulsion for the better part of a day. Multiple drops could keep a person in that state for over a week. I'd found references in my mentor's journals of a report from Uwhela about a plant named the Thorn of Byail. A religious cult used the compound on their followers to create unstoppable soldiers. The ruler of Uwhela eradicated the cult, but it looked like someone had discovered their secrets.

My biggest question still revolved around why. Astaria had many enemies and Everard even more, but the pieces didn't add up. The serum could control a human far more easily than it could an animal. Why have animals attack a magus for alarium when there were other sources to pillage? Most estates had multiple alarium lamps that were far easier to steal. The use of a Candalarian wind walker to control the animals and force them to attack the cult's enemies bordered on brilliant, but again, why not use humans under the influence of the compound? Humans doing horrible things would be so much more…commonplace. Every question spawned more questions and yielded no answers.

A knock on the door interrupted my thoughts. I slid my pistol under a stack of papers. After the adventure on deck, I didn't want to be caught unprepared. "Come in."

The door opened, and the smell of stew reached my nose. My stomach growled in response. *How long had it been since I'd eaten?*

"Lady Yorke," a masculine voice said. "Zora asked me to deliver your dinner before it got cold."

The door swung in, revealing Hook Nose from the other day. Until now, the tray had been left outside my door with a knock to let me know they'd dropped off my meal. Today was different. He held a tray with a bowl of stew, bread, and a mug of what I assumed was ale. I rose and took the tray from him.

"Thank you…"

"Isham, ma'am, but everyone calls me Ish," he said to my unasked question. "I wanted to apologize for me and the crew. We've been on cleaning duty since the captain said you refused to let him dock our pay. We all need the coin so thank you for that."

"Thank you, Isham. It's in the past." The stew smelled good, and my stomach made more noise.

Isham smiled. "I should let you eat."

"I appreciate you bringing me dinner. I'd lost track of time."

"Yes, ma'am." He rubbed his hands together. "I just want to tell you, Lady Yorke, that I am your man from now on. Cal got us all riled up and not using our brains. We all will do anything you ask, being you've been so generous and kind to us."

I had no idea what it cost Isham to say that, but I appreciated it, nonetheless. "I'll have need of you and the rest of the crew once we reach Uwhela."

"We're your men," he said with another smile. "Just leave your tray outside the door and I'll pick it up for ya." With that, he left, softly closing the door behind him.

I guess I'd made the correct decision with the crew, after all. I set my papers aside on the bed and devoured the stew, which had a spicy tang I didn't recognize. The slow heat of the spices warmed me as I ate. The ale was passable. In a matter of minutes, I'd finished as much as I could. The bowl would have fed a small army.

I placed the tray outside and retrieved my papers, setting them beside me on the cot. The captain had a mudstone lantern in his cabin. The yellowish light didn't provide great illumination, but I couldn't read in the dark.

I heard the clank of the metal tray from outside my door. The airship jerked slightly, but not enough to worry me. A few moments later, it happened again. *Strange.* I collected my papers and set them back in my luggage. The ship jerked much harder than before, sending my papers to the floor. After organizing my papers, I threw my duster on, settled my pistols in their holsters, and promptly hit the floor as the ship lurched like it'd been shot.

I clambered to my feet and pulled the door open. The tray lay upside down on the floor, with the remaining food sloshed across the planks. I ran for the stairs to the main deck and found the crew racing back and forth. Storm clouds hung low above us, and the wind tore at me. The ship bounced around like a cork on a turbulent sea.

"Lady Yorke, it isn't safe for you up here," Cal yelled as he tightened the cables holding the massive balloon to the ship. Isham and another crew member worked the lines on the other side keeping the balloon centered in the strong wind. The ship rocked back and forth in the gale.

"You need every hand you can get," I yelled back over the wind. The boat rocked again, and I momentarily lost my balance.

A hand grabbed me from behind.

"If you're going to be stubborn, you can at least be safe," Zora yelled. She looped a harness around my waist and tied off a lead rope to my back.

"Thank you!"

She ran off without another word.

Rain burst from the skies above, driving in sheets across the deck. Dragging my leash behind me, I crossed the deck to help Cal hold on to the port line before it pulled free of him. If the cables twisted, it could crash the ship or worse, explode the balloon. Water whipped by the gale making everything slick.

"Go beneath before you get hurt," Cal said.

"Forget it," I shouted back. "I'm not dying in a cabin like a coward."

"Much better than being smashed to bits up here."

The port line jumped again, threatening to take Cal along with it. I latched onto the rope and held it while he got a better grip. The hard hemp surface tore at my hands, but I wasn't letting go. Before I slid across the rain-soaked deck, Cal pulled with all his might on the rope, and we stabilized.

Crack!

Lightning flashed across the sky, leaving me blinded for a moment. The deck leaned downward. The lateral propellers tilted the ship downward. The captain must be looking to ride out the storm on the ground.

Another lightning strike left an afterimage. The thunder deafened me, stunning my senses. I concentrated on the rope and staying in place.

The ship lurched again, threatening to dump the crew from the deck. Cal and I wrestled with the rope to keep the balloon in place while we were in a rapid descent.

"Help them!"

I followed Cal's gaze and saw Isham and the other mate fighting to control the starboard line which had gotten loose. I released the port line and ran, well, stumbled across the deck.

Crack!

The deck dropped out from under my feet. Isham tripped, then started to fall toward the rail that was now below us. His harness line had broken, leaving him in freefall. I leapt, latching onto his ankle before he went any further. He pulled knives from his belt and drove them into the deck to hold himself.

The captain's voice reached my ears. "Starboard propeller is gone! Hold on!"

Winds grabbed the airship, tossing it around like a child's toy. The crew struggled to control the bucking airship. The mates screamed as they fought with the lines while we descended.

"Get those ropes taut," Zora yelled to the crew. "We are coming apart."

I crab-crawled across the deck to help restrain the stern rope. Isham joined us and the deck leveled out. My hands were raw and bloody, but far better than crashing.

Debris whipped around in the wind. We held tight to the rope.

"We are coming in hot!" Zora yelled.

A few moments later, we hit the ground, bounced, and hit again. The deck crewman next to me lost his balance and flew over the rail before I could grab him. The ship slid to a halt.

We'd survived the crash, only to be stranded in the wilds of the Candalarian grasslands.

If we lived long enough in Candalar, it would be a great story. That was a big if, though.

4

Two crew members were dead and three more injured. It could have been far worse, but the captain and crew had done their jobs well. The deck leaned to the port, but not enough to make walking impossible. Isham approached as I surveyed the damage.

"Lady Yorke, can you help the injured?" Isham asked, following me to the stairs down to the captain's quarters.

"I'll get my medical kit from my luggage," I said over my shoulder. All watchers received basic medical, weapons, and unarmed combat training. Looks like today I'd play doctor, and not in the fun, adult way. "Help get everyone away from the ship in case it blows."

"Yes, ma'am. Good idea. If those boilers go, we'd be blown to Norn."

He strode off at the rolling gait of a true airman. The rail next to the stairs made my descent much easier. I entered my room, threw my travel sack over my shoulder, and grabbed my medical kit. I hated to leave my luggage on the ship, but I'd suffered far greater losses than if my bags were blown to smithereens. My research needed to be gathered up since it had scattered like startled birds around the room.

I closed the door behind me and exited the ship by way of the rope ladder the crew had rigged. Scents of wet hay and earth greeted me as I climbed down. The ship laid in the middle of the grasslands with nothing to see but tall grass. The only good part was given the huge expanse of the

133

Candalarian plains, it was unlikely we'd be discovered soon. Not that I expected slavers to take the crew of the Kiss, but there would be a fight. I followed the crew carrying an injured female crewmate. From the litany of curses flowing from her mouth, I guessed she'd survive.

Zora supervised evacuating the ship and moving her crew a few hundred feet from the downed airship. She was instructing the crew in setting up the makeshift shelter made from tarps. The three injured crew were laid under the protection to keep them out of the rain. I walked over to her.

"Where is the captain?"

"He's closing down the boiler and assessing the damage to the Maiden's Kiss," she said before stomping over to a startled female crewmate who was securing a second tarp. "Nel, pull that rope taut our it will blow away in this storm."

"Aye," Nel responded, putting her back into tying the rope around the stake in the ground.

"Lady Yorke, if you could see to our injured crew, I'd appreciate it. Cal and his crew are searching for the bodies that went overboard. We don't like loose ends."

"Of course," I said. I left Zora to do her job, while I set to mine. The rain pounded on the tarp above my head. At least I was out of the worst of it. The occasional lightning flash and resulting thunder set my teeth on edge, but people needed me.

The woman I'd seen earlier was first in line. "What's your name?"

"Hope Marine," she said through gritted teeth. "I think I broke my arm, my lady."

The broken bone pushed against the skin but hadn't pierced it. I pulled open my bag and got a piece of clammum bark. "Chew this. I'll be back after I check on the others."

"What about my arm?" she asked a bit snarkily.

I raised my eyebrows and looked at her, and the color drained from her face.

"I'll chew this until you get back."

I move to the next injured mate. He had a deepening purple bruise covering the right side of his face. He didn't move, which wasn't a good sign. I checked his pulse and listened to his chest. Both sounded normal, but medicine wasn't really my purview. I opened his eyelids, and his pupils reacted, so I hoped that was a good indication that he'd recover.

From what I saw, the last man had minor contusions and no major trauma. "What's your name?"

"Bart," he said, more of a grunt than actual words.

"Well, Bart, what is the problem?"

His face screwed into a look that hinted I must be crazy. "I have cuts and I hurt my leg."

"Hmmm." His pant leg was soaked through with blood. The fabric tore as I pulled it, but it wouldn't come free. I pulled out my knife and sliced away the cloth and found a piece of metal had punctured his calf. I guess I was wrong about the no major trauma.

"Bad?"

I had no way of knowing for sure. The metal could have damaged any number of blood vessels or simply be caught on the muscle tissue. My medical training didn't cover surgery. I didn't know what would happen if I just pulled it out. "It isn't good. I'm going to suggest you leave it there."

"You can't leave it," he said, heat creeping into his voice. "I'll lose the leg."

I shook my head. "I'm not a sawbones, I'm an alchemist."

"Doc, you've got to take it out. We ain't gettin' out of here anytime soon. Old Haps died of an injury not half as bad."

"If I take it out you could bleed to death but leaving it in would be worse." I'd have to sterilize it and then cauterize the hole. Perhaps that would allow him to live through the trip to Thaclet. If I left it in, he'd probably die from the general dirtiness of the area. At least if I cleaned it out, he might stand a chance. I handed him a piece of clammum. "Chew this. I'll return momentarily."

I checked on Hope, who was still chewing, but her eyes were glazed over from the bark. *Excellent.*

Zora approached as I stepped back into the rain. From the looks of the clouds, we'd be under them for a long time.

"How are they?"

"Hope needs a splint, and Bart needs to have his wound cauterized. I'll need some straight pieces of wood, a bottle of the strongest alcohol you have, and a small fire set up in the tent near Bart."

"Yes, Lady Yorke." She paused. "Will Al be okay after this?"

I stopped. "Al?"

"He's got the bruise on his face. I've seen men turned to simpletons with a far less serious injury."

Oh, Al. "It's too early to tell, but I think he's just unconscious. Most of the damage was localized to his face. He'll have a hell of a black eye, though."

She laughed. "I've given him one myself. He'll survive."

I didn't say anything, but the joy of Zora's exclamation made me feel better. "Time to get to work. Can you lend a hand?"

Zora nodded. She left for a couple of minutes and returned with a few pieces of wood, a pile of kindling, and a bottle of whiskey. I pulled cloth ties from my bag while the first mate built a small fire. I handed her an old metal knife I had in my bag. She placed the blade in the fire and joined me.

Hope had dropped off from the bark. Zora held her while I reset the bone and placed the split. She'd sleep off the clammum and be sore, but fine.

Bart presented a different problem. The man slept from the effects of the clammum. I unrolled my tools and poured the whiskey over them to make sure they were clean.

"Seems like a waste of good whiskey," Zora said.

I took a swig and handed her the bottle. "You'll want this."

The first mate took a long pull and returned the bottle. The fire had gotten hot enough for us to start. "When I tug the metal free, I need the knife as fast as possible."

"Understood."

I started by cutting away the flesh from around the piece of metal. Blood trickled out, but that was to be expected. I retrieved my pinchers and got a good hold of the metal. "Ready?"

Not waiting for a response, I gently pulled on the embedded metal, and it slid but stopped. Another tug and it pulled free. Blood flowed but didn't gush. Zora went for the knife. I poured the whiskey into the wound, then pressed the blade of the heated knife against the hole.

Bart screamed and bucked.

"Hold him down!"

Zora flung herself over the struggling crewmate, while I finished cauterizing the wound. The smell of charred flesh was sickening, but the blood stopped.

"Geez, I take a nap and wake to you havin' a go with Bart," Al said from where he sat on the ground.

Zora sat up and laughed. I took another swig from the bottle and left so they could reunite.

I stepped out of the tent. The rain had stopped for now. Captain Breachcolm approached as I stretched my back. "Thank you, Victoria, for healing my crew."

"I can't guarantee anything," I said, wincing at the spreading pain. "Al woke up on his own. Hope's arm was a simple break, and with Bart, we'll wait and see."

"You also caught Ish before he flew over the railing. If not for you, he'd be dead, and I'd be down another crew member."

"Beginner's luck."

"I'm going to assemble a crew together and get help from Thaclet," he said, rubbing his chin. "From the last position of the ship, the city should be a couple of days' walk. Then I'll need to hire a crew to repair the Maiden."

"I'll go by myself," I said. I couldn't wait around for a week for the ship to be airworthy. Time held the key to catching the people behind the attacks on the Astarian Maguses. "I've got to continue my mission."

"We are in the middle of the Candalarian grasslands. The white ghosts aren't going to care if you are related to a Magus or if Everard is your personal butler. They sell captives as slaves if they don't just kill them straight away."

While I appreciated Captain Breachcolm's concern for my wellbeing, he didn't know the full story and never would. I couldn't use my Watcher's gear with another in tow. "One person can make better time than a group, and I need to find passage to Uwhela. I will go to Thaclet, broker a repair junket, and then be on my way."

"And if I say no?"

I laughed. "I doubt you'll fare any better than your ship, Captain."

He considered it for a moment. "Fine. What do you need?"

"I have supplies in my bag, but I will need to get to my luggage if the ship is stable."

"The boiler is shut down. It is safe to board her."

"Excellent," I said, rubbing my hands together, partly from the chill, partly from the readiness to be off on my mission again. "I'll leave within the hour."

The captain shook his head. "There isn't anything I can say to change your mind, is there?"

"You know I've always been skeptical of goodbyes."

The captain's brow furrowed. "You have?"

"Yes, they're a bit hand-wavy, aren't they?"

"I should have known." He turned and left, muttering under his breath.

I laughed and headed to the ship to gather my supplies for the journey.

No matter how well you plan, fate will always play a different tune for you to dance to.

5

From the air, the grasslands appeared flat. On the ground, the land rolled with hills and valleys that made the journey much more taxing. It had been a couple of years since I'd been in the field and my legs groaned in pain. A horse would have come in handy, but then I'd have other sensitive parts to complain about.

The grass reached my waist and hid holes and churned clumps of dirt. Numerous times I tripped, but only fell twice. I'd half expected an easy stroll to Thaclet and then on with my mission. Roland had lived for this type of adventure, but I'd rather be in the lab, working on a mysterious substance, than traversing the wilds of the Candalarian grasslands.

I retrieved my Watcher's mask from my bag and settled it in place. The optics dampened the glare from the sun and let me see farther than normal. Not that there was anything to see except grass and more grass.

Hours passed with no change in scenery. How anyone lived out here was beyond me. What did you do to keep yourself occupied? Stillhold contained the basics, unlike Iron Harbor that had everything you might ever want. As long as you didn't mind the smog and abject poverty of a large portion of the citizens.

The sun grew hot as time passed. I stopped periodically to check my directions and eat and drink. Of all the bad luck of being crashed by a storm. I should have been on my way to Uwhela tomorrow. Every day gave the drug producers a greater chance to make more of the blasted drug and create more monsters out of innocent animals.

"No sense sitting around," I said to no one at one such stop. A large rock made an excellent perch to enjoy my tasteless meal and stale beer. I should have brought along some of the crew for company, but in reality, I preferred to work by myself.

A sight off in the distance caught my eye. I dropped to the ground to avoid being spotted, creeping up to get a view without being exposed. It appeared to be a caravan, which could be a boon if they were Astarian traders headed to Thaclet. If they were Candalarians, it would be a fight if they saw me. Since Candalarians don't use many wagons, I guessed they were merchants headed to the market to ply their wares.

Thankful for the tall grass, I crouched and slowly made my way toward the caravan. The thought of riding to Thaclet made me want to run to catch them, but I was tired, not stupid. Watchers who were stupid tended to be dead Watchers.

The caravan rolled toward me and now I heard voices carried on the wind. They spoke Candalarian which meant slavers, given the wagons. My fantasies of riding with Astarian merchants into Thaclet vanished before my eyes. The important part now was that they had horses. If I stole a horse, I'd make Thaclet by nightfall tomorrow.

Generally, I abhor stealing, but in this case, saving lives trumped petty theft. The fact that Candalarians were mortal enemies of Astaria made it much easier to excuse the theft. They'd killed my fellow Watcher, Brulle, in an ambush on the Ramcoll border. It might be petty, but it felt like revenge.

An hour later, I hid off the barely noticeable trail in the sea of grass, and the caravan rolled on just ahead of me. I would have never found the route if not for the caravan. The guards ignored everything unless the captives made a noise, then they beat the bars with wooden clubs. None of this made me any less inclined to steal a horse. Roland would have some clever trick to distract them long enough to get a mount, I had no idea where to start.

I stayed low in the tall grass, avoiding the gaze of the Candalarian horse troops. A mixture of ghostly white men and women escorted three rolling carts. A giant of a man lead the procession. His braided hair fell past his waist. The warriors rode massive horses while they used smaller ones to pull the wagons. I couldn't ride well enough to handle one of those huge beasts, so I'd need a wagon horse to ride to Thaclet. On the back of each wagon stood an iron cage with a mixture of people of all ages, but mostly coppery-skinned Astarians.

"The children need water," a man yelled in Astarian at the guards. "They'll be no use to you if they are dead."

The caravan stopped, and the leader rode back. With a harsh laugh, he commanded the guards to remove the man from the pen.

"You're letting me go?"

He didn't even see the blow coming. The guard on the left smashed his baton into the man's lower back, driving him to the ground. The other guards gathered around and beat him. Without a word, the leader left, and the guards tossed the bloody man into the cage and locked it.

My temper flared, but I tamped it down. The man had been stupid to make demands. Candalarians had a brutal reputation, and the slave trade in Thaclet produced a lot of coin. The Norns, Uwhelans, even the remote Tofragrad merchants bought and sold human flesh there. If it was tradeable, you could find it in Thaclet.

The caravan continued on, though the silent captives looked haunted. As far as they knew, their lives were over, and slavery awaited them. Worse, there were a number of children in the cages. Under different circumstances, I would mount a rescue operation, but there were more lives at stake than a couple dozen Astarians. The life of a Watcher was full of horrible decisions.

I trailed the horsemen. The sun sank into the west, and they set camp for the night. No rations for the captives, only the loud sobs of the children.

Darkness fell. The horses were picketed off to the left of the wagons. A large fire burned, releasing the oh-so fragrant scent of horse manure into the air. Even with the filters in my mask, I could smell the reek. No wood made for fires with alternative fuels.

I waited in the dark until the guards and warriors curled into their blankets for the night. I counted fifteen warriors and guards. That meant they only had one person on guard duty. The soft nickers of the horses and an occasional creak from the wagons were the only sounds from the caravan. I crept closer to the horses, passing by the bigger ones, and headed for the wagon teams.

The first normal-sized horse I came upon nickered at me as I approached. I reached out, letting him sniff my hand. He nuzzled my hand, and I rubbed his forehead. The horse pushed into my hand, wanting more attention. I wished I had an apple with me.

"Mommy, it's a ghost," a shrill young voice came from the nearest wagon. "Is it here to save us?"

The sound of waking Candalarians came from behind me. Quickly, I moved without thought, running toward the long grass. I glanced over my shoulder to check for pursuit and ran square into the guard with a wicked-looking knife in his hand.

He lunged for me, but I feinted left, then pivoted right, chopping down on his weapon hand. The knife spun off into the darkness. I followed up with a punch to the throat to keep him from calling for help. He folded from the force of the blow. A punch to the back of the head knocked him out cold. I crouched, grabbing the warrior by his armpits and dragging him into the grass.

The rest of the Candalarians ignored the screaming child. They returned to their sleeping areas. An idea popped into my head, and I allowed myself a low chuckle. Why not get some help from the enemy? I dug into my travel sack, found the pure hypnotic serum, and injected a dose into my new friend. A few minutes later he woke and babbled in a very hoarse voice. He'd have a sore throat for a while.

"Do you speak Astarian?"

He nodded. "A bit."

It is nice when a plan comes together.

6

I explained to my new friend, Talat, what I wanted him to do. He agreed like we'd been close for years, not on opposite sides of a running war. I prepared my fire potion and checked my pistols. The plan required a large amount of confusion and speed. If I could get on a horse and away from their camp, I'd be in Thaclet far sooner than I'd planned. If I didn't, the Candalarians would kill me, and I doubted I'd care at that point.

"Go," I said to Talat.

The Candalarian ran through the grass without making a sound. I waited until I heard the first creak from the wagons. With a clang, the iron gate dropped, and he headed to the second. No one moved in the cage.

I ran toward the horses. "Run if you want to escape!"

"The Watchers have come to save us!" The voice belonged to a younger person, but they were right. Shadowy figures descended from the cage and fled into the night.

I threw the vial of fire potion into the midst of the now awake Candalarians. The explosion flared much higher than I expected. I must have put too much liquid into my attack. Flames shot fifteen feet into the air. Screams in multiple languages answered the sudden firestorm. Good thing it wasn't the dry season, or the fire would have burned for a long time.

Horses stamped and skittered at the explosion but didn't flee. Candalarians know how to train horses. The second cage opened with a thud and the captives fled. I reached my chosen horse and prepared to mount and ride.

A third clang announced the last gate dropping. Those captives ran after the second group.

Candalarians were everywhere, trying to restore order to the camp or chasing after the escaping slaves. Fire dotted the ground where flames had spread from the initial explosion. A couple of figures sprawled unmoving on the ground.

A solid blow of a thrown club struck me across my calves, knocking me down. I rolled until I was on my back facing where the attack had come from. A Candalarian warrior charged, a long blade at the ready. I pulled both legs to my chest and drove them into his sternum, throwing him away from me. He hit with a hard thud. I climbed to my feet, calf muscles screaming at the abuse.

The warrior leapt to his feet far more gracefully and launched another attack. With my Watcher's mask, I had the advantage of seeing as clear as day in the flickering light of the flames. My opponent didn't.

He swung overhand to stab me in the head or chest. *How rude*! I side-stepped the blow and delivered a punch to where his jaw attached to the skull. His head whipped around, and he fell to the ground. Time to leave.

No such luck. The Candalarian leader, wicked sword in hand, approached with two others flanking him. The fire was dying down, and the others were returning to the camp. I needed to end this quickly, or I'd be getting a ride to Thaclet in a way I wasn't interested in.

I pulled my pistols and shot the warrior to the left, dropping him in place. The second shot took the female warrior in the shoulder. She screamed in pain and slumped.

The leader sliced at me but missed by a mile. To his credit, he didn't overextend, and his backslash almost removed my head. I fired a wild shot that missed. He closed the distance between us, thrusting his sword at me. I stepped left and ducked under the sword.

"You will die," the leader said.

"I think not." I kicked out and caught his ankle, causing him to stumble. Another blow to the back of his knee and the big man collapsed to the ground. A lesser fighter would have given up, but he rolled and came up ready to attack.

The leader leapt, driving me back. Another leap and his weight bore me to the ground. He grinned and pushed the sword toward my throat. I used my pistols to keep the sharp blade from my skin, but I couldn't hold him off forever.

A guttural scream pierced the silence of the night, and the weight disappeared. Talat wrestled the leader, both men struggling to subdue the other. I pointed my pistol and fired, taking the leader square in the head. He dropped to the ground, dead.

Talat jumped up and ran to me. "What do I do now?"

The drug would wear off in a bit. I couldn't be anywhere near him when it did. "Leave the caravan and run back to your clan."

He nodded and loped off into the night. Hopefully, the captured Astarians would get away and return to their lives. I found my chosen horse and mounted. In a few seconds, I was on my way. I followed the trail into the night, happy to be away from the carnage.

<hr>

The sun greeted me as I rode toward Thaclet, the faint outlines of the city taking shape in the distance. I'd reach the gates and be able to discharge my responsibility. Then I'd find another airship to continue on.

Foreigners called the Candalarians all sorts of names, given their skin coloring and fierce fighting. They routinely sold their captives as slaves, so it was easy to see why they were feared and hated. As with most things, the majority of the Candalarians I knew were decent people, but the outliers made life tough for them outside their country.

I wondered how many Astarians had made it safely away from the Candalarian slavers? Given that the fire had killed or injured many of the Candalarians, there couldn't have been a lot of them left to chase down the captives. Maybe I should have killed them all to ensure the people's escape, but if I didn't stop whoever was behind the hypnotized animals and the attacks on the Maguses, no one would be safe in Astaria. I'd picked speed over justice.

The day wore on and the Candalarian capitol, Thaclet, grew larger with each passing hour. I'd been to the city many times before and knew where the safe houses were which I needed. The city was a trading center and unless there was a full-blown war, all nations traded there. The sun started to set as I reached the outer gates of the city. Two burly guardsmen eyed me up and down as I walked up. My hair was a mess and mud, grass stains, and blood covered my clothes and duster. My Lady

Yorke persona wouldn't be an advantage here in Thaclet, given her reputation, and revealing a downed ship would end up with slavers headed toward the Maiden's crew.

"State your business," the first guard announced as I pulled to a stop before them. He had the classic top knot the Candalarians preferred.

"Janice Bartlow," I said. "I'm a trader doing business with Mac Tan in the commercial district. My party was attacked by bandits overnight, and I made my escape."

The two eyed each other, before the second guard pulled a rope to sound the all-clear. The bell rang for a moment before the gates opened. "Trader Bartlow," the first guard said, inclining his head. "May your business be profitable."

I nodded, surprised by his exceptional grasp of Astarian. Most Candalarians barely spoke any languages but their own. Obviously, being a guard had taught him more than how to hold a spear. I rode through the gates and headed for the commercial district.

After a bit, I arrived at the Iron Shoe, a bar, and, more importantly, a Watcher safe house. The groom took the reins of my horse and led him away. I entered the front door into a cacophony of sounds. The warmth of the room was a welcome change from the cool night I'd ridden through to get here.

"Lillian Tamor," a booming voice said over the onslaught of noise. I started at alias I hadn't used in years. A second later Will Eskew, proprietor and inside man for the Watchers, greeted me with a stately bow. "What a pleasure it is to see you. Our mutual friend told me would be arriving on the Maiden's Kiss. It hasn't docked, but here you are."

I explained the situation, and Eskew sent runners off to dispatch help to the downed ship. "The guest room is all set for you. While my boys are getting ready to gather in the Maiden's crew, can I get you a drink?"

"A good bourbon would certainly be nice, along with a bath and a fresh set of clothes."

He nodded, and soon after, Master Eskew's sister, Mistress Eliana, escorted me to the saferoom under the inn. It was the only room I'd consider protected in Thaclet. Shortly thereafter I had a long, hot bath, a strong pour of bourbon, and clean clothing. She also laid out a sleeping gown and a missive from Everard.

I curled up on the bed, nursing my drink while reading the note from the Arch Magus Everard, though he signed with an alias.

My Lady Yorke,

Our mutual acquaintance informed me of the issue he encountered. He's assured me you are taking care of any loose ends. Once you've accomplished such, please return to visit me. I fear my time is short.

Lord Justin

I threw the note in the fire. Quinn had reached Everard with Cian. If the renegade Watcher had given over any additional information, he hadn't seen a need to mention it in his missive, not even in code. How had he known I'd be here? Or perhaps he sent the same letter to all the safe houses. I could only continue on my planned route and find whoever was behind this plot.

I finished my drink, thinking about how best to deal with Mac Tan. Tomorrow held new opportunities and adventure. A good night's sleep would clear my mind and hopefully point me in the right direction.

For now, sleep was the best medicine.

7

The next morning, I strolled through the markets of Thaclet on my way to meet with Mac Tan. The man left a lot to be desired as a human, but information was his business and I needed it now.

I walked down the dusty dirt streets to the Copper Kettle. All manner of people passed me. There were a lot of horse people in their leather riding gear, but also a number of Astarians, Norns, Uwhelans, Tofragrads, and some people I couldn't identify. A mixture of languages and dialects tickled my ears with their uniqueness. Most had weapons at hand, which was good in a place where anything or anyone could be bought for the right price.

I skirted an enormous pile of horse manure and entered the Copper Kettle. The place stank of stale beer, vomit, and more scents I didn't want to know about. In the back corner sat Mac Tan. He had a glassy-eyed girl on either side of him. The left one had long coppery hair and wore a sheer black dress that exposed more than it covered. The one on the right had short black hair and the same style of clothing. Mac's face held more scars than the most experienced warrior. His nose had been broken and not set straight, which gave him a strange hiss when he breathed. He wore an open coat with a linen shirt and a wide belt. His signature leather pouch hung from his belt just like every other time I'd seen him.

"Lady Yorke." He inclined his head. "What can I do you fer?"

148

"Mac," I said before sitting in the chair across from him.

The barmaid paused at my left shoulder. "Drink?"

I shook my head. There wasn't enough gold in the world to drink or eat anything in this dive. I worried I'd catch something just sitting on the dirty chair. I spoke to Mac. "I require information and am willing to pay for it."

He smiled, showing an array of missing or broken teeth. "The all-powerful always come to me when they want information. What exactly do you need to know?"

"A group is using animals to attack people in Astaria, and I have to find them."

"I've heard a few rumors and can get you more in a day or two, depending on your ability to pay." His greasy smile widened at that.

"Name your price."

"Now, no need to get antsy. I need you to get me something in exchange for the knowledge you want. Seems fair to me." He held his hands out in front of him like he was giving me a present. His gifts often came with knives in the back.

"What is this thing you need so much you'd rather have it than my money?" I asked, my hand settling on my pistol at my hip.

"Just a trinket," he said, his eyes merry with unexpressed mirth. "The owner of the antiquity shop—"

"You mean a fence?"

He shrugged. "Either name works."

"Only in your world," I said. My tone dripped with sarcasm, but it flew over his head.

"Huh?" He shook his head as if to clear it. "Whatever. She retrieved an artifact from a Tofragrad merchant, and I want it."

"Why don't you just buy it?" I couldn't afford to lose my temper and expect him to cooperate. Dealing with Mac always set my teeth on edge. There were always numerous games at play—none of which were honest.

He sighed. "I tried, but the skinflint won't part with it. Says she has a buyer already lined up. That may be true, but since she won't sell it to me, I'll get it another way. Deal?"

I eyed him as I thought it through. "How do I know you have actual information I need and aren't just stringing me along?"

"You make a good point," he said, rubbing his chin. "I'll give you this piece for free, then you can decide if we do business or not."

"Works for me," I said cautiously. "What do you have?"

He dismissed the girls, who traipsed back to the bar where men flocked like carrion birds. I turned to Mac, waiting for his information.

"There is a cult, called the Followers of the Alpha, south of Thaclet, who offered a business partner of mine a blue liquid that they swore would control anyone who took it."

I kept my features still, not wanting to give anything away. "Where is the cult located?"

Mac sat back in his seat. A huge grin crept across his face. "I gave you a taste. Now I want the metal rod Joelle Blackrose bought from the Tofragrad merchant. It's about a foot long and etched with runes."

"What does it do?"

"That, my dear Lady Yorke, is none of your business. Get me the rod and I will tell you the full story when you return with my rod later tonight."

"Tonight?"

He shrugged. "The deal for the trinket is going down tomorrow if the word around town is correct. After tonight there is no information for you."

"I can pay you for the information and you could send your people after the item."

"No, she knows my crew and would leave with the rod if she saw them creeping around. She keeps it in the second-floor strongroom of her store, the Peddler's Rest." Mac wore a self-satisfied smirk like the cat who caught the canary.

I stood, ready to be done with this place, and Mac in particular. I smiled at him. "Why was 6 afraid of 7?"

His eyes narrowed, but he responded, "Why?"

"Because seven was primed for revenge, and odds had to be evened." I laughed, though Mac didn't.

"I don't get it?"

"You cross me, and you'll understand far too well."

He gulped. I left.

<hr>

I spent the afternoon finding the Peddler's Rest which was tucked down a side street. It sat between two other buildings with a single door and a small window in the front. A well-worn sign marked with the shop's name hung over the door. I circled the building, noting the lack of exits from the second floor. In the back alley, an upper window over-looked the attached cobbler's shop. With its flat roof, it would make an easy escape route. The loading area had two wooden carts and a rain barrel in the corner. A stone ramp led to a banded metal door that was the only entry from the back. Getting in wasn't going to be easy.

What I needed was a reason to go inside to see what was there. I found a local vendor who sold me what he termed an antique sextant that the Norn sailors had used to find their way home, but the metal was cheap brass, and it might be worth a silver on a good day. I paid him three silvers and thanked him.

As the sun began to set and shops started to close, I entered the Peddler's Rest. Goods ringed the room with a massive counter at the rear of the store. The back wall had an exit covered with a black cloth. Low shelves in the middle of the room held even more merchandise. An odd assortment of devices from the mundane to the exotic covered every horizontal surface in the place. As it was flanked by buildings with no side windows, the front and back door, plus the one window on the second floor, were the only exits. Behind the counter sat a young man, polishing a trinket I couldn't make out. He looked up and called out a greeting.

I strode to the counter and placed my treasure in front of him. "My great grandfather used this on a Norn merchant ship. He said it has been in the family for hundreds of years. How much is it worth?"

He set down his work and picked up the sextant. "A few coppers at most. If this is over a couple of years old, I'll eat it."

I wrung my hands in false dismay. "Sir, I swear it has to be ancient. Are you sure it isn't worth at least a gold?"

He laughed. "Gold? Not likely. I'll give you a copper for it, just to be generous."

"You must be mistaken," I said, making my voice crack. I wiped at my eyes with my hands to clear the nonexistent tears. "Are you the owner?"

"No, Mistress Blackrose is the owner, but she's too busy to be interrupted."

"So you are trying to steal from me because you think I'm helpless?" I asked, pushing my voice into a shrill upper register. "I demand to see the owner or I'm going for the guards."

He held up his hands. "It's closing time and I want no bad blood with you, ma'am. Let me get her."

"Thank you."

He parted the curtain behind him and left. I heard him calling and the steady thump of his boots on some stairs.

I ran around the counter and pushed the cloth to one side. A set of wooden stairs led to the second floor and another doorway led to a small storage room with stacked crates and assorted other things. There didn't seem to be another way up. I retreated and searched behind the counter. Nothing out of the ordinary. The sound of someone descending the stairs warned me. I returned to my spot in front of the counter and waited.

The young man held the cloth open for Mistress Blackrose. In the mudstone lanterns, her blond hair glowed, but when she reached the counter, I realized it was actually gray. The woman wore a simple tunic the Norns favored and carried a jeweler's loupe in her hand. She had a long blade on the belt at her waist, and from the looks of her, she knew how to use it.

"Evening," she said, before picking up the sextant. She looked the piece over, then scratched at the surface. "This is worth a silver at most."

"But—"

"My lady, I assure you, I know my trade. This piece isn't Nornish. The runes inscribed on the back are Candalarian and they aren't even correct. Whoever made it had a bit of skill but couldn't do runes to save their lives."

I slumped my shoulders in defeat. "I'd gotten this from my mother. She swore it was an antique."

Mistress Blackrose pushed the sextant across the counter. "Sell it to a local trader. You'll get more for it with that story. I only deal in truly unique items."

I looked at my feet. "Thank you."

"It is closing time. Please let yourself out."

I left, knowing I'd be back in a few hours.

8

I returned to my room to collect my supplies. Watchers over the years had stocked the safehouse with weapons, armor, alarium devices, and a fair selection of potions. I hated this part. Did I need knockout gas? Fire potion? A big box of chocolates? My natural instincts screamed at me to take everything, but it wasn't subtle to show up with three men carrying assorted bags and boxes.

I settled on my pistols, a vial of forget-me potion, a fire elixir, and my thieves' tools for picking locks and assorted other tasks. At the last minute, I added a small vial of acid, just in case. It could come in handy given the mission.

I hoisted my mission pouch and headed out. The streets still held a fair number of people, though most ducked their heads and moved on quickly. It had reached the hour of the night when those who were out and about weren't up to anything good. I doubled back a couple of times to make sure no one followed me. I doubted Mistress Blackrose had concerned herself with me, but various unseemly folks might have other ideas.

After an hour of wandering in a random direction, I headed toward the Peddler's Rest to find the rod. I entered the loading area and made sure I was alone before proceeding. Clouds sailed across the moon, plunging the area into darkness. I settled my Watcher's mask into place and examined the door. I knew how to use lock picks, but a good thief would come in handy right about now. No sense wishing for things you didn't have.

I retrieved my tools and set to work on the lock. It took a pipe key, which made the job easier than a pin set lock, though still challenging. After many tries and curses, I found the proper diameter pick, and the door unlocked with a clack. I slid my knife along the inside of the door to make sure there weren't any traps. Nothing happened.

The door opened with a faint groan. I stepped into the darkened warehouse and looked around. Crates, furniture, barrels, and an odd assortment of what I'd refer to as junk covered most of the room. I crept around the room, careful not to knock anything over and make a racket.

A couple of things caught my eye, but I wasn't here to shop. I needed to find the wand and get out as quickly as possible. The faint outline of a door came into view just past a large stack of crates. I edged over and put my ear to the door, but no sounds penetrated. I pulled it open and peeked through. Not a person in sight.

After a minute of dead silence, I stepped into the stairwell. The curtain had been pulled back so I could see through into the store. I skulked toward the counter I'd been at earlier. Given the hour of the morning, nothing stirred in the shop, but it still set my nerves on edge.

"What are you doing?" a loud masculine voice demanded in the silence.

I ducked behind the counter and froze.

"Go home, Murph," a female voice said from outside the shop. "You stink like whiskey and your wife will gut me if she finds out you've been chasin' my skirt."

I padded silently to the front, where the window had been left open a couple of inches. The clerk must have forgotten to close it before he left. Once I got a glimpse of a drunk man pawing at a woman outside the shop, I let loose a sigh of relief. I doubted she gave away her affection being so early in the morning.

"Come on, Lil," he said, though slurred was probably more accurate. "Wife ain't got…"

Their voices diminished as they left. His wife was one lucky woman.

Once they had moved on, I crept to the curtained doorway that led to the upper floor. I listened for a long second. Nothing. The couple outside had spooked me, and I still had to finish my mission. How I wished Evangeline, the Watcher from Sarfin, was here. To call her an assassin was a major understatement. She was a brilliant thief, counterintelligence agent, master of disguise, stone-cold killer, and a whole lot more. This job wouldn't have caused her a moment's worry.

"Get it together," I whispered to myself before returning to the stairs. I stepped slowly, placing my feet on the outside of each tread to minimize any noise. The slightest sound accompanied my footfalls.

After an eternity, I reached the top. Sweat dripped down my back like the icy fingers of the reaper himself. A room opened up before me. It was a large space with items cluttering the tables that dotted the area. A massive desk sat at the far end. A painting of an old man hung behind the desk.

I searched the tables, making sure there wasn't anything that matched the description of the rod. Not that I thought Mistress Blackrose would leave such an item in plain sight. It was far too valuable if Mac was to be believed.

In the center of one table sat an exquisite bracelet. The main stone looked like amethyst, but smaller hematite stones were set in the silver band. I took the piece and studied it. It might have been the most inter-esting piece of jewelry I'd ever seen. A coldness seeped into my fingers as I held it, which seemed indicative of magic. Everard would know what purpose this piece had.

Since I'd become a thief, one more piece wouldn't hurt. I pushed the bracelet into my bag.

The wind rattled the shutters outside and the resulting noise brought me back to my senses. I could have been killed while I fancied the bauble. I concentrated on the task at hand. If luck was with me, the painting hid the strongbox. People really needed to be more creative.

The old man had a scowl on his face. Must have been a lovely gentleman to deal with. Running my fingers around the frame for traps yielded nothing but dust. I swear the man in the painting glowered at me as I lifted the picture from the wall and set it down soundlessly. At this point, I doubted anyone was in the building, but hasty thieves ended up dead thieves.

I took off my mask and examined the iron plate and locked door that had been set into the wall. Unlike the downstairs door, this one had an elaborate lock. Definitely a custom job. The keyhole didn't match any of my picks. I chuckled. *Nice try.* I retrieved my vial of acid and applied it to the hinges.

Smoke wafted off the metal while I put away the acid. When the smoke dissipated, I pulled on the door and the hinges snapped. The door was far heavier than expected and I almost dropped it. Finally, I got the beast on the floor without too much fuss.

The iron box held stacks of gold coins, piles of paperwork, and a couple of pieces of jewelry, though not as intriguing as the one I'd already taken. The one missing thing was the rod.

I took the gold, placing it in my pouch. I had to pay the Maiden's crew, so this would come in handy. I shuffled through the papers, looking for anything that might tip me off to where the wand was. Scrawled on a piece of paper were the words "Dockside. The Merry Traveler. 10."

I tossed the papers on the desk and peered into the now empty vault. All of this and no wand. I could probably force Mac to tell me about the cult, but then I'd have to kill him or risk a constant parade of hired assassins trying to "even" the score. If I knew other information brokers in Thaclet, I'd go check with them, but Mac was all I had. No, the only way out of this was finding the rod.

"The wand isn't here."

I jumped out of my skin and found myself staring down the business end of a pistol.

So much for an easy mission.

9

"irgil Wainswright, at your service."

The owner of the pistol, currently pointed at my head, was a rather tall man with long dark hair. He was thin as a whip and looked twice as deadly. He smiled at me.

"Well, if this isn't awkward," I said, holding my hands up.

"Lady Yorke, I presume?"

"How did you know?"

His smile widened like a cat with a cornered mouse. "It's my job to know, and I have need of your skills, Madame Watcher."

I straightened. "If you know I'm a Watcher, you also know I am not for rent."

"Rent?" he asked, obviously amused by the suggestion. "I am proposing a trade of sorts, beneficial to all sides."

I leaned against the desk, my hand resting next to my pistol. There was no way I could draw, aim, and fire the weapon before Wainswright shot me dead. He held the revolver like he knew how to use it. Powder-loaded rounds were temperamental and prone to misfire, but I wasn't about to risk my life on a gamble.

"I'm waiting," I said.

He cleared his throat. "Very well. My sister, Trader Joelle Blackrose, is in trouble, and the wand you are looking for is at the root of it."

"A wand? Really?"

"According to Joelle, it is an artifact from Tofragrad. The legend says it can do amazing things from healing wounds to controlling the weather. Who knows if any of it is true, but people are willing to pay for power, even if it isn't real."

"And this involves me how?"

Virgil smirked. "I will tell you where the deal is, and you will get the wand from my sister and kill the men she's meeting with before they kill her."

"Couldn't she just give you the wand? Seems like an awful lot of trouble to get something you already possess."

"I tried," Virgil said, annoyance clearly present in his words. "The amount the Norns are offering would make her a Master Trader and she wants that more than anything. She's stopped listening to me and has hidden the wand so I can't take it, which is why I need you to kill the Norns before they kill her."

"I am not an assassin."

"If they let you take the wand and leave, then you don't need to kill anyone."

I laughed. "That doesn't seem probable."

I'd dealt with treasure hunters, mercenaries, and murderers, and the worst by far were collectors. They had no bounds to the depths they would go to get what they desired. Were the traders in question collecting artifacts or simply attempting to reap a profit?

"No, but it's the deal I have. Save my sister, take the wand, and be off."

"Your sister is just going to believe me when I ask for the rod?"

"Of course not," he said with a chuckle. "That's why I'm going with you."

Wonderful.

We stood in the shadow of the wharfside warehouse, waiting for Trader Blackrose to show. The barely risen sun peeked out from behind the pinkish clouds. The temperature dipped, making me wish for a heavier coat. Since Virgil knew my secret, I wore my Watcher's mask to maintain my anonymity around Thaclet. The trade was to take place in the loading area for two warehouses. The buildings blocked the view of any random passersby.

"She should be here soon," Virgil said, resetting the pistol in his chest holster for the tenth time in as many minutes. "She'll enter from the land side."

As if summoned, Joelle Blackrose turned the corner and strode into the center of the cobblestone courtyard. She wore a leather coat over linen pants and a wide belt. She could be carrying a large variety of weapons under that jacket. I followed Virgil out of the shade to intercept his sister.

"Joelle," Virgil said as we approached. "You need to give this Watcher the wand and get away from here."

Miss Blackrose snorted. "Virgil, you need to grow a pair. This deal will establish me as the top trader in Thaclet. I'll be able to buy out my competition and crush the others."

"According to the legends, that rod is dangerous. Giving it to the Norns will start a war," Virgil said. "You can still become a master trader, but not if the Norns burn down Thaclet."

"They care nothing for Candalar," she said, eyeing me as she spoke. "They want to destroy Astaria, and frankly, who cares?"

"I do," I said, stepping to be next to Virgil.

"So I should give it to you so you can use it against Candalar?"

"No, you should give it to us as promised."

My head whipped around at the sound of the unfamiliar voice. From the far side of the courtyard, five towering Norns entered. The leader stood a head taller than me with a long black beard, leather bracers, and banded leather armor. A sword and knife hung from his belt. "I'll be taking the wand now."

The men spread out in a semicircle around us. I pushed back my duster and settled my hands on the butts of my pistols. "Go home."

"Ha," the leader barked out a laugh. "Cute. Now run back to Everard and tell him we are coming for him."

"Afraid not." My mask lowered my voice into a more menacing tone.

Trader Blackrose pushed me aside. "Wengo Akisson, give me my gold and the wand is yours. The deal's been struck, and the bargain made."

Wengo pulled a pouch out and tossed it at the trader's feet. She pulled out the wand from where she'd carried it under her coat.

I set my hand on hers before she could toss the wand over to the Norns. "Open the pouch."

She scowled at me but bent down and retrieved the sack. She loosened the drawstrings and upended the pouch into her hand. Pebbles filled the bag. "What is this? We had a deal."

The sound of swords being drawn filled the air. "We don't deal with the ghosts. Give me the wand or I'll take it."

I pulled my pistols, ready for a fight. I really didn't want to kill these men, but I had to have the information from Mac. If we didn't stop the drug from being used against Astaria, many more people and animals would be killed. While the loss of human life bothered me, using defenseless animals to kill those humans and then die miserably really bothered me.

"I am Firehelm. The wand is ours and we want it back."

Everyone stopped to look at the newest arrival. A short, round man stood with three muscular toughs, each covered with the tribal tattoos of the Tofragrad fire eaters. They rarely left their island nation, and few traders ever returned from those trade routes. Firehelm had the markings of a fire summoner which wasn't good. They tended to be nasty in a fight, throwing balls of fire to incinerate their foes.

"That is a sacred artifact that was stolen. Return it now."

"And who are you?" the Norn leader demanded, pointing his sword at the smaller man.

"You call me Firehelm."

"Firehelm?" Wengo laughed, his men joining in. "Little man, leave now before you get hurt."

Virgil stepped into the middle of the three parties. "This can be handled without fighting or bloodshed. Joelle will give the wand to Firehelm and everything will be where it belongs."

"What?" a chorus of voices answered.

"Enough!" Wengo yelled, slashing his sword toward Virgil, who dove to the ground to avoid having his head cut off. Three Norns rushed us.

I raised my pistols and shot the two ruffians who'd charged with their leader. The first took a slug to the leg and fell to the ground, screaming. The second shot grazed its intended target, a man in leather breeches and traditional Nornish arm leathers.

Blackrose met Wengo in the center of the courtyard, blocking his attack with a pair of wood and metal batons. She turned his blade aside and cracked him across the knee with the second baton.

Wengo screamed in pain but pushed his attack. "I'll kill you for that."

Blackrose laughed in his face. "You can try."

Virgil returned to the fight, firing and missing Wengo. He pulled a pair of knives out of his boots and met the Norn warrior attempting to flank his sister. The two fought like cougars, blades flashing in the pale sunlight.

"In the name of Ghuasis, I will have my due!" Firehelm yelled.

"Down!" I shouted as I dropped to the cobblestones.

With a mighty "whoosh!" a blast of flames streaked across where I'd been standing. The Norn who'd gotten behind me wasn't so lucky. Fire hit him squarely in the chest and bounced him across the courtyard like a dropped yarn ball. The flames grew higher as they consumed the screaming man. Seconds later, a pile of ash replaced what had been a person. The breeze picked up his ashes, scattering them into the air.

"Egil!" Wengo wailed at the sight of the burnt corpse. Ash danced in the air above where the man had fallen. He swung at Blackrose with renewed strength. She blocked each of his attacks and got in a few hits on the massive warrior.

As much as I wanted to get Virgil and Joelle away from the fight with the wand in my possession, Firehelm's power couldn't be left unchecked. I ran toward him, firing my pistols to stop whatever he was casting. One bullet tore into the edge of his shoulder, sending him to the ground. His party pushed between the two of us.

"Move," I said to the three. "I don't want to hurt you."

"Stop!" yet another unknown voice called over the chaos. Six leather armored guards sat on massive Candalarian mounts. "City guard. Put down your weapons!"

Just what we needed, the constables.

10

No one stopped fighting to comply with the newest entry into the battle. The clang of metal and grunts and groans of pain still flew around the courtyard. It would take more than yelling at people to drop their weapons to stop this brawl.

"Grunthal!" Firehelm called out, and then everything turned to fire and heat.

I dove to the ground and covered my head so as to not be hit by the plume of flames.

The rest of the courtyard burst into a panic. Fire poured through the air from the mage's fist, turning the courtyard into a furnace. His guards ran from the debacle. A massive figure formed from the flames resolving itself into a monster.

Virgil's opponent turned and ran. Blackrose pivoted, only to catch the hilt of Wengo's sword behind the jaw, staggering her. To her credit, she held onto her weapons, but the wand bounced off the cobblestones with a brassy clang.

I pulled myself up and spotted the rod on the cobblestones, well out of my reach.

"Get the artifact," Firehelm yelled at the monstrosity.

"Yes, master." The voice that answered was so deep that it shook the ground. In the center of the courtyard stood a fifteen-foot golem made of flame. Its ponderous head swiveled like an owl's until it locked on the wand on the far side of the courtyard. With a loud crack, it took a step toward the wand, leaving molten rock in its wake.

"Virgil, get Joelle out of here," I said, running toward the wand before the magma monstrosity could reach it. If Firehelm sent a fire monster after his precious wand it must be extremely durable. Wengo dove at my legs. I kicked out and caught his shoulder. He landed short of me, though I stumbled before regaining my balance.

Virgil ran, grasping his sister by the back of her leather coat, and propelled her away from the fight. She screamed at him the whole time, but at least they'd be alive.

"Kill all of the infidels," Firehelm called to his monster.

"Yes, master," the thing said. It pulled its arm back and threw a ball of fire directly at me.

I rolled under it, and its impact into the far building ejected debris into the air. The flames grew far more rapidly than any normal fire. The monster reared. A stream of solid lava flew at Wengo, who managed to avoid most of it. His impressive beard flared from the searing heat. He slapped at the burning hair until he put it out.

The sound of hooves caught my attention. The mounted city guards charged the beast, throwing their spears at the thing. The spears burst into flames before they hit the monster.

Wengo's punch would have taken me in the side of my head, but I got turned around enough that the blow struck my mask. Pain shot through my face. I heard bones snap but couldn't be sure whose bones they were. I fell flat on my back, driving the air from my lungs.

"Not so funny now, huh?" Wengo said, taking time to spit on me. He staggered to the wand and shoved it in the back of his belt.

"Get out of here," I said to the city guard commander. They ignored me. The good news is my mouth still worked so I'd probably escaped broken bones from Wengo's strike. The guard pressed their attack and I used it as a diversion to go for the wand. Not that it worked. From the corner of my eye, I sensed movement. It saved my life.

"Noooo," the monster roared. It stormed across the stones, blackening everything in its wake.

I pushed myself up and stumbled to the guard. "Get someone to put out these fires or the entire city will burn."

Pain flared through my face from where I'd been hit. I didn't want to think about how much damage I'd taken from a single strike. I shoved down the hurt and kept going.

The idea of a Candalarian warrior taking orders from a Watcher should have been a joke. Under the circumstances, he didn't pause.

"Sterling, get the fire marshal," the guard leader said. One of the guards saluted and charged out of the courtyard. The remaining horsemen wheeled their horses for another attack.

"Yes." He wheeled his horse, and the remaining guards charged the golem. With Virgil and Joelle out of the way, I could tackle the disaster at hand. The beast lobbed chunks of magma at Wengo. He dodged each, but not well. One slip and he'd be dead. I thought about sitting back to root for the monster, but I really needed to recover the wand.

I opened my travel bag, sorting through the wrapped vials until I found the fire potion. This was either a great idea or the worst one ever. If I was wrong, Roland could lecture me in the afterlife. I threw the vial at the monster and dropped to the ground.

The vial struck the golem, sticking like a burr in a wool blanket, and nothing happened. I lifted my head to get a better view. Where the vial had hit, the outer layers of the beast bubbled and seethed as it grew. A second later, the vial burst, and the resulting explosion could be heard in Terralon.

Pieces of monster exploded out, scattering pools of fire around the courtyard. I rolled to the side to avoid one such splash. The courtyard had turned into a lava field.

Wengo stumbled toward the space between the warehouses that lead to the wharf and, most likely, his ship back to Norn. I couldn't let him escape.

I climbed to my feet, aware of my injuries and assorted burns. No time to feel sorry for myself. I pushed my beaten body to something faster than a hobble, but not much. Wengo staggered as he tried to escape.

The distance between us closed before he realized I was after him. He swore in Nornish and attempted to increase his pace. I reached for my pistols, but I'd lost them in the fight. *Damn.*

"Give it to me, Wengo and you can limp back to your ship."

He turned to face me. "Watcher, one step closer and I'll gut you like a fish."

"We both know you are outclassed," I said, continuing toward him. "Last chance. Give it to me and you live to fight another day."

He pulled a long, thin boning knife and attacked. He came in overhand, which was a mistake against a faster opponent. I jerked to the side and lashed out to kick his right knee. The blow landed, but without much force.

Wengo stumbled, striking out and slicing through the arm of my duster. A trickle of blood trailed off the knife. He held it up to examine it. A wicked grin crossed his face. "Come closer, I don't bite...unless you ask me to."

"My taste in men runs to the more civilized varieties, not a barge rat like you."

He growled and threw himself at me. I caught his arm and twisted, using his weight against him. He went to his knees but still fought on. I twisted his arm harder until the knife clattered to the ground. I stepped over his legs, wrenching his arm in the process and retrieved the wand from his belt. I looked at the artifact for far too long.

Roland's first rule of fighting had been never let your concentration wander. I'd broken the rule and now paid the price.

Wengo grabbed my foot and tugged. My balance shifted, and I lost control of his arm. He swung his leg around and finished knocking me to the ground. I landed next to the knife, but the Norn straddled me, knocking the knife away, and got his hands around my neck. My mask covered part of my throat so he couldn't get a solid grip, but he was slowly crushing my windpipe with his weight.

I punched him just below the ribcage and he whoofed out air but managed to maintain his grip. "My ancestors will be waiting for you in the next realm."

"Lovely," I croaked.

Wengo leaned forward to put more pressure on me. I took advantage of the oversight as he put himself into range and grabbed a handful of his manhood. He squealed like a pig, and when my hands tightened, the pitch of his screams rose. He released my neck to pull my hands away.

I reached over and grabbed his knife and stuck it where my hand had been. Blood fountained from the gash. Wengo's eyes grew wide, and he fell to the side, grasping the wound. One last time, I got up and found my pistol on the ground nearby. I picked it up and aimed at Wengo.

"Greet your ancestors for me." I pulled the trigger. The slug took him between the eyes.

The sounds of fire wagons and shouting people warned me it was time to leave.

I had the wand, but why was it so important?

I should have headed directly to Mac's, but I needed to recover from the fight, and he'd need time to get the information I asked for.

Tomorrow I would get more information from Mac.

11

"What happened to your face?" Mac said as I entered his office instead of the rundown Copper Kettle. Today he wore a gray overcoat and matching trousers. "You look like a herd of horses ran you over."

"Always the flatterer," I said, trying not to wince. From what I could tell, nothing had been broken, but the bruises would be there for a while.

He cleared his throat. "My apologies."

"None needed, I do look quite the fright."

"Well, let's skip the chit-chat. Did you get the wand?" He leaned forward in his chair, eager for the information.

I slid into the chair across from him. Even a good night's sleep hadn't improved my looks or my mood. "I did, but you better start talking if you want it delivered."

"You have it," he said, a wide grin spreading across his face like a wildfire. "Can I see it?"

I shifted in the chair, partly out of discomfort, partly to get my pistol closer to my hand. "No. When you have answered all my questions to my satisfaction, I will bring it to you. Until then, it remains in my custody."

"What?" he asked, his cheeks flashing red. Candalarian skin bordered on translucent, so the touch of color looked odd. "That wasn't our deal."

"Our deal didn't include me fighting Norns, the city guards, Tofragrads, and a particularly nasty fire golem. Why do you want the wand?"

167

He grimaced during my list of bad guys. My guess was he hadn't known about all the interested parties.

He threw up his hands. "Fine. You win."

"I always do," I said, though my smirk hurt way more than it was worth.

"It is an artifact from Tofragrad. The legends range from it will heat your food to summoning the god of flame himself. I have a collector who wants it for her museum."

"You are prepared to hand over an unidentified, and possibly deadly, artifact to a rich matron?"

He grinned. "I am. She is an Astarian Magus, so no worries about it being used against you." Mac ran down all the details, which made me feel better. Mac was a lot of things, but he'd never been a liar, at least.

"As long as it is out of circulation." As much as I hated to admit it, he had a point. Other than under Everard's thumb, there wasn't a safer place than a Magus's mansions. "Now, tell me about your information on this cult."

"I guess I can trust you to keep your end of the deal," he said, though the look on his face was less than pleased. "The cult's name is the Followers of the Alpha."

"I know that."

"Allow me to start at the beginning." When I didn't object, he continued. "The cult worships the Ghuasis, goddess of the undead. At least it's as close as I can translate it. In Uwhelan religion, they cast her out of paradise and sent her to rule over the lost souls. And they want to bring her to this plane."

In a world where magic can do such amazing things, how was I to dispute that the cult could use magic to bring a goddess into our world? Stranger things had happened. I didn't understand how animal attacks and Cian's betrayal were connected to all of this. "What does this have to do with attacking an Astarian Magus?"

"You are so impatient," he said with a snort. "The Uwhelans believe if they send enough nonbelievers into the Goddess's realm, she will become powerful enough to break free and banish death forever."

"Now that is a lofty goal."

"It is," Mac said, pausing to take a drink. He set down his mug before continuing. "In order to do this, they are gathering resources like alarium, sacred runes, even artifacts from the Tofragrad fire tribes. Anything they can use to destroy the most people. They need a concentrated amount of death to fuel the ritual."

"Where will they strike?" This could be rather horrible or just terrible, depending on what they were destroying. "It has to be a place with a large number of people and a way to kill them. They could poison an entire city or set off a massive explosion."

"Or they need to bring a lot of people to the same place."

"War?"

"That is my guess. The battle at Chein saw almost two thousand deaths. Everard had destroyed most of the Norn fleet by himself. If they can prompt the Candalarians and Norns to attack the Astarians at a single location, the number of deaths would be huge."

"And they could use Everard to assist in the slaughter." Everard's defense of Chein was the largest battle I'd ever heard of. What Mac reported would make it look like a summer picnic. "I need more information. Where are the cult leaders now?"

"I don't know for sure," he said, stroking at his bare chin. "I heard a rumor that two days south of here is a cult outpost. Word is cult members have been spotted there. It is within a week's ride from Uwhela, so it's possible."

"Find out and then you can have the artifact."

"Wait! I didn't agree to that."

"Like I said, I didn't expect to have my face rearranged by a Norn warrior, but here we are. I'll be back tomorrow with your trinket."

His shoulders slumped in defeat. "I'll find out, but I have to have the wand tomorrow."

I stood to leave but couldn't resist one last jab. "What do you call it when a flower shop bursts into flames?"

Mac groaned, then answered. "What?"

"A florist fire."

I left before I was thrown out.

A secure room in a dangerous city was a blessing. I stored the wand in the hidden floor safe before bed. I doubted even Master Eskew knew of its existence. As soon as it was light out, I returned to Mac's to get any additional information he'd been able to glean about the situation. Thaclet ran much the same as the Astarian cities I was used to, but with a different flair. Horse traders, slave exchanges, and brothels were right next to the normal butchers, bakers, and candlestick makers of the northern nation. Plainsmen rubbed shoulders with merchants from faraway places. The whole town felt like a rustic outpost instead of the capitol of an entire, though sparsely populated, nation.

My boots kicked up swirls of dust from the hard-packed roads through town. My olive skin stood out compared to the Candalarians' bone white skin, yet none of the residents even gave me a second glance. A steady stream of traders and merchants of all appearances flowed through the capitol regularly.

The Candalarians who lived and worked in Thaclet wore loose fitting clothing and sturdy boots made of leather from horse, deer, or other animals of the plains. They went about their business, took care of their children, and in general were similar to the people I'd sworn to protect in Astaria. Politics and power made enemies of people who would be friendly under other circumstances.

"Ma'am, could you spare a copper?" asked a young girl in a dirty smock and tangled hair. "I haven't eaten for a day."

Her face bore a series of bruises that were covered with dirt. I fished two coppers out of my pouch and knelt close to her. I held a single coin up for her and slid the second into her smock pocket. "Take this."

I handed her a coin, and she held it in her tiny hand. "Thank you, ma'am."

Before she ran off, I caught her arm. "The one in your pocket is for you, not your boss, understand?"

A quick smile that vanished immediately told me all I needed to know. She still held the first coin where it could be seen. Smart girl. "Now off with you, scamp," I said loud enough for whoever was watching to be satisfied.

She grinned at me, then ran off into the alley between a general store and a leather worker. I hoped she'd at least get to eat with the second coin.

I reached the dilapidated building that Mac used as an office when he wasn't slumming in the Copper Kettle. People milled around in front of the stairs that led up to his office. I froze, examining the mob. After a minute, a constable stomped down the stairs.

"Nothin' to see here," he said to the crowd. "Old Mac finally met his match. Someone burnt him but good."

The man pushed past the onlookers who began to disperse. I stepped into the herbalist across the street and browsed her wares while the crowd left. After a few minutes, I left the shop and climbed the stairs the second floor.

A battered but solid wood door led to a hallway containing series of even more battered doors. The hall was empty, so I crept over to Mac's office door and tried the pull. To my surprise the door swung open. The constable had been nice enough to leave it unlocked.

Even though I knew someone had murdered Mac, I wasn't prepared for the site of his corpse laying on the floor by his desk.

The smell of sweat and feces hit me like a ton of bricks. I fought down the rising bile in my throat and focused on the mission at hand.

Or I tried to. My stomach lost that battle, much to my dismay.

12

After locking the door, I pulled my mask out and settled it into place. The respirator helped limit the stench, and the optics made use of the diffused light. My choice to wear the calling card of the Astarian Watchers put me at risk, but if anyone tried the door, I'd have time to remove the mask.

The desk was a sea of clutter. Mac wasn't the neatest person around, but it was still a shock to me. All of the drawers were emptied onto the floor. None of the contents showed any signs of char which made me think Mac had been dead before they had dumped the drawers. Given Mac's nature, I doubted he would sit still while someone ransacked his office. The cabinet behind the desk fared little better, but several mugs sat on the desk, all three with dribs of bourbon in them. Huh. Had Mac known his attackers, or had they helped themselves to his liquor after his murder?

Surely not. The smell would have put the most people off drinking unless they had a far greater intestinal fortitude than I.

I spent the next few hours sorting through the piles of paper, trinkets, and general mess. Some of the papers held information that might come in handy, so I stored them in my bag. Information was the currency of the Watchers, and more was always better. Under a receipt book, I found a very nice set of brass knuckles that I put in my pouch for safekeeping. Mac also owned an assortment of knives, daggers, and weapons I wasn't familiar with. None of them looked particularly interesting, so I left them. When the Thaclet authorities returned for Mac's remains, I didn't want it to be obvious someone had been there before them.

I'd been putting off examining the body, but that was the last step. I knelt next to the corpse and pushed him onto his back. Dark bruises stood out on the unburnt portions of his flesh. Dead was dead, but this wasn't an easy way to die. When I found the responsible parties, they'd regret their actions.

Mac had been wearing a long coat with a drooping collar over a tunic and trousers, which were charred like a burned out house. As I searched, I noticed the pouch he normally wore was missing. On the inside of his coat, the pockets were empty, but a crinkling noise caught my attention. I pushed my hand into his sleeve and found a folded piece of parchment. He must have hidden it before his attackers found it and his bent elbow had kept the flames away. I set the paper aside and finished searching Mac's lifeless body. I found nothing else.

I took the slightly burnt parchment and sat in Mac's chair. It tore a bit as I opened it, but it was still legible. It read:

Nimish Nimkar at The Ashen Farms. Ghost Hunter has returned.

A hand-drawn map showing The Ashen Farms in comparison to Thaclet was marked at the bottom. Mac hadn't wanted whoever it was to find this information. The real question was whether Mac's death tied into the cult's plot, or had his business practices had finally caught up with him. Finding Mac's killer would have to wait until after I'd stopped the cultists.

Boom, Boom, Boom! "Constables! Open the door," a man shouted from outside.

I jumped to my feet. Just as quickly, I yanked my mask off, stuffed it into my travel bag along with the parchment and other odds and ends I'd liberated. Last I poked myself in the eyes to get tears going and ran to open the door.

I threw the door open and sobbed. "Thank goodness you're here," I said, while choking back my fake uncontrolled sobs. "They killed my brother."

The constable's eyes narrowed. He wore the brown leathers of the Thaclet city watch with a steel tipped baton shoved into his wide belt. "I didn't know Mac had a sister."

Wonderful, I had to get the one person in law enforcement who knew Mac. "Don't tell me you can't see the resemblance."

Given that Mac currently was battered, bruised, and burnt to a crisp, there wasn't much you could do to verify our shared ancestry. The constable nodded. "Of course, my lady…"

"Ginni," I answered his unasked question. "Our mother was Candalarian, but my father was Astarian, which is why we don't look exactly alike."

"I'm sorry for your loss, Mistress Ginni," he said, trying to sound sympathetic. "I'll be needing you to leave. We are removing the body, and a lady shouldn't be present for such a thing."

I wiped at the tears on my cheeks. "Can I say my goodbyes?"

"I'll step outside to give you some privacy."

"Thank you, constable," I said in a choking voice. "I won't be long."

He nodded and left but waited just outside the open door where he could keep an eye on me.

I knelt by Mac and made loud crying sounds, holding onto Mac's lifeless corpse. The last thing I needed was the Candalarian city guard poking their noses into why I was here. I leaned close to Mac's ear and whispered, "Rest well and know I will settle the score for you."

I stood, straightened my duster to make sure my pistols were covered, and exited, stopping to thank the constable on the way out.

Now I had a vendetta to fulfill, a hypnotic drug to eliminate, and a cult to stop. No one ever said being a Watcher was easy.

<hr>

I spent the rest of the day gathering supplies for the trek south. My horse, who I'd named Azure, had been cared for by Master Eskew's stable lad. I'd purchased a proper saddle and tack for the upcoming journey. I doubted anyone missed Azure, since most of the slavers had been killed and their horses scattered. The inn provided all I needed and then some.

The next morning, after leaving a note with Master Eskew to give to Captain Breachcolm, I set off from Thaclet, guided by the crude map Mac had left me. A soft drizzle made the ride so much more pleasant, with the constant drops running down my back and the wet horse smell. The dirt roads out of Thaclet had turned to rivers of mud with the rain. I passed people wearing tall wooden shoes to keep out of the muck, though most went barefoot.

It took much longer than expected to find the trail that led south to the Ashen Farms. I wondered where the name had come from. I doubted they farmed ash, though stranger things were out there. Plainsmen were driving in herds of horses, cattle, goats, and a couple of animals I wasn't familiar with. I moved around these groups, though the smells followed me for a time.

Early in my time with the Watchers, I did a lot more field work, but I preferred mastering alchemy. I'd gotten to the point where I dreaded being away from my lab but investigating and stopping bad guys was what Watchers do. The next two days were a blur of rain, soreness, and boredom. Sleeping rolled in an oilskin didn't improve my mood. Azure took it all in stride but was lacking in the companionship category. Now I wished I'd brought a few of the crew from the Maiden's Kiss to handle the more mundane details, like setting up a camp and cooking food, though airship crew might not be any more of use than I was. Eskew's men had left the day before I did, so the captain should be headed back to Thaclet with his damaged ship by now.

The markings on the parchment meant little to me, but I followed the path the best I could, backtracking numerous times when the road ended or led to a settlement that wasn't the Ashen Farms.

Candalar consisted of a sea of grass, dotted with forests here and there. In the distance I could make out the outline of the woods I was riding towards. Given the distances over the flat land, I knew I still had a lot longer to go than my eyes told me.

The endless ride gave me time to think. I wanted to understand why Cian had betrayed us, how to stop a goddess from being resurrected, and how much longer the current tensions with the Candalarians and Norns could go on until full out war. Over my years with the Watchers, we'd fought off attacks from both nations, managed multiple uprisings of Maguses who wanted more power, and staved off a civil war. Peace was a term the Watchers never got to experience. I wondered how many more years I could handle the constant stress of the job. Once this was over, I needed to find an apprentice, assuming I lived to see the other side of this mission.

On the third day, I spotted smoke, probably from a chimney or campfire. According to the map, I was near the right place. I needed to scope out the site before making any moves. There could be many cultists or only a few. Either way, I wanted to be prepared.

I tied Azure to a tree where he could reach grass to munch while I explored the area. Unlike most of Candalar's vast plains, this close to the Uwhelan border, trees hid the buildings ahead. The sun was behind the clouds and night would be approaching in a few hours. I had to be quick.

I put on my mask in case of trouble and pulled a pistol. I slid between the trees, trying to be silent, sliding through the undergrowth. I moved cautiously to lessen the noise and reduce my chances of providing an easy target for anyone watching for intruders.

Minutes passed as I crawled through and under bushes and around trees. A log cabin sat in a fifty-foot clearing ahead. I'd expected more buildings, given that it was a farm. One building didn't really scream farm, but there could be more beyond the cabin.

The bush ahead of me shook, startling me. I prepared for a mouse or a forest animal, but instead, two golden eyes appeared out of nowhere. The loud growl froze me in place as the rest of the big cat shimmered into view.

I didn't dare move. The cat eyed me like I was lunch.

Being eaten wasn't on my things to do list for the day.

13

P hantom, what you got there?" a voice asked from the clearing.

As much as I wanted to see who it was, I didn't take my eyes off the beast in front of me. The big cat snarled as if answering the man.

The branches parted above us. "Well, I'll be. You caught yerself a Watcher."

"You'd best call off your pet before I am forced to take action," I said, hoping I sounded more confident than I felt.

"Victoria Wyndham, is that any way to greet an old friend?" he said with a laugh.

This time I looked up, and my eyes confirmed the last person in the world I expected to see. A tall man with a long, gray beard and the pre-mask style of Watcher goggles. He carried a multi-barreled rifle I hadn't seen since Leslie Gould had quit creating weapons for the Watchers and given the job over to Roland. Brulle Cobb stood before me.

"But you're dead."

"That might have been exaggerated. Everard doesn't much like retirement, so I faked my death," he said, glancing at the big cat. "Phantom, down."

Phantom looked over at Brulle before stretching out at Brulle's feet but continued to watch me.

"Nice cat," I said while standing up. Brulle had been "dead" for years.

Given the map Mac had left, though, this should be where the cult was. A shadow crept over me. Could Brulle be a part of the cult trying to destroy Astaria? "Why are you out here?"

He shrugged. "I don't care much fer people and the Plains folk trade me for what I need."

"And they don't try to capture or kill you?"

"Nah. Between Phantom and Gertie," he said, patting his rifle, "they decided to leave me alone. Come on in and you can tell me why you've come to my doorstep."

"I need to see to Azure before you get that story." We went and retrieved my horse.

I followed Brulle and Phantom down a path to the small house in the center of the clearing. Smoke trickled out of the chimney. A stable sat behind the main house and a shed to the far right of the clearing. Brulle took my horse into the stable and settled him in a stall.

"Right this way," Brulle said. We went to the front of the house where he opened the beaten wooden door for me.

"It's not much, but it's home."

"What is in the outbuilding?"

He glanced over his shoulder at me. "I use it for preserving meat to trade with the plainsmen."

Phantom, who loped alongside Brulle, growled at the hunter.

"Yes, Phantom eats it, too," Brulle said with a grin.

"You can understand him?"

"Yep," he said as he reached the front porch of the cabin. He held the door for me to enter.

I entered Brulle's abode. To my right was a small kitchen with a table. In the center of the room sat a large stuffed leather chair and a woven rug with an enormous fireplace beyond it. In the back, a closed door broke up the rear wall.

Brulle gestured toward the table. He pulled out a chair and took a seat. Phantom curled up on the rug. "Phantom is an Eriko cat from Pheimall off the coast of Tofragrad. The natives believe the cats are invisible, but their fur just makes it hard to see them until you are close enough to bite. When they bond with a person, they can 'talk' by putting pictures in their brain."

"Interesting."

Brulle leaned back in his chair. "What are you doing here?"

I'd known Brulle for years and found myself launching into my story without hesitation. I started with Quinn and the mysterious blue serum, explained the animal attacks, and finished with my trip to Thaclet. He nodded, asking a couple of questions along the way. I pondered on whether to divulge the information about Cian, but he needed to have the option.

"I left out one piece of information that may upset you, but I'll leave it up to you if you want to know. It's about your former apprentice, Cian."

"What did that fool boy do now?"

"He's working with a cult to destroy Astaria."

He shook his head slowly. "That was my worry when I took him on as an apprentice. I thought I'd calmed him down, but he was always hot headed. Always wanted to fight instead of looking at all options. Did you kill him?"

"No. He stabbed himself with a vial full of the serum. He was unconscious when I left. For all I know, it killed him."

"Serves the damn fool right for being so stupid," he said, though his eyes betrayed a hurt his words didn't convey. "This Quinn is Roland's apprentice?"

"No, Roland was killed on a mission. Quinn is the Watcher and artificer for Terralon."

Brulle's brow furrowed. "Roland was an incredible man and a great Watcher. I hope Quinn can fill Roland's shoes."

I didn't mention Quinn's magic, since that was his tale to tell. "Quinn will be a good Watcher and might be the best artificer we've had since Leslie died "

Brulle laughed. "When he can top Gertie, then I'll believe it."

"She is a beautiful weapon," I said, knowing how much Brulle loved his rifle.

"Where do you go from here?" he asked, his eyes glued to my face.

I pondered for a moment before answering. "Well, the rumor I was following led me to you, not the cult. I guess I'll start for Uwhela in the morning to see if I can track down the cult there."

"Let me see your map," he said. I tossed it to him, and he studied it for a bit. "Victoria, you are a great alchemist, but you can't read a map for nothin'."

I huffed. "I followed the map to the best of my abilities. It is hardly a work of art or precision."

He nodded in agreement. "It's not, but you are too far north. Did you take map reading? See this symbol? It marks the Uwhelan border. The cult camp is just over it. It's a day's ride and we'll be there."

"We?"

"You don't come traipsing in here, tell me that a cult is trying to resurrect a goddess, and expect me to sit here, do you? I didn't want to be an assassin, but this is bigger than Everard's petty squabbles with the Maguses."

"Honestly, I wanted nothing from you, though I wouldn't mind a hot meal and a dry place to sleep," I said, hiding my shock.

"I'll pull together some food," Brulle said, getting up from the table. "You can take the bedroom."

"Thank you." I hadn't realized how much I'd missed Brulle until he was back from the dead.

We set off the next morning to find the Ashen Farms. Brulle took the lead, though Phantom scouted ahead, returning to give Brulle updates. I spent the morning catching him up on all the gossip and doings of the Watchers, Maguses, and Astarian politics. He asked questions or told stories from his days as a Watcher. Most of them made me laugh, a couple so hard I almost fell off my horse. It was an excellent way to pass the day as we rode toward the cult's hideout.

About midday, Brulle moved ahead to check out something Phantom had found. I slowed Azure and waited for the all-clear. When I rejoined him, I launched into the question I'd really wanted to ask. "Why did you fake your death?"

Brulle glanced at me but said nothing for a moment. I figured he wouldn't answer, but he did.

"Everard asked me to do something, and I refused," he said, scratching his beard as he spoke. He resettled himself into his saddle. "We had an argument over the role of a Watcher. Protecting people is one thing. Being an assassin is another. I refused to kill for political reasons, but he pushed."

I nodded. "Everard can be quite insistent at times."

"That's a nice way to phrase it." He stared off toward the horizon for a minute. "Everard loves Astaria, but he blurs the boundaries of protection and murder. I'd had enough, so I left on the mission and never went back. I put a couple rumors out that I was dead and let the people do the rest."

"Sometimes you have to take a stand."

He shrugged. "Didn't matter. Cian ended up killing the man. Turns out he wasn't doing what Lord High and Mighty thought he was, so they killed an innocent man."

Though I was rarely at a loss for words, I struggled with what to say. I stared out across the sea of grass. A nice building or a tree even would break up the scenery a bit. "I'm sorry. Everard does what he thinks is best, but he's not infallible."

"He's not, that's fer sure," he said. Phantom returned to "talk" with Brulle. "There are people ahead. I think we've found the farm."

We left the trail we'd been following and tied both our horses to a stake driven into the ground. Brulle pulled a pouch from his saddlebag and set it on the ground. He opened the top of the bag and took out a chain of slug-shot larger than what I used for my pistols. With a snap, he clipped the first round into Gertie's undercarriage and snapped the fasteners in place. "I'm going to follow the path over there."

I didn't see a trail, but Brulle's the hunter. "And what do I do?"

"Phantom will lead you to the side so you can back me up if things go south."

I unholstered my pistols and checked them. "I'm ready."

"Good. Let's try to get information without any bloodshed."

I nodded but given my earlier run-in with Wengo and Firehelm, I doubted. I'd been wrong before. "Let's go."

Phantom loped off in front of me. I never thought I'd be attacking a farm with a talking cat. But then again, not much about this mission made sense.

14

I followed Phantom through the tall grass that surrounded the farm as he drifted in and out of sight. I'd love to study the big cat to find out how he turned invisible. My guess was a type of chemical reaction in the hair follicles would be needed to create the illusion of invisibility. That kind of knowledge would be highly useful, but I doubted Brulle would allow me to examine his friend.

I crouched down and crept into position, trying not to move the grass too much. I reached the edge of the clearing but stayed back in the grass. From my hiding spot, I could see the whole encampment. Five buildings sat in a circle with the path leading into the opening of the compound. The center building was the largest. Men and women wearing gray homespun tunics and pants worked around the buildings. There wasn't a child in sight, which made me think we'd found the right place.

Phantom growled softly. I followed his gaze and saw a wagon with a cage on the back.

"There's a wolf in there," I said to my companion. It appeared the cult was still using animals to do their fighting. It sickened me and I'm sure Brulle would like it even less. "Looks like we've arrived."

Brulle strode down the center of the dirt path. "Ho! I'm a traveler seeking a place for the night."

A woman with a dark ponytail down to her waist yelled from the main building's porch. "We don't take strangers. Leave or you will regret it!"

The old hunter held up his hands. "I'm just an old man looking for a place to sleep. I'd even take a place in a hayloft if you've got it. See here, I've got coin to pay."

The woman didn't soften. "Last warning."

Men and women converged on their leader, carrying swords, knives, and a couple of hunting bows. I'd need to target the bow users when the fighting started. I sighted my pistol on the woman holding the longbow. She'd nocked an arrow but hadn't pulled the bowstring.

"Well, if that's how you want it," Brulle said. "I've got business with the folk at Ashen Farms. If you could give me directions, I'd appreciate it."

The archer pulled and fired in one smooth movement, but Brulle dodged faster acid eating away parchment. Gertie swung around from behind his back. The barrels spun as he opened fire. The slugs screeched through the intervening space, tearing a hole in the leader's chest. She fell to the porch dead.

I opened fire as well, striking the bow user square in the side of the head. She dropped like a bag of potatoes. I fired again, taking out the young man who tried to get a shot at Brulle. The old hunter moved like the wind.

"Drop your weapons," Brulle yelled. "Don't make me kill you all."

No such luck. More people poured from the buildings and ran to attack. I took down two more before someone realized I was there.

"There in the grass!" one astute woman screamed, pointing at where Phantom and I were hidden. I shot her in the forehead, but the damage was done.

Two men charged at me. They had gotten too close for the pistols, so I stood, holstering them. I grabbed both knives from their belt sheaths. I ducked under the clumsy sword swipe of the first attacker, driving my knife into his throat, and pivoted to take down the second.

Phantom had other ideas. The big cat came out of stealth mode and raked his razor-sharp claws down the second man. The cultist screamed while his torso turned into a waterfall of blood before he collapsed.

I didn't have time to admire the cat's ferocious attack. Cultists hurtled toward us with a fervor reserved for the insane or true believers. It didn't matter. I danced a ballet of death through their midst with Brulle and Phantom carving their own way.

Without warning, a heavy weight struck me in the back, driving me to all fours. The snarl and snapping jaws told me they'd released the captive wolf from his cage. My duster stopped the worst of the claws raking across my back, but the wolf latched on to my hair and shook. He tore chunks of my hair from my scalp.

I screamed in agony, and then it was over.

Phantom knocked the wolf from my back as a spray of blood arced across the dirt from where my hair had been torn free. I pushed myself up and parried an over-handed sword strike with my two knives. Sparks flew as the metal blades scraped against each other.

"I'll kill you," the bearded man said as he reversed his strike, intent on disemboweling me.

I jumped back to let the blade pass and flipped my knife toward his head. The hilt end struck him in the eye. Good aim, bad throw.

He pulled back from the fight, trying to clear his vision. He didn't have a chance as my second knife tore his throat out.

Phantom and the wolf raged on. Both animals had blood on their fur. I pulled my pistol and shot the wolf in the head, earning a snarl from Phantom.

"Stop playing with your food. We have work to do."

Brulle, Phantom, and I stood amid a pile of dead and dying cultists. I spotted a man hiding near the wolf's cage. I called to Brulle. "I've got a rabbit here."

He walked toward the shaken man. "Son, come on out. We have a couple of questions. We have no want of hurtin' you."

The man, no, he was more boy than man, trembled uncontrollably. I noticed a wet stain down the front of his pants. "Stay away."

"Who is the leader here?" I asked in a calm voice. "We just need to ask a couple of questions."

"You killed her," he said, his voice cracking as he spoke. "We did nothing to you."

They'd threatened Brulle and attacked him without provocation, but I held my tongue. Mostly. "I understand. If you help us, we'll let you go."

"Ghuasis will eat your souls for attacking us!" he shouted, backing away.

"Who is Nimish Nimkar?" I asked.

He froze in his tracks. "Infidels shouldn't speak the name of the high priestess. She will burn you to ash for this insult."

Brulle swung Gertie up to fire, but I pushed down the barrel. "Where can we find her?"

The boy turned to run. I released the barrel of Brulle's rifle. "Wing him."

One of the best marksmen to ever live, Brulle fired a single shot that hit the boy in the side. He spun and fell down in a lump.

"Nice shot." I pulled my bag around and found the vial with forget me potion. The boy was trying to get to his feet when I reached him. I grabbed his face, forced his mouth open, and poured the greenish liquid in. He spit it in my face. I punched him in the gut, opened his mouth, poured more in. This time, I shoved his mouth closed and held his nose until he swallowed it.

He slumped back to the ground. I put away the vial while I waited for the serum to take effect. A minute later, he perked up.

"What can I do for you?"

"Alchemy has its benefits," I said to Brulle. I turned to the boy. "Where can I find Nimish Nimkar?"

He smiled. "She is at the temple at Onkhod. She is the spider goddess. When she sings, you can't help but do her bidding, Talasha told me. I've not proven myself yet, so I haven't been in her presence."

"See, we don't want to hurt you." I looked at Brulle to make sure he got the message. He nodded and slung Gertie over his shoulder. "Where is Onkhod?"

"Talasha said it is on the southern coast of Uwhela. The temple is on a small island outside of Zixraz."

"The city of the dead?" Brulle asked. "I thought the Uwhelans had destroyed the city to stop the necromancers?"

The boy shook his head. "I don't know. Talasha didn't tell me."

"What else did Talasha tell you?"

He grinned. "Ghuasis is returning to free all of us. Now is the time to worship her. She will place the true believers above all others. She returns on the day of crossing and will destroy all of those who don't follow her."

"Interesting," I said.

"She will kill you both and I will become immortal." He fell to the ground laughing uncontrollably. Brulle and I left him there.

It was time to go see a goddess about a war.

15

Two days of hard riding later, we reached the Uwhela city of Oras. We rode up to the city ready to go find the Followers.

I'd never been to Uwhela, but luckily Brulle had. "Zixraz is at the southern tip. Half the year, the rain is so strong, the natives built covered walkways to get around the city. Between the rain and the lack of travelers, the necromancers flourished for centuries. Now they have mostly been killed off, though if they are tryin' to summon Ghuasis, there must be a fairly powerful group of them in the Followers of the Alpha."

A tall stone wall ringed the town, with wooden shacks built around the outside. We traveled through a drizzle of rain that had started on the first day and not stopped since. The guards, not wanting to be out in the increasing rain, directed us to the closest inn and ducked back inside the comfort of their wooden shelter.

Brulle took the lead, Phantom nearly invisible by his side. The cat strode along but made no sound to give himself away. I'm not sure when I started to see his outline when he went invisible, but it was helpful. When we reached the inn, named the Sorcerer's Cauldron, Brulle went inside to secure two rooms. I stayed with Phantom and the horses. After a few minutes, a stable hand came out to take the horses. If he noticed Phantom, he didn't mention it.

The two-story building that housed the Sorcerer's Cauldron smelled of smoke, stale beer, and sweat. Brulle awaited me on the first stair. "We have rooms on the second floor. Suz has a key for you."

A tall, red-haired woman stood behind the bar, twirling a key.

"Ma'am, you look a fright," she said, handing me the key. I'd forgotten about my bruised face from the fight in Thaclet, though it felt much better than it had.

"You should see the other guy," I said with a grin.

"If you're with Master Tucker, I'm sure he didn't fare well." She pushed a mug of ale across to me. "I'm thinking you could use a drink."

"Lady Yorke doesn't drink that swill," a familiar voice said from across the room.

I turned to find Captain Breachcolm seated at a table in the corner of the room with members of the Maiden's crew. He stood and joined me at the bar.

The smiling Isham at the table. He raised his mug in salute. "Lady Yorke, a pleasure."

"Hello, Isham, Captain," I said with a tip of my chin. "So nice to see you both. I take it the Maiden's Kiss is repaired?"

"She's better than new. The crew worked on her all the way to Thaclet. The crew wanted to finish your mission with you. Master Eskew gave me the note so we came here to wait for you."

"Fantastic. We leave for Zixraz in the morning."

The captain grinned. "You do take us to some interesting locales, my lady."

I shrugged. As much as I would love to think these people were devoted to me, the promise of a gold coin at the end of the mission pulled them far more than loyalty. "We go where the money is, don't we?"

Isham grinned like a crazy man. "Coin is a god we can all follow."

"I will meet you here in the morning with my associate. We have two horses, so please make arrangements."

"Yes, my lady," the captain answered. "We'll be ready at the first bell."

"Excellent." I turned to leave, but Travis caught my arm.

"What, no joke?"

"Why, Travis," I said with a smile. "You should know a woman should never become predictable."

He groaned.

There are some people you can't ever please.

Rain hammered at the Maiden's Kiss as we flew toward Uwhela. I found myself on edge after the crash during the first leg of the journey. The captain explained the previous storm, a derecho with high-velocity winds and torrential rain, had been the issue. Our current conditions were normal rain, but it didn't make it any better. Brulle and Phantom were in the first mate's cabin. The captain hadn't been happy about bunking with the crew until Phantom appeared in front of him. He was more than happy to move after that.

I reviewed my supplies now that I had my full set of luggage at my disposal. The large leather-bound trunk had survived the crash intact. The outside was scuffed from when it tore loose from the wall during the rough landing, but the construction of the box had protected all of my clothes, equipment, and alchemical supplies. I opened the specially designed case that held my elixirs—twelve vials. Fire, forget me, and acid took up the top row. On the bottom row sat the vials of blue drug I'd been able to synthesize in my lab, as well as the concentrate of the floral-smelling compound in its pure form. I also had a vial of what I'd termed unlimited death serum. I'd never used it myself, but Watcher Timms had in the fight with Norn invaders. The elixir increased strength, speed, and numbed the body to damage. The unfortunate part is once it wore off, the user collapsed and died. Watcher Timms had been killed during the battle, so I didn't know if the drug had worn off or she had taken too much damage to survive.

I replaced my fire and forget me potions with full vials. I decided to add the unlimited death elixir to my bag. Not knowing the situation we were headed into made it difficult to decide what would be handy. Things like truth serum, climbing, and sleeping elixir wouldn't be of much use in a fight. I added healing elixirs, a strength potion, and a vial of acid too. If it came down to an all-out attack, I'd need any advantage I could get.

The wand I'd taken from Joelle Blackrose, I'd placed in my trunk when we boarded the airship. I studied the artifact, trying to decipher the runes. They were similar to Nornish runes but more curved and flowing. If I was deciphering them correctly, they meant, "By the will of the mistress." I had already tested it while it had been pointed out to sea, saying the words in a number of languages, to no effect, so it was wrapped in a leather cloth and set in the bag. It might come in handy at some point. I definitely wasn't about to leave it behind after all I went through to get it.

The bed wasn't comfortable, but it beat sitting on the floorboards. I retrieved my notes and set to updating them with what Brulle and I had learned thus far and the questions I still had. Would the cultists have the drug or were they getting it from someone else? At least we understood why the plot would be carried out. What would happen if there was a war, and no one showed up?

Given the Candalarians' and Norns' hatred of Astaria, I doubted we stood a chance of stopping a two-pronged attack, but if we eliminated the drug, we could possibly stop the cult and, by extension, stop the war. People would still die, but we wouldn't have an angry goddess to deal with, assuming the cult knew what they were doing. I had my doubts, but it's better to be ready than surprised.

I reorganized my notes and put them in the leather folder for safekeeping. Some of the papers had been damaged during the crash of the Maiden's Kiss. At least I still had them. The captain's skill had prevented us from a devastating crash that would have killed us all.

I lay back on the bed and thought about all the variables we could deal with and how to counter them. Tomorrow I'd know what we faced and needed rest more than thinking.

After a while, I drifted off to sleep.

16

The Maiden's Kiss docked in Zixraz at noon. The crew set to work tying off the airship and readying to enter the strange Uwhelan city. I had my travel pack ready, as did Brulle, who seemed agitated.

"Good morning, Brulle," I said as I met him at the gangplank that led to the tower we were tied off to. "I think I should enter the city and scout out any rumors of the cult."

Brulle scowled. "Ferget it, Victoria. Zixraz makes Thaclet look like a walk through a meadow of flowers. The crime families run the city, and there is no law other than what you can enforce on your own."

"I assure you that I can take care of myself."

"I agree, but..." He reached down and scratched Phantom's head.

I hadn't even seen the cat as I approached. Phantom was an amazing creature. "But?"

"Strangers are targets and a single woman doubly so. You'll deal with a lot less crap with me along."

Footsteps sounded behind me. I turned to see Isham and the rest of the mutinous crew approaching, along with Zora. "Master Brulle," Zora said. "I overheard you speaking with Lady Yorke, and I agree you should stay here. She'll be fine with the crew protecting her. There are still people who remember the Ghost Hunter."

"They are still calling me that?" he asked with a laugh. "So you think Victoria should go on her own? Are you crazy?"

She laughed. "No, me and the crew will escort Lady Yorke into town and make sure no one messes with her. We are known here, and the locals give us a wide berth."

"Zora split the head of a guy who got too grabby," Isham said with a great big smile on his face. "Plus, we swore to protect Lady Yorke with our lives after she spared us."

Brulle's gaze went to each of the crew. He finally nodded. "Fine. Phantom and I will guard the airship while Victoria uncovers information on the cult."

"The captain has canceled leave while we are in town. We are ready to make a fast getaway if needed," Zora said. She turned to the crew. "Get your gear, we leave in ten."

"I doubt all that is necessary," I said. "It is simply a reconnaissance mission. Nothing should happen."

Zora snorted. "No offense, but I've traveled with you before, Lady Yorke. Nothing with you is ever easy."

I wanted to disagree, but she had a point.

Things tended to go awry when I was around.

Six of us departed the airship. The gangplank was pulled up once we were off. Each of the six towers held three airships and stood fifty feet high. Each had an elevator for freight, but we took the circular stairs down the three levels to the ground. A large platform stood loaded with crates to be lifted to one of the awaiting merchants. The surrounding land was clear with roads leading to a series of warehouses and brokers who made their gold off the trade from the airships. Zixraz did a fair amount of trading which accounted for all the docking towers. I glanced back and saw Brulle sitting at the fore, Gertie out and loaded. The older man wiped the sweat away with a cloth before he waved once, then turned back to watching for trouble.

Zora assumed the lead, with Isham on one side of me and Cal on the other side. Three of the crew, Mattie, Cara, and Royce, followed behind. Knife hilts and batons stuck out of the fabric belts the crew wore. Zixraz consisted of wooded buildings with steeply pitched thatched roofs. Traders brought spices from the jungle, which lent the city a particular odor of sweet and spicy scents swirling around. The men near the airfield wore breeches and no shirts while the women added colorful sashes wound around their chests. I fought not to gawk like a tourist at all the unusual sights.

The townsfolk took one look at the seven of us walking down the street and gave way…quickly. A man stomped down the street toward Zora. He carried a wooden club like he knew how to use it. A crowd of people gathered to watch the impending confrontation.

"You got some nerve showin' yer face here."

Without missing a step, she drove her fist into his jaw, followed by a kick to the knee that dropped him to the ground. "Anyone else have a problem with me being here?"

The crowd wisely dispersed now that the prospect of a fight had passed. Zora was right, no one would want to deal with the seven of us. She resumed her pace, stepping over the prone man. Isham kicked him in the jaw when he tried to rise. The man collapsed completely.

I trailed after Zora through a warren of muddy streets, narrow alleys, and a couple of places I'd have labeled a dump, but people lived there. We walked for a bit before Zora stepped up to the entry of a seedy inn. She pushed open the door. Cal and Isham walked in first, with me next and the rest behind me. Hands sat on batons and knives as they stationed themselves outside the inn's door.

I stepped out from behind the crew. "I am in need of an information broker."

The barmaid traipsed over to me. Her eyes were wide and glassy. "You be needin' the Siren, then. You ain't her normal type, but you might have somethin' she wants. Follow me, your ladyship."

I nodded to the woman and followed her. Zora trailed me as we walked to the back of the inn. A ratty cloth covered the doorway into a secluded chamber next to the bar. The maid pulled aside the curtain with an awful attempt at a curtsy. Cal and Isham moved to flank the doorway.

Zora took my arm, stepping through before me. I entered after and walked into a dusky, dark room. A single mudstone lamp hung on the wall, putting out a whisper of light. A table sat in the center of the room with four chairs. One chair held a shirtless man who might have been very attractive, except for the darkened circles around his eyes and his rib cage pressing against his pale skin. "Please, Siren, I need more."

"Hush, my pet." The woman who sat next to him was broad of shoulder, with black hair that had been cut short. Scars crisscrossed her face and arms. "What can I do for you, Zora?"

"My friend needs some information, and we are here to get it," the first mate said, gesturing to me.

A slow smile spread across the Siren's face. "And does she have the coin to pay?"

"I do." I stepped forward. I disliked having others speaking for me, but Zora had been right about the town being rough and I wasn't about to argue now. "I need information on the Followers of the Alpha and a drug they've been using."

"Ahh, you've heard of the blue heron, have you?" she asked. A self-satisfied smirk crossed her face. "That kind of information is gonna cost you gold, missy."

"I have the coin if you have what I came for."

"I do indeed. The cult is no friends of ours." Her cheeks flushed red in the dim light. "The followers steal our soldiers and turn them into an army."

"Zora, it's getting crowded out here," Isham's voice warned through the curtain.

"It's fine, we are leaving soon," Zora answered.

"We have the same enemy," I said, pulling out a chair and taking a seat. The first mate stood off my left shoulder. "It would seem we can do business."

"Now, don't go gettin' ahead of yourself," Siren said, holding up her hands. "Just 'cause I don't like them doesn't mean I'm about to turn them over to you. For all I know, you're worse than them."

"I can assure you, I am far easier to deal with than the cult."

"So it would seem," Siren said. "Let me see the color of your coin."

I pulled a small pouch from inside my belt, slipped out a gold coin, and tossed it on the table. It rolled across to her, where she snatched it. She held it up, studying the crest and shield of the Astarian gold coin. "Astarian. I don't like Astarians. Cost will be double if you want anything."

I tossed a second coin to her. She slid the pair under the table, where they vanished from sight. "What do you need to know?"

"Where are they getting the blue heron from and where are they holed up?"

She considered for a few moments. "They harvest the pikku plant from the island of Onkhod. Rumor has it that they live in a compound there with a couple hundred soldiers."

Well, the information we had about the island was correct. Now that I knew which plant they were using I should be able to make a counter for the drug. "Interesting. Why didn't you stop them?"

"That will cost you another two, and here we haven't even been properly introduced. I'm a terrible host."

"My name is Lady Victoria Yorke," I offered in a pleasant tone. "I take it Siren isn't your given name."

She shook her head. "No, it isn't."

"May I know your name?" I asked, not understanding why Siren clenched her jaw repeatedly.

"My name is Trudy Spencer," she said. "I believe we have a mutual acquaintance, my brother Weaver Spencer."

Wonderful. Master Spencer had been a pain in my side for years. After he tried to extort Mrs. Habsburg and Quinn had stepped in, I'd poisoned him to keep him in line. I'm not sure if he died of natural causes or if he'd refused to take the antidote, but he was for sure dead.

Leave it to me to find his sister half a continent away.

Trudy lowered her chin and gripped the table like it held her up. "Looks like we've got more to discuss than the cult."

It had been going well. So much for that.

17

Siren threw the table at me, but I'd already started moving. The young man fell to the ground and began to sob loudly. I ignored him, concentrating on the knife Siren grabbed and drove toward me.

Zora lashed out with her baton, cracking it across the Siren's wrist. The knife fell to the floor, sticking into the boards next to my feet. She pulled me away from the cursing woman.

"I'll kill you both!" Siren screamed, holding her wrist.

"Time to go, a pleasure, I assure you," I said, then pivoted and ran from the room behind Zora. The first mate stopped short at the sight of the inn's taproom filled with armed men and women. Isham and Cal had their backs to the doorway next to us, knives drawn and a couple of bleeding men laying at their feet.

The first woman came at me, throwing a vicious punch at my head. I ducked under her arm and kicked her in the hip, sending her flying into a group of armed assailants. They fell like ninepins.

"Go!" Zora shouted, pushing me forward. Cal and Isham moved to help, but the surge of fighters threatened to overpower us all.

"Kill them!" Siren yelled from the doorway. She held her arm against her chest. Zora must have broken it.

"Buy me a moment," I said to Zora.

She grabbed a poorly constructed chair and swung it around her, pushing back Siren's fighters. On the second sweep, she connected with a heavyset man. The chair shattered, leaving a large piece of wood protruding from his abdomen. Blood sprayed his companions. One slipped on the pooling blood and fell.

"Down!" I pulled a vial of fire potion and tossed it at the bar. My crew ducked as the vial flew across the taproom. The explosion shook the bar, releasing a flurry of dust from the ceiling to cascade over the assembled fighters.

"Now, run!" I yelled into the cacophony of noise and flames. The bottles of alcohol burst, firing shards of glass into some of Siren's people. Screams added to the chaos of the room. I grabbed Zora by the back of her tunic and dragged her toward the front door with Cal and Isham in tow.

"Hurry, we need to get out of here," Cal yelled across to us.

As if I wasn't already moving as quickly as possible. I kicked and punched anyone who got near enough.

Zora pulled free of my grip and knocked over a table into another group of patrons. Drinks and people tumbled to the floor. The taproom had transformed into a full-fledged brawl. Everyone fought someone, but who and why made no sense.

A large man, fire racing up his back, lunged at me with a knife. I side-stepped him and threw him onto the downed table. The flames burst free, consuming the spilled alcohol.

Isham seized my arm and propelled me out the door into a whole new fight. Men and women armed with all sorts of weapons held the three guards in check.

"So much for a hasty retreat," I said, wishing Brulle was here with his rifle.

"We've pushed them back," Cara said. "There are a lot of them, though."

Flames grew inside the inn. Cal, the last one out, slammed the door closed and wedged a piece of a broken table into the handle as a makeshift lock. The door rattled as the people inside pounded on the door to get out.

"They killed my brother!" Siren yelled from the alley that ran alongside the inn. "Two gold for anyone that kills the woman in the leather coat."

Of all the times for my reputation to proceed me. Would Master

Spencer get his revenge from the grave? The world was a better place with him in the ground.

Siren snagged a young boy from the edge of the crowd. "Go tell Stavlat I've got a job that pays ten gold."

The boy nodded and ran off into the city.

The people in the street milled around. Unlike inside the inn, these weren't soldiers employed to do Siren's dirty work, only bystanders looking for the promised reward. They could be broken.

I unholstered a pistol and shot the closest person, a burly man with Tofragrad tribal tattoos covering his arms and face. He fell shouting for help as the slug passed through the soft part of his side. He should live, but given the filth of the place, it was a toss-up.

"Ten gold!" Siren screamed.

"Time to go," Zora said, hurtled toward the crowd, swinging her batons. Cal and Isham followed, creating a wedge that I fell into, firing my pistol at anyone the three didn't mow down.

Royce ran by my side, intercepting a woman with a wicked-looking hand scythe from removing my head. He drove a short lance through her. She stared down at the wooden shaft protruding from her abdomen and fell.

"We've got to get to the ship!" Cal called out as we broke free of the crush of people. We ran through the warrens of Zixraz. Pockets of people looking to collect Siren's bounty charged after us. Many others turned and fled at the sight of seven armed and angry warriors charging at them.

We reached the edge of the airfield and met up with a large group. The boy Siren had sent stood at the rear of the group. From the look of them, they were mercs, armed and battle-hardened. They each wore leather armor with steel plates sewn in for extra protection, and each had a dagger tattooed along their necks.

"Those are the Band of the Damned," Cara said as we stopped running. "We ain't beatin' them."

The leader stepped forward. He stood a head and a half taller than I. His arms were the size of a small tree. He carried a two-handed bastard sword in one hand. "Siren's put a bounty on her head." He pointed at me. "The rest of you can go. Just leave her with us."

Isham stepped forward, knife at the ready. "Pound salt. Siren's crazy and we've sworn to protect Lady Yorke. Go find a war to fight in, Stavlat."

The big man didn't respond, just shoved his sword at Isham, taking him through the gut. He kicked Isham off the blade like a piece of meat from a skewer.

I opened fire on the leader. The slugs hit, but the armor held up under the stress. He reeled backward at the impacts but didn't fall.

The others moved, but Stavlat yelled, "Stop!"

The mercs froze in place.

He straightened up and faced me. "No sense killing these people. Lady Yorke, if you can best me, I'll let you and your crew leave."

"I'd think you'd have an enormous advantage in a fight, doesn't quite seem fair."

He shrugged. "My boys can kill all of you if you'd prefer."

"Done."

"Are you crazy?" Zora asked, tugging me around to face her. "We signed on to protect you."

"Absolutely. Protect me, not die in a futile battle." I turned to Cal. "Get Isham on the ship and see if you can patch him up. The rest of you watch and report, but don't do anything to interfere. Understood?"

They all nodded. Royce helped Cal get Isham up so he could be carried to the ship.

"I'm sorry, Lady Yorke, I let you down," Isham said as he passed by me.

I reached out and squeezed his hand. "You did great. Let the captain get you fixed up."

"Aye." Isham's eyes closed. A worried look crossed Cal's face.

"Time is of the essence," I told Cal. He left at a trot to save his friend.

The wound looked far worse than I let on. I wanted to kill these people who'd harmed a man who was trying to protect me. I pushed the thoughts away. I needed to focus, or I'd be dead. I took off my duster and travel bag and handed it to Zora. I couldn't risk losing the artifact to this bunch. "If I don't make it, give this to Brulle."

She nodded, but her eyes were saying goodbye. I removed off my holsters and draped them over the coat. Both were empty, so unless I was going to throw them at him, they were worthless. The last thing I wanted was my pistols in the possession of a mercenary.

I turned to Stavlat. "I accept your challenge. Do I have a choice of the contest?"

Stavlat handed his sword to one of his men who staggered under the weight. "Of course."

"Excellent. I chose riddles."

"What!" a chorus of voices said in unison.

Stavlat laughed. "I'd heard you were a tricky one. Cornered me with my own offer. If I refuse?"

"Then I win, and you will let my people and I go."

"And if I don't agree and attack you?"

I tilted my head to regard him. "How much work do you think your band will get when word reaches employers that you reneged on a challenge? That you might, in fact, turn on them?"

His face twisted in a sneer. "Looks like I have no choice. Let us begin."

A battle of wits with an unarmed opponent. Should be a short contest.

18

I bowed to Stavlat. "Rules are each of us poses a riddle. If both answers are correct, then we do another round until one of us is wrong, and the other is right."

"I should just kill you, but my word is my bond."

"Excellent. You can go first."

Stavlat thought for a second. "How do warriors send secret messages?"

I laughed. The Norns were known for their warrior's code of war. "By the Norn code, of course. I hope you have better ones than that."

"You go."

"What goes up, but never down?" I asked. I started easy to give him a chance to get invested in our contest. If I knocked him out with the first riddle, he'd not take it well.

"Age?" he answered hesitantly.

"Correct."

His crew cheered and clapped him on the back. He beamed like a child given a sweet for good work.

"Your turn," I said as the ruckus quieted down.

He thought for a minute before he grinned. "Why did the potato cry in the bath?"

"Hmmm. Good one," I said, pausing like I had to figure it out. Stavlat's smile grew larger the longer I took. "Oh, because it got soap in its eyes?"

His smile fell. "Correct."

"That was tough," I said, trying to keep him in the game. "What do you call a baby rifle?"

I waited as he tried to answer the question. "A son of a gun?"

"Correct."

A crowd of onlookers had gathered around the unlikely group. They whispered back and forth, but no one interrupted the game.

After another celebration, he asked, "What did one wall say to the other?"

Another easy one. Stavlat was out of his league. "Meet you at the corner?"

His shoulders slumped. "Correct."

"What's a ship's favorite drink?" I asked knowing he'd know this old nautical joke.

A huge smile spread across his face. "Anything, as long as it's not on the rocks! My turn. When you need me, you throw me away. But when you're done with me, you bring me back. What I am?"

"An anchor," I answered. Time to finish this off, though this would always be my favorite fight. "What drink can't freeze?"

"Ha! Ale!"

"Incorrect."

"What?"

"The answer is hot water."

"But ale doesn't freeze."

"Stavlat, it does. My Da left a mug out in the stable last winter and it froze solid," one merc said. He looked very pleased with himself until he realized he contradicted his leader. "Oh, sorry, Stav."

A murmur went through the crowd as they awaited the outcome of the contest. A loud voice broke the almost silence. "Stavlat, I offered you ten gold to kill her. What is the holdup?"

Stavlat turned on Siren, his eyes blazing. "I am a Norn warrior, not your lapdog. Lady Yorke has bested me in a contest of riddles. She and her crew are free to go."

"Thank you, Stavlat," I said, bowing to him. "I look forward to seeing you again under better circumstances."

Zora handed me my holsters and duster. I carried them as we fled the arguing Norns and Siren.

"They are getting away!" Siren screeched like a fishmonger. "What good are you if you don't do what you are told?"

The crew and I raced up the stairs of the tower. Captain Breachcolm had guards at the gangplank to greet us. As soon as we crossed, the lines were loosed, and the ship floated up from the mooring.

"Where is Isham?" I asked, wanting to treat his wound before he lost too much blood.

"I'm sorry, Lady Yorke. He died from the Norn's sword."

Rage boiled through me. Isham had done nothing other than try to protect me. I pushed past the captain and crew to where Brulle still sat watch on the yards below.

Siren stood below us, screaming and shaking her good arm at the ship. "I'll kill you for what you did to my brother. I swear on my mother's soul that I'll have my revenge. Lady Yorke—"

I grabbed Gertie out of Brulle's hand, aimed, and fired. The slug hit her squarely in the forehead, cutting off her screeching. "That's for Isham."

I handed Gertie back to Brulle.

"Nice shot."

I ignored him, storming back to the main deck. "Captain, we are bound for the island of Onkhod. We will have a service for Isham in the morning. I am not to be disturbed before then."

If he answered, I didn't hear it or anything else said to me. I hadn't known Isham well, but I didn't have many friends and far fewer people who actually tried to protect me. I'd lost far more than I'd bargained for.

I entered my cabin, laid on the bed, and cried for the man who died for me.

***

In the morning, we were over the Middlenigan Sea. The captain and crew stood at the rail. Isham's body was covered in sailcloth and laid on the gangplank held by three crewmates on each side. I crossed the deck to join the crew. Brulle and Phantom were off to the side.

"Lady Yorke, we'd be honored if you said a few words," Travis said. The wind ruffled his dark hair.

I nodded. "Isham and I got off to a rough start, but he was an honorable man, and in the end, it cost him his life. I am sorry that I didn't have more time with him as I feel we would have become better friends."

Murmurs of approval came from the crew. I continued. "The mission we are on is life and death. I need your help, but I understand if any of you don't want to accompany me."

Cal spoke up. "Lady Yorke, you were far kinder to us than many of us deserved. Ish believed in you and your mission, and I, for one, will be by your side until we have won or died."

The rest of the crew answered aye. Captain Breachcolm cleared his throat. "The Maiden's Kiss and her crew are yours. There is more to life than coin and we have agreed to follow you wherever you go."

"Thank you," I said, refusing to cry. The time for grief had passed and now it was time to stop a cult from starting a war and raising a goddess to destroy everything in their path.

Travis Breachcolm stepped to the rail. "May Nitasis, Goddess of the Air and her sister, Tokta, Goddess of the Sea, shepherd Ish to paradise."

Cal lifted his end of the gangplank and Ish slid off the board and fell into the sea below. Everyone stood staring at the place Isham had been on the empty plank for a few minutes before the captain started calling orders. The crew dispersed to do their assigned tasks.

Brulle came to me. "You all right?"

Phantom pushed against my leg. I reached down and scratched the big cat's ear. The cat purred at the attention. I wanted to kneel down and hug Phantom but refrained.

"I'll be fine."

"Victoria, this life takes a toll on all of us. Some crack like Cian, while some go to their graves fighting for what they believe in. I know you don't want to hear it, but all of the crew could have been killed, and you stopped that from happening. Just remember that."

Brulle left for the fore of the ship. Phantom clung to me, unwilling to let me be alone. Tears trickled down my cheeks. Today was horrible, but I needed to be prepared to stop the cult, no matter the cost.

I was ready to unleash my pain over losing Isham on them.

19

A day later, we hovered over the shoreline of Onkhod on the opposite side of where we believed the cult compound to be. The large island itself was covered with thick jungle. Gulls and other seabirds flew around the airship, looking for handouts. We were low enough that unless you were on the beach we weren't visible. Captain Breachcolm approached where Brulle and I sat on the foredeck.

"Morning," the captain said. "How do you want to proceed?"

"We need to disembark and make our way on foot," I said, catching Brulle's nod of agreement. "If we fly into the compound, it will give them time to mount a defense or escape."

"We need to kill as many as possible so these Followers of the Alpha cultists can't just keep going," Brulle added. "Without the people who have the power to summon the goddess, we should eliminate the threat."

"I agree," Travis said. "The crew is requesting to go with you."

I thought that might be the case. "Zora, Cal, Cara, and Royce can accompany us, but that's it. We can't be stomping through the jungle with a whole passel of people. We need to maintain the element of surprise."

"Absolutely, I know the others will be disappointed. Ish was well-loved by the crew. They all want revenge," the captain said, disappointment filling his eyes.

"Travis, I would gladly have you by my side, but you are our pilot and our escape route. We need to head back to Iron Harbor as quickly as

204

possible after we finish here," I said, trying to save Travis's feelings. "No one else can handle this ship like you do. We'd be lost without you."

He nodded, mollified, but none too happy. "I'll follow your plan. You'll have to avenge Ish for me."

"Exactly," Brulle said. "You are the most important part of the mission, remember that."

He grinned a bit at that. "I'll have us down for you to disembark."

He turned on his heel and left. We both watched him for a moment before Brulle spoke.

"He's a good man and a fine captain," Brulle said. "You don't want him hurt, do you?"

I thought back over the past few years. Pirates, alarium smugglers, Norn assassins, and the list went on. "No, he's lost enough taking me on my adventures."

"His choice."

"I'd like to think so, but I'm also aware I can badger people into doing things."

Brulle chuckled and Phantom growled in what sounded like amusement.

"I once got into a fight with a pirate."

"Victoria, I am not listening to your jokes."

"You know, he had a mean right hook."

"I should have stayed dead," Brulle said with a laugh.

I left to get ready for a hike through the jungle. Something told me it was going to be a very long day.

<hr>

The captain lowered the ship so the six of us could climb down the rope ladder. Brulle fastened a harness for Phantom, and they sent him down after we'd reached the shoreline. The big cat was not impressed, but a twenty-foot drop wasn't going to work out well.

The sandy dunes of the beach were dotted with seaweed, dead fish, and other debris washed up in the last storm. The sand itself was hard-packed, which cut down on the blowing grit. Brulle and I had our Watcher's masks on. The crew had cloths tied over their mouths and noses in case the cult tried to hide their identities. Phantom prowled back and forth, irritated.

I'd become fond of Phantom, and I caught the edges of him "talking" with Brulle through the images he projected. They had a special bond that I envied. I'd hadn't been on a field assignment until Quinn showed up in Stillhold. He'd be handy to have on this mission, but he had Cian to deal with. How shocked would he be when he found out the cultists behind the animal attacks were trying to release a goddess to control the world?

Being a Watcher was rarely boring.

Brulle set off across the dunes toward the tree line. Once we reached the jungle, he turned left and followed the edge. After an hour, he halted the procession to examine the ground. I slid in behind him. It looked like more sand to me.

"See that?" he asked me but didn't wait for an answer. "Someone swept the sand to hide their tracks. If we walk to the water's edge, I bet the swept footprints lead to where a boat landed."

"Is there a trail we can follow?"

"Phantom, find them."

Phantom took off like a shot into the dense undergrowth. The fronds of the giant ferns barely rustled at his passing.

I sipped from my canteen and triple-checked my pistols to make sure they were ready. I made sure my belt and boot knives were all set as well. Under my duster, I had Isham's baton tucked into my belt. I'm not sure why I'd carried it, but it made me feel better.

Phantom slid out of the brush after a short period of time. I caught the image of a small group of houses. People toted baskets of greenery. My guess was picca plants for refinement. It looked like Phantom found our target.

Brulle stared at me quizzically. "Can you hear Phantom?"

"I see images, so I think so," I said, not sure if Brulle would be upset or not.

He pursed his lips. "Interesting. No one has ever bonded with Phantom but me. He must like you."

"That's reassuring. I like him as well."

"Are we on a date or trying to kill the bastards behind Ish's death?" Zora asked.

She unsheathed her freshly sharpened sword. Royce, Cara, and Cal followed her lead. This might be a mission to save the world for me but for them, it was avenging their fallen crewmate. I needed to keep that in mind since it could cloud their judgment.

Brulle took the lead, pushing through the dense underbrush. Once we passed the outer rim, the jungle was in perpetual twilight to the point I was glad I had my mask on. I'd expected brush and bramble would cover the floor of the forest, but it was the opposite. Giant trees towered above, blocking out most of the sun and limiting the growth in the process.

We wound our way through the giant trees. Vines grew everywhere. It was unlike anything I'd ever seen.

"Stay away from the vines," Brulle warned. "Some types like meat for their food."

"Really?" Royce asked, his eyes wide as portholes.

"Yes," Brulle said, reestablishing the pace. "Stay behind me, single file."

With Phantom up front with Brulle, we headed in the direction of the houses the big cat had found. The footing was treacherous, causing all of us to stumble at times. It wasn't what I'd call a walk in the park.

We kept going, but Cal drifted off to the side. "Cal!" Zora snapped at him. "Get in line."

He took one step to comply, and the ground gave out under him. The big man yelped and lunged for a vine to catch himself. His head and shoulders were visible as hung there. The sound of movement told me something lived down there.

Royce and Cara laid on the ground trying to edge over to where Cal hung in midair by a thick vine.

"Stop!" Brulle said, halting everyone. "A lurker lives down there. Don't move, Cal."

Cal stopped swinging back and forth and held still.

Brulle cut a section of vine that bled yellow pus from the wounds. He coiled the vine into a rope. Noise rose from the pit below Cal. It sounded like scales rubbing across rocks.

"I'm going to toss you this vine. All of us are going to hold it," Brulle said in a low, calm voice. He motioned for everyone to get behind him. Once we all had the vine, he motioned us to sit, alternating sides of the vine. "Don't make any noises. You'll fall a bit, which is fine, but if you scream, you're dead. Understand?"

Cal nodded once.

Brulle threw the vine so it landed over his left shoulder. We all tensed, waiting for Cal to grab the vine. Time ticked by and nothing happened.

"Cal, now, or it will eat you," Brulle said.

Cal's eyes went wide, but he grabbed the new vine. We all slid a foot or so with his weight. As a team, we lifted Cal from the pit. The growls increased the farther we got Cal out of the pit. It roared, and we all froze. All but Brulle.

"Keep pulling or Cal's done for," Brulle said between gritted teeth.

With a final heave from the group, Cal was back on solid ground.

"That was close," Brulle said before rounding on Cal. "What were you thinking? I told you to stay in line. The jungle is full of dangers."

Cal blushed. "I thought I saw an easier path."

"Damn, lurkers are clever. Ten minutes rest and then we continue. We need to be in position by nightfall."

I slumped where I was. All I wanted was a mug of ale and a warm bed, but the jungle didn't provide either.

20

The sun had started to set by the time we reached the cabins Phantom had spotted. We stayed beyond the brambles at the edge of the clearing and ate a quick meal while waiting for full dark.

Phantom returned from scouting the area. I counted about ten people in the images he shared with Brulle and me. The buildings were log construction with a large fire pit in the center. Smoke poured from the chimneys of the back buildings. Carts sat behind that same cabin.

"The right building looks like the place," Brulle said. "I'll take Royce and Cara around to the far side of the clearing."

I agreed. A two-pronged attack would allow us to eliminate the targets as fast as possible.

Brulle stood, motioning for Royce and Cara to join him. "I'll send Phantom when the time is right. I want to let everyone get some sleep before we attack."

"Makes sense," I said.

Brulle took his two and Phantom and disappeared into the jungle. Zora and Cal moved to sit with me. Cal hadn't said a word since the lurker pit.

"Cal, are you injured?" I asked him. If he was, I couldn't risk him in a fight. This mission had already cost Isham his life, and I refused to think I'd lose any more people. I'd known the risks when I signed up to be a

Watcher, but I still hated involving others. Unfortunately, death was another liability of this job.

He looked up like I'd surprised him. "I'm fine, Lady Yorke. Just shook from earlier. I'm ready to fight, no worries."

"I'm more worried about you than if you can fight," I said. After years as a Watcher, I had my fair share of dead bodies in my wake. Hopefully, the majority of people I'd killed had been bad people, but I didn't know for sure. Brulle faking his death made more sense the more I thought about it.

"We'll handle these cultists and then head for port," Zora said. "It might be time to set up a home and stop wandering around with Captain Breachcolm. The years are catchin' up with me, I'm afraid."

"I understand," I said, thinking she was answering my unasked question. When was it time to hang it up? "I've had similar thoughts myself."

"But you're a Watcher," Cal said. "You are needed. Captain can always hire another deckhand, but you protect people."

I chuckled. "I seem to remember you wanting to pitch me over the side of the Maiden's Kiss for my gold."

Cal stammered. "That was before I knew what a good person you are."

Could a murderer be a good person? What would I even do if I wasn't a Watcher? Make love potions and other elixirs or sell my skills to the highest bidder. Assuming I survived the upcoming war, I'd have to consider my future. Do my job right, there might not be a war.

Phantom ghosted out of the night. I nodded to him. "Time to go."

Cal and Zora got to their feet. "All right, time to execute the plan," Zora said.

This was the tricky part. We needed to subdue or eliminate as many Followers of the Alpha members as we could before someone raised the alarm. "We'll start at the closest building and work clockwise, unless Brulle signals."

We pushed our way through the bramble and entered the clearing. It must be two in the morning. There were no guards since no one would ever expect an attack in the middle of a jungle on a remote island. Without Phantom, we would never have found this place so fast.

"Follow me," I said. We stalked through the night toward the large cabin in front of us. Phantom sniffed at the door but returned to my side. When we reached the front door, I motioned for Cal to open it. He did. It swung in with a small squeak.

"Pissing again?" a deep, gravelly voice said from the darkened building. "I swear you are an old man."

"What are you talkin' bout? I'm still in bed," the second voice said.

"Then who opened the door?"

"Wind probably blew it open. I'll close it," the second voice said. The sound of bare feet on planks came toward us. I stepped into the doorway and the man gasped.

"Ghosts. I told you this place was haunted."

I closed the distance, clamped my hand over his mouth, and stabbed him with my knife under the arm to his heart. He tried to yell, but I muffled the worst of it before he slumped forward. Cal and Zora caught him and dragged him out of the cabin.

"What are you jammerin' about? Ghosts."

With my mask on, I saw the second man climb out of bed to check the ghost sighting. I closed the distance and stabbed him in the neck. He dropped to the floor. The taste of bile rose in the back of my throat. This wasn't a fair fight, it was an assassination, but the cult would kill everyone in an attempt to free their goddess. Even if their beliefs were unfounded, it wouldn't stop them from starting a war.

I checked the rest of the cabin, and no one was there. I found a mudstone lantern and turned it on so Cal and Zora could see. We searched the cabin, but other than personal belongings, there wasn't anything.

The next cabin played out in a similar fashion. These men were sound asleep and not expecting us. It was a slaughter. We stepped out of the cabin and saw two figures running toward the jungle. Phantom broke to give chase. I ran after him, but the cat was far too fast.

The door to the cabin with the chimney slammed open and three men with short swords ran out into the night. "Wake up!" one bellowed. "We are under attack."

Nothing else moved in the night. Brulle came up behind the men. "Drop your weapons."

One did, but the other two attempted to fight. Gertie made quick work of them. Phantom returned to Brulle's side. I was too far away to see the images, but when Brulle swore, I knew it wasn't good news.

"Kneel," Brulle said to the captive.

"Please don't kill me, they forced me to work here to make that awful stuff," the man said, his head on the ground as if he worshiped an ancient god.

We gathered around the prostrated man. "Two of them got away," Brulle said. "Phantom could have caught them, but being in the jungle at night is dangerous, even for him."

"Let's hope the lurkers get them," Cal said.

"They may have a cleared trail I didn't see in the dark," Brulle said. "What do we do with this one?"

I nudged the man with my foot. "What's your name and what are you doing here?"

The man lifted his head. "I'm Eli. I was captured by the Followers and brought here. There were twenty of us, but we keep dying and now there are only a few of us left. The priestess said there were more workers coming, but that was a while ago."

"Do you know what you're making?" I asked. I wanted to believe him, but something wasn't registering for me.

"Some sort of drug," Eli said, stammering out his words. "If you disobey, they test it on you. A lot of the first ones died terrible deaths, but lately, they give it to the workers and we do what we're told. They've turned us into puppets. I did what they told me so they didn't need to give it to me."

Interesting. To this point, we had only seen it used on animals. The ability to control people made it even more dangerous. "It must wear off over time. Have you seen them use it on animals?"

He nodded. "The Followers did and the poor beasts died in agony. They screamed for days before they died. If I never hear that sound again…"

A low growl came from behind me. I wasn't sure if it was Phantom or Brulle. "How do you know all this?" Brulle asked.

"For a while, we were forced to bury all the dead from the testing hut," Eli said. Tears ran down his cheeks. "I was a merchant. I'd sold my goods at a market in Uwhela and was headed home when my caravan was ambushed and they brought us here. They made me do such horrible things."

"I'm sorry," I said and meant it. No one should be dealt such a cruel fate. "I take it the deaths stopped after a while?"

"Yes, people were still dying but the animals were fine. It wasn't until Nimish showed up that they started using the animals to guard us. The Followers gave commands to the beasts and they'd kill one of us to make sure we stayed in line. Later they gave us the drug and we had no choice but to obey."

The early version must have only worked on animals. "Do you make it here?"

Eli shook his head so vigorously that I thought his neck might snap. "We harvest the picca flowers and boil them into a syrup. The leaders are the only ones who know how the drug is made."

"Show me."

He stood, eyeing Phantom and Brulle as he stepped past them. We followed him to the larger building with the chimneys. The structure inside was one large room with a series of fires with cauldrons over them. The smell was the floral scent of the distillate I'd produced. He stepped aside, flanked by Royce and Cara, while I studied the room.

Each of the cauldrons was half full of a sickly yellow flower suspended in a dark liquid. "What is it boiled in?"

"A mixture of tree sap and water. After a few days, it turns clear. We put it in those glass jars over there and they send them to the compound. The Followers turn it into the drug. When the cart out back is full, we take it to them. If we are late, they use the drug on us to make us fight or do other revolting things as punishment."

"If you agree to show us the way, we will free you when this is done."

"Oh, thank you, mistress."

"Don't thank me yet. We all have to survive the next step."

Given that two men had escaped, I wasn't expecting easy.

We'd find out in the morning.

21

Sun rose over the jungle, and we were still alone. At least we had that going for us.

Zora approached, leading Eli and our crew from the house where they'd guarded him overnight.

"Eli, can you show us the trail to the main compound?" I asked.

Eli nodded and led the way. Brulle cursed when Eli pointed it out. The hunter had missed it in the dark.

"Is it wise to take the path?" Zora asked. "Won't they know we are coming?"

"They might, assuming the prisoners didn't try to get off the island. If the escaped prisoners went to the Followers then they'll know we are coming. Either way, we'll be much faster on the trail. We also don't need any more excitement in the jungle. The plan is to get to the cultists, destroy the drugs and what they used to craft it, and make sure anyone with the knowledge is sent to their goddess," I said, ready to be off. Every moment gave the Followers that much more time to prepare.

"I hitched the team to the wagon and dumped the goo into the jungle. We will be far quicker than the two on foot," Cal said.

"Good idea," Zora said. "Get there fast and hit them hard. Then we can use a flare to call in the Maiden's Kiss and get out of here."

We all agreed. Half an hour later, all the buildings were burning, and

214

we were riding in the cart to find the cultists and stop their plans. I wanted to sleep in my own bed.

We rode for most of the day, Phantom loping ahead to detect any unwanted visitors. Just after dinner time, the big cat appeared in the middle of the road. I caught the image of a compound of buildings with a crumbling stone wall surrounding it.

"Time to go to work," Brulle said, jumping down from the cart.

Cal and Cara pulled Eli from the cart. They held him in place, though he was crying.

"We aren't going to hurt you," I said in a soft, reassuring tone. Eli had done what he promised, but I didn't want the extra baggage or the chance he'd betray us. After everything he'd been through, killing him might be a mercy, but I refused to kill the man out of convenience. "I am going to give you something so you will sleep until this is over."

"You're going to kill me," the man said through his choking sobs.

"No," I pulled a syringe out and loaded up a dose of the heron blue. He pulled back, but the crew held him in place. I stabbed him in the arm and depressed the plunger. A few minutes later, his eyes were glassy. "Eli, who normally delivers the drugs to the compound?"

"Jiles, but he's dead now."

"I want you to go to sleep in the back of the cart. We'll be back for you later."

"Yes, ma'am," he said absently.

"You have to do what I tell you."

"I am very tired." Eli climbed up into the cart and his snores could be heard almost instantly.

"Cal, can you be Jiles? I doubt the guards pay attention to the slaves."

He nodded. "I'll tell them my cart broke down."

"We'll be right behind you."

Cal set off at a good pace and the rest of us followed at a distance. He crossed the open space to the gate in the wall. He pounded on the gate. "Let me in. It's Jiles. My wagon broke down with the syrup."

The gate creaked open. A guard stepped out and Cal dropped him with a club before he could sound the alarm. Cal waved us in.

"Time to go," I said.

We ran across the intervening space and got to the gate before the guards could close it. The guard Cal had struck lay on the ground bleeding. We pushed the gate open and entered, weapons ready to use.

The cultist stronghold consisted of two-story buildings built out of biscuit, a combination of clay, sand, and pebbles. It dried to a hard consistency that resisted water. The roofs were a thick thatch constructed from the plant materials found in the jungle. The outer ring around the buildings was filled with vegetable gardens, and a large stone well stood to the right. A path wide enough to allow the cart to pass between them ran to the middle of the circle and ringed a large fire with a spit over it. Whatever they'd cooked last still clung to the metal.

The farthest building had a short bell tower attached to the roof of the long, low building. My guess was that was where they processed the blue heron. Low chimneys dotted the room, and the windows were all bricked up. The compound was minimalistic and bleak. Just what I'd expect from a cult bent on ending the world.

"Attackers!" someone screamed. Armed men and women swarmed out of buildings. Brulle and I opened fire while the crew engaged the cultists on the flanks. Phantom flickered in and out of view as he took out the unsuspecting attackers.

A bell started to clang from the tower at the far end of the compound. The Followers of the Alpha all turned and fled, headed to the building farthest from us.

This was going to be bad.

"Enough!" bellowed a familiar-sounding voice. Firehelm strode into view, a cadre of fire golems in his wake. These were like the enormous monster I'd fought in Thaclet, but man-sized. Unfortunately, there were ten of them.

Brulle shot at Firehelm, but one of the golems stepped in the way and the slugs struck it harmlessly. I had two fire potions in my bag, but that would leave eight golems and no visible way to fight them.

"Keep Phantom away from those things," I told Brulle as they burned their way across the packed dirt of the compound.

I fired my pistols, hoping to hit Firehelm, to no avail. The golems created a shield for the mage who'd summoned them.

Brulle opened up with Gertie. The rapid-fire rifle pushed the golems back but didn't do much, if any, damage to the creatures.

"Everyone fall back," I yelled, panic lacing my tone. I had no ideas on how to stop these things. "Get outside the wall."

Zora signaled her people, who ran to hold the gate. "Lady Yorke, we have to leave and regroup."

The golems continued to move, their glow intensifying as they passed between the two closest buildings. An idea struck me. "Brulle, aim at the base of the walls."

"What?" he asked, clearly believing me crazy, and I wasn't sure he was wrong.

"Fire a line down the base of that wall." I pointed at the building nearest him on the left.

Firehelm threw his arms in the air. "You will not defeat me with your evil ways! The goddess protects me and all who serve her."

"Didn't work out so well in Thaclet!" I called back to him. "Seems you ran away if I remember correctly."

The golems turned to focus on me.

"You will burn!" Firehelm yelled. "My pets will leave nothing left but ash."

"Brulle, now!"

The hunter opened fire, tearing out chunks of mud biscuit and sending dust through the air. He kept it up until he reached the end of the building. Nothing happened.

"Ha! You will burn!"

Crack!

"I don't think it worked," Brulle said. He returned his aim to the golems.

"Wait," I said.

Crack! Chunks of wall clattered to the ground. With a loud groan, the wall tilted.

"What did you do?" Firehelm screamed.

"I'm putting an end to you."

More chunks rained down as the wall splintered and fell. Large pieces hit the golems. Fire needed air to work, and the dirt and dust were doing their best to suffocate the fire creatures.

With a mighty snap, the whole wall gave way and collapsed across the golems, hitting all but the lead one. I'd taken out a much larger golem in Thaclet. This small one should be no problem.

The dusty air made it difficult to see where Firehelm was.

"Good idea, Victoria," Brulle said. "Only one left."

Then the monster started to grow.

Well, so much for that.

22

ow what do we do?" Brulle asked, watching the golem enlarge.

A motion caught my eye. Zora and the crew were all racing toward the golem, carrying buckets.

"Get away from it!" I yelled.

"We've got this!" Cal answered as he reached the golem first and threw his pail of water on the fiery monster. It hissed and plumes of vapor flowed into the air.

"In the name of the goddess, attack!" Firehelm screamed from beyond the swirling dust cloud.

Zora pitched another bucket of water on the monster, sending up more steam. Royce and Cara followed but hadn't reached the monster. The golem surged forward and grabbed Zora. The woman screamed in sheer agony before she crumbled into ash.

"Run!" I yelled as the first mate's ashes fluttered to the ground.

To their credit, the others delivered their water and ran before the golem could react. It had shrunk to about nine feet tall, but the golem was still whole. We'd need a boat full of water to douse this thing.

"Slow it down," I said to Brulle while I dug into my travel bag for a fire potion. It had worked in Thaclet. There was only one monster left and it was smaller than the one I'd fought before.

Brulle opened fire, the slugs creating a pattern on the golem's chest.

The monster lunged forward and vomited out magma. Brulle and I

218

dodged the attack, but the fire potion fell to the ground and exploded. Shards of glass peppered us both. A trickle of blood dripped from my forehead and down my cheek. My duster had taken the worst of the damage.

Brulle had been farther away, so he had only a few cuts. He unloaded Gertie at the flaming beast. "Victoria, we need to finish this."

That was when I heard the rifle stop with the *clack, clack* of an empty chamber. Brulle had run out of ammo. Good thing I still had one vial of fire potion left. I tugged it free and threw it into the chest of the approaching golem. The vial sank into the creature and right out the other side to explode harmlessly against the fallen wall.

What in the hell? My mind reeled to find a solution this problem.

"Did you think me stupid enough to fall for the same trick twice?" Firehelm yelled in triumph. "Kill them."

I closed the vial case and shoved it into my pouch. Cool metal touched my skin. I clamped around it and pulled out the wand I'd added as an afterthought to my kit.

"Time to die!" Firehelm yelled at us.

"Victoria, I think it's time to retreat," Brulle said, leading me away from the approaching monster. Phantom appeared at Brulle's knee. The big cat growled at the monster but stayed away.

"Run. I have an idea."

"Are you kidding?"

"I said run!" I didn't bother to see if he obeyed. I pointed the wand at the creature and said, "In the name of the mistress."

Nothing happened.

Firehelm laughed. "So you brought my wand with you. I'll take it from your corpse."

The words were wrong. I'd practiced this before so I knew what didn't work. I needed to find the correct phrase. "By the will of the mistress," I yelled, trying to force the wand to work. Still nothing.

"Give me the wand and I'll let you and yours go." Firehelm's voice held a note of fear. The fire mage's hands were clenched together like a worried mother.

Why would he offer...

Oh! Like a stroke of lightning, the answer hit me. Firehelm had given me the right words, and I'd not realized it. "In the name of the goddess, attack!"

The golem stopped advancing on me. "What are your wishes, master?"

It hadn't spoken, but I "heard" it in my head.

"Destroy the buildings, except the largest."

"Yes, master."

The golem spun and advanced to the nearest building. It punched the structure, and the walls crumbled under the force.

I turned to find the remaining members of the crew and Brulle staring at me. "What are you waiting for? We need to capture Firehelm."

"How did you do that?" Cara asked in disbelief. "Are you a magus?"

"No, it's the wand."

We ran past the center fire pit while the golem demolished the encampment. It was certainly effective. We avoided the destruction, instead, we concentrated on finding Firehelm. We rounded the massive building to find another path leading into the jungle.

Brulle stooped low. "Fresh tracks. They must have taken carts of the blue heron to get away."

"We've got to stop Firehelm," I said. "Cal, Royce, and Cara, you stay here in case anyone comes back. If Firehelm shows, you run."

"Yes, ma'am," they all said in unison.

Brulle, Phantom, and I trotted down the cart trail. I gave one of my pistols to Brulle, who looked it over. "Don't know how you get anything done with this peashooter."

"I usually don't require guns in my daily job as an alchemist."

"Good point," he said. He didn't hand me back the gun.

We rounded a corner and ran into the back of the fleeing cultists from the compound. They stopped pushing the overburdened cart, turning to bring knives and swords to bear.

"We've got no quarrel with you," I shouted. "We only want Firehelm."

No such luck.

Three of the Followers of the Alpha cultists charged at us as the rest fled. Phantom hamstrung the first easily and Brulle and I took out the other two. There might be a lot of them, but these weren't trained warriors, just scared people.

We repeated this scene until we reached a low tower in a clearing. Three airships were departing from the raised platform. We were too late.

The ships rose into the air, casting off the tie lines. They were out of range of my pistol, and my traveling bag wouldn't be of much help, either.

"All that, and they got away," Brulle said. The hunter looked twice as old as when I'd found him. His shoulders slumped in defeat.

The sound of cannon fire broke the still air. The first ship rocked as the projectiles smashed into the hull. I looked up and the Maiden's Kiss sailed into view. Another volley struck the floundering airship in the balloon, and it burst. The airship plunged into the sea, dropping people and debris as it fell.

The remaining two airships split directions. One went straight out to sea at full power. The other turned, heading toward the Maiden's Kiss. Captain Breachcolm swung his ship around to take on the second ship. While the cultists weren't fighters, they obviously had good air captains.

The cultist ship maneuvered close and threw out boarding ropes entangling the Maiden's Kiss. Instead of the crew jumping across to attack, they set their own ship on fire. Explosions in the belly of the ship flared, and the ship lurched precariously.

"If they don't cut those ropes, the Maiden's Kiss is going down," Brulle said. He was right.

The Maiden's Kiss attempted to climb, but the weight of the dying airship dragged at them. The Followers of the Alpha's ship wallowed as the fire spread. The cultist crew was climbing the ropes to the balloon. Once the Followers of the Alpha's ship lost its floatation, it would become an anchor that would tear the Maiden's Kiss from the air.

With an ear-splitting boom, the cultist's balloon burst in a cloud of fire and smoke. The dead airship plunged. The ropes attaching her to the Maiden went taut. I held my breath as I watched in horror.

The lines holding the two ships together snapped from either the weight or the crew had cut the ropes loose. The Maiden's Kiss swung away, then righted itself. With a whoosh, the Followers of the Alpha's ship plunged, crashing into the jungle.

"That was close," Brulle said. "We should go greet the captain."

We climbed the stairs to the docking area to help the crew tie off the damaged ship. The third ship had flown too far and was too fast for the Maiden's Kiss to stop them. If my guess was correct, Firehelm was on that ship. He'd be paying for all the deaths with his life. I swore an oath.

He would die.

23

After getting the Maiden's Kiss tied off, Brulle, Phantom, and I returned to the compound where Cal, Royce, and Cara were waiting for us. I dismissed the golem before he burnt the whole place to the ground.

I sat on the ground and let Zora's death wash over me. I'd tried to keep her out of harm's way, but in a fight, things never went as planned. Thoughts of the first mate ran through my head. She'd been a strong, smart woman and died far too early.

"We saw the Maiden go by. Is she okay?" Cara asked, her words a bit shaky.

I startled having not heard Cara approach. I wiped my eyes on my sleeve. "The Maiden's Kiss is docked and making repairs. The captain has requested your presence aboard the ship. You should go join the rest of the crew."

They nodded and left down the trail. I watched them go and thanked providence they'd survived this endeavor. Given what was coming, I wasn't sure who was better off, the living or the dead. A war the size the Followers were attempting to start would kill far more than we'd lost so far.

We crossed the blackened dirt and entered the large, low building. The vast space contained huge vats, boiling away with condensation tubes dripping the blue heron into glass jars. Other stations were set up to transfer the liquid into smaller vials. Cages holding animals and humans stood along the wall to the left. All of them appeared to be dead.

"Wow, look at this place," Brulle said. "They are preparing for battle. With this much blue heron, they could control half of Astaria."

"They don't want to control Astaria, they want to destroy it," a female voice said. A thin, stately young woman approached from the right side of the room.

Brulle's borrowed pistol snapped up to aim at her. "And who might you be?"

"My name is Miranda Oldfield, and I am the alchemist who created the blue heron."

"Give me one reason not to kill you," Brulle said, hostility laced lacing his words.

I placed my hand on his arm. "Let her talk."

Brulle lowered his arm, but Phantom paced, feeling Brulle's aggravation.

Miranda tipped her chin in way of thanks. "Lady Yorke, your reputation precedes you. You are a legend amongst alchemists."

"Save the flattery," I said, icicles dripping from my words. "To Brulle's point, why shouldn't we kill you?"

She held up her hands. "You have every right to kill me. I've unleashed this on the world."

"You aren't making much of a case," Brulle said.

"Please let me finish," she said. When Brulle nodded, she continued. "I created blue heron to help patients dealing with lunacy to find help. It worked too well. Nimish heard of my success and kidnapped me and forced me to make the drug for him to use."

"You could have refused," Cara said.

"Nimish threatened to kill my husband and children in Uwhela if I didn't help. I couldn't risk that."

At my core, I understood, but after losing so many people, I didn't want to. Zora and Isham had died along with others on the crew. All I wanted to do was retreat to my lab and hide until this was all over, but I'd sworn an oath to Everard and Astaria that I would protect her people, whatever the cost. Brulle had walked away from his oath, but here he was, risking his life for a country he no longer lived in.

"I'll give you two choices," I said. "We can kill you and your knowledge dies with you."

"That's not much of an option," Miranda said.

"Or you come with us. We will get your family and you will come to Astaria with us to help fight the evil you've unleashed."

"I'm an alchemist already," Miriam said stiffly. "I don't see either as appealing, but you are right. I did unleash this on the world so I should help make it right."

"No, you are a drug maker," I corrected her. "An alchemist would have seen the potential for abuse and mitigated it before ever using it when anyone could see the results. You are a little girl playing with toys you don't understand. If the next words out of your mouth aren't 'yes, Lady Yorke' then I will put you down like a rabid animal. You have three seconds."

"See here—"

"One."

"This is blackmail and—"

"Two."

She bowed her head. "Yes, Lady Yorke."

"Brulle, if you will escort Miranda back to the ship and restrain her. She is a prisoner until she proves her loyalty."

"You didn't say—"

"You will not speak until spoken to. You have killed more people than you can count, enslaved people, and have pushed us all to the brink of disaster. Be happy I don't let the golem burn you to death like it did Zora. Do we understand each other?"

"Yes, Lady Yorke."

"Excellent. The next time you backtalk me, I'll cut out your tongue and feed it to Phantom."

"Phantom doesn't eat offal," Brulle said with a smirk.

I bit back a laugh. Leave it to Brulle to make me chuckle at a time like this.

Brulle ushered Miranda out, Phantom following along.

I set to searching the facility.

<hr>

It took until the early hours of the morning to sort through the contents of the labs. In Miranda's research, she had a couple of promising leads into other compounds that might become useful in a medical setting. She had also drawn pictures of Firehelm and various people from the compound. Those would come in handy. If only she'd drawn one of Nimish.

In the end, I walked back to the Maiden's Kiss.

Cal helped me cross the gangplank and led me to my room. I slept until the next morning when a knock on the door woke me.

"Come in," I said, not getting up.

A flash of red hair announced Cara as she stuck her head in. "Captain has requested you to join us. He needs orders."

"Of course."

Cara flashed a brilliant smile that sparkled in her eyes. "I'm sure he'll be happy to see you, Lady Yorke."

The world had gone mad while I slept. "I'll be up shortly."

She nodded. "Captain says to take you time, ma'am." Cara pulled the door closed behind her.

I dressed and left the cabin for the warm and sunny main deck. Brulle and Phantom sat against the rail. Cara and Royce worked at the coiling rope while Cal sewed up holes in his clothes. The captain paced back and forth.

He turned to face me as I arrived on the deck. "Lady Yorke, I hope you slept well. We'll be ready to cast off as soon as the rest of the repairs are completed."

"Thank you, Travis, I did."

"Master Brulle filled us in on the situation. We are at your disposal. As you know, one of the cultist airships escaped."

I sat on the deck next to Brulle. "You had enough on your hands doing battle with the other one. Exceptional flying, captain."

Travis beamed with delight. "It worked out, though I wanted to down all three ships. What are our orders, m'lady?"

"I need to retrieve Miranda's family in Uwhela and then meet up with Quinn." I glanced at Brulle. "And you, sir?"

"Sir," he said with a snort. "I'm going to find a ride and go after Fire-helm. We have to stop him before Nimish can organize and attack Iron Harbor. I don't believe we've seen everything he has in store. Miranda said they had a compound near the border of Ramcoll. Since Cian turned traitor, I need to set the scales right."

I looked at the captain. "You have your answer."

"Yes, ma'am," he said with a crisp salute. "We'll be underway in the hour."

Travis stood there staring at me.

"And?" I asked.

"What, no joke?" the captain answered with a smirk on his face.

"Never make fun of a person who stammers."

"Why?"

"Because they'll get revenge…eventually."

With a chorus of groans, the captain started calling out orders to set sail.

The mission had been long and it wasn't over. I needed to get the Watchers mobilized for the upcoming fight.

Astaria was going to war.

The End

MACHINES & MONSTERS

BOOK THREE

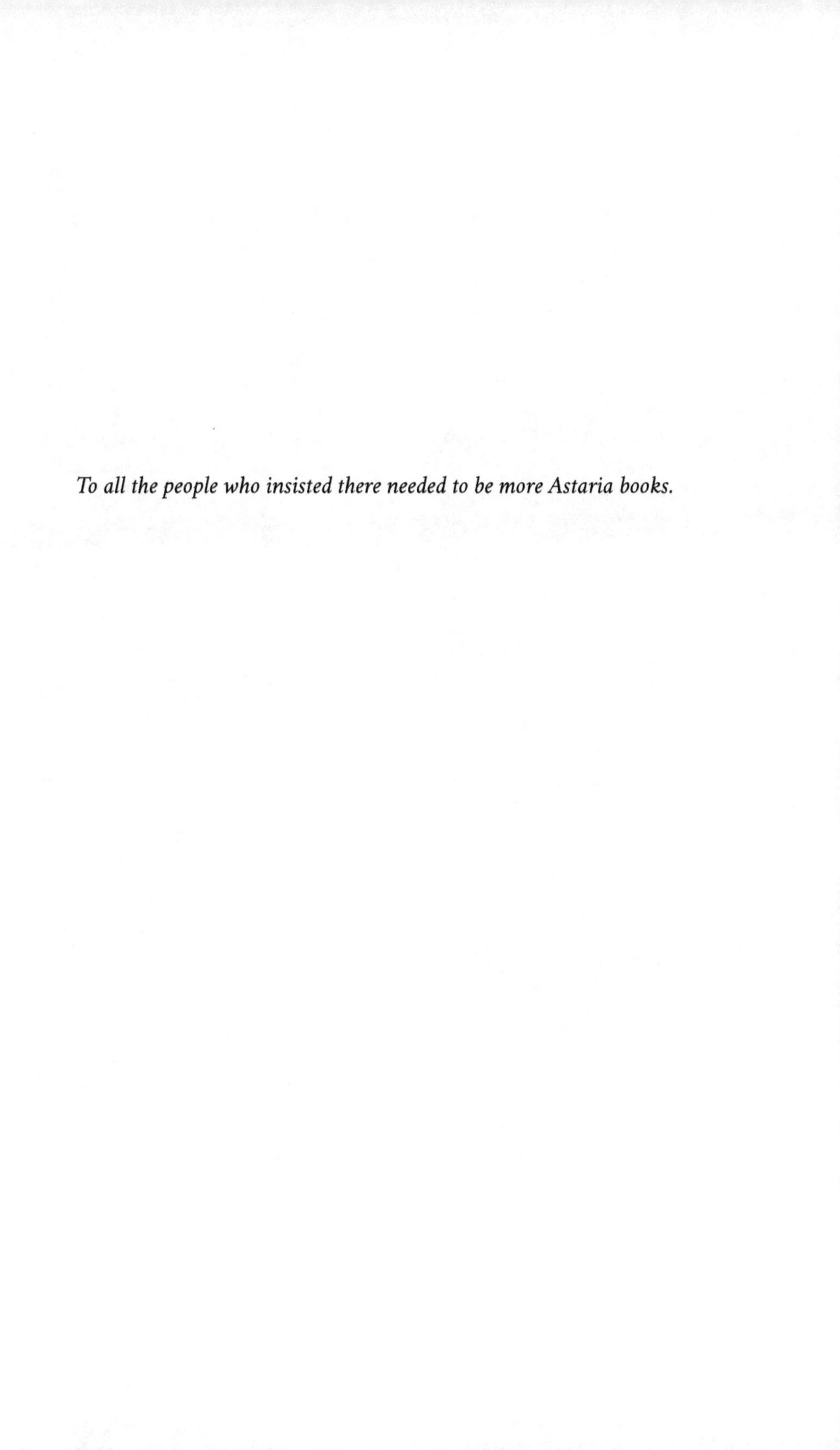

To all the people who insisted there needed to be more Astaria books.

1

BRULLE

My Grandma Jane always said, "Growing old ain't fer sissies." Her words floated in my brain as the aches and pains of the fight in the jungle set into my old bones. From the foredeck of the Maiden's Kiss, I watched the grasslands of Candalar pass below a sea of green, dotted with copses of trees like lost islands of darkness.

Phantom pushed against my leg with his head, which I dutifully scratched. The big psychic cat worried like a momma bird, feeling my discomfort.

"I'm fine, just remembering why we don't run off on adventures anymore. Once this is done, we'll go hunting and get away from people."

Phantom approved, rolled over, and closed his eyes.

I envied the large cat. Since the mission to Uwhela, my sleep had been filled with nightmares. I'd left the Watchers behind and didn't miss the killing and mayhem we protected the Astarian people from. My reintroduction hadn't been unwilling, because I was willing to help save the world, but that didn't mean it had been pleasant.

"Good morning," Victoria said. She jogged up the stairs to join us. She tossed a sausage to Phantom, which he caught mid-air. I received my breakfast on a plate with a mug of ale.

"Thank you," I said, taking the plate so Victoria could sit down. I snuck a bite, then another, then a third. The spices of the sausage filled my mouth and nose. I realized Victoria was staring at me.

231

"Hungry?" she asked with a smile. "I thought you might be."

I nodded, still chewing. I took a swallow of the ale and found it didn't live up to the meal, but it would do.

"I've spoken to Miranda, who is much more talkative now that we've got her family aboard. The Blue Heron compound she created was meant for patients at the asylum she worked at, but the cult leader got ahold of her and used the drug for her own gains," Victoria said, though her thousand-mile stare told me she was elsewhere.

"That's good. I know you trust her, but I have a bad feeling in my bones about her," I said, taking a pull from my mug. "You want to tell me what's bothering you?"

Her cheeks flushed. "You always did know me far too well for my liking."

"Reading people comes with the territory."

"It's just…" She paused.

I waited.

"The whole thing bothers me," she said after a moment. "First Cian betrays us, now we've killed all those people to stop Firehelm, and we are no closer to actually averting the war than when we set out. It all seems pointless."

I nodded. "Violence usually is, but if we did nothing, Astaria would be awash in the blood of all the innocents the cultists want to kill. Part of the reason I left the Watchers was to get away from the missions and the killings, but evil will grow when good isn't watching."

She scoffed. "Are you suggesting we are the good guys in all this?"

I thought about it for a moment. I never felt like a good guy while I was a watcher, but I also knew the end result was we helped people. "Not at all. We are the in-between."

"In-between?"

"If good is light and evil darkness, we are the twilight," I said, trying to find the words to a philosophy I believed, but had never spoken. "We long to be in the light but need to stay in the shadows to stop evil people from harming those who can't protect themselves. At its core, the Watchers are protectors. Everard turned us into assassins."

Her finger tapped her lips as she thought. "So we can't be in the light while functioning as a protector?"

"Maybe some can, but a good person couldn't have killed all the cultists, not knowing if they were captives or drugged to fight," I said, watching her face. "A good person hesitates when evil is required to fight a greater evil. You and I can walk the line between them so most people can lead a normal life."

Understanding flickered in her eyes. "Interesting, I hadn't thought of it that way. If that's how you feel, why did you stay away?"

I shrugged. "Once I was out, the thought of returning seemed impossible. Also, I figured Cian would grow out of his reckless phase without me standing over him. I was wrong."

She put her hand on my leg. "None of us saw it coming. He could have killed Quinn before he realized that Cian was a traitor."

"I'm looking forward to meeting Quinn," I said with a chuckle. "He sounds like a resourceful fellow."

"That is an interesting way to describe him," Victoria said, throwing a smile my way. "He's smart, driven, and a great artificer. If he can control…"

"Control?"

"Quinn is a very special person, but like all of us, he has his secrets that I'm not at liberty to discuss. I'm sure he will tell you, but he's asked me not to divulge anything."

The Victoria I knew would have told me in a second. I wondered what her relationship with Quinn was, but that, too, was none of my business. If I had to guess, she fancied him, but would never admit it.

"Like ya said, we all have secrets." I took a swallow of my ale. "What is the plan now that we have Miranda's family?"

"Miranda lived up to her end of the bargain we made in Uwhela. I will escort her and her family to Terralon. Once I'm there, I'll bring Everard up to speed and fetch Quinn so we can meet up at Iron Harbor to prepare for war. What about you?"

Part of me screamed to hide from the coming battle and the resulting horrors, but I couldn't turn my back on the people on both sides of the fight who were being used to further Nimish's scheme. My morals and training wouldn't let me do anything less than fight to protect those who can't protect themselves.

"I'll get an airship to Iron Harbor and see if I can track down Firehelm. If I can kill him before the battle, we might be able to avert the whole mess."

"So we'll plan to meet up at Iron Harbor in two weeks?"

"Certainly."

"Thaclet towers to the east," a call came from above.

"Looks like our time is about up." I forced myself to my feet, the creaking of my bones reminding me how sore I was.

Victoria sprang up, gave me a quick hug, scratched Phantom's head, and was off like the wind.

Damn, I hated being old.

I parted ways with Victoria and the Maiden's Kiss's crew at the Thaclet landing platform and headed down the spiral staircase of the tower. Phantom, fully visible, stayed next to my leg to avoid people. His appearance in the middle of the city drew a lot of stares and gasps as we moved away from the tower. Crowds and invisibility didn't work well.

Thaclet teemed with merchants and traders, which slowed us down. I needed to hire an airship to get to Iron Harbor and then track down Firehelm before he did any more damage.

The pungent odor of spices filled my nose as I pushed through the crowds to find an inn for the night.

"Is that you?" a woman asked, tugging on my sleeve. "Watch—"

I spun and the words died in her mouth. A smile crept across my face as I recognized Ann Tolo, the first mate of the Lunatic's Revenge. She had the light hair of the Norns, but the olive skin of the Uwhelans. Bandoleers over her brown vest held two double-shot gunpowder pistols. "Just Brulle will do, Tolo."

She shook her head. "Of course, Brulle. We'd heard you were dead."

"You can't believe everything you hear. Are you still flying on the Revenge?"

"As sure as tar is sticky. Captain Stokes will be glad ta see ya."

I'd traveled all over the world with Captain Edina Stokes and knew her to be a powerful fighter and a woman of her word. Everard had introduced us, and we'd flown together more times than I wanted to count. It would be good to see her as well. "As it happens, I'm in need of an airship. Lead the way."

Tolo laughed. "Just like old times." She turned on her heel and headed off toward a new tower. There above us stood the Lunatic's Revenge. We climbed the three flights of stairs to the loading platform.

"I'll be right back," Tolo said with a smirk.

A few minutes later, the captain yelled over to me. "Brulle Cobb, you know I don't allow walking corpses on my ship."

"Captain, it is good to see you as well," I said, smiling at my old comrade. Edina was a striking woman with dark coppery skin and black hair that hung down her back. I noticed a fair number of gray hairs, reminding me it had been more years than I liked since I'd last seen her. A mechanized bird golem sat on her shoulder. It squawked and flapped its metal wings in my direction.

"Watcher Brulle," Captain Stokes said. "I heard you were dead. I thought Tolo had lost her mind when she said we were taking on a passenger."

"It's just Brulle now. Tolo is a fine first mate," I said, glancing up to the woman on the quarterdeck watching us. "I recently got back from Uwhela, and I need to hire you for a mission, Captain."

Captain Stokes' eyes glittered. "My ship is booked. Letting the merchant in Bradenbridge down would be bad for business. She's waiting for a very important delivery."

I sighed. "Edina, under other circumstances, I'd haggle with you all day, but I don't have time."

"I guess you'll need another ship then," she said, turning to leave.

I tossed a leather pouch on the deck at her feet. It made a satisfying noise of coins clinking. "All yours, if you agree. Another payment after I complete my mission."

I probably should have mentioned the mission bordered on suicidal at best. I needed the ship if I wanted to track down Firehelm, Nimish Nimkar, and the Followers of Alpha who had escaped from our attack on their Uwhelan stronghold. Miriam, the alchemist Victoria and I captured during the raid, said Nimkar, the leader of the cult, liked to hide at an old temple just inside the Candalarian border. It was a two-day ride from Iron Harbor, which made it a perfect command post for an attack on the city.

Captain Stokes grabbed the bag and poured out a handful of silver. A smile grew on her face. "I'd ask how long this mission will be, but this will cover me and the crew for six months. Looks like you got yourself a ship."

"Excellent. We need to head to Iron Harbor now." I wanted to examine the safehouse and find out what Cian had left behind. I hoped he'd been as careless as usual and left me clues about why he'd turned traitor or information on the upcoming war.

"Iron Harbor? Returning home after all these years?"

"Something like that. The Watchers pulled me back in for old time's sake," I said, hating that I couldn't tell her what we were headed into. If the news got out, it would cause a panic, and I didn't want that. "We've traveled and fought together. You know how things go."

She laughed. "With you here, I'm guessing fire and destruction are in our future. Kind of like the time we caught the rogue Magus in Nanon. The way he was throwing all that lightning around, he was more storm cloud than man."

"At least he wasn't as tough as the Leopard Prince of Imfozron. I thought we were dead for sure."

The captain reached down and scratched Phantom's ear. The big cat purred like a kitten. "It was all good. You found poor Phantom there in those pens. The prince made rogue magus we fought outside of Sunchome look like a child."

"Edina, I need you and your crew as backup," I said. I knew the captain could be reckless and dishonest in trade, but she'd never let me down in the past. "This one could be bad."

She shrugged. "They are all bad, but…" The captain dumped the silver back into the pouch and slid it into one of the bunch of pouches on her belt. "I'll have Tolo set you up in my cabin. We'll be airborne in two hours."

"My thanks, Captain," I said with a nod. "I'll be on the foredeck if you need me."

"Aye," she said and started yelling orders to get the crew going.

Phantom trotted alongside me as I walked to the foredeck. I found a spot and started cleaning Gertie. She'd not been used this much since I'd left the Watchers. I needed to get ammo and supplies from the safehouse in Iron Harbor, assuming the inn was still around. I had a couple of fall-back locations, but I preferred to return to the place I'd once considered home. I'd never understand selling out the Watchers. While I didn't always agree with Everard, every member of the team put their lives on the line to protect innocent people. Even Cian had before he'd thrown his lot in with the enemy.

Memories of my time with the Watchers flooded back while my hands worked to disassemble the chain gun. Watcher Gould had given me Gertie after my pistols had run out of slugs in the middle of a fight. Each piece had been hand-tooled to perfection. The stock had two alarium crystals to power the gun. It held twenty slugs, or the weapon could be loaded with a chain of slugs with a quick shift. I'd seen the newfangled gunpowder-loaded guns the Astarian merchants sold, but nothing was better than Gertie.

My hands kept going while I considered the mess Victoria and I had uncovered. Mind control drugs, cultists raising a goddess, and a fire mage from Tofragrad had made for an interesting trip.

I'd known Roland, the artificer from my time in the Watchers, but I had been long gone before he'd selected his replacement. Quinn sounded like a good addition to the Watchers, but Victoria was holding back on me. I'd been friends with her for years before I'd retired. She could tell all the jokes she wanted, but she didn't fool me. Victoria's mind was keen and her wits sharp as a spike. She always knew far more than she ever let on. As long as it didn't hinder the mission, she could keep her secrets.

A low growl from Phantom brought me back to the present. A short woman in her early thirties, with blond hair and a scar running from her temple to her chin, stood at the top of the foredeck's stairs.

"Can I help you?" I asked since she hadn't spoken.

"Watch—"

"Brulle," I corrected her. No sense stirring up the Watcher business; other than a handful of people, everyone else thought I was dead. "I left that organization years ago."

"Okay, Brulle." She rocked from one foot to the other. "Captain says you just came from Uwhela."

"I did." Phantom laid down by my feet and started to softly snore. Obviously, he wasn't worried about our new arrival.

"It's just that… well… My brother Reuben got into trouble and ended up with some strange people. Last I'd heard, he'd run off to Uwhela with the lot of them."

"Uwhela is a big country and a lot of jungle." Considering all the nameless cultists we'd killed, had this girl's brother been among them? It was doubtful, but I had no way of knowing.

She shook her head. "I just wanted to know what the place was like. Reuben was always a city lad. Hated being away from the hustle of the crowds. It seemed like an odd place for him to go, is all."

An image of a shaking rabbit came to me from Phantom. I stifled a laugh. The woman was nervous, to say the least. "Once you're done with your duties, come find me and I'll tell you the little I saw of Uwhela, though a city boy wouldn't be happy in the jungle, is my guess."

She turned to leave, but I stopped her. "You haven't told me your name yet."

"Isabella."

And then she was down the stairs and gone.

2

BRULLE

Good to her word, Isabella showed up right after her shift with two large bowls of food and two mugs. The spicy smell of stew reached my nose. Phantom's head lifted as the scents roused his sleeping stomach. The image of a raw slab of meat came to me through our bond. Good thing this was a short trip.

"Cook sent me with dinner for you both," Isabella said.

I reached up and took a mug and bowl from her. "Thank you."

She lifted a raw piece of meat from her bowl. "May I?"

Phantom pushed himself up. She had his full attention. "Easy, boy."

An image of a running deer came into my mind. Phantom understood far more than people would ever expect. Well, except Victoria, who the big cat had bonded to more than anyone else. Phantom had never liked Cian, so maybe I didn't give him enough credit for his insights, either.

"Hold it out and he'll take it," I said to Isabella.

She did and Phantom carefully grabbed the piece of meat and dropped down to gnaw on his dinner. I started eating my food at a speed usually reserved for growing boys.

In between bites, I answered her questions about Uwhela without divulging the details of our mission in the jungle. If she was worried about her missing brother, talking about killing people wasn't my best option. She took a moment to get me a second ale while we talked. She had a lot of questions and a curious mind. After a while, she fell quiet.

238

"Nothing else?" I asked with a low laugh. Honestly, I was enjoying my time talking with Isabella.

She sat on the deck across from me, pecking at her food, but kept glancing up at me.

I took a drink of ale. "I'm sensing there is something else you want to say?"

Her cheeks flushed. "There is, but you'll think it's stupid."

"Nonsense." I set the empty mug down. "Shoot."

She set her bowl down in the crook of her folded legs. "How do you get to be a Watcher?"

I stroked my beard, thinking back to my initiation into the watchers. Everard had found me hunting wolves around Bexley and brought me in. We were encouraged to keep an eye out for talented apprentices. The trials to be admitted were grueling and deadly to a lot of apprentices, but I'd survived—thrived, even. "Well, first off, you need to be Astarian."

"I was born in Worlf. My da was a miner and my ma worked for a butcher. I joined the Lunatic's Revenge's crew about three years ago."

"Being a watcher is dangerous. Why not stay on with the captain and enjoy your life?" I gestured around to the ship. "Plenty of adventure, new ports of call, everything a wanderer could want."

"It's a good life, but I want to protect people. Both my parents were killed in a Norn raid. After their deaths, I joined the captain in hunting them down, but they got away. If I'd been trained as a watcher, I could have protected the people I cared for."

I thought back to another wide-eyed kid who'd followed me around, begging for a chance to be a watcher after I'd freed him from the Candalarians. Cian had been a good kid, but also a lot of trouble. His anger had led to rash decisions and a lot of misery for both of us, but he'd passed the testing. Isabella's age made her a better choice if I wanted to take on an apprentice, but the fact I'd chosen Cian and he'd turned traitor left me wary and unwilling to choose another. Hell, I wasn't officially a watcher anymore, though I doubted Everard would turn down a trained replacement. Still, I didn't trust anyone at this point.

When I didn't answer, Isabella continued. "I'm good in a scrap, can gut anything you kill, and I'll learn anything you care to teach me."

I shook my head. "I can't take on an—"

"Is it because I'm a girl?"

"Nonsense. Some of the best watchers I know are women. Can I finish my sentence or are you going to argue yourself out of an opportunity?"

Her eyes got wide, but her mouth shut.

Over the years, most candidates fled after seeing what being a watcher was all about. If the long hours, travels, the endless months of training weren't bad enough, we didn't lie to potential Watchers about their chances in the testing. We lost as many who declined the honor as we did to the tests themselves. Isabella had to be tough and competent to survive on the Revenge for this long, and Captain Stokes was extremely picky about her crew. Maybe it was worth taking the chance. "Thank you. We'll call this mission your audition. You stick with me, listen, do what I tell you, and I'll consider you for an apprenticeship if you do a good enough job. Best I can do. If you are still interested, you can speak with Everard about the official testing process."

"Seriously?" she asked. Her tone went up about twelve octaves. "Thank you, Watcher—"

"No watcher, just Brulle. Before you go agreeing, you need to understand that this mission will be dangerous. I can't guarantee your safety or that you won't be killed. Think about it tonight and when we dock in Iron Harbor, be ready if you are going with me. No shame if you don't. Hell, I'd rather be on the captain's crew than take on what we'll be doing."

"I'll consider it. I hadn't considered that you would accept me."

Maybe there was hope for her. Cian never thought anything through, but neither had I when Watcher Hartness had trained me all those years ago. The man had been larger than life and the best hunter I'd ever met. He'd never taken to the alarium-powered weapons that most of us used now. Instead, he'd sported a bow I couldn't even draw and an iron-tipped club. I'd seen him take down a bear twice his size with just the club.

"Well then, I guess I'll bid you a good night," I said to her. As much as I hoped she would turn me down, I doubted it.

An image came into my mind of a goose turning on a spit.

"Really?" I asked Phantom.

I swear he laughed at me.

<hr>

Just after breakfast, the captain docked us at the Iron Harbor airfield. Twelve tall docking towers dotted the broad expanse, more than half with airships tied off at the tops. Isabella stood in front of the gangplank waiting for me to emerge from belowdecks with my gear.

"I understand that traveling with you will be dangerous, but I want to protect the people of Astaria."

I nodded to her but turned my attention to Captain Stokes. "Morning, Captain."

"Isabella told me she's headed off on an adventure with you," she said, her voice only mostly a snarl. "I can't say I like it, but she's a grown woman and I'll not be taking her choices away from her."

"I warned her it was dangerous, and she still wants to go," I said in what I hoped passed as a placating voice. Worry gnawed at my belly about bringing a raw recruit into the fray. Was I making a mistake? What if she died in the process? "If she fails to pass muster, I'll get her back to you."

"She won't fail." The captain turned to Isabella. "You've got a place here if you change yer mind."

Isabella tipped her chin to the captain. "Thank you. I'll do you proud."

"We'll wait for your return, Brulle."

"We won't be but a few hours. Let's go," I said to my new trainee.

Isabella settled her knives into a better position and hoisted her ruck-sack. She followed me as I crossed the gangplank and took the spiral stairs that ran around the outside of the tower The Lunatic's Revenge hovered beside. The ship cast off and was redirected to a long-term dock. My guess was the captain would let the crew take leave while they waited.

Smog clung to Iron Harbor's air like grease on water. The forges pumped out smoke faster than the wind could move it out to sea. Urchins and beggars ringed the airfield. Guards patrolled the perimeter to ensure no one bothered the flow of people and goods from the airships.

"Where's Phantom?" Isabella asked suddenly. "He was just here and now he's gone."

"Hush," I said, not wanting to be overheard. "You can't see him, but he's next to me."

"Oh," she said, a mixture of awe and skepticism in her tone. She jumped when Phantom became visible for an instant in front of her.

I stifled a chuckle, but the big cat enjoyed scaring people, me included. "We don't advertise his presence. Most innkeepers worry about having a large predator in their establishments."

"Are you talking about Phantom or yourself?"

Well, she did have a point.

3

VICTORIA

The Maiden's Kiss bumped against the mooring of the Presics airship docking tower. Miranda, her husband, and her daughter stood at the rail, a small pile of bags beside them. We'd been lucky to get them out of Uwhela before Firehelm had time to fulfill his promise of killing them. Once I had them settled, I'd continue on to meet up with Everard and Quinn.

"Lady Yorke," Captain Breachcolm said, descending the stairs to the main deck. "How long will we be here?"

Good question. I'd need time to get Miranda settled and inform Magus Caitlyn Drisyer about our newest alchemist and have her set her up with a small lab to get started. I handed Travis ten silvers. "Two days. Please allow the crew a night in town on me as a thank you for their assistance."

"It's not necessary, but they'll appreciate the thought. Do you need a porter for the alchemist's gear?"

The look on his face told me he still didn't approve of our passenger. "No, I think we can manage. We are going to a house Watcher Callahan has for emergencies. It should do well until she's set up with the magus."

"You shouldn't trust her. She could be lying about her situation," Travis grumbled. "I don't want to sound like a mother hen, but shouldn't you be armed? You don't know these people well."

It had been a long time since anyone had worried about me, and it hit me like a pistol slug. I cleared my throat to get rid of any emotion. "I appreciate the concern, but walking around with my duster and guns will draw attention that I don't want. I have my bag of tricks with me if anything goes wrong."

"Can you drop them off with the magus?"

"No. Miranda will be a great addition to Astarian medicine. Blue Heron showed a lot of promise before it was subverted."

Travis nodded. "Two days?"

"Two days." I turned and went to Miranda and her family. "The house is close, so if you can carry your belongings, we'll be off."

"I can handle it, ma'am," Miranda's husband Ezra said. He hoisted the two larger bags, leaving Miranda and Iris, their seven-year-old daughter, to carry the smaller bags. A stuffed teddy bear was under Iris's arm.

"And who do we have here?" I asked Iris. I love kids since they always laughed at my jokes.

"Master Emerson is his name. He goes everywhere with me," Iris said. Her smile lit up the whole area.

I returned her smile. "I'm sure he is a fierce and loyal protector."

She nodded solemnly. "Oh, yes. When I go to sleep, he stays with me to keep the monsters away. Uncle—"

"Lady Yorke doesn't need a history lesson, poppet," Miranda said, interrupting the child. "Her uncle Phineas gave her the bear when she was small."

"Mama."

"Iris, hush," Ezra said not unkindly. "Lady Yorke is helping us, and we are grateful. Once we are settled, you can tell her more."

"Promise?" Iris's eyes grew to the size of dinner plates, waiting for my answer.

"Of course," I said, tapping her gently on the cheek. "I can't wait to hear all about him and your adventures."

Iris beamed with excitement. At least she would be happy for a bit. "If you'll follow me, I'll take you to the house you'll be staying at. Tomorrow, I'll introduce you to Magus Drisyer and we can get a proper home and lab set up for you."

"Thank you, Lady Yorke." Miranda had begun this as our enemy, the manufacturer of the Blue Heron that had enslaved animals and people to do the cult's bidding, but freeing her and her family, who had been held hostage, had quite possibly earned the Watchers her loyalty. "My family would be dead if not for you."

"You can thank me by helping us reverse the Blue Heron effects. Let's be off."

I strode across the gangplank onto the tower proper. Once I was sure Miranda and her family climbed on the lift, we were lowered like so much cargo down to the ground level.

Presics was a medium-sized city that traded in seafood, lumber, and more recently, iron ore. The capitol of the Drisyer region had grown from the influx of people moving in to exploit the mountain mines that had sprung up to fulfill the flourishing steel industry in Iron Harbor.

The city itself reminded me of Terralon with the stone buildings and ornately detailed columns that decorated the more prosperous structures. Everything was a wash of grays and browns. I followed the boulevard leading to the center of town.

"How far is it?" Iris asked with a touch of whine in her voice.

"We are almost there." We reached the butcher shop and turned to the right. A few short blocks later, we arrived at the safehouse. A cobblestone path led to a squat stone building with a heavy wooden door. Empty window boxes sat beneath filthy windows. The place had seen better days.

I moved the small planter on the side of the house and retrieved an old pipe key. The door swung open, revealing a small living area with a cast-iron stove for cooking and a couple of wooden cabinets with a wash basin. A battered table and chairs sat on a worn rag rug. Two doors decorated the back wall. Each led to a small bedroom.

"This is lovely," Miranda said, stepping into the house. "It will be perfect while we are getting settled."

"I think lovely is a vast overstatement," I said.

Ezra laughed. "Either way, we appreciate your help, Lady Yorke. Compared to our last…accommodations, this is a palace."

"Yes, indeed," Miranda said, reaching out to take Iris's hand. "Let me get Poppet settled in her room."

"Good idea," I said. "Ezra, would you mind accompanying me to the market so we can get some food for the next few days?"

Ezra hesitated before Miranda chimed in. "Perfect, that will give me time to unpack. Please see if there is a couple of sweet treats for Iris. She's been through a lot the past few days."

"I will." Ezra sketched a slight bow. "After you, Lady Yorke."

"Why, thank you." I exited the house and took the cobblestone path to the street. "We'll stop at the butcher on the way back so we don't have to carry meat around with us."

"Excellent," Ezra said. He sped up to walk next to me. "May I ask why you saved Miranda?"

I quirked an eyebrow at him. "Honestly, I wasn't sure for a bit, but when I found out she was an unwilling accomplice, I couldn't do anything but save her. The world is cruel enough without me adding to it."

"I, for one, greatly appreciate you saving Miranda. Our captors didn't explain what was going on. I hadn't realized a cult had dragged her into service, I only knew we were all in danger. Frankly, I wondered if I'd ever see her again."

"Seeing your family back together is thanks enough."

For the next hour, we picked up an assortment of fruits and vegetables, plus a treat for Iris. We purchased a piece of beef for dinner that night. I'd leave some coins so they could purchase daily instead of relying on salted meat.

We returned to the house, and I opened the door for Ezra. Miranda's voice came from the back bedroom. "I'll be out in a moment."

"We'll put the supplies away," Ezra called back to her.

We busied ourselves with putting the food away and I took inventory of cooking gear. While not in the best shape, it would hold them over for a bit while I made arrangements for a more suitable home for them.

"Lady Yorke, what is that building over there?" Ezra asked from the kitchen where we looked through the dirty window.

I joined him. The top of a tall spire could be seen over the houses behind us. "If I'm not mistaken, it is a watchtower from when Presics was smaller."

Iris pulled away from Miranda, and the patter of running feet came up behind us. The child bounced with excitement. Miranda stepped next to me, a smile on her face. A flood of warmth spread through me. I'd made this reunion happen and was so glad I did.

"Papa, Mama says we are going to go see Uncle Firehelm," Iris blurted out.

Firehelm?

Uncle Firehelm?

I pivoted too late to stop Miranda from plunging the syringe into my upper arm. Cold spread through me as the Blue Heron surged through my system. I batted her arm away, but it was too late.

"Stop!" Miranda said before I could strike her down.

My arms lowered to my side. Internally I screamed and fought, but the drug spread over my thoughts like a wet blanket.

"Very good, darling," Ezra said. "Ah, her eyes are tinged blue. She's under control of the drug. Firehelm will be pleased. Does she still have the artifact?"

Miranda pulled the strap of my bag over my head and emptied it on the table item by item. When she extracted the wand wrapped in cloth, a smile lit her face. "We've got it. Nothing can stop us now."

Ezra stepped in front of me. "We need to keep her drugged and you need to stay near. She's bonded by you now. Time to go to sleep, Lady Yorke. We'll make arrangements to deliver you to Firehelm."

"Go to the bedroom and go to sleep," Miranda said, and my body complied.

I should have listened to Brulle and Travis. I'd walked right into the trap Miranda had set for me. All her stories were lies, and now I'd pay the price for trusting her.

I reached the bed and lay down. My eyes grew heavy as I fought not to sleep.

I knew I needed a nap, but until now I didn't realize how much.

4

BRULLE

couple of hours later, Isabella and Phantom were safely tucked into an upstairs room at the Black Diamond Inn. I left Gertie with them, settling for a couple of boot knives and two metal-tipped batons under my leather duster. Guns and crowded cities weren't a great match. Now I could go check the safehouse and hopefully find some sort of clue as to what had transformed Cian. His betrayal stung. I'd been gone for enough years that it shouldn't have, but it did.

The filth, stench, and noise of the city assaulted my senses. I'd forgotten what Iron Harbor was like in the years I'd lived alone in the wilds. Rivulets of grime left stains down the stone walls of the buildings, giving the impression they were alive. Scents from cooking food, sweat, and rotting garbage mixed with the sulfur of the forges and smelters that sat north of the city. I almost wished I had my mask on, but then everyone would know I was a watcher.

I followed streets I'd once known like the back of my hand. I stopped in Hicks' bakery and got a pastry from the owner Dino. We both sported long white beards now, so he didn't recognize me, but the treat was as amazing as I remembered.

Both men and women wore faded breaches and shirts of industrial workers. A few middle-class ladies passed by in ankle-length dresses accompanied by men with their stiff overcoats over linen shirts. Children in rags and no shoes sat in the mouths of alleyways or panhandled anyone walking by. I shooed them off, not wanting to draw attention to myself by being generous.

After all these years, I'd decided to get back into the watcher's business, much to my surprise. My hands reflected the passage of years as did my gray beard. If I were honest, the chance for one last adventure was too good to pass up. I passed Mayo's Clothing Emporium and the Nettle's Glass Rose. Once, I'd known all of these folks, but now I was a stranger in my own town.

I wove through the streets and alleys, making sure I wasn't followed. Most of the world thought me dead, but given my long history as a watcher, I didn't want to take any chances. I twisted and turned like a snake with a belly ache, but it didn't work. Three toughs followed at a distance, but they never deviated from my path. Time to lose them.

I took a sharp turn into an alley and then took another left and waited. The alley smelled more like a rotten animal than anything. Puddles of waste dotted the broken cobblestone path that ran between the buildings. If I remembered correctly, this led to one of the main roads to the dock. If I was wrong, I had just walked into a dead end. The alley cornered hard to the right. I pulled both batons from my belt and waited for whoever followed me.

Nothing.

Seconds passed and still nothing.

A few moments later, a splash sounded from behind me. I froze, not wanting to give away my position. Seconds crept by and the echoes of the hurried trot of my pursuer reached me. A shadow crossed in front of me. I grabbed them, throwing them against the wall and lifting a baton to strike.

"What? A girl's looking for a bit of coin and you've got to rough her up?"

I lowered the weapon and stepped back. The woman wore a tattered smock over a stained blouse and britches. Her long, dark hair had been pulled up. She couldn't be twenty if she was a day. "Why were you following me?"

"Well, I was standin' on Loomis Street, and I saw you headed back here. Thought I'd see whatca were lookin' fer and make a bit of coin," she said with a wink.

I stepped away from her. "You might ought to think harder before you follow a stranger down an alley."

"I had that thought myself," a new voice said from off to my left. Three men, if you could call them that, stood to my left, blocking the alley. Each wore torn-up pants and shirts, with the leader adding a faded and torn vest to the ensemble. The boy on the right had a severely crooked nose and tapped a club in his hand. The one on the left had a shaved head with a couple of scars running over his cheeks. He held a length of pipe. The leader's dagger was rust-pitted, but it looked sharp enough.

I moved so that I could see the four of them. No sense leaving the girl at my back. She hadn't shown a weapon, but her smock could hide a lot. "I'm not looking for trouble with any of you. Let me pass."

The leader laughed. "Hear that, Bess?" he said to the woman. "You go to all that work to find us a rich pigeon and he wants us to 'let him pass.'" The last bit was delivered in a mocking approximation of my voice.

I spun the batons in my hands, loosening my wrists. "I'll try not to kill you lads, but…"

Bess' eyes grew wide. "Titus, maybe we should do as the man says."

"Jahn, Vin, you hearin' this?" Titus said with a barking laugh. "Bess wants us to let the old man go. I think she forgets who runs this gang."

"We can take an old man," the pipe wielder said in his thick accent.

"Vin, you're right. Old man, you should hand over your pouch before ya get hurt," Titus said with a sneer.

"Bess, you should probably leave," I said to her. She started edging away as I spoke. "I don't want to hurt you."

She ran back down the alley as I squared up on the boys.

"Bess!" Titus screamed after her. "Come back here!"

I brought the batons to a ready position, just like Watcher Hartness had taught me all those years ago. "You should follow her lead."

"Screw you, old man," Titus said. Clearly, anger fueled his poor decision making. "Get him."

Jahn and Vin moved toward my sides, but the narrow alleyway didn't leave them enough room to flank me. Vin came in high with the metal pipe swinging for my head. I caught the bar on my baton, stopping the stroke, and jammed my second baton in his belly. The air whooshed out of his lungs and he went down.

Before Jahn got his club over his head, I kicked out and took him square in the knee. He screamed at the force of the blow. The club clattered to the ground. Neither wound would kill, but an injury in this city made you a target for everyone looking to score some coin.

Titus's knife cut my wrist, shooting pain through my right hand. My blood-spattered baton tumbled to the cobblestones.

Titus drove the knife toward my gut. My left baton clipped the blade, knocking it aside. Titus swore, but he dodged to my right and stabbed. The tip scored on the arm of my duster, preventing the worst of the damage. The warm trickle of blood told me it hadn't completely stopped the knife.

I responded with a back-handed blow that should have broken his arm, but the boy danced out of reach.

"Not so tough now, are you, old man?"

I grunted. My hand throbbed from the first slice. "Tough enough to deal with a street rat like you."

Titus snarled and lunged.

First mistake of fighting. Never let your emotions take over. The baton came down across his outstretched arm, and I heard a snap from the bones. The knife flew from the boy's broken grip. He screamed, clutching the arm to his chest. Tears ran down his face.

Footsteps caught my attention. Vin was back on his feet, but his eyes were wide with fear. "You said this would be easy, Titus. I'm not dying for a couple of coins." Vin ran the same way Bess had.

Jahn still lay on the ground, holding his knee. I doubted I'd busted it, but he'd be a while healing. I turned back to Titus. "Get yourself over to old Doc Kennedy and he'll set that arm."

"Doc Kennedy left years ago," Titus said through gritted teeth. "Go pound salt."

I tied off the wounds on my right arm, retrieved my baton, and left the two boys there. If luck was on their side, they'd get to a safe place and heal up. If not, the predators of the city would get them like they'd tried to get me.

First day back and it was like I never left.

5

BRULLE

Half an hour later, I reached Sover's Tavern. Alex and Sarah Sover had taken over the inn a year or so before I'd retired. Great beer, but more importantly, it contained one of my safehouses. I slid between the inn and the stable, which led to the root cellar in the back.

The area behind the inn butted up to the back wall of a warehouse. Merchants and traders stored their goods in it while they waited for ships to load up the supplies. The sounds of the harbor were ever-present, which made stealth unnecessary. Plus, the place was empty.

Stone stairs ran along the back side of the building to the solid wood basement door. I crouched down and found the loose rock and retrieved the key. Unfortunately, after I slid it into the lock, it didn't budge.

"You are either the world's worst thief or you are Master Brulle," a strong female voice said from the top of the stairs. She had long black hair. She also had a loaded crossbow pointed at my head.

I raised my hands. "Good to see you, Sarah."

She laughed, unloaded the crossbow, and held out her arms in greeting. Tears raced down her cheeks as she waited.

I climbed the stairs and hugged her. She laughed harder. "Your beard tickles."

She pushed me to arm's length. "It looks good on you, especially for a dead man."

251

"About that—"

"No worries. Cian filled us in on the whole watcher's safehouse and all. We just thought you liked our beer."

I groaned inwardly. Leave it to big-mouthed Cian to tell the Sovers about our hidden safehouse. I have no idea how he survived as a watcher. What people didn't know, they couldn't reveal. "I had to 'die' to get away from the watchers. I didn't get to tell anyone goodbye."

"I'm just glad you are alive. We haven't seen Cian in a few months. Is he okay?"

I nodded. Guilt poured over me like an upended bucket of icy water as I lied to my friends. "He's on a mission. He could be gone a long time."

"Well, the bar isn't going to clean itself." She tossed me a brass key. "Cian changed the lock on the door, but you can use ours. Stop in for a beer when you're done. I can't wait to see Alex's face."

"I will."

She gave me another hug, grabbed the crossbow, and was gone.

Another person I'd worried by being a watcher. I hadn't considered all the people I'd left behind when I retired. I pushed my melancholy thoughts away and got back to business.

With the new key, the door swung open without a sound. I followed a path through kegs of fermenting beer to the back. A rack of supplies covered the entrance to the safehouse. I pulled on the shelves, and they moved to the side.

I found the alarium lamp sitting next to the door and turned it on. The room looked like I remembered it… mostly. A large case of cabinets stood across from the entry. Cian had left his gear, papers, and dirty mugs laying over the table and the chairs that took up the center of the room. The cot in the far corner hadn't been made, and from the looks of things, the bedding needed a good washing. I wondered if he had been living down here, which would explain the Sovers' familiarity.

I cleared a space for the lamp on the table and opened the top cabinet. Disarray could be used to describe the mess that I found. Every weapon, device, and supply had an appropriate place, and none of them were in the correct location. I dug around in the lower cabinets until I found a first aid kit. All my safehouses had them, for just such emergencies.

After cleaning and bandaging my arm, I stitched up the cut in my duster. I had a couple of hours before dark, so I set to righting the arsenal cabinets. I found an old satchel, which I loaded with two chains of ammo, plus a basket of single shot. With the upcoming war, I'd need all the supplies I could get my hands on. I had five safehouses in Iron Harbor. Each should have the same gear, though after Hurricane Cian, I wasn't sure.

I took each weapon out of the cabinet, verified it still worked, then put each back in its proper place. I found two of Roland's explosive devices, which I added to the satchel. I switched out my boot knives for better quality ones, still razor sharp after all these years. Cian had left two alarium pistols here, backups to the ones he normally wore. I put them and the holsters in the satchel. Once the reorganization of the cabinet was done, I started on the contents of the table.

First off, I needed to get rid of the mugs. I stepped into the cellar and found a couple of wooden boxes. One I filled with the mugs to return to the tavern. The other I filled with trash. More weapons and supplies went back into the cabinet. I threw clothes onto the bed. Given the situation, I doubted Cian was returning for any of this.

I collected up all the papers and laid them out on the now cleared table. I sat and read through each before either placing it in the trash or keeping it to share with Victoria and Quinn when they arrived. Nothing earth-shattering, but it might be useful.

A piece of paper held a communication from Everard. It said:

Watcher Cian,

You are to meet Watcher Quinn in Murkwood. Someone or something is attacking the inns of the villages in the area. Candalarians are the most likely culprits, but I want you to work with Quinn and teach him what you can.

Everard

One page was covered with runic symbols. A few had notes as to what they meant, but most were just the drawing and the name. They didn't mean anything to me, but it seemed important. Crude sketches of different devices I set in the keep pile as well. Bad poetry about a woman named Chloe went in the trash, along with attempted portraits of various people. I tossed a handful into the box, but one page floated out, landing on the floor.

I stooped to retrieve it. This one actually looked like a person. A striking woman with short hair and a jagged scar down her jaw line. "Nimish" was scrawled under the picture. Huh. This seemed to be the cult leader, meaning somewhere at some time Cian had met her or seen a portrait of her. I pulled the rest of the drawings out and went through them again, but this was the only useful one.

After shoving the papers in the satchel with the ammo, I grudgingly tackled the bed. I don't know why Cian leaving the safehouse like this bothered me so much, but it did. Bad enough that he betrayed the watchers, but he also trashed the things I'd left behind for him. Maybe I never really knew Cian at all.

I gathered the clothes, emptied the pockets of loose coins, and threw them in a pile. Cian's old leather duster got set aside to give to Isabella. I'd figure out what to do with the rest of the clothes later. The bedding stank of sweat and old beer. Everything came off the stuffed mattress and topped off the pile of clothes. I slid the bed away from the wall so I could free a shirt that was pinched behind the frame, only to discover a strongbox underneath.

Odd.

I picked up the box and took it to the table. It wasn't locked, but it could be trapped. Wrapping an old shirt around my knife hand, I pushed the blade into the lock. Nothing happened. I kept the knife inserted and opened the lid slowly.

Click!

A metal needle ejected from the lock, embedding itself into the fabric protecting my hand. Cian didn't want anyone looking in this box. I carefully removed the needle and stabbed it into the tabletop, where a black ring spread out from the tip. Poison.

I moved to the far end of the table with the box. Inside it was a handwritten note to kill Quinn if he could. The map showed the farmhouse Victoria had told me about where she and Quinn had faced off against Cian. A couple of runed pieces of metal went into my bag, along with a small knife. At the bottom of the box sat the real prize. A sketched-out map with directions to what I assumed was a cultist camp. The date at the bottom was in three days.

And just like that, I knew where I had to go.

QUINN

I knocked on the carved runic door to Everard's office. Worry flooded me since Everard had said he was dying. The old man was still alive but for how much longer? Hopefully, the device I'd forged would help.

The runes surrounding the door glowed softly. I'd seen enough magic to know these were protection glyphs. The Arch Magus's magic didn't use runes, but I was pretty sure he found a way.

"Come in," Everard said, though it was weak enough to be barely audible.

I pushed open the door and stopped dead in my tracks. Everard sat behind his desk, but he didn't look much like himself. The powerful Arch Magus had been replaced by a hunched old man.

"Arch Magus," I said, trying to hide my shock. "You requested to see me?"

He chuckled then coughed for a moment. He cleared his throat and took a drink from a goblet in front of him. His hands shook as he set it down. "Quinn, thank you for coming. Take a seat."

I did as he suggested, removing the pouch from my belt so I could get into it easier. "What can I do for you?"

"Making me young again would be nice, but I think that is beyond either of us. After a couple of hundred years, you'll feel the same I expect. Your magic will keep you young for a long time, but not forever."

"Maybe, but I did bring you something that may help."

The old man quirked an eyebrow at that. "Really? Exactly what did you bring?"

I opened the pouch and removed a brass medallion with a worked leather strap. It had taken a couple of days to get the piece forged. The magic tingled in my left hand. "This might help."

"What does it do?"

I bounced the piece in my palm. "If I crafted it right, it should restore your health enough to get you moving again. I don't think it will stop your decline, but it should buy us more time."

"Well, don't just sit there, put it on me."

I stood, hoping against hope that this would work. This piece was far more complex than the levitator or any of the simple things I'd forged since I'd gotten my magic. I undid the clasp that held the leather straps together. The runes I'd taken from the Candalarian wind walkers' control box glowed slightly in the darkened room. I settled the metal against Everard's chest and set the clasp.

Everard pulled the medallion away so he could examine it. "Nice rune work. I can feel the magic pulsing inside it. I don't feel any different, though."

"I keyed it to a word, so it would only work for you."

"What's the word?"

"Roland."

"That's it?" Everard asked.

"It is."

"Roland." Everard's eyes widened as the medallion's glow intensified. He gasped when the glow flowed up his arms and into him fully. The ashen color fled from his face as the spell took hold. His back straightened slightly.

"This is wonderful," Everard said in awe.

An invisible flow of energy pulsed from me into the amulet. I stumbled back to the chair. The activation of the medallion had drained me, and I thought I might pass out. Creating massive amounts of magic exhausted me like nothing else. I'd thought once I forged the piece, I was done, but a surge of magic had deserted me to "heal" Everard.

"Using magic definitely is tiring," Everard said lightly.

I settled into the chair and took a couple of deep breaths. My head stopped spinning, but the weariness remained. I'd have to get some sleep before I did anything else. "Do you ever get used to it?"

Everard shrugged. "You will build up your tolerance the more you use it. I passed out after destroying the Norns at Cheim. Everything comes with a price."

The sparkle in Everard's eyes intensified. The effects would fade eventually, but hopefully, I'd bought him enough time to help with the upcoming fight. I could recharge the medallion to continue to keep him going, but all magic had a cost.

According to the staff, messengers had been coming to Everard from all over Astaria. He had an avalanche of papers covering his desk. "It looks like you've been busy."

Everard nodded. "Usorin is governing the country, but they insist on bringing every report to me."

"Usorin should be dead," I said, more hotly than was proper. The man had cut off my arm. "He's a coward."

"Usorin has changed, and he did release you so you could stop Ovro from taking my magic. You can always accept the Arch Magus position and rule after me. A few hundred years of settling magus squabbles and stopping attacks will change your mind about being Arch Magus, I'm sure.

I shuddered. The idea of forcing people to obey a government run by false maguses turned my stomach, not to mention the current system of authoritarian rule by one man made it even worse. "No, we should just remove the magus from power and install a new government. Let the people rule themselves."

"How long do you think it would take for those people to realize the amount of gold that alarium would bring?"

It always came back to alarium. My magic came from it as well as the rigs the maguses used to appear to control magic. It kept the other nations at bay, but at what cost?

Everard continued. "What would stop the other nations from invading once the reserves were gone and there wasn't any alarium to fuel your magic?"

Damn it. He made a good point. "Laws could be enacted—"

Everard laughed. "Quinn, laws are temporary at best. By trusting a very small number of people with the knowledge of alarium, we've kept Astaria safe."

"Safe for who? Ovro killed Roland and almost killed you and Usorin," I said.

"Speaking of Walden Ovro," Everard said, sorting through the piles of paper. He found one and held it out to me. "You might be interested in this."

I read the page and my jaw dropped. "Ovro was spotted in Terralon? Why hasn't he been arrested for Roland's murder?"

"Not for lack of trying," Everard said with a long sigh. "He's dangerous and is playing the long game to overthrow Astaria and become its dictator. The watchers are the only ones who can stop him."

"Who, though? I tried and he got away," I said. While I was being granted my magic by Lady Maelyrra during the fight over Everard's magic, Ovro escaped. I'd thought he'd left the country since I hadn't found any traces of him after the incident. "Any other news I need to know?"

Everard's face darkened. "Cian is awake."

7

BRULLE

Isabella's raised voice reached me as I entered the hall at the top of the Black Diamond Inn's stairs. I raced down the hall, yanking out a baton, which made the wounds on my hand flare, but I needed to protect her. I threw the door wide open and stopped.

"Give it back, you beast," Isabella shouted from where she stood on her bed.

Phantom lay across Isabella's sack, a self-satisfied smirk on his catty muzzle. The image of wrestling with cubs entered my mind with what I'd grown to recognize as the big cat's laugh.

"He's playing with you," I said, closing the door behind me. "He thinks it's funny."

"Well, it's not," she said with a huff. "It's not like I can take it from him."

I scratched Phantom between the ears, and he lifted his paws off the bag. The big cat rolled over to let me give him a tummy rub. Isabella jumped off the bed and grabbed her sack.

"In the morning, we are going to ride south to see if we can spot a camp," I said, not taking my attention off the very happy Phantom. "It will be dangerous."

"From the looks of the blood soaking the bandage on your wrist, Iron Harbor is dangerous."

She had a point. If I was going to let Isabella in, I had to trust her even though I'd been on high alert since finding out Cian had converted to the cult. "A group of street toughs decided they could take me in a fight. Didn't work out so well for them."

Isabella crossed her legs while sitting on her bed. "I'm in, but it would be better if I knew what we were doing."

Cian was the traitor, not Isabella. She'd been on the Lunatic's Revenge long enough that I doubted she was a cultist. It wasn't fair to ask her to risk her life when she didn't know why. If she lived through the upcoming events, she'd have earned the right to be a watcher. Everard could decide after if she needed to prove herself through the testing and training.

"Sit back. It's a long story." I started off with Quinn and Cian and the rogue bear, went through Victoria's journey, and what happened in Uwhela. Isabella peppered me with questions, but they were good ones and showed she had thought it through.

"So let me get this straight," she asked once I finished. "We are going to scout out a camp that could be filled with crazed cultists bent on resurrecting a goddess and possibly animals programmed to kill?"

"Sums it up." I looked her dead in the eye. "A smart person would run back to the Lunatic's Revenge and get as far from here as possible."

She shook her head. "Astaria is my home. If I can help stop these people, it's worth the risk."

I pulled out the satchel and retrieved the two pistols I'd taken from the armory. "Here."

"I don't know how to use a gun."

"I'll teach you." I helped her settle the holsters under her arms and showed her how to pull the weapons. "We can practice while we ride."

"Good," I said. "I'm going to change these bandages and go to bed. We leave at dawn."

Dawn came and went. I'd not taken into account how much Isabella didn't have for a trip into the wilds. Plus my poor battered body didn't heal as fast as it once had. By the time I got her a horse and tack, food, weapons, and supplies, it was lunchtime. We spent the afternoon riding south from Iron Harbor, keeping the ocean in sight. If the map was correct, the camp should be a two-day ride along the coast before turning inland toward the Donnastall Forest.

As we rode, Isabella practiced with the pistols. She turned out to be a fair shot but needed a lot of practice before she'd be up to my standards. Hopefully, she had plenty of time to learn, though I wondered if that was true.

Night closed in on us, forcing us to stop. I found a gully near a small stream to camp. At least it was a warm night and clear. The moon hung low in the sky as we ate a meal of stew. I kept the fire small enough to not attract attention, but large enough to cook on. I'd hate to start eating jerky this early in the mission.

Isabella proved to be a good companion. She knew her way around the campfire, chopping vegetables and meat for the stew pot and tossing the extras to Phantom, who gladly made short work of them. We swapped stories over the flames as we ate our stew.

"I'll take first watch," I told her as she laid out her bedroll. "I'll wake you up to switch."

"Can I take first?" she asked. "I'm better off up late than to bed early."

"Sure." I pulled the blankets over me and got as comfortable as possible given we were sleeping on the ground.

Phantom stretched out next to me.

"Keep an eye on her," I whispered to my companion. He pushed himself up and went over to sprawl next to Isabella. After a moment of uncertainty, she put her hand on his head. Phantom purred like a kitten.

"Can he really talk to you?"

"In his own way. I see images when he wants to tell me something. He can let me see through his eyes if it is really important."

"Will he talk to me?" Isabella kept scratching at the fur between Phantom's ears.

"Maybe," I said, thinking about how Victoria had bonded with Phantom. "Before I would have said no, but he's taken a liking to Victoria and could with you as well."

She smiled.

I rolled over to go to sleep.

"**B**rulle, wake up," Isabella whispered in my ear. The urgency in her voice snapped me awake in an instant.

"What is it?"

"Voices, over there." She pointed to the west of us. "Phantom went invisible, and I don't know where he is."

I grabbed Gertie and threw my satchel strap over my head. After a moment of concentration, the scene through Phantom's eyes grew clear—a group of armed horsemen fifty feet in front of the big cat. Phantom lay in the tall grass hidden from their view.

A ball of flame hovered over one of the rider's outstretched hands. "They are here somewhere. Find them."

The horsemen dismounted to start their search. Each drove a stake into the ground to tie off their horses.

"Tofragradians," I said, keeping my voice low. "They are looking for us."

Her eyes grew wide. "Do we run?"

Given the fire mage's abilities, I doubted we could lose them. They had tracked us to here without any warning. "No, they'll hunt us until they find where we are. They have a fire mage with them. We need to remove them as a threat."

She nodded, though sweat beaded on her upper lip.

"Follow me and stay low," I said, hoping she was up for a fight. Through my bond with Phantom, I knew they were close by.

Isabella readied the pistols I'd given her. She nodded.

We crawled to the top of the hill we'd been camped behind and I spotted the ball of flame in the distance. The good news was the Tofragradians would be night blind with the fire illuminating the surrounding area. The bad news is they had a lot of power and didn't care who got hurt.

We crawled until we were just outside the circle of light.

"They have to be close by. Nimish said they were seen traveling this way."

I tapped Isabella on the shoulder and pointed to the right. "Move twenty feet or so over so we aren't a single target."

After she complied, Phantom stalked up beside me, invisible. I felt him brush against me. I wanted to charge in, but I was hoping for more intel before we dropped them.

"Flameguard, we found their camp, but they are gone," one of the men said from the edge of the circle. He was within a few feet of Isabella. A second later, I heard her voice as she fought off whoever had caught her.

"Let me go, you bastards. I'm the first mate on the Lunatic's Revenge and have nothing to do with you."

A large man pushed Isabella into the light. He grabbed her arm and put a knife to her throat. "Should I kill her?"

Flameguard waved the man off and climbed down from her horse. She wore a metal helmet and banded armor. "You were seen leaving Iron Harbor with one of the watchers."

"You are wrong," she said hotly. "I'm traveling to Thaclet to take on as Captain of the Harbor's Crone."

"Enough," Flameguard said and slapped Isabella across the face. "I know you are there, Astarian. Drop your weapon or we'll kill the girl."

This was not how an apprenticeship should start.

8

BRULLE

I stood and dropped Gertie to the ground. My satchel still hung by my side, and hopefully, they wouldn't notice it. I held up my hands and whispered, "Phantom down."

"Ah, Firehelm will be happy to have you," Flameguard said with a huge grin on her face. "I will sit at the left hand of Ghuasis as her disciple."

I wasn't sure what these cultists were drinking, but they were all crazy. I needed a distraction to get Isabella away from the knife before I could take care of Flameguard and her crew. "Look, I am just taking the captain to her new ship. I was a watcher but haven't been for years. I'm just doing some guard work for coin."

"Nonsense," Flameguard said with a sneer. "Our spies have been watching you. We know you assisted Lady Yorke in destroying the Blue Heron factory. You will make a fine sacrifice to the goddess."

"Horse."

Flameguard's face twisted into a full-blown scowl. "Horse? What does that mean?"

She made a mistake in thinking I spoke to her instead of Phantom. The big cat slid around the perimeter and came up behind the mage's mount. The animal bucked at the scent of the predator that was suddenly next to it.

That was when the fun started.

The horse reared and kicked Flameguard in the chest, knocking her forward and causing the magical fire to go out. A loud crunch sounded from where Isabella stood. I grabbed Gertie and knelt to get a better aim.

Flameguard's magical light reappeared, showing me the scene. Isabella had broken free of her captor, who had blood running down his face and a broken nose. She held the cultist off with a knife. Three other guards fought to gain control of the panicked horses.

"Kill them both," Flameguard said. She pulled back her arm and lobbed a ball of fire at me.

I rolled forward to avoid the flames, came up to one knee again, and fired a single shot. The bullet hit the cultist sparring with Isabella in the shoulder and knocked him to the ground.

Isabella didn't waste any time. She pivoted like a dancer and threw the knife overhand, striking Flameguard in the chest. The throw was perfect. So was the armor the knife hit. It bounced off and tumbled to the ground.

"Infidel, you dare strike me," Flameguard bellowed, running behind the others who were still trying to control the horses.

Phantom flickered between the animals, further stirring up the chaos. With all the moving bodies, I couldn't get a clean shot at Flameguard.

Flameguard scattered fireballs like a toddler having a temper tantrum. "Protect me!" she screamed, fear thick in her voice.

Two of the cultists released the animals and turned to face me. Unfortunately for them, they forgot about Isabella. She fired a pistol at the closest. It hit him in the leg with a spray of blood. The man screamed and dropped to the ground.

The second man took one look and whirled away. Gertie shot him down quick. He crumpled like a rag doll to the ground. The horses bolted, exposing a very startled cultist and a crazed fire mage. I shot the cultist before he could run. We were too close to the cultists to let any of them return to their camp. Watchers deal death like an alchemist dispenses potions.

"Ghuasis, protect me," the fire mage called. The surrounding ground bubbled with fire like a volcano. Heat and the smell of sulfur built as the spell came to life.

"Isabella, Phantom, to me," I called. I snapped off a couple of shots at Flameguard, but the heat between us melted the shots midflight.

"Stay close and if I say run, run."

In front of the mage, a clawed foot appeared from the boiling flames. A second followed shortly before the lizard's head broke the surface. Its long, split tongue tasted the air as its black scales gleamed with trails of fire.

"What in the name of Nitasis is that thing?" Isabella's voice was soft but didn't have the notes of fear I'd expected. If we survived this, she might just make it as a watcher.

"Fire lizard of some sort," I said, a little concerned about the size of the monster emerging from the broken ground. "Don't fight it in the flames. We've got to get it out of the flames."

Isabella stared at me with a disbelieving look on her face. "You know how to fight these things?"

"Hang around with Everard long enough and you see a lot of crazy stuff."

"Kill them," Flameguard called from the middle of the lava-filled crater. She balanced in a three-foot circle of earth with a firestorm swirling around her. Her hands danced over her head as if she were controlling the lizard like a puppet.

The lizard pulled free and leapt out of the flames. It landed on the injured cultist, who screamed as the giant beast's jaw clamped down on the man. In another horrifying second, the monster had eaten its prey.

"Not him, them," Flameguard screamed.

The lizard's head snapped around and locked its gaze on us. I raised Gertie and fired three shots into its head. The scales cracked where the bullets struck, but if the lizard noticed, I doubted it.

The beast shook its head from side to side, throwing fiery spittle across the ground. It lifted its head and growled, baring its jagged teeth in the process.

I sighted Gertie and pulled the trigger. The bullet was true and hit the beast in the eye. It reared back in pain. So it could be hurt.

"Attack," Flameguard commanded. The fire around her intensified, forcing us to scurry back from the heat.

The lizard charged. The thing was far faster than it should have been. When it pounced, both Isabella and I lunged aside.

It turned on Isabella, giving me a chance. I aimed Gertie and snapped off a couple of rounds into its rear behind its leg where the scales should be the thinnest. "Aim for the soft spots."

Fire and a green goo exploded from the slugs as they penetrated the weaker scales. The creature reared back, screaming in pain.

Isabella took her chance and fired into the underside of the thing's throat. More green ichor gushed from the wounds.

"Move!" I yelled at Isabella. She did, but not fast enough. The head whipped down and crashed into her as she backpedaled. She went down hard.

I fired another round into its front leg to distract it from my fallen comrade. The beast screamed, but it was more interested in eating Isabella than stopping me from harming it.

Phantom flashed into view between the prone Isabella and the monster. He raked his claws across the lizard's remaining eye and jetted out of range.

Isabella used Phantom's distraction to crawl away from the fight.

The beast went wild, snapping and lashing its tail. In its death throes, it almost mashed Isabella with its tail.

"No!" Flameguard screamed. "I will summon the fire lord to destroy you, Watcher."

The heat from the swirling pit of fire intensified to the point we had to back up even farther. The ground buckled and geysers of fire burst forth. It was like being inside a volcano.

"Manath, obey me!"

The sound of breaking stone filled the air. Around the mage, pillars of molten stone emerged from the mass of lava.

"Nitasis protect us," Isabella said. If the goddess of air favored Isabella in any way, we could use all the help we could get.

The stone pillars were now taller than the fire mage. They flexed like giant fingers, protecting the delicate human in the center.

"Destroy the infidels!"

A booming "No!" filled the air and made the ground shake. The protecting hand snapped together, encasing Flameguard in its fist. The hand sank into the ground and was gone.

The lava pit still burned, but the wild, swirling winds died along with the mage.

"Are all your missions like this?" Isabella asked, sweat dripping from her face.

I shook my head. "No, most are really weird."

9

VICTORIA

I woke to the rocking motion of a wagon. Since Miranda had commanded me to stay still and silent, I couldn't move. My mind exploded with rage. I'd spared her life so that she could help undo the damage her creation had caused, and she'd turned on me. I should have just killed her.

The longer we rode, the angrier I got. At fairly regular intervals Miranda would appear, command me to eat and use the bathroom, then drug me again. She always gave the same commands. Stay still and silent, then sleep. As much as I fought to avoid the effects of the drug, it didn't matter.

I had no idea how long we'd been traveling when I was woken up by Miranda and told to come to stand next to her. My body ached and I may have groaned as I got up. I did as she told me, not that I had any choice in the matter.

"Well, look who we have here," Firehelm said as he strode across a grassy field where the wagon had halted. He wore a linen shirt with a dark brown coat. "Did she have the artifact?"

Miranda produced the wand and handed it over to a grinning Firehelm.

"Lass, you did good. I worried she'd killed you back at the compound."

"The others wanted to, but Victoria thought she'd save me and my family from your clutches. Fortunately, she didn't realize just how many places one can hide vials of Blue Heron. Once we got her alone, we took her prisoner and headed to the rendezvous."

"Good thinking." Firehelm turned to me. "No mouthy comments this time, I see."

Given I'd been commanded to stay silent, I didn't have much of a choice. All I wanted to do was rip out the fool's throat and put a stop to Nimish before they did any more damage. Under the current circumstances, I wasn't getting that chance anytime soon. I'd fallen into her neatly arranged trap. So much for being the smartest alchemist around.

"I told her to stay quiet. Have you heard the awful jokes she tells?" Miranda asked, rolling her eyes. "Iris thinks they are hysterical, but she's a child."

Firehelm's smile grew broader. "She won't have much time to make jokes. We will sacrifice her to Ghuasis on the new moon in a few days. It will save us from using one of the slaves."

Internally I seethed. All I needed was a small opening and I'd get out of here and bring down the watchers to finish these fools off.

"Let her speak," Firehelm said.

"You may speak," Miranda said. "But no jokes."

My mouth popped open as if the lock had been released. The muscles protested at the sudden movement. I shifted my jaw back and forth to loosen it up.

"Well, what do you have to say?" Firehelm asked.

"Nothing to the likes of you," I said, though my voice cracked from my throat being so dry. "You know Brulle will find me and end you."

Firehelm chuckled. "We are in remote Candalar. None of the watchers will have the remotest idea of looking down here."

"The airship captain is the only one who knows the plan. Everard and the rest will think she is delayed establishing me as the new Astarian alchemist. She'll be dead before she's missed."

Dammit. I should have kept my mouth shut in front of Miranda. I could have discussed plans with Travis in private. My foolishness would cost me my life.

"Excellent," Firehelm said. "Bring her this way. We'll get her situated in camp, and then I have work for you, Miranda."

"Yes, sir," Miranda said, shoving me forward. "You don't need me to guard her and keep her drugged?"

"No, have Ezra bring her travel bags to her tent. Even if she were to break free, there isn't a city for days."

"Yes, sir." Miranda instructed me to follow her.

Like an automaton, I did, clomping along while my stiff muscles screamed at their forced use.

"I'll be in shortly, so we can discuss the situation," Firehelm told me before he returned to the camp.

Miranda set off at a brisk pace. The camp was in a large clearing surrounded by trees and brambles around the outer ring. We passed numerous tents, most of which were patched to the point that they looked like quilts. The clashing colors gave me a headache.

Small fires dotted the openings between tents. Huge casks were placed along the makeshift walkways for water or ale. Men, women, and children wandered the camp doing whatever it was they did here, many with the tell-tale blue-tinged eyes. Firehelm and his people must go through a lot of Blue Heron to keep the workers under control.

After a few minutes, we reached a white tent at the edge of the encampment. Miranda opened the flap and gestured me inside.

I went.

She told me to sit in an old wooden chair.

I sat.

She set on a chair in the center of the tent. "You may talk, but you are not to leave without my permission." She pivoted and exited the tent.

The inside of the tent was fairly sparse. A single cot and a chamber pot were along one wall and a small table sat on the other. The front and back of the tent had large flaps, but the ones in the back were tied shut.

Ezra entered after a while and set my travel bags and my duster on the bed.

"Why are you doing this?" I asked, more out of curiosity than anything. Given the situation, the information I was gathering about Firehelm's operations would only be going to my grave.

Ezra studied me for a moment before he answered. "Nimish has promised us our own region of Astaria after Ghuasis is set free. We will rule over the masses for her and provide her the souls she needs to feed upon."

"Do you believe that?"

He nodded. "I do. And more importantly, Miranda does. We had a business in Port Alarin making tinctures to cure diseases and help the average person. The magus's personal alchemist complained about our goods, and we were shut down and forced to move. We lost everything on the whim of a magus. Once Ghuasis takes her rightful place, we will destroy the Astarian maguses and punish them for their sins against people like us."

"Why didn't you go to Terralon and tell Everard?"

Ezra laughed. "Everard doesn't care about the little guy. He's kept the evil maguses in power for hundreds of years. Plus, we would be dead if we had tried. There are scores of dead people who challenged the maguses. The regular people are the ones who pay."

He sounded like Quinn. The artificer was convinced that governing by maguses had to end, but what would replace it? Anarchy was my guess.

I was about to respond when the tent flap opened and Firehelm entered. "Ezra, Miranda needs you at the main fire."

"Yes, sir." Ezra left the tent.

I wondered if Quinn was right about needing to change the way Astaria was governed. If the maguses were abusing their power at the expense of the people we were sworn to protect, then why were they still in power? Why would Everard have allowed it, when the whole point of the Watchers was to protect the people of Astaria? Wasn't it?

"Your gear is in your bags. I've stationed two guards outside the tent. If you need anything, tell them."

"Give me my pistols and I'll take it from there."

He produced my pistols from under his coat and tossed them on the ground at my feet. "I took the liberty of removing the slugs, but alarium magic disrupts the natural flow of my power. You can have them for what they are worth. On the new moon, we'll burn you as an offering to Ghuasis."

I didn't reach for the weapons, thinking it was a test and Firehelm might kill me out of hand. "Aren't you just going to drug me?"

"No, the amount you had will keep you in here until the ceremony. I want to make sure you fully understand that I've won. Your death will help to bring about the new world."

"Aren't you worried I'll escape?"

"Go ahead. The Candalarians already want to make an example of you. You are only safe inside this tent."

I shuddered at what they would do to me or any watcher they came across. I'd heard horror stories about the slavers and their methods of breaking willful people.

"I see we understand each other," Firehelm said with that stupid smile on his face.

Unfortunately, I understood far too well. My only option was to wait. And probably die.

If I could at least tell jokes, that would improve matters. I'd have to wait for the drug to wear off.

10

BRULLE

Not wanting to waste the lava pit, Isabella and I tossed the bodies of the cultists in. The flames consumed them in seconds, leaving no evidence of what had passed. The horses had fled into the night, and if they carried anything of any use, it was gone.

"Look what I found!" Isabella called from where the cultist had held the knife to her throat. She held up one of the pistols I'd given her. She had a couple of pretty good-sized cuts on her arm and shoulder and some scorched hair where the burning lizard had struck her but otherwise seemed unharmed. "I thought I lost her in the fire."

"Good job. Let's get you looked after," I said to Isabella. I motioned her to follow me back to camp. "Sure you want to do this?"

Isabella smirked. "Someone has to watch your back."

Phantom growled at that. We both laughed.

We crested the hill to see our camp hadn't been affected at all. The horses grazed where we'd tied them up. The bedrolls were still in the same place. It was hard to believe that a short walk from here was a temporary volcanic pit.

I threw a couple of pieces of wood on the fire so I could see better. My hands had a reddish tint from the heat of the lizard fire. Isabella's skin showed the same slightly burnt complexion. The stench of burnt hair followed her like a bad seed. I pulled the first aid kit from my satchel and got to work stitching up her injuries.

"Lizard's teeth hit me when its head came down," she said, almost apologizing. "I thought I had enough room to shoot and get out from under it."

Phantom wandered over and sprawled out next to Isabella. She ran her hand through his fur while I worked.

"They don't teach this stuff. If you want to be a watcher, you've got to think on your feet," I said, getting out the sewing thread. "You did great, especially for your first fight."

"Back home, we always were fighting giant lizards," she said with a laugh. "This must be old hat to you."

"Not really," I answered honestly. "Most of the time, the watchers deal with rogue magus, slavers, or raiders. Since the cult has shown up, things have definitely become challenging. Fire mages are a deadly sort."

"We never traded in Tofragrad when I was on the Revenge. Captain liked to keep to the eastern shores." She winced when I tied off the knot on her shoulder.

I got up and pulled a bottle of whiskey out of my saddlebag. I popped the cork and handed the bottle to Isabella. "You might want a drink."

She nodded and took a large swallow before handing it back. I poured a bit over the newly stitched flesh, eliciting a hiss of pain from my patient.

"Damn, that hurts."

"I'm sure it does." I took a swallow of whiskey and returned it to my bag. "Why don't you get some sleep? I'll watch for the rest of the night."

Isabella stood to go, but stopped and looked at me. "Thank you, Brulle. That thing would have eaten me if you hadn't stopped it."

I laughed. "Don't thank me, thank Phantom. He jumped in to distract it."

She scratched the big cat between his ears. "Thank you, Phantom."

Phantom growled his response and Isabella rolled over to get some sleep.

I got Gertie and started cleaning and checking her out. I considered loading in the chain shot, but it made her less maneuverable and I didn't have a lot of extra chains. I field stripped the weapon, checked the alarium crystals, and reassembled her.

The rest of the night passed with no major events. As the sun came up, I walked up the hill to see what was left of the fire pit. Coals and small flames smoldered in small sections, but most of the firestorm was gone. Isabella joined me.

"It could have burned the grasslands down," she said. "These people have no sense of what they are doing."

"Power is all they understand. The cult wants to bring Ghuasis to this world so they can rule it. Not to feed starving children or stop wars. They don't care who is hurt as long as they get what they want."

"I'm not so sure. Most people want to be nice, or at least think they are. What if they are doing this for what they think is a good reason?"

Interesting. Over the years, I'd met some truly awful people, and if I was being honest, I was probably one of them. I'd done terrible things to protect Astaria. Did that make me any different than the cultists? They believed Ghuasis would fix the world. What if they were right? Did creating a better world justify the killing of thousands of people? If Astaria could be safe, would I make the same choice?

"I don't know."

"Me neither, but for now, we need to stop them before they kill a lot of innocent people."

"Yes, we do. Saddle up."

***

The sun was setting when we reached the edges of the Donnastall Forest. We tied off the horses where they could graze and followed a small game trail I'd spotted. Phantom was in the lead, Isabella behind me.

We crept down the path, keeping the noise at a minimum. The birds chirped and a couple of deer ran past us, but nothing out of the ordinary. We kept going until I saw an image from Phantom. He'd found the camp.

"Camp is about a mile ahead."

Isabella unholstered her pistols. "What's the plan?"

"Scouting only," I said. "We need to see how many cultists are there and what kind of armaments they have. Every scrap of information we have gives us an edge in planning to stop their attacks. By the time Victoria and Quinn are in Iron Harbor, we need to know what we are facing."

"Got it. Look, don't shoot."

"Unless necessary."

"I get the feeling with you, Brulle, the shooting is usually necessary."

I smiled. "It usually is."

I t was twilight by the time we reached the edge of the area the cult had cleared for their camp. Tents of all sizes were haphazardly arranged around the open ground. Stumps still stood between tents, showing the haste they'd cleared the forest with.

Phantom lay next to me as we watched the comings and goings around the camp. They didn't have a guard posted, but with a couple of hundred cultists and at least two fire mages, I doubted they were concerned. Most carried knives, clubs, or swords. A couple carried crude powder rifles. These were elite troops, for sure.

We settled in for the night, while the food was passed out. Isabella and I contented ourselves with a meal of jerky and water. Somewhere in the camp, music and singing could be heard. It was more a rover's camp than a military base.

"Aren't they worried they'll be found?" Isabella asked, her voice low.

"We are away from the trade routes and farms. The odds of anyone finding them are slight. If Nimish is here, I'd think there would be a lot more people."

The music got louder, and two cultists marched over to the tent nearest us. They went in and, after a few moments, emerged with a woman held between them.

I gasped.

"What in the world is Victoria doing here?"

11

BRULLE

T his is not good. Victoria should be with Quinn," I said, worry flooding my brain.

"From the looks of it, she's in trouble."

"Unhand me, you brutes," Victoria shouted as she struggled between the two men. "I am Watcher Victoria Wyndham, and you will release me now before…"

Her words faded as they turned the corner to drag her deeper into the encampment.

"Change of plans. Phantom, follow Victoria, but do not be seen."

The big cat vanished from view and jumped out into the clearing in tracking mode. I watched through his eyes as he navigated the shoddily constructed camp. With all the people converged in the center, it made for an easy trip.

The center of the camp held a rough wooden stage at the far end with a large open area where the cultists sat in groups around small fires. A larger fire sat off to the side, with tables holding food and large casks of ale.

The two men pulled Victoria onto the stage. A third man joined them. The new addition wore robes with runes running down both sides. His face bore the traditional tattoos of the Tofragrad tribes.

My brain went into overdrive trying to think of a way to free Victoria.

Phantom's thoughts intruded into mine, making it more difficult to think. He knew Victoria was in danger, and he didn't like it. Not one bit.

"Brothers and sisters!" the man said from the center of the stage. His voice reached us at the edge of the clearing. Seeing through Phantom's eyes and hearing through my ears led to a strange duality.

"We've captured the infidel that stole the sacred wand of Nabal. Tomorrow we will put her to death. Nimish will burn her as a sacrifice to Ghuasis. We will use her ashes to paint the symbols that will bring our mother back to this plane."

A cheer went up from the assembled cultists.

"We've got a problem," I said.

Phantom returned to our hiding place beyond the edge of the encampment. The tall grass and scrub trees screened us from prying eyes, though after they'd fetched Victoria, we hadn't seen any more guards. A bit later, a defeated Victoria was dragged back to the tent. The guards laughed as they departed.

"Let's go get her," Isabella said. "They won't be expecting anyone to rescue her."

"True, but if we let them feast, we won't have as many able-bodied cultists to fight. Let them celebrate their triumph and get lots of ale in them."

Isabella chuckled. "Good idea. It will be much easier."

Famous last words.

<hr>

Once the camp quieted down, Isabella and I prepared. I hooked an ammo chain to Gertie and set my batons and knives in place. I pulled out a couple of explosive packs and handed one to Isabella.

"What do I do with this?" she asked, turning the brick like a weapon over in her hands. "Throw it at the bad guys?"

"No, but if you pull this metal tab, it will explode a minute later. We'll each drop one of these and then make our move."

"How big of an explosion?"

"Big enough that you don't want to be nearby," I said. "You and Phantom will go to the left. Once you are near a good-sized tent, tell him to find me."

She snapped her fingers. "He can find you just like that?"

"Yes. I can 'see' him when he's invisible, and he always knows where I am. Place the brick outside the tent, pull the tab, and then run to where Victoria is being held."

"What are you going to do?"

"I'm going in the opposite direction. I'm going to destroy their supplies. Hard to march troops without food."

Isabella pulled a pistol out. "I'm ready."

"Count to twenty, then move out."

I pushed through our screen of bushes and out into the camp. I sped across the grounds between the tents as quietly as possible. No sense in giving away the plan before the explosions started.

Though I encountered nobody awake, snores and other nighttime noises made their way to me as I snuck past the empty canvas structures. I rounded a large pavilion to find three cultists sitting around a fire. The supply wagons sat just beyond them. After holstering Gertie, I slid the explosives into my satchel and got my batons out to keep the noise down.

The one farthest from me appeared to be asleep, but the other two spoke in hushed tones. They'd need to be neutralized first. I crept in, striking the closest cultist in the back of the head with the metal tip. He crumpled forward, almost falling into the fire. My second swing caught his friend under the chin with a hearty thump and dropped him onto his back.

The third man opened his eyes, but I threw my baton and caught him in the face before he could make any noise. Three down and minimal commotion. I retrieved my baton and made sure the man was out cold. Finally, something had gone right.

I moved to the supply wagons and placed the charge. A couple of moments later, Phantom showed me Isabella pulling the tab on her explosive. I did the same.

A branch cracked off to my right. A man walked into the firelight, tying his belt as he went. "Don't go over there for a while."

I hurled my baton at him. The baton glanced off his shoulder, and he took off as fast as a startled hare.

"Intruders! We are under attack!"

I swore before running toward Victoria's tent. I scooped up my batons, jammed them into my belt, and got Gertie ready. Cultists swarmed like a kicked wasp's nest. I shot at them as I ran, forcing them to take cover. I turned the corner and spotted Isabella and Phantom moving in the opposite direction.

"Get Victoria out while I hold them off."

Isabella and Phantom tore the tent flap aside and disappeared. More cultists ran in every direction. The first to approach had enjoyed his ale a bit too much. He swung a heavy ax at me but missed by a mile. I kicked his knee, hearing the telltale snap. He flailed on the ground in pain.

More rushed at me. I opened up Gertie with a sweeping motion. Cultists fell as the slugs tore through the mob. Some fled, others kept coming. I spun and sprayed slugs in the other direction to keep the mob at bay. I only needed to hold until Victoria was free.

A huge man covered in banded leather armor approached. I fired several shots at him, but they didn't strike. "Damn magic," I swore, pushing Gertie into her holster. I pulled my boot knives and prepared.

The assembled cultists cheered as the juggernaut strode toward me. He pulled a club the size of my leg off his back. "Your bullets can't touch me, infidel. I will kill you in the name of Ghuasis."

"You can try," I said and stepped in to attack. He swung the club at my head, but I got under it and slammed a knife into his arm between the bands of studded leather. Blood spurted. He grunted, but still managed to punch me with his off hand. The blow staggered me, but I rolled to the side before the club crashed down where I'd been standing.

"Why fight it? I will promise you a quick death." The club arced on an upswing and almost caught me in the head. I dodged and sliced my knife across his gauntleted hand. It didn't even scratch the armor.

He backhanded me and sent me flying. Blood flowed down my face from my nose and mouth, making my beard a mess. I rolled over and was rewarded with a kick in the side. It threw me a good ten feet, where I hit one of the tree stumps. The world spun. I tried to push myself up, but I couldn't manage it.

The giant lumbered over and knelt before me. He plucked up my knife, as I'd only maintained a grip on one of them. Pretty sure it was my right, but my vision swam and blurred.

"You are a worthy opponent. I grant you an easy death." He lifted the knife over his shoulder.

BOOOM!

The first explosive went off. The whole camp shook. The big man steadied himself. People screamed and ran as the night turned into day with the fiery explosion. He brought the knife back into position just as the second explosion tore through the night.

BOOOOOM!!!!

The bomb from the supply wagons went off with a much larger eruption. My opponent pitched forward, landing on my legs. The world snapped into focus just long enough for me to drive my blade into his exposed neck. His eyes widened as he realized I'd killed him. He slumped onto the ground next to me.

Isabella, Phantom, and Victoria emerged from the tent. Victoria ran to me as I crouched behind the stump. "Are you okay?"

I nodded and regretted it. "I hit my head, but I'll be fine. Help me up."

It took Isabella and Victoria to hoist me to my feet. Victoria availed herself of Gertie and opened fire on the cultists milling around. Screams erupted from the group as they fell or fled. Either suited our escape.

A single woman walked toward us. She wore a long black robe and had gems woven into her hair. She looked familiar, but my addled brain couldn't place her. She raised her hands. "I seek parley."

"Speak your piece," Victoria said.

I stared at the woman and suddenly I knew her.

Nimish had arrived.

1 2

—————

BRULLE

Nimish Nimkar, leader of the Followers of Alpha and the designer of the plan to resurrect Ghuasis, stood before us. A shimmering globe of energy surrounded her like a halo. The artist of the picture I saw hadn't done the woman justice. She carried herself like a queen, or maybe more like a goddess.

"Nimish, you need to forgo this insane plan and leave Astaria in peace," I said. My head spun and my stomach threatened to betray me, but I held it together…barely.

Victoria straightened up to face our foe. While a bit worse for wear, Victoria still acted as if she was in charge. Her pants and shirt were torn in places, covered in dirt and blood, but she still could command a general to do her bidding.

"The Nimish?" Isabella asked.

"Yes, child," Nimish answered for me. "I am the high priestess of Ghuasis and will bring her to this plane in all her glory. She will punish the unbelievers and make the world into one of peace and harmony."

"You will kill thousands of innocents on a plan that won't work," Victoria said. "Leave us in peace."

Nimish cocked her head to the side. "Why? The Astarian have killed thousands of Norns, Candalarians, Uwhelans, and Tofragradians. You are barbarians that use your magic and alarium to subjugate the rest of us. For centuries, Everard has killed anyone who challenged Astaria's place in

282

the world order. He is the monster here, not I. We are seeking retribution for a long list of grievances, and the Astarians will pay for their sins. Once we've destroyed you, Ghuasis will reign, and all will be welcome to worship her. There will be no more war, just peace."

"And if we don't want to worship her?" Isabella asked. My would-be apprentice had her hand on her belt knife. I reached over and tapped the hand. She got the message. No suicidal attempts today, at least not for her.

"Then you shall perish to allow the rest to live their lives. Don't we put down sick animals so they don't kill off the flock? It is not so different."

"What do you want of us?" Isabelle would have a far better shot at killing Nimish, but if any of the three of us was to die here, it would be me. I still held the knife in my right hand. If I could get close enough, I could end her, and the war would never come to pass. I doubted I could penetrate the shield she'd surrounded herself with, but if the opportunity presented itself, I'd gladly trade my life to take hers.

"Nothing, Watcher Brulle."

That stopped me cold. What game was the woman playing? The watchers were key to the defense of Astaria. She could kill us and be that much closer to her goals. "Nothing?"

"You are free to leave. In five days, the massed might of the Norns, Candalarians, and Tofragradians will attack Iron Harbor. I expect you all to be there to lead the resistance. All of you will die in order to fuel the spell to bring the sacred lady into this world. I will allow you to perish in service to Ghuasis."

"I'm done with this," Victoria said. She fired a stream of slugs into Nimish's chest. The bullets dropped to the ground. Victoria rose from the ground, thrashing to break loose. Her hands were scrambling to get free of whatever was choking her. Suddenly, she crumpled to the ground, gasping as she started breathing again.

Isabella knelt at Victoria's side and helped her to her feet.

"I will pardon your rude behavior this once. Know I could kill you all here, but that won't serve the greater good. You may leave or I will burn you where you stand. Your choice."

"Let's go," I said to Victoria and Isabella. Nimish stepped aside and watched as we retreated into the woods and back to where our horses were tied off.

Our first encounter with Nimish was a colossal failure. If this was the best we could do, we were all in grave danger.

W̲e reached the horses an hour later. The fact that Nimish so easily bested Victoria and we'd face her again in five days had a demoralizing effect on all of us. Taking into account the two-day journey back to Iron Harbor, to say we were pressed for time would be a vast understatement. How could we marshal troops in time to stop the combined forces of the Norns and Candalarians?

"How did they capture you? Last I saw, you were on the Maiden's Kiss headed to Terralon," I asked our esteemed alchemist.

Victoria sighed. "After I met with Everard and Quinn to discuss what we'd found. Everard sends his regards, by the way."

"I should have known you'd tell him," I said, sounding sulkier than I wanted. "I take it he's upset with me."

Victoria shook her head. "On the contrary, he was overjoyed that you are alive. He's rather fond of you. Anyways, I took Miriam to a safehouse to get her and her family settled, and she drugged me."

"We should have killed her. Where is she now?" I wanted to tell her "I told you so," but what's done is done and we had bigger game to hunt.

Victoria shrugged. "No idea. I've been in the camp for three days and I haven't seen her or her family since the first day. Considering the circumstances, I couldn't care less."

"Well, you aren't too bad off," I said, glad to see she hadn't been hurt while being held by the cultists.

"No, but Firehelm took the wand from me. Everard could sense the magic and thought it somehow controls things."

"We knew that after you used it on the fire golem."

"Yes, but he thinks it can control anything given enough power. If it is true, we've lost a devastating weapon to our enemies."

"That's assuming Firehelm can use it for anything other than golems." I filled her in on our fight with Flameguard and her death at the hands of her summoned creature. "I don't know if the fire magi can control anything outside their sphere."

"Flameguard was scared," Isabella added. "She panicked when we attacked. Are all of the Tofragrad magi used to fighting?"

"From what I overheard, it sounds like most of the magi spend their time worshiping the fire gods of their nation. Firehelm is out of the ordinary, but let's assume he's trained the others. There is a lot of power at their disposal," Victoria said.

"We have Everard to counteract anything they throw at us," I said. "Once the Norn leaders spot him, they'll turn tail and run."

Victoria's face fell. "This can't go beyond us, agreed?"

When Isabella and I both nodded, she continued. "Everard is dying. It is amazing he's lasted this long. His magic has faded to almost nothing."

My stomach dropped out of my body. Everard? Dying? "You have to be mistaken. He's hundreds of years old."

"I wish I were," Victoria said, wiping at a stray tear that ran down her face. "It is only a matter of time. Our hope is that when the assembled armies see Everard has taken the field, they will retreat."

"I don't like the sound of that." News of Everard's mortality was a shot to the gut. There are people who you never think about getting old or injured. Everard was larger than life in many ways, but his energy and commitment to Astaria had never wavered. "What happens if Everard's presence doesn't stop them?"

"We fight and hope we win."

Not the best pep talk ever, but the reality of the situation was what it was. The sun had crept up from its bed while we were talking. "No sense sitting here. We need to get back. Victoria, can you ride with Isabella?"

"Sure, let's be off."

I realized as I mounted my horse that this might be the last time I traveled anywhere outside of Iron Harbor because the war was coming.

Time to roll the dice and hope I didn't throw snake eyes.

13

QUINN

ian paced his cell like a caged animal. The two-inch-thick bars and triple locks would keep the former watcher safely out of the way of the upcoming events.

"What do you want?" he snarled when he noticed me standing across from his new home. "If Victoria hadn't meddled in this, you'd be dead."

"Why?"

"Why what?"

"Why did you betray Everard, the watchers, and Brulle?"

"Brulle's dead. I doubt he cares."

I shook my head, suppressing a smile. "That's what we thought. Turns out he was just retired."

"You're lying to me," Cian snapped. "You are Everard's pet."

"Victoria was here and told us all about Brulle faking his own death to get away from you. Hells, Brulle might be along eventually to tell you himself. I'm sure your mentor is quite proud of your accomplishments and eager to tell you all about it."

Cian's face flushed red. "Liar! Brulle is dead. I'm not telling you anything."

I leaned back against the stone wall of the prison and let Cian rage. The more I goaded him, the more likely he was to slip and say something useful. To say his language drifted into the colorful range was an understatement. I waited until he calmed down.

286

"Look, you can answer my questions or Victoria will have something to loosen your tongue. Your choice."

"Fine, I'll answer before the witch uses her potions on me." He folded his arms.

I pushed down the urge to laugh at the fact he looked like a pouting child and asked my first question. "Why did you join with the cultists?"

Cian settled on the floor, legs crossed. They'd removed his shoes and he only wore a long smock. They weren't taking any chances with him.

"I was on a mission for Everard to find and eliminate a Tofragradian spy. He'd broken into the home of Magus Terbitta and attempted to steal the alarium harness he used, but the guards chased him off."

"How did he know they were from Tofragrad?" I asked more out of curiosity than anything.

"The tattoos," Cian said with an eye roll. "Didn't Roland teach you anything?"

I ignored the dig. Roland hadn't been alive long enough to teach me much. "Go on."

"I tracked him to a small farm in Aldon. I went in planning on killing him and everyone else, but he had the family hostage. We spoke for a while, and after a day or so, Firehelm showed up."

Interesting. I slid down to sit with my back against the wall. "Continue."

"Firehelm told me about Ghuasis and how they were going to bring her to our plane so that all would be treated equally. No more starving children, slavery, or wars. I told him to stick it, but then he offered me what I truly wanted."

"To destroy the Candalarians?"

Cian's head came up and he gave me an appraising look. "Yes. He told me the plan involved killing off the horse troops and then we could rid the world of the Candalarians, since they would never submit to Ghuasis's rule."

This Firehelm knew how to read an audience if he'd figured out the key to Cian so quickly. After his family was killed and he was sold into slavery by Candalarians, Cian would do anything to get even. "You could have gotten revenge without betraying us."

"No, Everard forbid me from attacking them unless I was in danger. He cast some sort of spell on me to stop me from killing Candalarians."

Now that, I could understand. Cian's hatred knew no bounds. "What changed?"

"Firehelm took me to a wind walker who removed the compulsion. I was free of Everard's arbitrary rules."

"You trusted a Candalarian to remove the spell?"

"If I wanted to be free, I had to," Cian said, running a hand through his tousled brown hair. "Firehelm kept me from killing the man, but I left the camp and killed a group of outriders. I took my time and made them pay for what they had done to me."

I didn't know Cian well, but cold-blooded murderer wasn't something I'd expected from him. "So you went from protecting people to becoming a murderer."

He spat on the ground in front of me. "Quinn, you sicken me. You are a dog lying at the feet of your master, eating the scraps he leaves you. The Candalarians are barbarians who murder and rape anyone they come across. I'm protecting the average people of Astaria by killing off the maguses who would turn us into slaves."

Nothing like beating on a piece of slag and expecting to make a knife. "Other than killing, what are you getting out of it?"

Cian laughed. "Freedom. I can do what I want, and no one will stop me."

"How is that working out?"

Cian glanced around, a smile creeping across his face. "Funny. Quinn, you could join us. With your power, you would be revered above all others. You could break free of the watchers and rule over the world."

I shook my head. "I don't want power; I want to protect the people of Astaria. One day, we'll have peace, and the watchers won't be necessary."

"You are a fool," Cian said with a sneer. "Ghuasis says only the strong will survive the purge and I'll be sorry to see you go, but you had your chance."

I pushed myself to my feet. Everard hadn't killed the rogue watcher yet, so he must have a plan for him. I wish I understood what it was. "Cian, you will die in here. We will stop this crazy plan and your goddess will stay where she belongs."

"They will free me and then we will destroy all of the structures and rule in their stead." Cian started to laugh.

I left, his mocking laughter echoing down the hallway after me.

1 4

BRULLE

Iron Harbor came into view as we rode across the Harvest Bridge into the city. The Allernora River flowed into the sea and provided easy transport of goods to the Aldon region of Astaria. During times of war, it served as a barrier between Astaria and Candalar. Four main bridges crossed the half mile-wide river. If history repeated itself, the battle would be fought on those bridges.

The battlements were open, but scores of armed and armored troops stood inside the wall that surrounded the city. Siege engines that hadn't seen battle in years were being worked on, oiled, and tested for the upcoming fight. The ballistas could throw spears across the river if needed, but they could also clear the bridges of invaders.

"State your business," an officer demanded as we entered the city. He had a pencil-thin mustache and a goatee, both liberally sprinkled with gray. Troops and porters clogged the staging area behind the gates as the war effort was in full swing.

"Aren't you a bit old to be playing soldier?" I asked Captain Herbst. He'd retired from the service for a life as a trader years ago. They really were calling up all available units if he was back.

He adjusted his glasses as he peered up at me. "Since they've enlisted corpses, I guess I'm fine."

I slid off my horse and gave the old scoundrel a rough hug. "Been a long time, Kent."

"Well, since one of us was dead, it cuts down on the social obligations. You look old, Brulle," he said with a twinkle of mirth in his eyes. "If what they are sayin' is right, you probably should have stayed that way."

"And miss the fun? Where are the generals holed up?"

"Harbor Admin buildings." Captain Herbst clapped me on the shoulder. He turned and yelled at the troops stationed behind him. "Clear the way."

I climbed back up on my horse, saluted the captain, and led the way into the city proper. Soldiers moved through drills off to the side of the courtyard. People of all ages and sizes carried bundles of supplies to the top of the wall or deeper into the city. Carts loaded with children and the elderly were departing, in anticipation of the upcoming battle. Hopefully, they would make it to Hillbase or Sunchome before the attacks started.

"Never thought I'd see the day," I said to Victoria as she pulled her horse next to mine. Isabella rode behind us. Phantom walked under my horse, invisible to all the people we passed.

"It's been a long time coming. We knew at some point all-out war was a possibility."

"I just never thought I'd live to see it."

We rode through the city, which felt more like a ghost town now that all the citizens had fled or locked themselves inside. We reached the Harbor Administration buildings the city leaders were using as the command center. I tied off the horses while Victoria headed into the building. I waited as Isabella dismounted.

"I'm going to go check in with the captain. I figure they'll be wanting all the airships they can muster for the fight," Isabella said.

"Good idea. Tell Edina to be ready. We may need to fly out of here, depending on the plan."

Isabella nodded to me. "Will do." She wheeled her horse around. "Hey."

I looked up at her. "Yes?"

"Did I pass the audition?"

"Absolutely. Everard may make you go through training, but as far as I'm concerned, you've passed. Welcome to the watchers."

She smiled and rode off. I wondered how long she'd have to enjoy her accomplishment.

The room was filled by the tribunal, a mixture of military types, maguses, and administrators. A large wooden table dominated the center of the room with high-back chairs ringing it. Bookshelves with large tomes of shipping ledgers and tidal patterns took up the entirety of the right wall. They had laid out refreshments along the left wall where many of the maguses were standing like this was a party, not a war council.

Everard wasn't here, but there was always friction between the maguses and watchers since we reigned in any that got overzealous in their pursuits. At least they weren't wearing their alarium weapon harness, so we wouldn't need to dodge lightning.

I glanced at Victoria. "You want to take the lead?"

She rolled her eyes but took charge. "Members of the tribunal. I am Watcher Victoria Wyndham, and I would appreciate your attention. I need a full rundown on where we stand and what plans have been put in place."

Magus Porter, wearing the robes of her office as head of the Petdon region, stood at the head of the table. She was a short woman in her forties with streaks of blond through her dark hair. "We will call for the watchers when they are needed. Leave this to the Magus Tribunal to handle. Iron Harbor will not fall."

Oh boy. Here we go.

"Magus, you don't speak for the tribunal. If Usorin or Everard are present, I will step aside, but the watchers handle the security of Astaria."

"Yes, we are well aware that your mishandling of the situation has brought us to this juncture," the Magus said harshly. "Everard is set to arrive in the morn and has instructed the tribunal to make plans for the upcoming defense of Iron Harbor."

"And those plans are?" Victoria asked. Her tone could have frozen a waterfall in place.

"We have sent emissaries to the Norns, Candalarians, and this Nimish person. We expect to strike a treaty any time now and stop this insanity. If we had tried diplomacy before the watchers attacked the cult, none of this would be happening." The magus pulled herself up straighter. "We are recommending that the watchers be dissolved immediately as part of our offer to the other nations."

"What?" Victoria stammered out. "Of all the stupid things I've heard in my life—"

"Stupid?" The magus' shrill voice cut through my eardrums like an ax through a watermelon. "How dare you? I am a magus, and you are a peasant that Everard sent off to cause trouble. You will curb your tongue when you address me."

"Phantom," I said softly. With all the commotion, no one paid attention.

The magus rounded the table, approaching Victoria. "One more word—"

Phantom appeared directly before the startled magus. He bared his teeth and growled at the woman.

"What my friend is trying to say is that you should mind your manners around Watcher Wyndham," I commented from my spot next to the door.

"Who let this beast in here?" the magus squawked as she retreated behind the table.

"I let myself in," I said, earning an amused look from Victoria. "In case you don't recognize me, I am Watcher Brulle Cobb, and we have information the tribunal will need."

"Watcher Brulle is dead," another magus offered from the far side of the table. If I was right, that was the new Magus Holrough. He looked like his late father.

"Jefferson Holrough, you were a boy who loved to put frogs into ladies' beds. I remember a certain time—"

Magus Holrough's face turned a proper shade of pink. "It's Watcher Brulle."

I approached the group. The map of Iron Harbor was laid out on the table. Miniature carved figures showed troop placement and the latest reports on the Norn and Candalarian positions. Their reports must be old because the enemy wasn't close enough to attack in three days.

"Regardless of who you are," Magus Porter continued in a huffy tone. Phantom had scared her but good. "We are in charge, and once the emissaries reach a deal with the aggrieved parties, we will all return home."

"The cult is using a drug called Blue Heron to control the leaders of the other factions. When have you ever known the Norns and Candalarians to agree on anything, except hating Astaria?" Victoria said.

"Ridiculous," Magus Porter responded. "You've created these wild tales to keep your place as the Magus' keepers. Once this is over, we will be eliminating the watchers and each region will police their own borders."

The door to the room opened and a younger man entered. He carried a large sack with him. From the metal arm, I assumed this was Watcher Quinn.

He strode across the room and upended the bag onto the table. Two human heads rolled across the map. When one jolted to a halt, its lifeless stare fixated on Magus Porter. "The Norns just delivered these as an answer to your offers of truce."

No one said a word.

"Now, if you are done abusing Watcher Wyndham, I am Quinn, and the watchers will be taking over the defense of Iron Harbor." He glanced at the assembled guests. "Anyone have an issue with that?"

Quinn knew how to make an entrance.

15

BRULLE

"We have bigger issues than who has the biggest hammer," Quinn said to the assembled group.

"Hammer?" Magus Porter asked.

"Hammer. You know you use it to beat metal at the forge. You've never used a hammer?"

Porter sniffed. "I am not a commoner who dirties their hands to make a living. I have the power of magic at my disposal."

Quinn pulled up a chair and sat down. "Show me."

This was bad. Astaria was ruled by the maguses. Each controlled their territory through the use of their artificially generated magic. What the world didn't know was that it was all fake. The watcher artificers over the centuries had developed harnesses for the magus. The alarium power of the devices allowed individuals to throw lightning or fire and generate a shield. Part of Astaria's power rose from the belief that magic was widespread, though the cultists knew the secret since Cian had gone rogue. Why else would the animals be forced to attack the maguses?

"Show you what?" the magus asked.

"Your vast and powerful magic. I'm sure we would all like to see you wield your power so we can all leave this pesky invasion to you to handle. Everard could use a break."

I bit off a laugh, as did Victoria and a couple of the maguses. Without her harness to use alarium to create "magic," she was useless.

294

Magus Porter stuttered. "It's too dangerous to use in here."

"Even better. We can walk to the harbor and you can sink the Norn scout ship sitting offshore. That will send a clear message to the Norns, right?"

"Ummm," Porter stuttered, trying to find a way to save face.

"Since I'm Roland's successor, you might want to stop boasting and think about your magic and how you get it."

She blanched and stayed quiet.

"Anyone else?" Quinn looked around the room. No one met his eye, let alone volunteered to defend Magus Porter. "Can we get down to business? We have many issues to discuss."

"Let's hear from Watcher Wyndham about what they saw in the field," Magus Holrough said.

Victoria launched into the story of the camp, the meeting with Nimish, and our return to Iron Harbor. "So we are expecting the attack three days from now. As a matter of fact—"

"This is all the watchers' fault," Porter interrupted, her voice climbing in volume. Everyone ignored her. "We are all going to die because you are incompetent."

"As a matter of fact, the only reason we know anything is that three watchers put their lives on the line to get the intel we have," Victoria said. "On the third night, Nimish will attempt to bring Ghuasis to our realm."

"Thank you, Victoria," Quinn said once she wrapped up her report. "We have other issues as well. Reports arrived earlier that the Candalarians attacked Sunchome last night."

Gasps of dismay and shock filled the room. "How could this have happened?" Magus Holrough asked. "I thought the point of attacking Iron Harbor was to force a huge death toll all at once...if what Watcher Wyndham said is accurate."

"Can we believe the watchers?" Porter asked. "They have killed or imprisoned many of the maguses. Quinn killed Magus Ovro because he challenged his 'authority.' Can we trust that they aren't working with the cultists to destroy us all? One was a traitor and maybe these three are as well."

"Magus, the watchers here are trying to save as many lives as possible," Victoria said. "We need to concentrate on the incoming attack."

"Watcher Quinn, it could be a feint to draw out our forces to weaken us," one of the generals said. "If we send troops to aid Sunchome, we will be out of position when the major attack comes."

Magus Holrough chimed in. "Those barbarians are probably sacking the city and taking everyone they can as slaves. This whole war could be a bluff to lure our troops away from the border."

"Sunchome's defenders held them off, but a contingent of riders bypassed the city," Quinn said.

"Why would they leave the city intact?" the general asked.

We'd been flanked while the maguses were standing around arguing and sending diplomats to their deaths. These people had no clue as to mounting a proper defense or the strategies involved. "It's a brilliant move. They don't want the city. They are using its bridges to cross so they don't have to deal with the river here," I said, marveling that none of the maguses thought to protect the surrounding area.

"We can fight the hordes on land or over the river. It makes no difference. They can't stand up to our combined magic."

"I'd agree if it was just the Candalarians," Victoria said from where she sat next to Quinn. "With the Norns and the cultists, we are fighting on three fronts with limited weapons."

"Quinn said many issues. What else has happened?" I asked. From what I knew of Quinn from Victoria, if he was concerned, I wasn't sure I really wanted an answer.

"The cultists established a base on Coveg Island. I couldn't get close enough to see numbers since the island has a good bit of forest on it. There were numerous ships docked on the far side, though."

"That is just off the harbor," Magus Porter exclaimed. "How did they do that without the watchers knowing?"

Quinn rubbed his face, whether from exhaustion or irritation I wasn't sure. "There are thirteen watchers. Four are dead from the earlier attacks, one turned traitor and is imprisoned, and three are here. The other five have been gathering intel and mobilizing troops. Meanwhile, the Tribunal has sat here doing nothing the whole time our enemies were gathering in force. So you tell me, Magus Porter. How did they take the island?"

"You are a fool. We have been doing our best to divert the upcoming invasion that the watchers caused. How dare you—"

"Enough," I said, loud enough to get everyone's attention. "What's done is done. The question is how do we turn the tables on our enemies?"

Quinn smiled. "I'm glad you asked."

An hour later, we were on the Lunatic's Revenge flying to Sunchome. Isabella sat off to the side, petting Phantom while he napped. Quinn wore a leather vest over his homespun shirt and pants, a forging hammer tucked into his belt.

I studied the young man who'd replaced Roland. The mechanical arm was a feat of engineering genius. It moved like my own arm but held a lot of power that most watchers could only dream of. We didn't make use of the alarium "magic" like the maguses, but each of us had weapons that used the powerful crystals. However, since most of us relied on Roland to create those weapons for us, we had better hope that Quinn was up to the challenge of creating them.

"You planning on setting up a forge?" I asked, pointing at the hammer.

"Something like that," he said before asking, "Would you mind if I looked at Gertie?"

I handed her over and Quinn examined her like a fine piece of art. Watcher Gould had designed Gertie to fight the Candalarian raiders that troubled me constantly. From the look on Quinn's face, he'd never seen such a weapon. I thought back to all of the times I'd relied on that weapon to get me out of seemingly impossible situations, and it had never let me down.

"Gould was a genius," he said as he worked the feed chamber of the rifle. "Roland said she was the best artificer around, but I'd not believed it until now."

"Gertie has gotten me through a lot of tough scrapes."

"I'm sure." He handed the rifle back so I could holster it. "So, why are we flying to Sunchome?"

Quinn shrugged. "I figure we can get an idea of the size of the forces they've moved across and delay any additional reinforcements. We only need to cost them two days to keep them from bringing all of their forces at us from the landed side of town."

"And you think you and I can do that?" The only one who could stop the Candalarians, in my opinion, was Everard. Quinn might be a great artificer, but he wasn't stopping anyone by himself.

"We'll see. If we get there and the odds are bad, we can fly back, but at least we'll know what we're facing."

"This sounds like a Roland sort of plan." I'd known Roland for many years and the man was a tactical genius and a master artificer. Without him, Astaria was far more vulnerable than ever before.

"I wish Roland was here," Quinn said softly. "He'd know what to do, but we're stuck with what we've got. He always told me you can't plan for everything, just do your best."

"Sounds like him. You don't seem like the seat of your pants type, though." It was tough to remember that Quinn was still a kid in a lot of ways. He'd had the role of watcher thrust on him and now here he was trying to help us stop an invasion of Astaria.

"I'm not. All I wanted to do was be a blacksmith and work with Master Ruari. Usorin robbed me of that opportunity when he cut off my arm. The Norns finished the job when they killed my family at the smithy."

I didn't know what to say. I'd known Usorin was a hot head, but cutting off an apprentice blacksmith's arm was beyond even his worst deeds. The fact Everard planned on making Usorin Arch Magus had to chafe Quinn something fierce. "I'm sorry."

"I was devastated, but I learned from Roland and he built me a new arm. I delivered all the harnesses Roland had created on my way to Iron Harbor. The maguses' families and trusted allies are being trained on how to use them. We should be able to field about fifty fully functioning maguses when the fighting starts. Hopefully, it will be enough."

"It will have to be," I said. I'd been older when I joined the watchers, but life wasn't always fair and you played the cards you were dealt. I leaned back and closed my eyes while we coasted toward the next fight.

I jolted awake when Captain Idina yelled, "Sunchome dead ahead."

Isabella and Quinn joined me on the foredeck. We watched the city grow larger as the landscape slid below us. The sun was about to set, so this was the last good look we'd have until morning.

Smoke billowed from the bridge that ran into Sunchome. According to reports, the Candalarians had moved about a thousand troops across, but the remainder of their troops were on the far side of the river. A force of Astarian pikemen and archers held the bridge, with a raging bonfire blocking the center. The fire wouldn't destroy the stone bridge, but the troops would need to continue to feed the flames to stop the horse troops.

Large rafts carried Candalarian troops and horses across the river, but it would take a year to get the rest of the army to the other side. From the look of it, some of the rafts had sunk, given the bodies along the downstream part of the river.

"Captain, can you get us to the bridge in the dark?" Quinn asked.

"Certainly," she said.

"Close enough for me to jump?"

She looked at Quinn. "Wait, you don't mean park next to the bridge, do you?"

Quinn grinned ear to ear.

"That's exactly what I intend to do."

Well, if nothing else, it would be an interesting way to die.

16

BRULLE

Once the sun had fully set, the Candalarians stopped trying to attack the Astarians protecting Sunchome on the bridge. The river width made night crossings extremely dangerous. The fire still burned on the bridge, but the horsemen had retreated from the city. The Candalarian leader was smart and resourceful to have prepared for a counterattack. Why risk it now by letting the enemy attack under the cover of darkness?

Quinn waited until the middle of the night to enact his plan, though I wasn't sure his idea counted as a real plan.

"Captain, take us in. I need to be able to get on the bridge and off again very fast."

"And if we don't go fast?" she asked, though I'm sure she knew the answer.

"Then I'll need to wade through a mass of Candalarians and this was a waste of time and lives." Quinn turned to me. "Do you see all the rafts there?"

He pointed to our left where the Candalarians had fires built along the riverbank.

"I do."

"Once I get on the bridge, I need you to open fire on the rafts and destroy as many as you can."

I scoffed. "Gertie can't tear up that many rafts."

"I can help with that," Isabella said from behind us. She produced a small wooden box. "Victoria sent these with her regards."

"What are they?" I asked.

"Fire potions. She sent them along in case we needed them. I'm thinking we can drop them on the rafts and let the fire take care of the rest."

"Brilliant," Quinn said. "Victoria thinks of everything. Change of plans. Captain, get me to the bridge. Once I've done what I need to, we'll fly over the rafts, drop the fire potions, and Gertie can keep anyone back until they are fully engulfed. If this all works, the Candalarians will either need to build more rafts or ride two days to Iron Harbor and be on the wrong side of the river."

"Sounds good," the captain said. "Are we ready?"

"As ready as we can be," I said, and hoped we would survive this night.

The captain set her crew to work. We tied ourselves to the rails to prevent falling off the ship if we needed to make sharp maneuvers, though I had to put Phantom in the captain's room for his own safety. The ship sped up and the nose tipped down. The wind whistled past us as we descended.

No shout or alarms were raised as the airship raced over the waters of the Allernora. Quinn had put his watcher's mask on and had his forging hammer in his hands. He'd have been better off with the devices built into his metal arm or on the gauntlet he wore on his left arm. They carried a lot more firepower than a hammer ever would.

The fire on the bridge grew clearer until I could pick out the individual troops. Lucky for us, the fire blinded them to us flying down the river. The captain swung the ship at the last minute, bringing us parallel with the bridge. Ropes were thrown over to steady the ship, though Quinn leapt without waiting for the all-clear.

Now we waited for Quinn to do…whatever it was he had planned.

17

QUINN

The ship bumped gently against the bridge. I unhooked my rope and jumped across, landing on the stone bridge. I ran to where the Astarian troops were standing guard. I was most definitely not a Candalarian warrior, so they waited for me to approach.

"I'm a watcher and we are here to help. I need to talk with your commander, but we need to stay quiet. Do you understand?"

He nodded. "Captain Unlai is in command, Watcher. I'll take you to him."

I helped the man to his feet. He only glanced at my metal arm, which I was thankful for. I didn't have time to answer questions right now.

We crossed through the sleeping troops to where a small tent had been set up. The guard outside nodded and held the flap for me to enter. Captain Unlai stood over a map of the area contemplating strategy even at this late hour.

She looked up as the flap closed. The woman was short but stout. I had no doubt she knew how to use the sword strapped to her back. "Watcher, to what do I owe this pleasure?"

"I thought you could use some assistance," I said. "I have an idea, but I'll need your cooperation."

"We will all be dead tomorrow, so please, I will do whatever you ask."

"Here's the plan."

BRULLE

I watched through my binoculars from the foredeck as Quinn crossed to the commander's tent. He entered and, after a few minutes, he emerged with the leader. She quickly rounded up the closest members of her army and sent them off, running in all directions. After ten minutes, the troops were assembled near the foot of the bridge.

Quinn swung his arms over his head and the troops set off at a trot toward Sunchome. So far, I hadn't heard anything that would tip the Candalarians off that something was up.

Quinn ran to the center of the bridge and readied his hammer. A cry went up from the Candalarians on the Sunchome side of the river. More shouts went up as the men and women of Sunchome ran to the gates of the city.

Quinn shouted and swung the hammer with all his might. The impact was deafening. The bridge bucked like a wave hitting the shore. He swung again and the center of the bridge splintered and started falling in massive chunks to the river below.

"Get ready!" the captain screamed as the ship lurched from the sudden shifting of the bridge. The crew raced around readying the ship to get away.

Quinn ran for the side of the bridge, but another shock wave sent him sprawling. He pushed himself up and tried to get moving, but it wasn't the vibrations from the collapse, Quinn was in trouble.

I jumped over the rail onto the bridge.

"Brulle, no!" Isabella screamed at me as I stumbled over to Quinn. The Candalarians on the far side opened fire with arrows. Their short bows didn't have much range, but it was enough to target the ship.

"I've got you," I said to an exhausted Quinn as I hefted him up and helped him across. We reached the rail when the first of the Candalarians rode up the far end of the bridge. The captain and Isabella leapt over and helped Quinn get on the ship.

I swung Gertie around and opened fire at the approaching horsemen. Two tumbled out of their saddles, while another fell off the side of the bridge into the water far below. More horsemen galloped onto the bridge, but then the air was full of arrows. The Sunchome troops rallied and struck at the approaching riders.

I took the opportunity to jump across to the airship, landing with a thud.

"Go!" shouted the captains as the approaching Candalarians' arrows struck the side of the ship. If the balloon burst, we'd all be dead.

The ship spun to the left and started to rise. Isabella ran to the rail and lobbed the vials of fire potion onto the rafts below us. They burst into flames, and we sped off into the night.

I found Quinn perched against the rail, drinking from a water skin. "You okay?"

He nodded. "Using that much strength just weakened me. I'll be fine in a few minutes."

With that, the savior of Sunchome leaned his head back and went to sleep.

VICTORIA

I watched as the Lunatic's Revenge flew back into the airfield. We'd set up temporary docks for the airships inside the walls of Iron Harbor. The normal towers were too far outside the city to be considered safe from attack. Fifteen airships had answered the call to defend the city from the approaching invasion.

Captain Breachcolm stood next to me on the balcony as the ship tied off to the makeshift tower. "Doesn't look like she took any damage. Must be nice," he said, flashing me his best smile.

"I guess Captain Stokes is a better pilot," I responded sweetly.

He laughed, and I joined him. The staff had moved a table and chairs onto the balcony so we could enjoy the nice weather. Given we all might die soon, it was a thoughtful gesture.

After a while, Quinn, Isabella, and Brulle joined us on the balcony that overlooked where the airships were tied off.

"It went well?" I asked as they took seats around the table. Phantom appeared and nuzzled my hand. Images I associated with fear swam through my brain.

"I wasn't in any danger, tattletale," Brulle said to his companion.

"Now this I have to hear," I said while petting Phantom's head. He purred like a kitten.

Brulle, Quinn, and Isabella took turns telling me about the fight at the bridge. All eyes turned to Quinn when Brulle described Quinn destroying the bridge with his hammer. "And it only took two blows to bring the center of the bridge down."

"It should have only taken one," Quinn grumbled.

"That's a mighty powerful hammer," Captain Breachcolm said when the story was complete.

"It's not the hammer, is it?" I asked. It was time for Quinn to own up to his true powers. If we were all going to fight together, the others needed to understand what Quinn could truly do.

He shook his head but didn't say anything.

"Leave the boy alone," Brulle said to me. "He's been through enough tonight."

"No, I need to tell you," Quinn said, then glanced at the captain. "I'd appreciate your discretion."

"I'll take it to the grave with me."

Quinn launched into a story, though I was surprised that he started with working on a project for Usorin instead of just explaining that he could do actual magic. He began with losing his arm, then the death of Ruari and the rest of the blacksmiths he considered family, fighting the Ovros, and finally Lady Maelyrra granting him the power to protect Astaria with magic.

"Now that is a story," Brulle remarked when Quinn went silent. "Lad, I'm sorry for all that you've endured. It would have broken most people."

"I thought it had when Roland died, but I found a way to get through it. Now we just have to stop an invasion and a goddess if they can summon her."

"We are in this together," I reminded him. "Quinn, we are your family now, and even if we don't all make it through, there will be others who step up to be part of the watchers."

"Thank you," Quinn said, then changed the subject. "What has happened since we left?"

"The Norns are moving ships into the northern part of the bay. The good captain can fill us in better," I said, shifting uncomfortably in my seat.

Breachcolm unrolled a map and placed it on the table. "This one doesn't have blood all over it," he said with a quick grin at Quinn. He jabbed his finger into the map. "The Norn fleet is here. They are moving siege weapons onto shore from their transports. They have about seventy ships if you include the transports. Probably a couple of thousand troops in total."

"That's three times the number that Everard destroyed at Cheim," Brulle said. "Without Everard, we are in trouble."

"He'll be here, though I'm not sure how much help he'll be." Quinn had pulled out his hammer and set it in his lap. "We need to take out as many siege engines as we can."

"I'll handle that if Brulle doesn't mind giving me a hand," I said with a smirk. "You know why Brulle is great at cooking?"

Everyone groaned, except Isabella, who asked, "Why?"

"Cause he gives sage advice."

I met Quinn at the smithy he'd taken over to work on his devices. He looked up when I entered. Dark rings hung under his eyes and his shoulders slumped, but under the circumstances, all of us were doing what we had to do. If we stood any chance of beating Nimish, we would need Quinn at full power, not an exhausted ragdoll.

"Victoria, I'm glad you are here. I have an idea for a new weapon if you have fire potions left," he said, stretching his back as he stood.

I'd given Isabella six vials, which left me with eighteen. It would take months to replace it, but if things went poorly, it wouldn't matter. "I do."

He picked up a long tube and a metal ball. He gestured to follow him as he headed for the door. "Let's go have some fun."

"Your idea of fun scares me," I said, though I went along. "How are you doing?"

"I'm fine," he said with a shrug. "We need to cut down the numbers on the opposing side before they can get to the walls."

I'd seen Everard eliminate thousands with a single spell. I wondered if Quinn's magic would be able to do the same. "That's not what I'm asking."

"I'm not sure what you mean," he said when I didn't continue.

Nothing like diving in headfirst. "That was quite the display how you stood up to the maguses the other day. I'm very impressed, though it's not very Quinn-like. I'm worried about how you are holding up."

He looked embarrassed. "While I was working at the smithy, the magus would come in and demand things, ridicule or humiliate Master Ruari, except Usorin. He was frightening in his power, but always respectful. I found myself looking up to him as what a magus should be."

"Then Usorin injured you." My heart raced at the thought of having your arm unceremoniously amputated by a man you had trusted. What a massive betrayal. I'd heard Usorin had a temper, but this was unacceptable.

"Worse. He was trying to kill Ruari, and I got in the way. He would have killed him for a mistake the magus himself made. Ruari warned him not to add alarium to the firebox, but he wouldn't listen. The heat destroyed the whole furnace."

The missing piece of the puzzle clicked in. "The maguses are arrogant, but they do protect the people."

Quinn swiveled and stared me straight in the eye. "A few do, but most of them decided to stay in their keeps and let us die to protect them. I guess I'll give Porter and Holrough credit for at least being here. I don't know if they'll fight."

"More of the maguses arrived last night. Everard will be here later. They will fight because they have so much to lose." I knew Quinn had an ax to grind with Usorin, but the others hadn't wronged him. While the governing ability of the maguses could be problematic, they usually took care of their region.

"We'll see." He resumed walking. "The watchers will be the ones who win this fight if we can find a way to stop the cult. The war is just a distraction for bringing the goddess here."

I scoffed. "A distraction that can kill you is quite effective."

He chuckled. "True, but we need to focus on the main objective."

We reached the harbor wall, put our masks on, and climbed the stairs in silence. Levelheaded Quinn was hurt on a much deeper level than I'd imagined. No wonder he was hostile toward the magus.

"Permission to come up," Quinn called to the guards' station on the wall.

"Master Quinn, permission granted."

When I climbed up, the guards snapped to attention. "Greetings, watchers. To what do we owe the honor?"

I gestured to Quinn. "My associate wants to show off his new toy."

"I hope this one works better than the last," one of the guards whispered, drawing chuckles from the others.

"You blow up one tube and everyone is a critic," Quinn said with a laugh.

This was his element, being with people who worked for what they had. People were drawn to Quinn. He led with his heart, not the cold, calculating eye of a watcher. I wondered what others thought of me.

"So what does this do?" I asked as the guards looked on.

"If it works," Quinn said with a sidelong glance at the guards. He hefted the spiked ball. "We'll be able to throw this a long way. When it hits…boom!"

"Boom sounds dangerous," I said.

"Let me demonstrate." Quinn placed the fist-sized projectile in the hatch on the black metal tube. He fastened the lid down and set the tube on the wall. "Step back."

All the guards already had, so I joined them.

Quinn pushed a button on the back of the tube and ducked, covering his ears with his hands.

Thump!

The tube belched out a flame and the spiked ball flew out and landed well in the harbor.

"No boom," I said.

"That's where you come in."

Ahhh. Behind every good man sat a better alchemist.

BRULLE

ood evening, Brulle," Victoria greeted me as Phantom and I entered the meeting room. She wore all black, which meant there was a mission coming up. Quinn was dressed the same. "May I speak to you for a moment?"

Isabella stood talking with Quinn as she gestured to the row of tubes laid out on the table. Something interesting was going on. "Of course."

Victoria stepped out into the hallway and closed the door behind me. "Tomorrow is the last day before the attack."

"If Nimish was telling us the truth."

She nodded. "Regardless, I need a favor from you."

"You know you don't have to ask."

"This time I do." She looked back at the door like she wanted to make sure it was still closed. "When I signal, grab Quinn."

"What?" Victoria had a wild sense of humor, but she was dead serious. I wanted to know what she was up to.

"I need you to trust me. I'm doing this for his own good."

"I don't know Quinn well, but betraying his trust isn't a great idea." Whatever she was planning, I wasn't sure I wanted any part of it.

"Which is why I'm not giving you any details. If he's angry, it will rest solely on me." She put her hand on my arm. "I swear I'll not harm Quinn in any way."

I nodded. "You have my trust. I'll follow your lead."

"Thank you." She opened the door and returned to the table.

What was Victoria up to? Since she knew Quinn far better than I, I let it go. If things went sideways, I'd deal with it then.

I joined Quinn, Isabella, and Victoria at the conference table once again, though the maguses weren't present. I wasn't sure if they hadn't been invited or they were staying away after their run-in with Quinn. He had dark circles ringing his eyes and his eyelids drooped. I wondered how much longer he could keep going.

Travis Breachcolm entered the room. "Sorry, I'm late."

"Thank you for coming, Captain," Quinn said. "From the Maiden's scouting, we know the Norns have assembled their siege weapons and are now moving them into position behind the front line of their troops. We have tonight to take advantage of the situation."

"How so?" the captain asked. "We don't have enough airships for a flanking attack."

"We only need one."

All eyes turned to Quinn. The smirk on Victoria's face told me she knew what Quinn's plan was. It would be nice if they shared more information with me.

Quinn picked up a metal tube. "These will deliver a projectile filled with fire potion. A swift flyby attack and twelve of these will eliminate a fair portion of their weaponry."

"Why not wait until they are in position?" I asked, not seeing the benefit of a night-time attack. "We'd kill far more enemies with troops protecting the engines."

"First, that would add to the deaths the cultists need," Victoria pointed out. "Second, they won't have as many archers watching for airships this far in advance."

"Victoria and I will fly on the Maiden's Kiss under cover of night, make a single pass, and destroy as many engines as possible. With the range of the cannons, we can shoot from outside bow range. Every machine we destroy will save lives," Quinn said as if that explained everything.

I turned the plan over in my head. Night attacks were tricky and often more dangerous than they were worth. Things went wrong under the cover of darkness, and you didn't always realize it until too late. I started to protest, but then I realized that they were right. Nimish needed a lot of people dying at a certain time, and we needed as few people to die at that time as possible. This was a fairly low risk way to prevent some of the deaths. "I'm in."

"Me too," Isabella said. "Anything I can do to help."

"Excellent." Victoria stood up, throwing her hands wide. "This calls for a toast."

Victoria went to the table where the food had been laid out for the maguses and brought back five goblets filled with wine. She handed the first to Quinn, then the rest of us. "To our success."

We all clinked glasses and took a drink. I set my cup down on the table. Quinn, standing to my left, set his down, then stumbled.

"Brulle."

I grabbed Quinn and got my arm under him. His head lolled to the side.

Victoria's expression softened, showing the worry she felt. "Quinn hasn't slept in days. I put a sleeping potion in his drink. The mission still goes as planned, but we'll leave Quinn here to sleep."

"And if his devices don't work?" I asked. Quinn started to snore lightly on my shoulder.

"Then we drop the projectiles like Isabella did at the bridge and return home."

A cough sounded from the doorway. "You seem to have broken Quinn," Everard said from the entry.

The Arch Magus had arrived.

<hr>

The captain and I carried the sleeping Quinn to a room and got him settled on the bed. Asleep, he looked more like a boy than a man. The metal arm reminded me that Quinn had lived through more than most people of any age.

I closed the door. Phantom rubbed against my leg, sending an image of sleeping kittens. "Yes, he's one tired cub."

We returned to the conference room. Everard sat in a chair, a goblet of wine in his hand. His face had lost most of its color since I'd last seen him, leaving him ashen. His hands trembled as he took a sip from his cup. "The illness has spread, but I've been conserving my strength. I don't have much time left, but I'd rather go out defending Astaria than lying in bed."

"Good to see you, old friend," I said to Everard and found I truly meant it. The reason I'd left the watchers seemed inconsequential under the circumstances.

"It is good to see you too, Brulle."

"You don't seem surprised that I'm alive."

"I knew all along, but you'd made your decision, so I honored it."

My heart sank at that. I knew it was stupid, but I'd always assumed if Everard had known I was alive, he would have convinced me to come back. To realize all along I could have just...retired? I pushed the emotions away. "I wish we could have reunited under better circumstances."

"Me as well, though this seems right. We've fought together more times than I can count. It is good to be back with you all. I sent the other watchers to command the ground troops along with the magus we trained to fight."

"That is good news," Victoria said. "We are going to hit the Norns tonight. Each blow weakens them."

"I'm leaving Astaria in very good hands," Everard said, stopping to take a drink. "Quinn has the magic to protect Astaria now. You will need to be there for him as he grows into his power. He is far stronger than I ever was but will need friends to help him."

"We'll take care of Quinn." I looked over at Isabella and decided it was time. "I have one piece of Watcher's business for you, Everard."

He waved his hand. "And that would be?"

"I'd like to introduce Isabella Kettell. She is my apprentice watcher."

Isabella stuttered. "I'm not sure I'm ready, but I'm happy to join the watchers."

Victoria laughed. "None of us is ever ready, but you have earned your place amongst us."

"Isabella, please approach me," Everard said, pushing himself up to stand. "Given the unprecedented nature of our situation, we'll bypass the normal testing and training."

Isabella did as asked and knelt before the wizened old arch magus. "Isabella Kettell, I entrust the Aldon region of Astaria to you when Brulle has deemed you ready. Until such time, you are a watcher in full and will learn from Brulle as many have before you. Do you accept this charge?"

Tears streamed down Isabella's face. "I do," she stammered out.

"Then rise and take your place as a watcher of Astaria."

We all cheered as Isabella got to her feet. Hugs were exchanged for a fleeting moment of joy. It was over far too fast.

Captain Breachcolm cleared his throat. "I'm off to prepare the ship. We set sail in twenty."

I stopped to shake Everard's hand. "Until we meet again."

Everard's eyes pierced mine. "In this life or the next, old friend."

It was time to go.

***

The Maiden sped across the clear sky, taking us toward a sneak attack on the unexpecting Norns. The wind was at our backs and the crew was ready. Victoria instructed the crew on how to load and use the cannons. A box of fire potion had been secured to the deck, loaded with projectiles.

"Whatever you do, don't drop these," she repeated for the third time. "None of us want to walk back to Iron Harbor."

"Captain, we've got 'em. Norns are up ahead," Cal called from above.

"We'll sweep in and broadside them. Everyone to your places."

I grabbed up my cannon and waited to be told to load. Below us, I could see the fires from the Norn camps and the wagon-drawn siege engines in the center of the ring of fires. They were protecting them from ground attack, but not from the air. This was a master stroke.

"For the love of all that's holy, we've got company!" Cal yelled.

A shadow crossed the bow of the airship. We weren't alone up here.

BRULLE

All hands to stations!" Captain Breachcolm yelled, running for the deck.

The crew scrambled to take up positions. I unholstered Gertie and prepared to fire. Another airship swooped down out of the cloud cover above us. We'd thought the siege engines were unprotected, but the Norns had outsmarted us.

"We need to protect the captain," Victoria shouted. She signaled to Isabella, and we both followed, with Phantom taking the lead up the stairs.

"Hold on!" The captain spun the wheel, and the Maiden turned and pointed back to Iron Harbor. "We'll make a run for it."

"Ship at forty-five, Captain," Cal called from the crow's nest. "She's moving in for a stern rake."

"Damn," the captain said as he spun the lift wheel. The nose of the ship rose as the port and starboard propellers twisted.

The cannons on the approaching ship fired. The Maiden rocked as a couple clipped the aft portion of the ship.

"Phantom, go to Victoria," I said before I moved to get a shot at the approaching vessel. Once at the aft of the ship, I sighted Gertie and let fly. Screams came from the other ship as the slugs dappled their balloon.

"We've got another coming in hot!" Cal yelled.

I kept my sights on the first ship and fired another series of rounds into the ship's balloon. The balloon rocked with the stress of the slugs striking it. I was too far away to punch straight through the toughened cloth, but a series of shots should weaken it enough to burst.

Another round of cannon fire came from the other ship, and I was thrown to the side. I got to my knees, loaded, and fired another salvo into the approaching ship. Shouts and curses from the enemy crew were clear until the balloon burst, dropping the airship like a rock.

I scrambled back to the helm to find the captain steering the ship toward the new arrival. The captain yelled, "Prepare to repel boarders!"

At his side, I aimed at the intruders crossing onto the Maiden and pulled the trigger. Nothing happened. I opened the feed chamber, where a deformed slug was stuck in the breach. Misfires happened seldomly, but when they did, it was at the worst time. I pulled my knife out and worked at freeing the obstruction.

"I've got a jam," I said to Isabella. "Watch my back."

"Got it," she yelled, standing over me with her pistols while waiting for the ships to meet up.

She didn't need to wait long. The Maiden's Kiss shuddered as the enemy ship slid alongside. Ropes were thrown across in an attempt to take the ship.

"Repel boarders!"

The damn slug was still jammed solid as the first wave of Norn attackers jumped across to land on the deck. The first to arrive was greeted with two shots from Isabella and Victoria's pistols. He flew backward and fell between the ships to the ground below.

Phantom raked his claws down the chest of the next attacker, taking him out of the fight. I shove Gertie into her holster and grabbed my knives. The captain, Victoria, Isabella, and I stood shoulder to shoulder, protecting the command deck, as more Norns jumped across the breach. A wooden baton spun through the air, striking the captain. He slumped down next to me.

I reached down and felt blood, but he gripped my hand to show me he was alive. "Protect the captain," I said to Isabella, stepping in front of him.

Phantom prowled behind us to deter anyone from taking the stairs up to the helm.

"Fire!" a Norn screamed from the bow.

Victoria shot the nearest Norn and kicked him out of the way. "That's not good."

With all the boxes of explosives affixed to the deck, ready to take out the siege engines, we were in trouble if the fire spread.

A Norn landed in front of Isabella and knocked her to the side with a massive club. He raised the weapon to finish her off. I got in close and rammed both my knives into his chest. Blood sprayed, and the club dropped from his fingers. He grabbed me by the duster and fell backward.

"Brulle!" Victoria screamed as she raced to my side. She pounded on the dying man's grip, trying to break me free before he pulled us both over the side.

"Leave me," I said, attempting to push her away.

"Never."

She pulled one of my knives out of the man with a sickening sound. She stabbed it into his wrist and turned the blade. His hand loosened, but he still held firm with the other.

"I've got you," Isabella said, now at my side. She pushed her pistol into the Norn's other wrist and fired.

A plume of blood sprayed everywhere, and the Norn's weight carried him over the side, minus a hand.

"Damn, those were my best knives."

"We'll get you new ones," Isabella said as she shot another Norn who landed on the rail. He screamed as he fell.

Cal ran onto the deck. "Captain, the ship is overrun."

Damn. I pulled Gertie from her holster. "Time to go."

The Norns had congregated to the breach in our defenses and swarmed the ship. They would overrun the Maiden's Kiss in a matter of minutes. With the ground a mile below and the fire definitely spreading, we needed to swipe the Norn vessel if we were going to live through this.

"Get everyone across, now," I said. "Cal, get the captain over."

Phantom knocked a heavyset Norn down the stairs into the raiders following, buying us time to abandon the ship. Cal and Victoria got the captain across.

"Phantom, now."

The cat phased out of sight and ran to the rail. With a single leap, he was over. Isabella and I were the only ones left. "Come on!"

I turned and ran for the rail. Isabella jumped across. "Cut the ropes!"

She pulled her belt knife and started cutting the two ships apart. The Norn warrior returned, reached out, and grabbed my ankle. Without thinking, I drove the rifle butt into his face. His head slammed into the deck. The ping of metal caught my attention. The slug had popped free from the force of the blow.

I climbed the rail and leapt across the increasing distance as the rear of the boats swung apart. I jumped, catching the rail with the tip of my boot, and went sprawling across the deck. Not my most graceful move ever.

Captain Breachcolm was on his feet and mostly ready to fight. "We need to secure the helm."

"I'll take the captain, Cal, and Phantom to get to the ship under our control," Victoria said, as calm as if we were discussing a picnic. "There are two more ropes. Isabella and Brulle, cut them."

I loaded Gertie and said to Isabella, "Let's go."

She had a knife in one hand and a pistol in the other. She looked every bit the Watcher, minus the mask.

I took the lead, shooting any of the crew that had stayed behind. Loud thuds came from the quarterdeck. Hopefully, they had control of the ship. Isabella ran ahead and started cutting away the bow rope. I fired a series of shots into the middle rope, and it fell apart, along with a good section of the railing.

The Norns were still attacking the remainder of the Maiden's crew left on Breachcolm's ship. The Norns possessed overwhelming numbers, and even with the watchers and our toys, we'd be hard pressed to overcome such a disadvantage and save the Maiden.

I raised Gertie and directed a stream of slugs into the Maiden's Kiss's balloon. It burst. The gondola crashed into our new ship, and I heard the fore rope snap. Screams of surprise and panic came from the Norns on the Maiden. The ship spun, throwing bodies from the deck.

Victoria appeared at my side. "We didn't stop the siege engines."

The explosives! I'd forgotten the box that was now surrounded by fire on the dying Maiden's Kiss. They would explode sooner or later.

"Captain, get us as high as possible!" I yelled.

The nose of the ship rose, and we accelerated upward. I could feel the engines below deck struggling to match what the captain demanded.

A muffled thud followed by a huge explosion rocked the ship. I grabbed the rail and held on as the blast wave dissipated.

"What happened?" Isabella asked when she reached us.

We peered over the rail at the chaos below. The Maiden's Kiss had fallen into the middle of the Norn siege engines. While it didn't destroy as many as we had hoped to, quite a few of them were now crushed and on fire.

"The fire potions. Don't drop them."

Victoria sniffed. "I guess the Norns didn't follow directions well."

"And we are all happy about that."

22

VICTORIA

"Brulle, that was dangerous," I said to him, though I knew he'd made the only choice he could. More people dead, and we weren't even fighting the main battle yet. "But brilliant nonetheless."

Brulle nodded. "I feel bad for the crew, but we'd have died trying to save them."

I fought back the tears that threatened to overtake me. Travis Breachcolm and his people had lost everything because I'd gotten them involved. I want to scream at the unfairness of it all, but many more people would die over the next day. At least their sacrifice hadn't been made in vain.

While the damage from the Maiden's Kiss explosion hadn't destroyed as many siege engines as it could have, a good section in the middle of them were gone after the ship fell on top of them. It would slow the Norns down enough to help.

Captain Breachcolm christened his new ship the Maiden's Arse and we made our way back to Iron Harbor. We helped man the stations since Cal had been the only crew member to survive our encounter with the Norns.

The sun was well up by the time we limped into the city. We tied off, and the watchers returned to the conference room. Everard and Quinn sat at the table. Their discussion stopped as we entered, looking far worse for wear.

"What happened?" Quinn asked.

"Long story," I said. I went to the table and poured myself a large cup of wine. "Would anyone else care for one?"

"I think I'll pass," Quinn said.

That stung, but I'd been justified in my actions. I hoped Quinn saw it the same way. "Yes, I'm sorry for having to knock you out, but you needed sleep if you are to be any use tomorrow."

"I don't like it, but I understand, and you are right, as usual."

I took a large drink. "How are things looking?"

"Not great," Everard said from his seat at the head of the table. "The scouts have been reporting."

Brulle grabbed a cup of wine and handed it to Isabella before bringing his cup and the bottle to the table. "Is the map up to date?"

Quinn nodded. "There are about a thousand horse troops on this side of the river and another two thousand on the far side."

Small horse markers sat outside the Iron Harbor on the map. A square wooden block sat on the island of Coveg. "Ran out of pieces?"

"No," Quinn said. "We don't know what or how many people are on the island. One of the airships made a pass over it, but the Tofragrad threw fire at it, so they left. There are three or more ships anchored off the back side of the island, but they appear empty."

"Do you think a preemptive strike would be in order?" Brulle asked, though he didn't sound thrilled at the idea, considering how the siege engine preemptive strike had gone.

"We discussed it," Everard said. "If we destroy the camp, then Nimish would relocate and do the ritual somewhere else, somewhere we might not be able to find in time. She needs to feel safe enough that we can launch a strike tomorrow night. Two airships are watching the back side of the island. Once she is there, we go."

"So all the people who die defending Iron Harbor are sacrifices so we can stop Nimish?" Isabella asked.

"Unfortunately," Brulle said to his apprentice.

I watched Isabella's eyes cloud up. Being a watcher was far more difficult than anyone would ever guess. With the power to protect the people of Astaria came an inordinate amount of decision making that led people to die. In order to protect the world, we had to make sacrifices. I gestured to the wooden army men on the north of Iron Harbor, more to change the subject than out of a need to know. "How many Norns?"

"We're guessing fifteen hundred or so, but they are fierce and each one is worth three of us."

"We know," Isabella said before emptying her cup. Brulle refilled it.

Brulle ran down the fight with the enemy airships. I pushed back the tears again. They would have to wait until this was all over. The thought of joining Brulle and Phantom in the middle of nowhere sounded really appealing.

"In the end, we destroyed a good number of engines and took two airships from them. I doubt they have many more, but we'll need the wall troops prepared in case." Brulle reached into his satchel, then froze.

"What is it?" I asked, wondering what had made Brulle pause.

"I'd forgotten about these."

He pulled a sheaf of papers out of the bag and handed it to me. Nimish Nimkar's likeness peered back at me. "Where did you get this?"

"Cian had a poison-trapped lockbox at the safehouse. I found those inside. There are charts of the runes and other papers that looked important. I thought the three of you might make sense of them."

I handed the picture to Quinn. "So this is the mysterious cult leader."

"She's far more attractive in person," Isabella said before she blushed. "If you are into the super evil type."

Quinn chuckled. "Nah, I get enough evil on the job."

He handed the picture to Everard. "Striking woman."

I started laying out the assorted papers on the map. "Quinn, are these the runes from the wand?"

"They are. Do you still have the etching from the wand?"

I rummaged through my belt pouch. A folded piece of parchment sat at the bottom.

"May I?" Everard asked, his hand outstretched.

I handed the Arch Magus the sheet, and he looked it over. "I don't know what rune this is." He pointed to a three-sided rune.

I looked at the parchment Brulle had given me. "It means strength. The one next to it means freedom, but it is sideways to the others."

"That is a control symbol. The wand can control anything the wielder had the strength to overcome. That wand is dangerous," Everard said.

I swallowed hard, not wanting to reveal what I knew I had to. "I lost it when Nimish captured me. I should have left it with Quinn to study. I'm sorry."

"You couldn't have known you'd be captured," Quinn said, putting his hand on mine. "The knowledge of what it can do is enough for now. When the wand comes into play, we need to eliminate it."

"The key here is the wielder has to be stronger than what is being controlled. If they use the wand on you, you can resist, if you are more focused than the user," Everard said.

"Interesting," Isabella said. "If they try to make one of us do something, we have a choice?"

I thought back to the fight in the compound. I'd used the wand to control the fire golem. It had spoken to me, which I hadn't thought unusual at the time, but now I realized it had been testing me to see if I could control it. Was strength of will the key? It was the only thing that made sense and could be the loophole we needed to neutralize the wand's effects. "If your will is stronger than the user, you can resist the wand. At least, I think so."

Isabella nodded and sat back in her chair.

I selected another sheet. It held a drawing of a circle with symbols etched around it and a swirling design in the center. Words were written at the bottom, but in a language I'd never seen before.

Everard took the page. "This is written in a dialect of Tofragrad. If I'm reading it correctly, the summoning needs to take place on the thirteenth moon cycle. That would be why the attack has to be tomorrow. If we can delay it, there won't be another thirteen moons for at least a hundred years."

"That is a long time to wait. No wonder they are in a hurry," Brulle said.

Our conversation was interrupted by horns blaring on the walls. We went out on the balcony. In the distance, the cultists and forces of Norns and Candalarians had arrived at Iron Harbor. Tomorrow the attack would come, and at night Nimish Nimkar would attempt to summon a goddess to our plane.

Time to get ready for a fight of historical proportions.

23

BRULLE

The sun came up over Iron Harbor the next morning. Phantom and I looked out over a sea of Norns from our vantage point atop the north wall. Quinn had gone to the bridges and Victoria to the west wall to fight the Candalarians.

The Astarian troops gathered inside the base of the wall. A mixture of lancers, archers, and pikes stood at the ready. I wanted today to be over with. The waste of all these people on every side, all for Nimish's desire to bring a goddess to this plane, seemed ridiculous.

"The commander reported they are ready," Isabella said as she ascended the wall. She wore a watcher's mask that Quinn had provided. I'd also accepted a mask from Quinn, but it sat in my satchel. It didn't work well with my beard, and I wasn't shaving ten years of growth to wear the damn thing.

A loud crashing noise announced the Norn's attack. The heavy siege engines threw giant barbed arrows at the city. How many shots had they dragged along with the engines? Given that we'd destroyed a good portion of their engines, they would have more shots per machine, but the reduced number of weapons would slow their ability to breach the walls.

"Down!" the wall commander shouted. We all got behind the stone wall.

Screams came from my right as a bolt that slammed into the stonework sent razor shards of shrapnel through the air. Medics ran along the wall to pull the injured away from the fight. More bolts slammed into Iron Harbor's defenses. Each shook the walls, but they held firm.

"They're on the move!" the commander shouted. "Ready the gates."

I snuck a peek over the crenels. A black wave of Norns charged at the city. From the far left I saw the telltale plumes of dust from the horsemen bringing their troops into the fight, but Victoria would have to hold her wall.

"Watcher Wyndham, the Candalarian calvary is charging," the west wall commander reported. He was far younger than I would have expected, but the scars on his face spoke to his past as a fighter.

"Are the archers ready?" I knew they were, but wanted to keep the commander engaged. If things went sideways, I'd need him to react quickly.

He nodded.

"When the front lines reach the mark, blow the horn. I'll signal the retreat."

"Very well."

We watched from between the crenels, which bucked at intervals as the Norns pounded the north wall with their siege engines. The Candalarians were open ground fighters, so no engines accompanied them, but if they got close enough to the city, pitch-soaked fire arrows would come into play. The last thing we needed was a fire inside the walls.

Over the last few days, the troops had dug holes at night and camouflaged them with woven grass mats. Each hole held five archers. Other holes were empty but would down horses as they charged. The goal was to weaken the attack, but each death provided the source of power Nimish needed for her ritual to work.

The first wave of riders got to the mark we'd agreed on and the horn blew. The lids were thrown aside, and arrows filled the air. The horsemen were too close to the archers to avoid them. The arrows ripped through the front ranks, dropping warriors and horses alike. The riders who survived their horses' fall were picked off by Astarian arrows or trampled by the riders behind them.

Well, that had worked as planned. Would miracles never cease? I'm sure they would, but I'd take any good luck we could get. "Call the retreat."

A second horn blew, and two hundred lancers charged out of the western gate and hit the side of the disoriented attackers. The archers ran for the port doors set into the wall. The Candalarians riddled the retreating archers with their own arrows but had to turn to face the lancers as they struck the left flank.

Chaos ensued as the lancers fought hand to hand with the Candalarians. The wave of riders had broken, leaving small groups to fight off the armored lancers. Their javelins gave the Astarians the advantage in this kind of fight, but it wouldn't last.

"Call off the lancers," I told the commander. He did and the remnants of the soldiers disengaged and fought their way back to the city. A cheer went up from the walls, but I'd guess only fifty of the lancers made it back alive. From the corpse-littered battlefield, the Candalarians had lost significantly more.

That battle had swung our way thanks to surprising the Candalarians, but our trick was gone and they had a lot more troops to throw at the walls. If only I'd stopped the Blue Heron before they had gotten to control the Norns and Candalarian leaders. What might have been was a waste of time though, so now we had to hold Iron Harbor until the true fight began.

All we could do was wait. Unfortunately, I forgot my needlepoint back in Stillhold.

⸻ ⬦ ⸻

Quinn

I was finishing my preparations on the Iron Harbor's main bridge for the fight ahead when a young aide ran up to me. "Watcher Quinn, we've spotted the enemy."

I resisted telling the lad that I could see that for myself. Massive piles of boulders completely blocked the outer bridges, leaving the center and largest of the bridges to hold off the attackers. Everard had suggested destroying the bridges, but tackling the one bridge at Sunchome had exhausted me, and these bridges were twice its size. Instead of completely blocking off the center bridge, the engineers had constructed six stone barricades across the main bridge. We could close off all the bridges, but Everard pointed out that we need to spread out the opposing forces so they didn't overrun the city's defenders through numbers.

Each barricade held a contingent of Astarian warriors and archers. The gorge the Allernora ran through prevented the horse people from going around the bridges. If they wanted access to the city, they'd have to break through our layers of defenses.

Trumpets sounded from across the river, and the Candalarian warriors flowed onto the bridge like a flood. The first wave wheeled their horses, firing arrows at the stone barricades of the Astarians. While the defenders ducked for cover, a contingent of Norn berserkers charged the fortifications.

What were the Norns doing fighting with the Candalarians? They were blood enemies, but Nimish had found a way to make them fight alongside each other. We hadn't prepared for this turn of events.

"Stand ready! Norns approaching!" came from the top of the wall behind us. The amplification device I'd crafted worked wonders. If the rest of the devices I'd developed worked as well…

"Archer's fire!"

The sounds of twanging bow strings and the hiss of flying arrows filled the air over the barricade, slamming into the Norns and Candalarians alike. The fact that the two nations fought together showed just how deep the cultists controlled the leaders.

The fighting raged on when I spotted a breach in the barricade in front of us. "Magus, close the gap," I yelled, moving into the fight.

Three Norn warriors cleared the top of the barricade with their axes, dropping defenders like saplings. More pushed into the hole, forcing the defenders to give way. Another hole developed off to my left as the Magus from Conrik Handley and her three chosen junior magus arrived.

"Watcher Quinn," the magus said as she reached my position. "What are we to do?"

"Spread out, two on each side of me. I'll call the retreat, and once the defenders are out of harm's way, we'll sweep the wall with lightning."

She nodded and got ready to fight.

"Fall back!" I yelled, using the magnifying stone ring to enhance my voice.

I ran to the largest breach and fired lightning into the closest Norn warrior. The bolt took him in the chest and drove him into his mates behind him.

With the break in the fighting, the defenders retreated to the next barricade. I saw the Magus and her people had followed suit and given the troops a chance to get back.

The Norns cheered and charged the first barricade. Hundreds of Norns climbed over the five-foot rock barricade. When the first reached the top of the barricade, I yelled, "Fire!"

Five arcs of lightning shot out of the alarium harnesses. Each of us swept back and forth in front of us, hitting as many of the Norns as possible. A club spun through the air, striking the junior magus to my left, dropping him. Defenders ran to pull the man free as the Norns tried to push forward.

"Rally!"

The archers fired, sweeping the first barricade. The defenders and magus climbed over the second barricade to cheers. The maguses and I had survived the first barricade. If we could hold the rest of the day, it would be a miracle. We hadn't counted on the Norns fighting alongside the Candalarians. Nimish had far more control than we expected.

Magus Handley returned, minus one apprentice magus. "I haven't used my magic in years. I'd forgotten how awesome and terrible it is. How many do you think we killed?"

"Not enough."

The afternoon wore on, falling into a pattern of holding the barricades, using magic to clear them, and then falling back. The Candalarians had abandoned their horses and fought on foot using their bows to offset our magic.

The sun was lowering in the west, but we held the last barricade before the city. Runners reported that the other two walls still held, as did the harbor. Once night fell, the fighting would cease. We would then have to stop the real threat, Nimish.

Our enemy readied for a last push, resting just outside bow range. We'd inflicted huge damage on them, but had lost too many defenders to guarantee holding the bridges. If the enemy got inside the city walls, it would be absolute butchery and Nimish would definitely get her death wish.

It was time to unleash our secret weapon. I sent word with my assistant to tell the commander we were ready. A few minutes later, our last gasp effort would play out. Hopefully, it would work.

"Candalarians, cease your attack or I, Everard, Arch Magus of Astaria, will bring my magic to stop you!" Everard's voice boomed across the bridges.

The man definitely knew how to make an entrance.

QUINN

"Retreat now," Everard said, his voice echoing over the battlefield. If the rings we'd placed around the city walls to amplify Everard's command worked, all the attackers would be hearing the same. If not, there was nothing I could do now.

A roar went up from the mobilizing attackers. Warriors rushed the last barricade.

"Stones aloft!" Everard commanded from above. Now we'd see if the magic I'd crafted would function for Everard. The boulders we'd placed began to rise at his command.

"Down!" I yelled.

The defenders all dropped to the cobblestone bridge. I activated my shield on my left arm, and the blue protective sphere encompassed me.

The largest stones we could find ringed the city. At the Arch Magus's command, they floated up as one, then sped over the massed attackers. With an ear-splitting detonation, all the rocks exploded, cascading the Norn and Candalarian warriors with stone shrapnel. Screams of agony erupted from the carnage.

A few minutes later, a tall man on a horse rode forward alone. He held a red cloth on the end of his spear. The Candalarians were requesting parley.

Everard had broken the attack.

I climbed over the last barricade, not falling flat on my face from exhaustion, and made my way to the horse rider. Shock flooded through my brain. I knew the Candalarian warrior who waited for me. Dakao, who Cian and I had met while first investigating the animal attacks on Astaria magus, sat rigid in his saddle. His long black beard had been woven into a braid. He slid off his horse to greet me.

Dakao had demonstrated a deep sense of honor when we fought together a few months ago. What could it hurt to take a shot and save as many lives as possible on all sides? "Dakao, are we meeting as friends or enemies?"

The huge warrior shook his head. "Quinn, it is unfortunate that we must meet this way. I am requesting an hour to collect our dead and wounded before we resume the battle."

I looked at the setting sun. Nimish needed death to fuel her ritual, and we'd provided it in droves. "Why are the Candalarians attacking us?"

"The Clan of Chiefs told us that it is in the wind to destroy Astaria and take the lands for our own. We are following the call of our ancestors."

"Do you remember the wolves we fought? The ones who attacked us in the forest?"

Confusion played over the big warrior's face. "Yes, but what does that have to do with our battle?"

"The wolves behaved in a way that we both knew at the time was not like wolves because they were controlled by a drug called Blue Heron. It works on people. My guess is the Clan of Chiefs is being forced by the drug to bring the might of Candalar against Astaria. I'm certain the Norns and Tofragrad are the same."

He tugged at his beard. "How is this to pass? Astarians will say anything to get what they want."

"You can fight here and one or both of us will die, or you can return to the Clan of Chiefs and look them in their eyes. If you see a slight blue tinge, then they are being controlled by Nimish."

"Where did you hear that name? She is a witch and a heretic."

"She is the one who started all this. You asked me to end the evil when we last met. She is behind the animal attacks, your missing wind walker, and this war. In order to restore peace and end the evil, I must kill her."

Dakao studied me for a long minute. "I cannot go against the Clan of Chiefs."

I rubbed my face half from exhaustion, half out of irritation that the warrior wouldn't even try to stop Nimish. I sighed. "I grant you until sunrise to see to your injured and perform the rites for your fallen. In the morning, Nimish will be dead and your people freed or I will be dead and you can resume your attack."

"Done." He held out his hand, and we grasped forearms. "I will send word to the others to cease their attacks until the morning. Good hunting, Quinn."

With that, the proud warrior of Candalar rode off the bridge to organize hundreds of funerals in a single night.

It was time to pay Nimish a visit.

Victoria

Quinn entered the command room dripping sweat and generally worse for the wear. He grabbed a slab of meat, bread, and ale and sat at the table. "We've declared a truce until morning. It should buy us enough time to take care of Nimish before she can do her ritual."

"You hope," I said, trying to keep the worry from my voice. "How are you holding up?"

He shrugged. "Victoria, I'm fine." He built and started eating his sandwich.

"You've pushed yourself to the limit and we have more ahead of us."

"What's all this about?" Everard asked as Brulle and Isabella brought him into the room. Everard looked tired, but there was a bit of color in his cheeks and he stood a bit straighter.

"I'm worried about Quinn," I answered. The Arch Magus lowered himself into the chair at the head of the table. Brulle placed a goblet of wine and some fruit in front of the older man.

"Quinn, that was fantastic," Everard said.

"How did you manage it?" Brulle asked, taking a seat. He tossed a chunk of meat to Phantom, who devoured it. "You put on quite the show of strength."

Quinn didn't look up. Killing people didn't set well with our artificer. After a long minute, he spoke. "I created a small metal spike that levitated the stones like my arm band does. It's paired with a second spike that we drove into the walls to counteract the lift needed."

I thought back to Quinn trying to lift a wagon and putting himself into the ground instead. "Much better than sinking yourself into the dirt."

He smirked at me, understanding the reference.

"With a second command, the spike burst, destroying the stone and turning it into a bomb. It worked far better than I expected."

"One last tale for my legacy," Everard said, a gleeful note in his tone.

Quinn didn't say anything else, just ate in silence. I doubted he would ever gloat about killing people.

I changed the subject. "We still need to find and stop Nimish or all this has been for naught."

"Only if she can summon a goddess," Brulle said around a mouthful of food. "If she can't, she just killed a lot of people for no reason."

"Can she summon Ghuasis?" Isabella asked. "No one has ever said if she can or can't."

"It is possible," Everard said, his hands steepled in front of his chest. "I studied the design of her ritual circle, and it looks correct. The questions are does she have enough power to open a portal to Ghuasis's plane and will the goddess accept her invitation to rule mortals? Those are things we don't know."

"Then Nimish doesn't know either," I said, forcing myself to stay calm. We weren't talking about turnip prices after all; these were people's lives hanging in the balance. "It's not like she could practice the ritual. For all she knows, she's not strong enough to accomplish it."

"No, she doesn't," Everard agreed. "She is a child playing with matches and not knowing if she'll burn her fingers or burn the world down."

"All this death on a maybe," Quinn said.

"The truly powerful rarely consider the costs of their planning. Nimish thinks she is saving the world, so no cost is too great." In this light, Everard looked like an old man, not the most powerful mage in Astaria that he once was.

"So what's the plan?" Brulle fetched more meat for Phantom and a mug of ale for himself. "Sun's down. When do we leave?"

Quinn finished his mug of ale. "I need time to recharge Everard's medallion so he's ready—"

"What?" Brulle and I said at the same time.

"He's not in any condition to go into a fight," I said to Quinn. "Everard can barely walk."

"Listen to Victoria, she's right," Brulle said, though I swore I heard "usually" added under his breath.

Everard held up his hand. "Quinn gave me a device to restore my energy for short periods of time. I have the most knowledge of the arcane ritual Nimish is using. I can't give advice if I'm not there."

"There is no way we can risk Everard in a fight on an enemy-controlled island. It is beyond stupid," Brulle said. Phantom growled his agreement.

Something sounded off, but I couldn't put my finger on it. "Quinn, are you good with this idea?"

"I don't like it one bit, but Everard is the Arch Magus, and he knows more than any of us. He's capable of making his own decisions." Quinn sunk into an open chair.

"Thank you, Quinn," Everard said with a nod to the artificer.

"No matter how dumb they are."

This was going nowhere fast. "How long do you need, Quinn?"

"An hour."

"We meet at the Lunatic's Revenge in an hour." I grabbed my satchel and prepared to leave.

The final showdown was at hand, and I had forgotten my gloves.

BRULLE

Captain Stokes lowered the Lunatic's Revenge to the sand, allowing us to disembark onto the island. I'd argued to leave Everard behind, his age making him a liability, but I'd been overruled.

Quinn wore a leather satchel over one shoulder full of devices he'd created. I hoped they were as powerful as Everard's magic had been. I'd heard of Quinn's fight with the Candalarians on the bridge, but the wall guards claimed Everard had been the one to turn the battle. Everard always controlled the narrative.

"Phantom and I are going to check ahead while you get Everard ready to travel," I said to the group.

"We'll catch up," Quinn said. "It takes a few minutes for the medallion to kick in."

I nodded, and Phantom and I took the trail the scouts had reported into the forest of Coveg. The trees blotted out the moonlight, leaving the trail pitch black. I stopped and got my watcher's mask out. Beard or no beard, I needed to be able to see. The forest was quiet as death as Phantom and I stalked our prey. Nimish was here on the island. One slug and this would all be over. If only it was that easy.

Ahead a clearing opened up, so I brought Phantom back to keep him out of the line of fire and approached. Gertie was ready to handle anything that awaited us. I dropped to one knee and sighted the rifle.

Nothing moved. The ground didn't show any markings for a ritual, so this wasn't the place.

We crept into the clearing on high alert for anything out of the ordinary. No people were in sight. No sounds. Just silence. I relaxed a bit.

"Let's go get the others," I said to Phantom.

I started to turn, but couldn't. No matter how I tried, I was stuck like a statue.

"I thought I might find you lot here," Firehelm said as he stepped out from behind a tree on the far side of the clearing. He looked around. "Where's that awful woman you travel with?"

I couldn't answer. My face was as frozen in place as the rest of me. The only thing I could do was breathe.

"Oh," Firehelm said after I hadn't responded. He pointed the wand, and my jaw came loose.

"They are back in Iron Harbor to fight off the invasion." I pushed against the paralysis with everything I had, and nothing happened. My will had to best Firehelm's if I was going to get free.

Phantom slunk across the space. He became visible right before he pounced and froze in his crouch.

"Not so fast, kitty cat." Firehelm reached over and pet Phantom. The big cat's growl was a warning that the Tofragradian ignored.

Images flowed through my mind in rapid succession. Trapped, fear, freedom, and more as my partner struggled with what was happening to him.

"Phantom, it's fine." The images slowed a bit but didn't stop. Panic filled me. Now I had to liberate myself so I could save Phantom as well. I threw my will against the invisible wall that prevented me from moving.

"Phantom, what a great name. I'd keep him as a trophy for killing you, but I don't think we'd be friends if I stopped holding him."

"Why don't we try it and see?" My hand twitched. Even a small crack in the barrier would help. I pummeled the mental barrier, fighting for both our lives.

Firehelm laughed. "I have a better idea."

Phantom growled and struggled, but slowly he turned to face me. "I've always heard these big cats are effective killers. Let's see."

Panic raced through me. My companion and protector was being set against me. I wasn't breaking through fast enough. I renewed my assault. "Phantom, kill him. He can't control you if you fight."

"So you've found out the true nature of the artifact," he said with a smirk. "Not that it will help you."

Phantom took a halting step toward me and then another. My shoulder moved slightly as I tried to get Gertie aimed.

Another crack in the barrier.

"You can stop him," I said, projecting images to him of breaking free. Everything I sent didn't stop him from walking toward me. "Phantom, I'm sorry."

"Kill him." Sweat beaded on Firehelm's bald forehead. He was struggling to control us both.

I fought to free myself, hoping it would loose Phantom from the wand's effects. My arms moved. Gertie swung to the ready and I fired. The shot went wide of Firehelm.

Phantom reared back on his hind legs and dragged his claws down my chest, opening me up like a butchered hog. Images flooded my mind of how sorry he was. "I love you."

"Brulle," Victoria's voice came across the clearing.

"Kill her," Firehelm shouted.

A shot cracked from behind us. Firehelm's wand went flying as the slug from Victoria's pistol struck his arm. Phantom's head jerked up as I fell to the ground.

Firehelm, holding his ruined arm against his chest, fled from the clearing. Blood trailed behind him as he ran.

"Kill him," I said to Phantom from where I lay on the dirt. I didn't want him to see me die.

Phantom wheeled around and took off after the fleeing fire mage.

Victoria knelt before me. Her hand was over her mouth and her eyes were wide. "Take care of Phantom. It wasn't his fault," I said as my vision dimmed around the edges. I thought about the years I'd spent alone with Phantom as my only companion. I'd never again hunt with him or have him curl up next to me to sleep. I'd lost everything and yet I felt at peace. I died as a watcher protecting Astaria's people.

Tears flowed down Victoria's face as she wept for me. "I'll keep him with me."

"He'll probably like that better. You're far prettier than I am. Especially now." I laughed, feeling the bubbles of blood on my lips. The world narrowed until I only saw Victoria's face.

"I love you. I'll see you on the other side," she whispered to me. It was the last thing I heard.

Everything went dark.

⸻ ⸺ ⸻

Victoria

I don't know how long I sat there, but Phantom nudged me out of my stupor. I hugged the big cat as he sent me questions about why Brulle wasn't moving. From the blood coating his muzzle, Phantom had ended Firehelm. I wished I could have done it, but Phantom had earned the kill.

The others arrived in the clearing to find us sitting next to Brulle's lifeless body. I had taken off his mask since he hated the thing and I didn't want him to be uncomfortable anymore.

"What happened?" Isabella said after she ran to Brulle's side and hugged her dead friend.

"Firehelm made Phantom kill Brulle," I said in a monotone that sounded strange to my ears.

"I'll kill the bastard," she hissed between clenched teeth.

"Phantom beat you to it."

Isabella nodded but didn't add anything.

"We need to keep going," Quinn said, putting a hand on my shoulder.

I stood and rounded on him. "Brulle is dead, and you want to just keep going? How about some respect for the dead?"

Quinn stood stock still as I yelled at him. He didn't deserve it, and I knew it, but the wall broke and my emotions poured out. I needed to hurt someone like I'd been hurt by losing my friend.

"Brulle died to save a lot of people's lives. Do you want to let Nimish summon Ghuasis and have his sacrifice mean nothing?" Quinn asked quietly.

That hit me far harder than it should have. Tears poured down my face, but Quinn was right. I wanted, no, needed, to stop Nimish so my friend could rest in peace. "You're right."

I carefully removed Gertie's holster from Brulle's body, along with the satchel. I handed them to Isabella. "He'd want you to have these."

She shook her head. "You were much closer to Brulle. You should keep them."

"No, you were his apprentice and a watcher of your own right now. This is your legacy."

"Brulle told me you would be a formidable watcher, Isabella," Everard said from where he stood next to Quinn. "Those items are yours as the watcher who'll replace Brulle. Take up his weapons and continue the fight. We are going to avenge Brulle this night."

Isabella nodded.

I helped her into the harness, and Quinn loaded Gertie with a chain of slugs. She placed the satchel over her head.

"There are two more chains in the bag if you need them," Quinn told her. "Hopefully, you won't."

Isabella looked at each of us. "I swear to live up to Brulle's legacy and avenge his death or die trying."

"We've lost enough today," I said. "You will not throw your life away. That wouldn't make Brulle happy."

"Understood, Watcher Wyndham."

"It's Victoria to the watchers, which includes you now. Let's go."

I didn't look back, only straight ahead. I was a watcher, and we lost people, but at the end of the day, we were there to protect Astaria's civilization from threats like Nimish. Brulle had returned to fight when we needed him the most. Who was I to stop and let the world fall?

I heard the others walking behind me. Phantom was at my side. Confused images filled my head, but I don't think the big cat understood what had happened. I projected an image of Firehelm stabbing Brulle and the cat seemed to understand. I would tell him that lie every day if it saved Phantom from hurting.

After a few minutes, we stumbled across what was left of Firehelm. Phantom had avenged our fallen brother. Now it was time to finish the job.

VICTORIA

Quinn led us through the forest in search of Nimish. I didn't want Phantom out of my sight after Brulle's death, so we didn't send the big cat to scout. Plus I wasn't sure if I could "hear" Phantom at a distance. After twenty minutes, Quinn stopped. "Fires are burning up ahead. This is the place. Ready yourself."

Isabella double-checked Gertie while I readied my pistols. Phantom nuzzled my leg, images of Brulle swimming through my brain. The cat was in agony over losing Brulle, as was I, for the second time. You should only have to mourn a friend once.

"Something feels off," Everard warned. "I think Nimish has already started the ritual."

"We need to move in," Quinn said, stepping into the open space and moved to the left. Phantom and I entered the thirty-foot-wide clearing and went right. The center of the clearing held a huge bonfire, but no symbols or other indication of magic.

"We should hurry," Everard said quietly.

"I'm glad you could all join me," a familiar voice called from the far side of the clearing. Cian stepped out of the shadows flanked by two enormous armored bears with glowing red eyes. He wore a magus harness and his watcher's mask, but it was him. "Nimish will be thrilled to have you all for her final sacrifice."

"Not likely," Isabella said, opening Gertie up to deliver a stream of slugs at the rogue watcher.

A blue shield sprang to life around Cian, stopping all the slugs. They fell harmlessly to the ground. The bears growled. Phantom answered them but stayed by my side.

"How did you get out of prison?" Quinn asked.

"It's good to have friends in low places," Cian said with a smirk.

Someone had broken Cian out of the prison Quinn and Everard had put him in? He'd been in a coma the last time I saw him. I wanted to tear his eyes out. I wanted him to suffer the way I was after losing my friend.

"Roland really knew how to pack the devices on these magus harnesses. It's a shame Walden Ovro gutted him like a stuck pig."

"I took you out once. I can do it again," Quinn said.

"But this time, I have this." A bolt of lightning streaked across the clearing, striking Quinn's shield. "You think you can take me in a fair fight?"

"Quinn, he's baiting you," I said, to no avail. The artificer was too tired and hurt to think straight.

"Bring it." Quinn turned to the rest of us. "If he wins, you have to stop Nimish."

There was no way Quinn was up to a fight with a rested Cian. The hunter knew all the dirty tricks that Quinn would never stoop to. "Quinn, no! We need to stick together."

Too late.

Cian opened with a blast of fire, forcing Quinn to step back. One bear rumbled around to block the fight from the three of us. The other came up behind us. Phantom snarled with rage but stayed put.

Quinn closed the distance between them and punched the hunter's shield, which flared blue. Cracks appeared. The force delivered by Quinn's mechanical arm was immense, driving Cian backward. Quinn pressed his advantage and kept punching. More spidery cracks laced Cian's shield.

Without warning, Cian dove away, rolling to his feet to fire a lightning bolt into Quinn. This time, the artificer didn't get his magus shield up in time. The energy struck him and threw him back fifteen feet to land in a heap on the ground.

"Quinn, get up," Isabella shouted, lifting Gertie to take another shot, but Quinn didn't move.

I caught Quinn's eye and he winked. I placed my hand on the barrel. "Wait."

"So much for that," Cian said, approaching an unmoving Quinn. "Not much in a fair fight, are you?"

Cian reared back and kicked Quinn.

Quinn's arm shot out, blocking the kick. Cian's leg bounced off the metallic limb as if he'd kicked solid stone. The hunter jumped back, but with an injured leg, he stumbled.

The instant Cian was distracted, Quinn opened up with a gout of flames. The hunter barely threw himself to the side in time, rolled, and fired another bolt of lightning at Quinn, which missed. The lightning exploded against a tree on the far side of the clearing.

Quinn dodged left and came in hard with a punch to Cian's head. Cian countered with his shield and backed away, pulling a long dagger from his belt. The two circled each other.

"You should have killed me when you had the chance, Quinn."

Quinn feinted to the right before dancing out of the knife's range. "I won't make the same mistake twice. Brulle was ashamed to hear you turned traitor."

Cian laughed. "Funny about that. You keep saying he's alive, but Brulle's not here, now is he."

"Brulle's body is down the trail. Firehelm killed him."

"What?" Cian's hand dropped and his eyes grew wide with shock.

Quinn moved in faster than I thought he could and uppercut Cian, knocking off his watcher's mask and driving him to the ground. Quinn dove to pin him, but Cian slashed out with his knife, cutting across Quinn's belly. He backed off, checking the cut.

"Liar!" Cian screamed, his voice breaking. "Brulle died years ago. He would never have abandoned me."

"Brulle left because he believed you would carry on his work, not betray it," Everard said from where he stood next to me. "He thought of you as his son, and it hurt him to find out you turned your back on Astaria."

"Go look for yourself," I said. "We'll grant you passage to pay your last respects to the man you failed. You are an embarrassment to the watchers, and especially Brulle, who raised you."

"I'll gut you just like Ovro did Roland," Cian said to Quinn. Acid dripped from his words.

Cian launched himself at me, but Quinn intercepted him. Cian struck Quinn's energy shield full force, pushing Quinn toward the nearest bear.

Quinn dropped his shield and caught his opponent's knife in his metal fingers. He twisted and snapped the blade. Cian's fist hit Quinn's face, knocking the artificer into the bear behind him.

The bear spun, swiping a massive paw at Quinn, who blocked it with his shield. Quinn stumbled and fell to the ground. The animal reared and landed on the shield, which began to splinter.

Isabella drew aim on the bear, but I stopped her. We could disable the devices controlling the bears if we got close enough. The other bear snarled and snapped at us. She lowered the weapon. "We've got to help Quinn. Cian is cheating."

"Quinn's fine, but if that bear charges us, we can't protect Everard."

Everard stood at the edge of the light, transfixed by something I couldn't see. "Something is wrong, something is wrong. The power is nearby and growing."

Isabella stepped between me and the second bear who snarled at us. Gertie might stop the armored bear, but it was not a sure thing.

Quinn activated the levitator on his gauntlet, and the bear flew through the air to land on Cian. The hunter managed to get out from under the massive beast, but it took several precious seconds. He got to his feet as Quinn reached him.

Cian twisted away from a punch to the head and fired lightning into the ground at Quinn's feet. The artificer went down hard, and Cian jumped to the prone man's side. He grabbed Quinn's metal arm and pulled. The buckles stretched but held.

"Can't do anything without a good connection, right?" Cian shoved the dangling arm out of his way and started to pummel Quinn.

"Quinn!" I shouted and prepared to fire.

"No!" Quinn yelled. An instant later, a ball of flame shot out of his left hand and hit Cian in the chest, driving him away from the prone blacksmith.

I looked at Everard. "Did you do that?"

He smiled. "No, Quinn is using his magic."

"But he said he has to build a device for the magic to work?"

"The devices are a crutch. He doesn't need them."

Quinn stood up, blood running in rivulets down his face from a series of cuts. His nose was off center, and one eye was swelling shut. "This is done!"

Quinn pointed his left arm down and threw himself into the air. He landed with both feet in Cian's chest and knocked him to the ground. The hunter tried to roll away, but Quinn held a knife to the man's throat.

The fight was over.

"Enough!" Nimish Nimkar roared as she entered the clearing. "Sleep."

With that, the lights went out.

27

QUINN

I awoke to someone slapping my cheek. I opened one of my eyes. The other wouldn't or couldn't open. Cian's bloodied and bruised face swam in through my blurred vision.

"Nice of you to join us," Cian said, standing up. "They are all awake, Mistress Nimkar."

I looked over and saw Everard, Isabella, and Victoria all tied to trees. Phantom was nowhere in sight. I mouthed the big cat's name, and Victoria gestured toward the forest with her eyes.

Well, at least one of us had gotten away.

A stone altar sat in the middle of a circle made of ashes. Nimish stood behind the altar chanting quietly. Dark rivers of dried blood covered the ancient rock. Ruins of the stone temple that once stood here were evident around the wide clearing. I saw our weapons and gear. Along with my metal arm, our weapons were piled on one of the shattered pillars off to my right. My forging hammer still hung from my belt. Cian carried Gertie, which enraged me. He'd betrayed Brulle and now carried his legacy like he'd earned it.

I pulled forward, but my left arm was tied behind my back. We hadn't considered anyone would free Cian, but he was right about one thing: I should have killed him when I had the chance.

"Why did you betray us?" Victoria asked. "We were friends."

The hunter glared at her but answered. "Friends? Hardly. Everard used us as pawns to further his goals while leaving us to die. With alarium weapons, we could rule the world, but his ego kept us weak so he could flaunt his magic."

"Cian, I never left you to die. There isn't enough alarium—"

Cian kicked the old man's feet. "Stop your lies! Ovro and Nimish told me that the alarium is key to your magic, and by keeping us without, you maintained your dominance over Astaria. Looks like that is over, doesn't it?"

"My goal was to protect the people of Astaria, not rule the world."

"Shut it, old man, before I end you."

Everard stopped talking, his head lowered to his chest.

"What is all the commotion, Cian?"

I knew that voice. Walden Ovro, the man who'd murdered Roland, rounded the altar. A smile split his face as he saw me. "Quinn, welcome to the end of the world, well, at least for you. The high priestess thanks you for your sacrifice."

"I should have known you'd be mixed up in this."

"After you so rudely took the magic that belongs to me, I was forced to flee Astaria. Best decision of my life. I met Lady Nimkar and learned of her plans. We created the runes to control the animals and the Blue Heron to hypnotize the people in power. Now, we are about to remake the world into one that is fair to everyone, not just the chosen few."

Nimish walked around the altar, her face painted in a strange pattern of light and dark. "It is time to begin the ceremony."

She stood at the end of the altar, with Cian and Ovro on either side. The two men started to chant while Nimish burned a fragrant herb in a bowl in the center of the stone lintel. She swayed back and forth, weaving patterns of magic in the air. I'd never seen magic flow like that before.

My eyes traced the magic as if she wrote it in ink, not air. The runes from the sheet we'd found in Cian's possessions popped into being, then floated to hover around the outside of the ash circle on the ground. The air hummed with potential as she fed a constant flow of magic into the ritual.

Something tugged at the ropes that bound me to the tree. Phantom. A couple more yanks and the ropes went slack. I didn't react, keeping my arm in the place it'd been tied.

Phantom's invisible face nudged my shoulder. I could kiss him. "Get my arm," I whispered to the cat. He purred before the pressure let up. Victoria winked at me, though she appeared to be tied still.

The ritual intensified as the runes drawn on the ground burst into blue-black flames. The shadows danced with unrestrained power. I didn't know if the spell could bring Ghuasis to this plane, but the power grew at an alarming rate. It held a taint I'd never experienced before. I wondered if that was what Everard meant by wrong.

Slowly, I worked my left wrist free of the rope. It took far longer than if I'd had two hands, but you forged with the tools you had. The light surrounding the altar brightened and receded at intervals as new aspects of the spell came into being.

Everard's eyes were wide as he watched the ritual unfold before him. "To think of all we could do with that much magic, but it's fueled by death."

"Take over the world?" I said somewhat sarcastically.

"Indeed, but we could cure disease or feed the hungry with so much power."

Nice thoughts, but in my experience, power bred corruption, not an altruistic heart.

I caught a glimpse of my arm sliding from the pile. With the chanting and currents of magic floating around, no one else seemed to notice.

"Goddess, accept my sacrifice." Nimish picked up a knife and sliced along the inside of her left arm. The blood dripped onto the stone altar. "I am your faithful servant now and for eternity."

Cian and Ovro did the same, pledging themselves to the goddess they sought to bring here.

Phantom's paw batted my shoulder. Next to me sat my arm. "Thank you, Phantom. You get all the meat and belly rubs you want if we survive this."

I reached over and pushed my metal arm under my duster. Though they were occupied, I didn't think standing up to attach my arm would go unnoticed.

"Quinn," Everard said from off to my left. "If they take me to the altar, you know what to do."

"No, I don't," I said in a panicked voice. "What are you talking about?"

"Channel your magic to me."

"How?" We'd practiced passing magic back and forth, but not a one-way channeling.

"Just do what you did fighting Cian."

"Lose?"

"Like we practiced in Terralon. You'll understand when the time comes."

"Goddess, we offer you up the life of our adversaries. You may feast on them like you will on all the infidels on this plane."

Cian and Ovro stepped away from the altar, heading for Victoria. I was about to speak when Everard called to Nimish.

"Nimish, I am the strongest here. I've thwarted your plans, destroyed your armies, and brought the watchers to destroy you. You have beaten us and I offer myself up so you might spare the people who followed me."

Her head whipped around, and her eyes narrowed. "Everard, why would you sacrifice yourself?"

"My death will be powerful enough to fuel your spell, but you have to promise not to kill anyone else. I'm an old man, and if it will save my people, I'll willingly sacrifice myself."

Her features twisted into a sneer. "You are weak, but I will grant you the peace of not watching all of your watchers die before you. Bring him."

They came and cut Everard loose. The Arch Magus didn't struggle, just let them take him to the altar. Nimish cut away his robes, leaving him standing in his underclothes, the health medallion, and the stone ring I'd created for him to broadcast his voice during the battle.

The stone was an amplifier. I created it to increase sound, but it would function the same with any energy source it interacted with. Understanding dawned on me.

They hefted up the old man and placed him with his head in front of Nimish.

"Goddess, we sacrifice the Arch Magus of Astaria to you. His power is yours to consume."

Nimish lifted the dagger, chanting and drawing runes of power around the steel blade. The knife glowed like it had just come out of the forge. The dark red-gold pulsed with the power that Nimish fed into it.

The fight with Cian was key. I hadn't needed my arm or any other devices to create the fireball of launch at him. I opened myself up and felt the edges of the magic. *How had I done it?*

"Goddess, we forsake all others in your name. Hear our pleas."

I stared at Everard. He would die if I didn't do something, and fast. Fear quickened my heart, and magic retreated from my grasp. Panic filled me. I clawed to bring back the magic I needed to end this. It slid even farther away.

"Goddess, bringer of judgment, accept our offering."

What had I done? I needed to beat Cian and the magic had responded. That wasn't right. No, I wasn't scared. I wasn't angry. I just did what I had to do. I cleared my mind and pictured the magic flowing to the stone ring.

The magic flooded through me like heat from an open flame. I did my best to direct it toward the ring, which vibrated as the new magic source swirled around it.

Nimish stopped chanting. "What is happening?"

"I'm ending this," Everard said, his words echoing across the clearing.

With a flash so bright it left an afterimage on the back of my eyes, Everard exploded into pure light and vanished. The altar cracked but didn't break.

What would we do now?

28

QUINN

The clearing plunged into darkness in the aftermath of Everard's departure. I wished my mask was on so I could see. I pulled my arm on, feeling the tingle as the cup affixed to my stump. The straps were a tangled mess, and I didn't have time to sort them out. As my eyes adjusted to the dark, I noticed the altar glowed with an eerie light, lighting the clearing. I threw a blast of lightning at the Ovro, blowing a good chunk out of the altar stone, but missing Ovro in the process.

Victoria shimmied out of her ropes, leapt up, and ran to where the gear had been laid out. Isabella joined her. Moments later, the air was full of metal slugs as Isabella fired Gertie and swept the altar. Cian screamed as slugs tore through him, and his body crumpled to the ground.

"That's for Brulle, you bastard," Isabella roared.

Her celebration didn't last long. Nimish threw a smoky globe at the apprentice, which struck her in the chest. She fell to the ground, gasping for air.

"You stop Nimish, I'll take care of Isabella," Victoria yelled as she ran for our fallen ally.

Nimish's magic took on a life of its own. We needed to end this before the magic became uncontrollable.

Flames burst into being atop the altar. Nimish and Ovro reared back from the heat coming off the stone altar. "Ovro, kill him before the ceremony is destroyed."

Ovro rounded the altar, pulling two knives. The former magus of Orsoro was a pompous ass who thought himself better than everyone and had tried to steal Everard's magic for his own uses. I'd stopped him and received the magic he coveted. Things had gone downhill from there.

I got the strap over my head enough to connect my arm. I pulled the connection tight and shot lightning at him. He used the blades to block the energy. The knives glowed white. "You aren't the only artificer in Astaria."

Ovro closed on me. He drove the left knife at me, followed by a stab with the right one.

I pivoted, using my momentum to carry me away from the second knife. The backslash of the first knife grazed my right shoulder. The jolt of energy it released caused me to stumble, but I maintained my balance. My arm swung loose, and I lost the connection.

"Like my newest invention? It delivers an extra punch."

Nimish started chanting again and the clearing burst into light as the runes reasserted themselves. Everard's ploy hadn't stopped the ritual, only delayed it.

Phantom appeared behind Ovro and slashed his claws across the back of the man's right leg. Ovro's leg buckled, but he stayed upright.

"Phantom, go!" I yelled. The distraction gave me the seconds I needed to reattach my arm. The connection tingled as the contact was fully restored. I managed to get one strap in place to hold it on at least temporarily.

Ovro limped as he circled me, but now I had two arms. He stabbed at my belly. I dodged. If I blocked with my mechanical arm, he could fry the alarium and my arm wouldn't work. The knives must have been imbued with a way to trap energy and release it when they struck. Normally I'd love to examine them to find out how Ovro had done it, but now wasn't the time. I had to be careful.

Another flurry of attacks and I managed to avoid the charged blades.

"So you don't like being hit by lightning?" Ovro asked. "I guess you've never been on the receiving end of your power. It hurts."

"I'll make sure to take your head off quick, so you don't feel anything."

"Tsk, tsk. You are so rude to your betters. You were born a peasant and you'll die the same."

Nimish's chanting picked up speed. Victoria helped Isabella to her feet.

Nimish threw another orb at the two watchers and they froze. "Quinn, we're stuck," Victoria called.

I dodged the first knife, but the second slid along my ribs. The jolt of power almost knocked me from my feet. With a swift punch, I drove Ovro back long enough to run my good hand along the wound. Dry. The energy must have seared it shut. At least I wouldn't bleed to death.

Ovro threw a knife at me. I dove to avoid it, landing squarely on my forging hammer. The pain lanced through my hip. I got to my feet and pulled the forgotten hammer out.

"You brought a mallet to a knife fight?" Ovro laughed.

I ignored the barb and closed the distance between us. Ovro swung overhand at my head, but I caught the blade on the top of the hammer. The clang was deafening as the knife discharged its energy into the solid steel head. The knife smoked, and the glow faded to nothing.

"Let's see how tough you really are," I said, preparing to strike. I swung the hammer back and delivered a blow to his sternum. The magic I'd stored in the hammer had cracked a solid stone bridge, and it did far worse to Ovro.

The man shattered into a million shards of Ovro. In under a second, he turned into a red cloud of mist.

"No," Nimish screamed as she saw him die.

"That was for Roland." I spit where my foe had stood not seconds before. I hefted the hammer and went to meet Nimish.

"You fool. Do you think that will stop the goddess from coming? You've sacrificed more of her believers. The spell is done. Rise, Ghuasis."

Nothing happened.

"I don't think she's coming," I said as I reached the altar. "The spell must have been disrupted or under fueled."

"Then I will kill you all myself."

I raised the hammer to destroy the altar, but Nimish was far faster. A black ball of energy struck me in the face. The heat seared my skin, causing me to scream in agony. I dropped to my knees and rubbed dirt across the burnt skin to stop the pain.

I staggered to my feet. Nimish stabbed me in the left shoulder with her ceremonial knife. "Ghuasis, I send another infidel to you. Hear my prayers. Come, mother of death."

The pain coursed through me. My left arm shuddered, and I couldn't feel it anymore.

With a sickening noise, she wrenched the dagger free and pulled me by my hair, raising my chin so she could cut my throat. I pointed at the ground and triggered my levitator. My body slammed into Nimish, and we flew across the clearing. When we smashed into a tree, Nimish acted like a cushion, absorbing the force of the blow. The knife fell to the ground near where we landed.

I pushed myself up and prepared to finish the fight with a bolt of lightning.

Nimish had other ideas. She threw a handful of black powder into my face. The acid burned as it touched my eyes and skin. I raked at the burning, but it only made it worse. I tripped and rolled across the ground in agony.

Nimish started chanting again, but I couldn't see her through the flood of tears as my eyes tried to clear themselves.

"Ghuasis, rise and smite your enemies!"

"I'll be doing the smiting," said Victoria. I heard her pistol fire multiple times.

Before I knew it, water was being poured over my face, washing away the acid. After a few minutes, my vision began to return. Nimish's body lay sprawled next to me, blood flowing across the ground. The glow from the altar had died down though we could still see by the light it gave off.

Phantom came over and rubbed against my shoulder. I scratched him between his ears. "You saved the day. All the steak you can eat once we get back to Iron Harbor."

The big cat purred in approval.

"We should gather Brulle's body and signal the Lunatic's Revenge," Victoria said, looking around the clearing. "Should we destroy the altar?"

"I don't think it's necessary, Nimish is gone, and the rest will scatter now that she's dead. Everard thought Nimish's spell would work. I'm glad he was wrong."

"And the Candalarians and Norns?" Isabella asked.

"Without Nimish controlling them, I assume they'll retreat. There's been enough death already." The two watchers helped me to my feet. I was ready to return to the Treetop Workshop and spend more time learning my magic. The hole Everard left made me feel hollow inside.

"Let's head for home," Victoria said. "We've lost far more than I care to think about."

"Agreed."

We turned to head back to the Lunatic's Revenge when the ground began to shake. The trees swayed as if a windstorm had popped up, but the air was still. Light flared from the stone altar.

Ghuasis, the goddess of the undead, rose from the massive stone slab.

"I have been reborn!"

"I told you we should have destroyed the altar!"

VICTORIA

Ghuasis, the goddess of the undead, stood atop the stone altar. She had a hooked beak and six arms, three to a side. Each hand had long talons the color of dried blood. A ring of skulls wrapped around her neck, and metallic scales covered a body that ended with an eight-foot-long serpent's tail. If a snake and a bird of prey had a baby, you'd get Ghuasis.

Quinn grabbed my arm. "You and Isabella get out of here. You can't fight a goddess."

I pushed him away. "We are in this together."

Isabella only nodded. Her eyes were as wide as dinner plates.

"Phantom, go to Brulle," I shouted, and the big cat sped out of the clearing. I'd not sacrifice Phantom in a suicidal fight.

"Mortals, which of you called me to this plane?"

"She did," I said, pointing to the corpse of Nimish where she lay on the ground. "Go back to your plane in peace."

"Peace?" Ghuasis laughed. "I have been freed from harvesting the souls of those trapped between good and evil. Your world has fresh souls. I can smell the evil and death. I will feast here."

Quinn stepped in front of Isabella and me. "Return to your place. We've got no quarrel with you."

The queen of the undead slithered forward, dropping off the altar.

"You may not have a quarrel with me, but you have killed my high priestess, so I will take your souls in payment."

"We are not so easily defeated," I said, though I felt rather disposable at the moment. The goddess radiated an immense aura of power. I fought to stay standing and not kneel before her might. Her presence threatened to blot out all rational thought.

"We shall see," the goddess said before her tail lashed out at Quinn.

Quinn's shield burst to life and deflected the blow, though it drove him back into us. "Scatter!"

Isabella ran to the left, and I went right. Quinn swung his hammer, and the ground shook with the force of the blow. Ghuasis fell back, only to recoil her tail for another strike.

Isabella opened up with Gertie, unloading the remainder of the chain into the overgrown serpent queen. It didn't faze her in the least. "Mortal weapons are of no use against me."

I ran to place the altar between me and the fight. I needed to help Quinn, but my pistols weren't of any use against a goddess. My foot bumped into something solid. Cian's lifeless body lay next to me.

Quinn struck with the hammer again and the surge of power knocked me back, causing me to trip and land hard next to Cian. The light flickered across the brass of the magus harness he wore strapped to his right arm. I pushed with all my might to get him to flip over so I could unfasten the buckles.

Shock waves from the fight tossed the ground around like an airship in a gale. I released the first clip. Pieces of stone cascaded over me while I worked on the other two clasps. I heard Isabella open up with Gertie, and I worried that Quinn might be down if she was firing the rifle while they fought.

The ground rippled again as the fight progressed. There was no room for error. If we didn't find a way to rid the world of Ghuasis, the rampaging goddess would threaten all life.

The last buckle came loose, and I got the harness off of Cian. I slid my arm in and hooked the straps around my shoulder and torso. When I turned it on, the arm piece buzzed with energy. At least the alarium hadn't been damaged.

I got to my feet. Quinn and Ghuasis battled. "Quinn, down!"

I threw a stream of lightning straight into the back of the goddess. She lurched forward from the impact of the blow. Black scorch marks covered her from her neck to her knees.

She spun in place. "How dare you use magic against me?"

"Quinn, your arm."

He threw a stream of lightning into the back of the enraged goddess. She hurled a piece of the broken altar at me. The chunk, about the size of my head, impacted my left shoulder and knocked me solidly onto the ground. The world swam around me and I vomited.

Isabella ran to my side. "Let's get you out of here."

I shook my head. I was injured but not out. Quinn needed all the help he could get, and I wasn't running away from this battle. I owed all the people who'd died the effort to stop the goddess. "We have to fight. She'll kill Quinn without us. Take the harness and help."

She pulled it off me as carefully as she could, jolting my shoulder in the process. I threw up again from a mixture of vertigo and pain. I had no doubt something inside me was broken. Isabella strapped the harness on and opened up on the serpent goddess. Between Isabella and Quinn, they had her flanked, but they weren't banishing her.

I sat up and wiped my mouth on my sleeve. All I had left were my pistols and what good were they?

Magic.

She called the alarium lightning magic, not power or energy like we assumed the alarium produced. What had Cian said about the alarium being the source of Everard's magic? If the goddess could be hurt by lightning generated from the crystals, then the crystals themselves should be pure magic.

I took out one of my pistols and unloaded the alarium from the stock of the gun. It was a challenge to do one handed. The crystal was about the size of my thumb. I pulled a torn piece of fabric from my shirt and got the piece out. I didn't let it touch my skin so it didn't burn me.

I stumbled against the bucking ground to stand up. The fight was still going full force, with Ghuasis pushed against the altar. Sooner or later, the alarium in the harnesses would run out and we'd lose. There was only one way to finish this.

"Stop!" I called as I made my way around the stone altar. "I surrender."

"What?" Quinn said in disbelief. "Are you crazy?"

I winked at him, and he backed down. Isabella lowered her arm, and the lightning stopped.

"Goddess, I understand just how powerful you are, and I regret standing against you. If you will have me, I would be your guide on this plane."

A shrewd look crossed the goddess' face. "Mortal, do not toy with me. You stand with the infidels against me. Why the change of heart?"

I thought of all the bad things that had happened and let the fear of losing Quinn and Isabella rage through my mind. I let the panic wash over me so Ghuasis could feel it, taste it. I needed her to believe I'd changed sides.

"I don't want to die."

"No mortal wants to die, yet they do."

"If I pledge myself to you, will you grant me immortality? Nimish promised any who joined her would be given the gift of agelessness."

"My embrace can grant such power as long as I am on this plane."

I knelt before her. "Goddess, I would be yours, so I never have to die."

"Victoria, don't. Think of Brulle and Everard. They sacrificed everything to stop this evil from entering our plane."

I glanced at Quinn over my shoulder. "Even with your hammer, you can't banish a goddess. You would need pure magic."

He didn't say anything, but I saw the smirk appear.

"Victoria, no," Isabella said from the side. Tears ran down her face.

"I'm sorry, but it is the only way."

"Enough. I accept you as my acolyte, then you will kill these two for defiling this ritual."

Real fear grabbed my heart and threatened to stop it, but I stepped up and allowed the six arms to close around me. A surge of her magic passed through me, pressing down on my thoughts, as she claimed me as hers. My thoughts boiled as Ghuasis's power settled over me. It took every ounce of will, but I pushed the alarium crystal into the eye socket of the center skull in her necklace before she released me.

"Daughter, slay these infidels and prove your loyalty to me."

"As you will, Ghuasis."

I turned to face Quinn. "Strike me down if you can."

Quinn charged. His hammer over his shoulder to attack. At the last second, I dove to my right, landing hard on the ground, and Quinn brought the hammer down on the alarium crystal. The crystal shattered, releasing pure magic. "I banish you to your own plane, Ghuasis."

"No!" the goddess screamed as a swirling white vortex of energy pulled her into the earth to return her to her own realm.

When she was gone, Quinn raised the hammer and slammed it against the top of the altar, shattering it into pieces.

"There, I destroyed the altar."

I lay on the ground and laughed until I cried. We had defeated a goddess.

All it took was getting hammered.

3 0

VICTORIA

Two days later, we were gathered on the deck of the Lunatic's Revenge. After Nimish died, the leaders of the assembled invaders fled the battlefield. It would be years before they would have enough troops to launch any kind of assault against Astaria again.

My arm was in a sling from the fight with Ghuasis. Quinn, Isabella, and Phantom stood near me with Brulle's body wrapped in sailcloth. We had said our goodbyes and now it was time to lay Brulle to rest.

Quinn had asked me to say a few words before we sent Brulle over the side to rest with Tokta, the sea goddess. After the fight with Ghuasis, I didn't want to deal with any more angry gods for a long time.

The breeze had picked up and the sunset continued on like it did every day. The ship hovered over the sea outside of Iron Harbor. Captain Stokes nodded. It was time to begin.

"Brulle had been a friend for a long time. His first death shook me to my core at the loss of such an amazing man. We were given a second chance to know him, and we are all the better for it."

I paused to release the sob that choked me. Quinn rubbed my arm and handed me a cloth to wipe my eyes. Isabella held Phantom while she cried.

"Brulle sacrificed everything to save Astaria when she needed him most. He will be missed."

Phantom let out a plaintive whine.

"By Phantom most of all."

The crew of the Lunatic's Revenge lifted the board that Brulle was laid out on. Captain Stokes stood by the rail. "Nitasis, we are but travelers through your domain of the air. Brulle was a good man, so please ask your sister Tokta to shepherd him to the eternal plains where he may wait for us to join him one day."

The cannons fired in salute to our fallen comrade. With a nod from the captain, the crew raised the end of the board and Brulle slid off to a watery grave. I hoped there was an eternal plain where Brulle could cast off his lifetime as a watcher and enjoy the peace.

We all stood in silence for a while before the airship returned to Iron Harbor.

I turned to Quinn. "Where will you go now?"

He shrugged. "Back to the workshop for now. We lost a lot of maguses and equipment in the fighting. I will need to forge new harnesses and train a whole new group on how to use them."

"You are going to train maguses?" I asked, somewhat shocked. "I'd have thought you would tear down the system for something fairer."

"Usorin and I are hammering out details of a new set of articles to govern Astaria. We'll be increasing the watchers so they can provide counsel to each of the thirteen regions. We are also convening a governing body of those watchers with Usorin as head to keep things in line."

I gasped. "You are working with Usorin?"

Quinn flushed red. "Yes, Victoria. I am. Everard was right. Usorin changed after Ovro almost killed him. He listens to my advice now, and I think we can have a more stable Astaria for all the people, not just the powerful ones. Change takes time, and throwing out the current system would lead to anarchy. I can't let my ideals destroy the country Everard, Brulle, and countless others died to protect."

"You would make a fine Arch Magus."

"I don't want it," he said with a grim smile. "I'm an artificer and a mage. I'll work from behind the scenes to keep Astaria safe."

Isabella joined us. "Quinn, what do I do now? I've never been a watcher before."

He smiled at the newest watcher. "Watcher Spider will be here tomorrow. She'll get you situated in High Keep as the Aldon watcher. She'll be the adviser there. You'll learn from her. Watcher Riz will be recruiting and training the new watchers. It will take a while, but we'll survive."

The Lunatic's Revenge docked in Iron Harbor, and Quinn headed for the gangplank. "Victoria, I'll meet you in Stillhold in a month. We have lots to discuss."

"I'll see you then."

He stepped onto the gangplank, then stopped. "No joke?"

"Not today. Next time I see you, though…"

He groaned, then laughed. "I'll look forward to it."

And off Quinn, the most powerful mage in Astaria went.

Isabella stayed on the Lunatic's Revenge so the captain could drop her in High Keep. Phantom and I went to where the Maiden's Arse, the replacement we'd captured from the Norns, was being retrofitted. Captain Breachcolm greeted me as I arrived.

"Watcher Wyndham," he said with a nod.

"Today, it's just Victoria. How much longer until the Maiden's Arse is ready?"

"A few days, though the crew and I decided to rename her."

"What will she be called?"

"Victoria's Servant."

I groaned. "Leave the jokes to me. What are you naming her, really?"

"Hunter's Haven."

Brulle would approve. "Good choice. I'll see you in a few days."

"Yes, ma'am."

Phantom and I departed the ship. The Norns and Candalarians had retreated when Ghuasis died. The Blue Heron's compulsions had lost their hold once Nimish had died. Anyone who had pledged themselves to her was pulled into the underworld along with her. After that, the leaders had taken their battered forces and left. I picked out the abandoned siege engines to the north of the city.

I had a couple of days to figure out what my next move was. Usorin would be the new Arch Magus with Quinn as the leader of the watchers. I wasn't sure if I wanted to continue as a watcher. Phantom and I could leave and live out our days back at Brulle's old house.

But after all, we'd been through, when the chips had been down, Quinn had come through and saved Astaria, and I had played a significant part in it. I probably shouldn't just leave him to it without backup. The watchers idolized him, but he'd need a confidant to help him through the waters ahead.

As we walked through the empty streets of Iron Harbor, I came to my decision. I'd stay on as an advisor and train a new watcher. My true passion was alchemy and I wanted to do that. As long as Quinn agreed, I'd retire from the fighting and concentrate on alchemy.

In the end, we had stopped a war and banished a goddess.

Not too bad.

THE END

ACKNOWLEDGMENTS

In your hands is a monument to reader perseverance. I wrote Fate & Flux as a stand-alone novella, in between books in my Darkest Storm trilogy, as a change of pace. Well, from the feedback, Quinn was a popular character, and many readers voiced their opinions there needed to be more books in the series. A few years later, the Watchers of Astaria novellas were born.

The journey from idea to book is a long one and involves a lot of people. Jody Wallace did a fantastic job editing the series and had the idea to add in more Quinn/Victoria chapters in Machines & Monsters which made a huge difference in the final story. She makes sure that you, the reader, can understand the stories that go from my brain onto the printed page.

Kristen Gould did the copy/proof edits on all three books to make sure we eliminated as many typos as possible.

My mother, Betty Rose, did the final proofread and caught that I'd switched names on a character in the middle of Machines & Monsters. When your mom was a professional proofreader, it's ok to say my mom likes my books.

At this point any typos or errors are my fault, but after so many passes, I consider them more Easter eggs than errors. You never catch all of them no matter how hard you try.

The physical production of the book requires all of my artsy friends. John Hartness did all the layout, from the map to the icons and everything in between; he makes it look great on paper and in digital formats. It is always amazing to see it go from a boring word doc to the polished book.

Davey Beauchamp created the icons that decorate each of the chapter headers. He knocked them out of the park. Davey also designed the Darkest Storm covers and it is always a pleasure to work with him.

Evin Kierans created the map based on my chicken scratch drawing of Astaria. I think it came out great.

If you bought a copy of the book, you probably were amazed by the cover (I know I am). Natania Barron did the cover for this and all of my other steampunk novellas. She has an incredible eye, and I've sold more books to people who are enamored with her art. She's also an amazing author which is totally not fair to be so talented. If Arthurian Legend is your thing, go check out her books.

Of course, none of these amazingly talented people would have gotten to spend countless hours helping me craft these books if didn't have amazing family and friends to support and encourage me. All of my peeps in my Facebook Patrick Dugan Book Readers group give feedback on covers, answer polls, and yell…err… request that I write faster. Whenever I feel like things aren't going great, they are always there to cheer me on.

At home, our kids are constantly cracking me up and inspiring me to be a better person and dad, which keeps me pursuing my goals, while watching them conquer the world. Blaze, our cavalier, is my writing buddy. He lays under my desk while I work and reminds me cookies are far more important than books. And this list wouldn't be complete without appreciating my wonderful wife, Hope. She is truly the most patient person in the world. Among listening to me go on about new stories, to giving my space to work long hours to get books written and edited, to always being there to celebrate the wins and picking me up when the bad times come. I'd truly be lost without her.

My last thank you is to my readers. I have been so fortunate to have such amazing people supporting me. From coming out to cons to meet me, to leaving reviews when they've loved my books, to opening my monthly newsletter (though I'm sure that is mostly to see pictures of Blaze). Without you, none of this would be possible. I don't remember a time in my life when I wasn't creating fantastic realms to set stories in, and now, I get to do that for many more people than I ever thought possible. So, from the bottom of my heart, thank you for allowing me to keep chasing my dreams.

Until the next book,
    Patrick
    June 2023

ABOUT THE AUTHOR

Patrick is the author of the award-winning Darkest Storm Series published by Falstaff Books. Other titles include Never Steal From Dragons, The Shadow Blade series, and Watchers of Astaria series from Distracted Dragon Press. Other publications include Fairy Films: Wee Folk on the Big Screen, a collection of fairy essays from Educated Dragon Publishing. Patrick is a member of SFWA.

Patrick resides in Charlotte, NC with his wife, two children and their spunky Cavalier King Charles, Blaze. In his spare time, he's a PC gamer, homebrewer, 3D printer enthusiast, and DIYer. You can usually find him in the Hearthstone Tavern or wandering Azeroth as a Blood Elf Warlock in the evenings.

You can find out more at https://linktr.ee/patrickdugan